LEGACY OF DANGER

LEGACY OF DANGER

Patricia A. Guthrie

Fresh Ink Group

Guntersville

Legacy of Danger

Copyright © 2021
by Patricia A. Guthrie
All rights reserved

Fresh Ink Group
An Imprint of:
The Fresh Ink Group, LLC
1021 Blount Avenue, #931
Guntersville, AL 35976
Email: info@FreshInkGroup.com
FreshInkGroup.com

Edition 1.0   2016
Edition 2.0   2021

Book design by Amit Dey / FIG
Art by Anik / FIG
Cover design by Stephen Geez / FIG
Associate publisher Lauren A. Smith / FIG
Edited by Beem Weeks / FIG

Cataloging-in-Publication Recommendations:
FIC027120 FICTION / Romance / Paranormal / General
FIC024000 FICTION / Occult & Supernatural
FIC022080 FICTION / Mystery & Detective / International Crime & Mystery

Library of Congress Control Number: 2021915555

ISBN-13: 978-1-947893-26-9 Papercover
ISBN-13: 978-1-947893-27-6 Hardcover
ISBN-13: 978-1-947893-28-3 Ebooks

DEDICATION

This book is for all those family and friends who wouldn't let me give up, even when it meant re-writing a whole novel.

Especially: Lois and James Guthrie, Micki Peluso, Diane Patricia Scalici, Bren Cubbage, Neva Franks, Lyn Alexander, Bruce Berg, Mary Berg, D.L Finn, Linda Daly, and the Fresh Ink Group.

Table of Contents

Chapter 1

Cemetery

Evanston, Illinois

"I was murdered."

Startled, Elena Dkany searched for the source of the whisper. Nothing. Undertakers lowered Magda Dkany's body into the ground.

A breeze blew in from Lake Michigan, dropping the temperature as Elena Dkany watched her grandmother go from ashes to ashes and dust to dust. A flock of seagulls squawked overhead.

A voice, floating from nowhere, whispered again.

"Elena."

Elena froze, but the chill didn't come from the air.

No voice except the priest praying over her grandmother's coffin. Hearing non-existent voices was not a good thing.

She shook her head and, hopefully, the cobwebs from her brain. Must be imagining things, a result of the long and tragic week.

Briar Hill College's faculty and staff stood close by under the shade of the oak trees. They'd abandoned their classes to pay tribute to the widow of their college president.

As the coffin disappeared into the ground, a vapor materialized by Elena's side, and a scent of roses surrounded her. Its perfume overpowered the smell of the pines and moldy earth. Strange. No rose bushes grew in the small cemetery.

Roses without a rose garden. Freezing when it was hot. Her grandmother, lying in a coffin. Dead. *This is not happening.*

But it was. Her grandmother stood by her side as though she'd never died—like they were attending somebody else's funeral. And nobody seemed to notice. No startled looks, no wide eyes, no 'Oh my God's.'

The ghost of Magda Dkany spoke. *"You must find your son."*

"Who are you?" The voice jolted Elena into an unpleasant reality. *My son? But he died nine years ago before he'd been a month old.*

Elena focused on the apparition. Beside translucent, Magda appeared as she'd looked only two days ago.

"Elena, I was murdered. Now y*our life . . . in danger. Your . . . son in danger. Find Alexander. He can help you."*

Her heart pounded fast enough without hearing her life might be in danger, and Alexander Brancusi was not someone she wanted to see.

The apparition thinned, and the voice softened.

"Go to Dkany. Find your son." Now she was hardly an outline.

"But . . ."

The vapor dissipated along with the scent of roses.

Magda's presence knocked Elena off balance, and she scrambled to keep from toppling onto the casket now halfway into the earth. A man with a mild scent of musky aftershave caught her arm.

Father Christofides, the American-Romanian Orthodox priest who'd baptized Elena, appeared strange and intimidating. A large crucifix hung around his neck like an ominous albatross of death. Everything moved in slow motion, a surrealistic emptiness of space and time. "Eternal your memory, Magda, our sister, worthy of blessedness and ever-remembered."

Elena turned to thank the man, but her friend Marina Brancusi now held her. She didn't know when Marina and the stranger changed places.

Dkany home, Evanston, Illinois

Elena leaned against the wrought iron railing of her grandmother's patio and inhaled scents from the wide variety of Magda's flowers. The garden of exotic blooms had attained somewhat of a local legend status in the neighborhood. A secret garden hid from view by towering white pines allowed in an occasional blue patch from Lake Michigan. A lone apple tree hugged the house—nature's perfect playground. Elena played in that tree as a child and delighted in climbing into her grandmother's window.

Life had a way of balancing miseries. Elena lost her parents at an early age but grew up in this wonderful old Victorian house, a child's fantasies come true. But life also played a nasty trick on an old woman overflowing with energy and love, her future snuffed out by a hit-and-run driver. *But murder?*

Funeral guests came and went. Elena barely heard their condolences.

Only one man remained on the patio the whole time as friends weaved in and out. At the edge of the railing, he too, gazed at the garden. His attire—a white starched shirt, dark blue suit, and maroon tie—painted him elegant, dashing. He stood tall and thin. Well-muscled. The man from a lifetime ago, Alexander Brancusi.

"How are you doing?"

Startled, Elena spun around and nearly knocked a glass of Scotch out of Marina's hand.

"Sorry." Elena eyed her friend, who juggled two glasses to keep them from tipping. "Your brother is standing over there. I don't think I want to see him right now."

"He'll be here in a minute. Drink this. I think you need it." Marina handed her the glass.

Elena sighed, took the glass, and tossed down too much of the swirling liquid. The warmth of the whiskey burned her throat as she swallowed. A cough shook her body.

"Watch how you drink that." Marina patted her on the back.

Elena wiped her mouth with her hand, breathed deeply, and took an easier sip. Maybe it would dull the edge of the depression that threatened to overwhelm her. "I'm trying for drunken oblivion." Elena tried to smile but ended up fighting tears.

Marina put a hand on her shoulder. "Honey, it's okay to cry. It'll be hell for a while, but it'll get better, you'll see."

Elena sighed. "Maybe."

Alex raised his glass and moved toward them.

"He's coming, be nice," Marina whispered.

"Mari, we were over a long time ago. I haven't seen him in almost ten years, so it really doesn't matter anymore."

Elena regarded the man, then glanced back at his sister. She smiled at their differences. His skin tanned by too much sun, hair a dark brown–almost black, except for a strange streak of sun-bleached red, a trait he'd inherited from his father. Marina was fair-skinned with copper hair and green eyes, like her mother.

Along with Elena's brother Freddy, they'd all been close from early childhood, playmates, and buddies throughout school. But Alex—Alex was a whole different story. What had been a childhood friendship turned into a teenage crush, then a relationship she didn't want to dwell on.

Elena came back to reality. "Listen, while we're still alone, there's something I want to tell you."

Marina raised her eyebrows. "What?"

"I've decided to go to Romania."

"You've decided to *what*?"

A breeze blew Elena's dark hair into her face. "Magda wanted me to travel with her this summer, to go through my brother's things, and settle the estate." She couldn't exactly say her grandmother's *ghost* told her to go.

"You should take someone with you," Marina said.

Elena cocked her head. "You want to come with me? We speak Romanian. We'd have a great time, roaming around the countryside and meeting the locals in Dkany. We could explore the castle and visit the monastery."

"I'm starting my internship, but I was thinking about Alex. He's not teaching this summer."

Dear God, no. "Marina, I'll be fine by myself. I lived there, remember?"

Silence

Inwardly, Elena winced. Nobody wanted to talk about her life in Romania. "I'm perfectly capable of taking care of myself."

The man approached through a cluster of people, and the scent of his after-shave filled the air. He'd been the one supporting her at the cemetery.

Marina clutched her arm. "Elena, yes, you do. You're very capable, but Romania isn't the same as . . . Well, it's still wild in spots, especially in Transylvania."

Alex spoke up in a clear baritone voice. "She doesn't need my help, and Romania isn't in my plans this summer. Hello, Elena." He kissed her on both cheeks. "It's been a long time. I'm sorry we had to meet under such lousy circumstances."

Elena's gaze locked onto the eyes of Marina's older brother. The drink in her hand trembled. His eyes invoked bittersweet memories from their shared past.

"Thanks." She forced a smile. "And thanks for catching me at the cemetery. I nearly fell on top of the casket."

Alex wrinkled his nose. A grin bent his lips. "Yeah. You were a bit unsteady on your feet. Falling on a casket wouldn't have been graceful. By the way, who were you talking to?"

Elena dropped her gaze to the patio and focused on sparkling bands of sunlight reflecting off the concrete. Heat warmed her cheeks. She glanced at him and considered her answer.

"My grandmother," she admitted. "I was talking to Magda. Does that sound strange?"

Alex shook his head. "No, not really." Pain shadowed his face. "I'm sorry about Magda. I visited her often while you and Marina were away at school. I thought she was lonely, then discovered she had more friends than she knew what to do with."

Elena managed a smile and nodded. "I know. She told me. She also mentioned you'd gotten your doctoral thesis on Romanian history published."

He shrugged. "Yes, I did." His arms crossed. His body leaned nonchalantly against the railing. "Heard you went to Romania and got married, and you'd gotten your master's degree from the University of Indiana."

"Magda kept you informed."

"She did. I heard about every test you took."

But, somewhere in there, Elena had lost her entire family. He didn't mention that.

A woman crossed the patio and waved at Alex.

Alex told Elena, "Excuse me. I have a student I need to talk to."

"Thanks for catching me this morning," Elena responded to his back.

He halted and spun back to her, his gaze scrutinizing. "I'm glad I was good for something."

Alex pivoted toward his student and walked her into the house.

Elena turned toward Marina. "So, who the heck is that?"

"That," Marina replied, "is a Mrs. Brancusi wanna-be." She shook her head. "Not going to happen."

Elena shrugged. "Why not? What's wrong with him?"

Mari stifled a laugh. "You," she said.

Chapter 2

Me? The reason why someone hadn't snatched Alex up long ago was *her*? He hadn't wanted her then, why would he want her now? She watched.

Alex held court with several professors and some pretty female students. Girls flocked to this young, handsome, and witty language professor. A bit on the exotic side, Elena thought. They stood close, leaned over him, and looked sorrowful. She caught snatches of conversation.

"I'm so sorry. I know how close you were to Mrs. Dkany. Maybe I could find a way to cheer you up?"

He smiled at them and muttered. "Thanks. She was special. Talk to Elena. She has some great stories about Magda."

He was sending these women over to *her*?

They remained by his side. They were offering condolences, probably other things, too.

This wasn't the Alex she remembered.

Once or twice, Elena caught him shooting glances her way. She turned toward a small crowd of neighbors.

"That man has bedroom eyes," Mrs. Rice, her next-door neighbor, said. "Oh, Elena. I'm glad you're here. Now, I've brought over some . . ."

Elena lost the name of what Mrs. Rice brought. She glanced at Alex but pulled away when he turned and stared. Yes, he did have bedroom eyes. She'd heard about his reputation. Alex must have changed a great deal.

The last of the women dropped a piece of paper in Alex's coat pocket as she left. Maybe a phone number? When she closed the door, he tossed the note into the nearest trash can. So much for the Mrs. Brancusi wanna-be.

A tall, thin man with an abundance of graying hair and a high forehead stood in the corner of the living room. A good-looking man, Elena thought. He wore a familiarity, but she couldn't quite place him. *I know you. Why do I know you?*

He played with his highball glass, talked to guests, glanced at her, then surveyed the room. Elena wondered if he was waiting for everyone to leave.

When the last of the guests left, the man remained, standing in silence—observing.

"Raven hair and blue eyes, you are the lovely Elena Dkany." The man bowed. "Although, I must say you are prettier than the last time I saw you."

Lovely? Her? She didn't think so. What did this man want? When had she last seen him? Elena tried to recall, but with Alex watching her, her mind went blank. Alex appeared amused. She glared and sent his head back into the book he held in his hand.

The man shook his head. "No, no. I do not wish to stir the bad memories." Then, she remembered. Gregory Balogh. Her grandmother's solicitor from Romania and the family's castle caretaker. The man who'd saved her life. The man who loved and cherished her grandmother. She hadn't seen him since that awful night, but she loved him all the same. "You're Uncle Gregory."

Gregory Balogh bowed and kissed her hand. "It is a compliment that you remember me." He turned to Marina, "And, from the bright red of your hair, you must be the younger sister of Alexander? I'm told you will be a resident in Internal Medicine at the Northwestern Memorial Hospital. I offer congratulations to a brilliant and beautiful lady." When he kissed her hand, a blush raced straight into Marina's face.

Elena raised her eyebrows. *He certainly knows how to dish out compliments.*

"But, please to sit," he said, stretching out his hands to all three.

Elena didn't know why, but they all obeyed like good, dutiful children.

"So, there it is. I know everyone. And, perhaps you remember me, as Miss Elena did. Gregory Balogh at your service. I arrived late. I am desolate to miss the dear lady's funeral. But I am here now, no?" He sat straight up in an uncomfortable-looking wingback chair. "A tragedy— a waste. Magda was a dear friend, Elena."

"Uncle Gregory," Elena said, her spirits rising. "I'm sorry I didn't recognize you. You saved my life." She remembered him, so long ago, bending over her as she lay on the living room floor in her apartment in Bucharest just before she passed out from pain and loss of blood. The memory of the attack she'd locked away.

"Yes, and that is now over, yes? We put the past behind us." He set his glass on the end table, leaned forward, and said, "I am, of course, an uncle only in friendship."

Alex sat on a bench and plunked a note on a walnut upright piano. They'd played it together while they were dating. He'd taken his left hand, her the right, during a rousing, hilarious rendition of 'Chop- sticks.' His glance sent a slight shiver down her spine. He appeared to remember too. She turned away—that was then, this is now.

"That's okay," Elena said with a sigh before returning to the con- versation. "My family loved making relatives out of friends."

"Yes, this is true, which is why what I am about to tell you should come as no shock." The tone in his voice roused her curiosity. "I am here, of course, not only to pay my respects but to read Magda's will." He raised his hands. "Of course, on this night, it seems not right. But it must be said—what the Dkany and Brancusi families wished for their children."

Elena glanced at Alex.

He shrugged back.

Marina said, "I didn't know Aunt Magda or mother had any specific plans for any of us." She smiled. "Except for us to be successful and, hopefully, happy."

Gregory nodded. "Yes, of course, my dear lady. You are all successful. But of what I speak does not concern you directly."

"Oh. Thank goodness." Marina looked visibly relieved.

Gregory coughed. "The Dkany Castle has always been owned by the Dkanys. With the passing of your brother, Miss Elena, Magda realized the castle would come to you and could eventually pass from the Dkanys if they had no heirs. She spoke with the Brancusi family. They felt a marriage between you and Alexander could bond the families forever. A match to ensure the Dkany Castle would remain within the ancestral circle. It was a marriage your families had hoped for since you were in your teens."

Elena's jaw dropped. The cuckoo on the wall chirped seven o'clock. She abruptly looked up at the wooden bird and wanted to wrench the stupid thing's neck. The past week's emotions finally caught up and walloped her in the form of giggles that wouldn't quit.

He frowned, shifted in his seat, and said, "It's not that funny."

"I'm sorry," she gasped. "An *arranged* marriage? I didn't think families did that anymore." She took several deep breaths and swallowed the nervous laughter. "Look, I'm sorry. It's been a horrible week."

Alex focused on the oriental carpet. Realization hit.

"You knew about this when we were dating?"

He tossed his gaze through the patio door.

A sourness arose from the pit of Elena's stomach. Her eyes fixed the floor to hide her hurt. "So that's why you wanted to date me. Our families forced you into it."

Alex's eyes darkened with defiance. "Magda obviously didn't force you into anything. You ditched me and married someone else."

"You wrote and said it was best we date other people. So, I did." Elena stood, her anger aimed at Gregory Balogh, who clasped his hands and looked uncomfortable. "You people are too much. You think you can force a boy and girl to marry in the twenty-first century?"

Alex raised his hands in protest. "Elena—"

"No. This is really too much." Trying to control her anger, she rose and turned toward the door.

Gregory stood and held out his hands. "You would be surprised. There are still many arranged marriages in our societies. Many work out very well. Please, Miss Elena. If this had not been an agreeable solution, the families would never have suggested it. Alex did not object."

Elena spun around and replied, "But I might have." She stared daggers at both men. "I've never heard about this. Weren't my feelings considered at all?"

Gregory shrugged. "It didn't seem important. You and Alexander . . . close friends already, no? We thought you liked each other. Unfortunately, complications prevented the union from taking place." He smiled. "They no longer exist."

How could he be so blasé about the death of her husband and baby?

The solicitor continued, "Of course, nobody can tell you whom you should marry."

"Thank goodness for that," Elena said.

Gregory frowned, raised his highball glass, and finished the remains. "I am charged with the responsibility of informing you of the family's wishes, that is all."

This was no joke. Their families had meant for them to marry. She'd wanted to marry him someday. She thought he'd wanted to marry her. She'd been wrong. This conversation and the memories it invoked were too overwhelming. She needed out. The French doors were only a few feet away. She tried to retreat.

"Elena, I would have married you."

Elena jerked around. "What?" Her gaze found Alex, who was staring at her with his sad and damned bedroom eyes.

A shadow clouded his face again. "But I'm sure you did a lot better with Janek Ivanov."

"What in the world do you mean?" Elena asked, staggered by the defeat in his tone and his sarcasm. She wanted to hit him; instead, she stood in the middle of some bizarre Victorian drama.

Uncle Gregory placed his hands in a prayer motion. The reflected colored lights of the Tiffany lamp on the end table falling on skin pulled taut over gaunt cheekbones. "Elena, I beg of you. Please . . . do sit. There is more to say and do."

Elena averted her eyes and gave it some thought. Her head tipped a nod before she settled back on the sofa.

Reaching into his briefcase, Gregory pulled out a plain white square box and handed it to her. "This is for you."

Surprised, Elena opened it. She removed a silver box with figures of fifteenth-century boyars appearing so accurate in detail, a gift likely created it in that era. Her breath refused to exhale, and she finally gasped. "The army of noblemen of Romania," she whispered, half to herself. "This is exquisite."

"It is so. Pure silver, but . . ." Gregory said, his eyes shining. His tone lowered to a whisper. "Look inside." The penetration from his eyes narrowed like a laser to the box. "This has been in safekeeping. Open it."

When she opened the case, she clapped a hand to her cheek and couldn't speak. A large blood-red ruby lay on a backdrop of white velvet. "My God," Elena murmured. She fingered the stone. "The color of blood." She looked up. "And passion."

Marina, who'd been quietly looking on, rose and peered at the stone. She turned to Gregory. "It's gorgeous."

"This ruby was embedded in an altar-cross, and the monks presented it to Viktor Dkany for valor on the battlefield." Gregory stood silent for a moment then said, "He'd killed Prince Vlad Tepes, and for that, he was highly rewarded. The stone has quite a history."

Elena whispered. "You mean this ruby dates back to the fifteenth century?"

"Probably older, my dear," he replied. "Remember, the Turks possessed it first."

Alex picked up *The History of the Romanian Empire* from the coffee table. Elena couldn't tell whether he was fascinated with the topic or bored with Gregory Balogh. His sister threw her brother a look, and he put down the book. "So, where's the cross, now?" He asked.

"Ah, destroyed in an earthquake. Only the ruby survives." Gregory remained solemn. "It remained in the castle vault for over five hundred years. Now, you are its sole possessor."

"Earthquake," Alex said, thumbing through the pages. "Romania is plagued by them. A big one hit in the '70s."

Gregory nodded. "Yes, that is correct in 1977. Over 1500 people were killed in Bucharest alone. But the earthquake also hit farther than the capital. The town of Vrancea—"

"Was the epicenter," Alex said. "Vrancea Mountains in the Eastern Carpathians."

"Yes, true. However, the Vrancea Earthquake was not the one that took the cross."

"Oh," Elena said, turning away from the ruby. "When was the cross destroyed?"

"In 1523. The last time anyone saw the cross before it disappeared."

"You're just full of cheerful facts," Marina said. "But wasn't there one just recently?" She glanced at the ceiling then nodded. "Believe it was somewhere in Transylvania, maybe even in Dkany. I read about it on the Internet in *The Romanian News.*

Gregory nodded again. "The Internet. A useful, if not sometimes a deceptive, source of information. But that is correct. There was an earthquake not far from Dkany only a week ago."

"Any damage?" Elena asked.

"Yes, unfortunately, that is so. Some of the underground passages were blocked by the rubble. The chapel organ was damaged. The instrument was unique. It had golden pipes. Such a shame. We hope this is not a, how-do-you-say, a prequel to a more serious tremor?"

Elena sighed. A castle in Romania, complete with a historic organ and underground passages. A rare ruby from the time of the Turkish Empire. How lucky could one girl be?

She stood gazing into the ruby's crystalline center again. Apprehension and foreboding wound their tentacles down her spine. Her eyes closed. Something inside her head rotated, like the whirling movement inside the stone.

"What's wrong?" The voices came from all around, but they echoed far away.

Her eyes opened again. Inside the center, a bloody battle full of fifteenth-century boyars raged in the background. Silhouettes of impaled Turks lined the horizon.

Switch. A young boy searched for something or someone. Then he disappeared, and a vision appeared of a monk executing a young woman in the present. She didn't know the boy. The woman, she knew.

Her.

The room took on a surreal quietness that seemed to extend to the outside. Even the birds stopped singing.

Cuckoo.

The clock broke the trance that hovered over the room. Elena tried to scream, but no sound came. She grabbed out for something—anything, but the walls started to spin, and the ground came rushing toward her. She fell into Alex's outstretched arms, and the ruby fell at his feet before darkness swallowed her consciousness.

Chapter 3

From Romania to Evanston, Illinois

"Done. The old lady is dead."

Elite among international assassins, Federal authorities considered Hadean Petrov one of the most dangerous killers alive. They remembered Bolivia's situation, which took down experienced DEA agents, and the drug runner's ambush on the Black Sea. All Hadean Petrov. Now, he was on another mission.

His baritone voice crackled in the static of his cell phone. "The funeral—held today."

"So . . ." The speaker on the other end trailed off then spoke again. "Who was there? At the funeral."

"I was not present, but I caught a glimpse and heard the conversation. Many people from the college, Elena Dkany, Alexander Brancusi, and his sister, and one Gregory Balogh, who comes from Romania. He is also Magda's solicitor. Uh, he was late but showed up at the house afterward."

"Yes, I knew he would be there. It is as I thought. Good." Another pause, almost as if the thinking came through the crackling of the phone. "The death, it was quick, yes? How?"

"Do you want details?" The assassin laughed. "How was it done?"

"Accident?" Voices, not from the speaker, overrode his voice. "Just one moment." Muffled conversation, then he was back. "I am free."

"Good. So, hit and, how do you say . . . run? As a tree branch topples in a storm."

"Did it look like an accident?"

"I made it look so."

"Good."

A man with a fishing pole came up alongside him. Petrov swung his feet over the rock, retrieved his sandals, and walked away.

"What now? Do I leave, or do you have another job for me?"

"You wait. I will have more for you to do."

"Do you have money for me?"

"Oh yes. You will have the money. Look in your Romanian bank account. It is all there."

"I thank you. It is good doing business with you." They clicked off their cell phones.

Hadean Petrov walked across the park and across the street where he'd killed Magda Dkany.

Chapter 4

Dkany Home

Evanston, Illinois

The afternoon after the funeral turned out as miserable as Alex's mood. Who'd want to run down an old woman like Magda? One witness account convinced him this had been a carefully planned attack.

Someone murdered her, but why? Had the old woman known a secret that would prove dangerous to someone? Was she eliminated? Again, the nagging question. Why?

Then there was Magda's granddaughter. Ten years was too long to brood over any girl. But from the moment he'd caught her in the cemetery, he'd found his heart just as vulnerable. He had to be careful. She didn't appear to give a damn about him. Especially when Gregory Balogh suggested marriage.

The fog was like pea soup—so dense he nearly walked into one of the pine trees bordering the sidewalk to Elena's front porch. Waves crashed against the rocks of Lake Michigan's shoreline, and the lonely moan of a nearby foghorn became his acoustic landmark. Something about its plaintive requiem forced the hairs on the back of his neck to stand on end. A premonition? Crazy. He didn't believe in them. He sighed, turned away from the tree, and used the gift box he carried as a shield to press their piney branches back.

Alex finally reached for the doorbell. He hoped the box Magda left with him might help soothe Elena's pain.

Marina opened the door. She gave up a yawn. Bloodshot eyes almost matched a ringlet of her red hair. "Hey." She might as well have hung a sign around her neck that read 'just got out of bed.' He grinned. His sister was hung over—a first.

Marina frowned. "What's so damned funny?"

"Drink too much?"

"Yeah. You look like hell yourself. What time did *you* get up?"

"About eleven," Alex answered. "And I always look like hell."

"We're just having coffee. Come on in before you melt into this fog."

He stomped the dampness from his shoes and followed his sister inside.

Elena sat at the kitchen table, drinking coffee.

His gaze rested on her black silk Chinese robe, violet lace peeking out from under the opening. Her hair disappeared into the collar, except for stray tendrils that escaped from her clip.

His heart thumped, and a residue of old heartache washed over him like the fog outside. He needed to make it *perfectly* clear—he would *not go* to Romania with her.

"I just wanted you to know, I can't go to Romania. My schedule . . ."

She raised her eyebrows and stared at him.

Alex redirected his sentiments to Marina. "In case there was any misunderstanding."

Elena waved his comment away and sipped her coffee. "This isn't a sightseeing tour, and I don't need a translator." The word *jerk* was there in her mind. "I didn't *expect* this would be a vacation."

Marina's eyes shifted, and she gave her brother a half-smile. "You mean you wouldn't help a friend in need? That's very unlike you."

Elena lifted her coffee cup to her mouth, then put it back on the table. "Listen." An edge crept into her voice. "I appreciate your concern, Mari. Really. However, I don't think either of you knows my reason for wanting to go. I don't need—or want—company." A strand of hair fell into her coffee cup. She removed it and pushed the stray lock behind her ears.

Alex watched, fascinated.

"Magda wanted to convert the castle into a school," Marina said. She eyed her brother. "A college prep for poor children."

Elena tapped her finger on her coffee mug, a shadow of annoyance crossing her face.

Strange girl—the one he'd let slip from his grasp. He scrutinized the blue eyes that broke his heart whenever he thought of them.

"Why?" Alex sat on a kitchen chair, leaned back, and folded his arms. Magda had mentioned one day she thought the castle might make a good school. Had that been her intent?

Was that contempt in Elena's eyes? It appeared and vanished quickly.

"Why not? My ancestors, including my brother, enjoyed years of luxurious living at that castle. Why not give something back?" She shrugged. "I'll be back to attend Briar Hill in the fall."

Alex nodded. The new Briar Hill, PhD student. Magda told him she'd come. "You expect to do all that in the next two months?"

"I'd like to think it's possible."

Her desire to go back to Romania surprised him. She had a lost look in her eyes—haunted even. The sweet innocence that defined the girl he'd loved was gone. Replaced were hints of sorrow and a strong sense of determination for something—but, for what? Her grandmother's school?

He changed the subject. "Here," he pulled out the box from behind his chair and sat next to her. "I brought you something."

Her eyes brightened with surprise. "Thank you. I didn't expect . . ." She tilted her head and looked puzzled.

Alex finished her sentence for her. "It's not from me. Magda wanted me to keep it for you until the time was right." He sat back waiting for her to open the box.

Elena crossed her arms. "So, this isn't a gift from you."

Alex sighed. "No. But, I thought it might cheer you up."

"What is it?"

"Don't know." Whatever it was, he'd hidden it in his closet for years, with the promise he wouldn't look inside.

A smile crossed her face. "Okay, Alex." She held out her hand. "Friends?"

"Friends." He pushed his mug out of the way and took her hand. Her touch sprouted images of fresh sheets and warm bodies, and he didn't want to let go. That worried him, and he pulled back a little too abruptly.

Elena looked at her hand, then at him, and bit down on her lip.

"Okay." Her tone implied it wasn't.

She blew out a deep breath, then opened the box and pulled out a Romanian peasant wedding outfit.

"Oh my God," Marina's mouth fell open as her eyes narrowed at her brother.

"What?" he asked. An authentic Transylvanian wedding costume. So? What was causing all the looks? A white blouse decorated with rose-colored stripes surrounded by flowers. She pulled up another layer of tissue paper. Hidden in the wrappings lay a matching skirt with an eyelet hem and a border of blue, green, and red flowers.

"Where on earth . . . ?" The color washed from her face.

Tears flowed down her cheeks. The bright flowers on the skirt hem mocked the misery in her face.

"What's the matter?" Alex got up for more coffee. Distracted, he missed the edge of his cup and spilled hot liquid over his hand. The carafe slipped and slid onto the counter.

"Damn!" He jumped back and leaped two steps to the sink, allowing cold water to douse the burn.

"Alex?" The two women started to get up, looking ready to pounce with first aid remedies.

Damn. Damn, damn. "Don't get up. I'm okay." Sure he was. His hand ached.

He mopped the spill with a dishrag, poured another cup, and came back to the table.

"Will someone please explain the significance of that costume?" Alex asked.

Marina shot him a 'shut up' look, the kind siblings cultivate with each other. *Some things shouldn't be discussed.*

"It's okay." Elena's glance moved between them. "This was my wedding dress. Maybe Uncle Gregory or Freddy sent it to Magda after they flew me back to the states. They probably didn't think I needed to see it."

This he didn't need. Alex's stomach lurched, thinking this was the wedding dress she'd worn when she'd wedded—and bedded—another man. Just great.

He settled back in his seat and took a sip of coffee, refusing to let her emotions get to him. He wasn't prepared for the wallop his stomach took.

A dog-eared leather-bound album lay in the bottom of the box. Photos Alex didn't think he wanted to see. *Please, just put it back into the box.*

But Elena didn't appear to be reading minds this morning. She opened the yellowed pages, dropped it as though stung, pushed back, and knocked over the chair.

Alex looked down at the album. Staring back at him was the pretty seventeen-year-old he'd taken to the senior prom standing beside a blond youth, their fingers entwined. A priest stood behind them. Curled up on the tissue was a silver cross with the chip of a red ruby.

"Oh no." Elena doubled over. Marina tried to catch her, but she pulled out of her arm, grabbed the box, and ran from the room.

Alex heard her footsteps running up the stairs.

How could he have been so stupid? Or—

Marina's eyes filled with tears. "I'm sorry, Alex. You couldn't have known. Maybe that's why Magda didn't want this in her house until the time was right."

"The time wasn't right," Alex whispered, still numb.

"The time may never be right." Marina's voice came from far away, and the temperature dropped.

"What the . . . ?" Alex glanced at the kitchen thermometer that read forty deg rees. A few minutes ago, seventy-five.

Why the sudden change?

Elena sat on her bed. The sobs from shock and sadness subsided, but she still shook from the memories.

Almost ten years ago, a drug-crazed student from the University of Bucharest broke into her apartment and murdered her family. She managed to kill him but almost succumbed to her own wounds. Her brother and Mr. Balogh stayed at the hospital every day until she recovered. Freddy must have sent Magda the package after he'd cleared out her things and moved them to his cottage on the castle grounds. Her heart slowed with bereavement. If she felt this way now, how would she react when those ghosts confronted her in Romania? Maybe going back was a mistake.

No matter. Her life had gone up in smoke, knifed in its very heart. And, when she returned home, Magda whisked her off to the University of Indiana. There had been no discussion of getting back with Alex. He'd gone to study in Washington, and she hadn't seen him since—until yesterday.

The years hadn't been entirely kind to Alex, and his reputation preceded him. He could make a woman tremble with desire and then send her spiraling into a deep depression when he'd finished with her. Marina had warned her. Be careful. Look, but don't touch. Touch, but don't get hooked. Alex would not marry you. But just this morning, he'd said—No, forget it.

Elena pulled her robe closer to her, not exactly cold but chilled from the shock. This wasn't his fault. He hadn't known what was in that box. Magda was secretive in her ways, but she'd never have hurt Alex by showing him the wedding costume. Still, she needed to blame someone.

The temperature was hot and oppressively humid. The ceiling fan struggled to circulate the air.

Marina peeked inside; her hair was wet beneath a towel. "Are you all right?"

"No," Elena replied softly. "I'm not all right. But I will be. It was just the shock of seeing my life jump out at me. It wasn't your brother's fault. It's something I have to deal with."

"He felt terrible about it. You know he didn't . . ."

Elena smiled. "He didn't know. I'm not blaming him."

"Do you want me to put this costume on the top shelf in your closet?"

"No. Leave it here. I'll put it away later. I need to hold it for a minute."

"That may not be so healthy for you, but okay."

Marina turned to go and hesitated. "Alex is going to stay until after Mr. Balogh leaves tonight. Is that okay with you?"

"Yes, it is." She suddenly realized his friendship was important to her.

The dress lay on the bed, smelling of mothballs and lemon-scented detergent stored in—ice? Strange. The inside of the box had been warm when first opened. Now, a frost vapor trail materialized as if the package had emerged from cold storage.

Apprehension turned into shivers, and a loud thumping resonated in her chest. She shot up and stared down at the garment. How had this dress caused such a panic attack?

The presence of someone in the room filled the air. A miserable someone.

Another *ghost?* She'd never even seen one, and now two? Magda again? Or . . .

Slowly, she backed out of the room, avoiding the onslaught of any specters that might reside inside the folds of the skirt.

"What's wrong?"

Startled by the new voice at her side, Elena let the breath go she'd been holding.

Marina looked at Elena, then into the room. "What in the world is wrong?"

Nothing. She couldn't squeak out a response.

"Elena!" Not a ghost, but a friend.

"Something's wrong. I can feel it."

Marina gripped her arms and turned her around. "You're white as your bedspread. What's in there?"

Keep control. "I could have sworn . . . I'm just on edge. I . . ." Elena stepped back. "I'm not prone to hallucinations."

Marina shook her head. "No. You're one of the most practical women I know. So?"

Elena frowned. "It must have been the strain of the past week."

"What must have—?"

She cut off Marina's question, disallowing any more phantoms. "Let's go back and check out the costume again."

The garment lay innocently on the bed. The blouse felt warm again. No signs of ghostly specters. Was she nuts?

"I'm not sure why I . . ." Her brows drew together from shock. The album she'd slammed shut lay open. A photo of Jan with his broad, handsome smile no longer rested in the collection. It had flipped onto the bed.

Marina grabbed her arm. "Honey, I believe the album's unleashed Jan's ghost. He's here."

"You believe, then?"

"Of course. You know I do."

Searching for a plausible explanation, Elena came up with nothing but uneasiness. "I'm putting this away." She boxed the album and costume and pushed them onto the top shelf of her closet. The cross she clasped around her neck.

The fog lifted, and blue patches slowly emerged from behind gunmetal gray clouds. Alex stood with his back against the patio railing, checked to see if anyone was in the immediate vicinity, and pulled out his cell phone. He dialed a number in Romania.

A gravelly voice answered, "Alex?"

"It's me."

"Good. Alone?"

"Yeah. You wanted to talk to me."

Alex Brancusi had a secret he kept even from his sister. He worked undercover for the Federal Bureau of Investigation, assigned to Tony Donatelli's special operations field team, *Operation Heroin Sucks,* who worked with the Romanian government. A trail led heroin exportation from Afghanistan to Romania, where it remained until transported to the United States.

Tony had been handpicked to lead the United States Department of Justice team because of his success in eradicating a cartel in South America. Tony was merciless in tracking down criminals, yet he could be one of the nicest guys Alex had ever known.

"So?" Tony asked.

"No question. Magda was murdered. Guy planned it to the second. Nighttime . . . headlights were off. Ran her down."

"How do we know the headlights were off? Witnesses?"

"Yeah. A couple walking home from the park, not far behind Magda. They saw the whole thing but couldn't give a description. The driver sped away. They were more concerned about Magda."

"Suspects?"

"None."

"Funeral?"

"Mostly Briar Hill faculty and staff. No one I haven't seen almost every day."

"Dead end, you think?"

"Look, I've wormed my way into the lives of the entire Briar Hill community. I've kept my ear to the ground through the student and staff grapevine. Some weed—no heroin. However, drugs are coming into Chicago, it isn't through Briar Hill."

"You seem pretty sure. Your judgment isn't being clouded by your proximity to home, is it?"

"Shit. Would you really have sent me here if you thought I'd be prejudiced?"

"No."

In fact, he'd done some despicable things. "Look, my reputation in town is shot. The women think I'm a first-class louse. I've wined, dined, and some other things I'm not proud of, all in the name of patriotism."

"Sometimes playing hard to get is a good thing." Tony chuckled. "Look, there are a few interesting developments. Magda's Romanian solicitor, Gregory Balogh, arrived from Dkany. As sole heir, Elena inherits the castle."

"Yeah, so?"

"She wants to go to Dkany this summer. Alone."

He heard Tony take a deep breath into the phone. "She does? She give a reason?"

"She hates me. Outside of that, I think she's exerting her independence. Magda wanted to convert the castle into a school."

"So she said."

"Elena is determined to continue in her footsteps. I'll say that for her. Also, Gregory Balogh will be coming again tonight."

Static shot out from the other end of the phone before it quieted down. "Gregory Balogh's a heavy in Dkany. You might find out something we don't already know."

The fog was lifting, and although the sun peaked out from behind the clouds, the atmosphere still felt heavy. A storm was brewing.

"Tony, do you know anything about an earthquake that hit Dkany last week?"

"I heard about it. Shook buildings. Some peasant shacks toppled. Most of the stronger structures held. Not horrible, why?"

"Balogh mentioned the castle had some damage."

"I didn't hear much. Seems okay. Why?"

"Checking out what Gregory told us. Just curious."

Tony's tone changed. "I found something you ought to know. I'm looking at the Dkany Hall of Recoord's site on the Internet."

"Dkany. Why?"

"Cross-referencing a list of names. But that's not what I'm looking at," Tony paused. "What was Elena Dkany's husband's last name, again?"

Alex sighed. He felt the familiar tug of emptiness whenever someone mentioned the name. He sighed. "Ivanov."

"Okay, listen to this."

Alex didn't want to listen.

"Janek Ivanov was born in December of 1986 and died November 2005 . . ."

"Why are you rehashing this? We know when he died."

Even though Elena's mentioned as his wife, a child is noted as being born in '05, with no record of the baby's death. Listen. This is from an article written by an American correspondent in Bucharest.

'Political activist Janek Ivanov died early this morning from injuries sustained in an attack in his home. Mr. Ivanov appeared to be defending his wife when he

managed to subdue and kill an unidentified attacker. Both Mr. Ivanov and his wife expired shortly after police arrived.'"

The news hit Alex like a bucket of ice-cold water. "What? No," he almost whispered. He cleared his throat. "Can't be. Must have been a mix-up of some kind?"

"That's what I thought until I read the obituary. It says Janek and Elena Ivanov died in the attack. No mention of a child."

Suddenly Alex had a hard time breathing. Why the hell had the report stated Elena had been killed?

"What did it say about the suspect?" Alex asked.

"A student from the university. No criminal background. Good student. Nothing outstanding. Maybe some kind of vendetta. Look, what have you found at Briar Hill?"

"Nothing."

"Maybe there's nothing to be found. But, Alex, face the facts, there's a lot of weird shit concerning the Dkany's. Their ownership of a castle that might be inhabited by a gang of drug dealers—"

"Or not."

"As you say. We still have other suspects. But think about this. Elena married her brother's best friend, who lives in Bucharest, and he's murdered. Then, nine months ago, Freddy Dkany dies of a heroin overdose. Next, Magda Dkany's killed. Now, Elena's going to the castle. Coincidence?" Tony's tone made Alex nervous. He was hitting hard on his family's best friends.

"Do you believe in coincidences?" Alex asked. He started pacing, nearly slipping on a wet spot. "And you think Dkany Castle stores the heroin? That's why you thought Briar Hill was the point of entry into Chicago? Elena's grandfather was on the board of directors for two decades. We're not investigating the college, we're investigating the Dkany's."

"Very good, Alex."

"Bullshit." Alex pressed down the 'End Call' button.

If this was true and Elena was unaware, she might be in grave danger.

Chapter 5

Dkany Home

Evanston, Illinois

The chimes on the doorbell clanged.

Elena jumped. "Dear God." She let out a sigh and bent over, almost hyperventilating.

Marina swung around. "You okay?"

Elena shook her head and placed her hands on her knees. She gasped and realized she really *could* breathe. Then she giggled. "I don't think so, not with Jan wandering around here unannounced."

"Elena Dkany—ghostbuster." Marina turned, and they walked down the stairs. Any remnants left of her inner peace turned on its tail and ran deep inside, refusing to emerge.

Marina opened the door.

"Good evening, Miss Marina." Gregory Balogh took her hand and kissed it in his old-world-style greeting.

Dear God. I forgot he was coming. She looked up the stairs to see if there might be a shadow lurking in a corner, then turned back and greeted her uncle.

Gregory Balogh stood in the threshold, wearing a suit and tie regardless of the ninety-degree weather. "You were expecting . . ." He looked over Elena's shoulder and blinked several times.

The movement of a dark shadow disappeared into an upper bedroom. So, Uncle Gregory had seen the ghost, had he? Now what? Pretend she hadn't noticed? Thinking about it, she knew Jan wouldn't harm her. So, why was he here? Why had he been haunting the box with the wedding dress?

"Uncle Gregory?" Marina turned and shrugged.

Slightly pale, Gregory asked, "What was upstairs? Do you have another guest?"

Elena gave Gregory her best dazzling smile. "The only other person here is Alex, and he's outside, I think,"

"Ah." Doubt shadowed his face.

So now what do I say? We have spirits floating around? Not a bad idea. "Yes. We have our own resident ghost. Didn't Magda tell you?" She laughed and poked Marina in the ribs. Marina picked it up and laughed too.

"It was only my fertile imagination. I am sorry." Gregory kissed the two women on each cheek. He looked up the staircase before centering back on Elena. "I trust you are feeling better today?"

He escorted the women into the parlor, his darting eyes communicated uneasiness. "You must forgive my intrusion, but I have your grandmother's will in my briefcase. I wish to go over its contents and have you sign some documents before I leave."

"I'm really not feeling up to this just now. Do we have to do this today?" Elena pulled out from Gregory's arm and stood in the middle of the parlor, looking around. Alex. Where was Alex?

Marina settled in the rocking chair.

"I, too, feel the sadness over your grandmother's death." Gregory put his briefcase on the coffee table and sat on the sofa. "We'd shared so much over the years. I prostrate myself before you with humble apologies, but I must return to Romania." He clasped his hands together and put his fingertips to his lips. "As the last remaining Dkany, everything comes to you. This house and property, all possessions. Your grandfather was an astute businessman. He left Magda well off. And, except for your education, Magda was frugal."

In general, that had been true. But Elena had never wanted for anything: tuition, clothes, spending money, a car. She looked at the numbers and nearly fainted. The financial holdings proved more than she could have dreamed.

"Any questions?" Gregory asked.

She shook her head. In reality, she had a lot. How could a college president stash away so much money? They'd been part of Romanian royalty—inherited perhaps? She wished she'd asked Magda more questions about her family.

Gregory answered her unasked question. "Ah, you want to know how your grandfather accumulated such wealth."

Elena nodded. "College presidents make a good salary, but not that much."

Gregory fingered his jaw before he spoke again. "Old money. You come from an aristocratic family."

That explained it, or did it? "Ancient royalty doesn't mean much today."

"No. That is true," Gregory said, "but he also played the stock market and played it well. We were in constant contact."

"Oh, I see." Did she? Why the inkling of doubt?

Gregory nodded. "So, we move on to Romania."

Elena scooted forward, anticipation settling into the pit of her stomach.

"Dkany Castle belongs to you."

She started to speak, but Gregory held up his hands.

"What's left of it." He reached into the briefcase and handed her several eight-by-ten glossy photographs. "Please, take a look at these. I am sad to show you such pictures. I tried to tell Magda many times, but your grandmother would not listen. She lived in the past, you see? She remembered her mother's time when the castle hosted foreign dignitaries and ladies wore ball gowns and danced in great halls."

The photos showed piles of rubble and ruin, fronting a tall brick and mortar façade. The front of the castle looked intact. Crumbling fifty-foot walls encircled the structure, and a splintered wooden drawbridge crossed a weed-strewn waterless moat.

The castle looked sad and forlorn ready to topple into the past.

Elena fingered the photo. "It looks like Sleeping Beauty waiting for her prince to wake her with a kiss."

"And who is *your* prince?" All three turned in the direction of the French doors. Alex stood braced against the door frame.

"She probably doesn't need one," Marina said, eying her brother. Elena wondered how long he'd been there.

"Alexander." Gregory stood, acknowledging his presence before he sat again. "I'm afraid the restoration of this castle will take more than a kiss to wake its beauty." He directed the conversation back to practicalities. "Elena will be well off, but I'm afraid the assets won't be enough for rehabilitation of this magnitude. The castle is barely habitable."

Elena raised her eyebrows. "My brother lived there."

Gregory smiled, but his eyes remained distant. "Your brother lived in the caretaker's cottage. Sadly, the castle's upkeep ate up its resources years ago. I am afraid this Sleeping Beauty will never awake unless someone pours much money into repairs. It is . . . how do you call it? A pink elephant?"

"A white elephant," Elena said. Gregory's English was near perfect, but he wasn't familiar with some of the less common idioms he liked to throw around.

However, what he said wasn't at all humorous. Magda's dreams of a school seemed to be shattering by the minute.

"There is some good news." Gregory touched her arm. "You are wondering how you would be able to unload such a sore eye?"

"Eyesore," Alex said. He walked across the room and sat in the chair next to his sister.

"Ah. I stand corrected once more."

"And what is this good news?" Alex asked.

"The City of Dkany has made a generous offer for the property. It is a historic site, after all."

Elena studied the photographs. She remembered old photos of the castle's better days. In the middle of this present-day ruin, her great-great-grandmother had danced in a gold beaded gown, curls of auburn hair piled high on her head. Coachmen had driven expensive horses and carriages across this now rickety old drawbridge. Magda's mother had ridden her pony in the fields as a little girl, the castle towers rising high in the background. She put down the photos. "I'd like to postpone making a decision. I want to see the castle for myself."

Gregory frowned, and his stare penetrated like a laser. He was a bit unnerving.

"I do not think that would be wise."

Marina had been quietly rocking on the chair, but she stopped the creaking motion and looked up. "Why not?" Her eyebrows narrowed. "It's her castle."

He made a dismissive gesture with his hand. "In some respects, Romania is still very wild, not only in landscape but in behaviors. The roads are full of dangers. Gypsies are everywhere, and they are good at the manipulations."

"That makes no sense, Mr. Balogh. I've lived in Romania."

"You lived in Bucharest," Alex said. "I agree with Mr. Balogh. I don't think you should go alone either."

What kind of conspiracy was this? Elena gave a determined, if somewhat angry sigh and started to speak in Romanian. "I've spoken the language since I was a child. I know the culture. One of my friends is from a gypsy family."

A slow smile crossed Alex's face. "But . . ." he said, "I still think it's too dangerous."

"It's not your business," Marina said, shooting him a 'shut up' look.

He shot one back.

"Why?" Elena stared at Alex, uncomprehending. Why should he care what she did?

Alex replied, "Your grandmother—"

"Was run over in front of this house, not murdered in Romania."

"Yeah, but Freddy was."

"No. He made the stupid mistake of getting hooked on drugs. It wasn't murder. It was *suicide*."

Gregory gave a grudging nod. "I see you are determined." He shut his briefcase. "You are a strong young lady, and once more, you have proved me wrong. If you come to Dkany, you shall indeed have my protection, and I shall provide you with every amenity. The City of Dkany would welcome their famous ancestor."

Elena looked for signs of reluctance on Gregory's part, but if he had any, it didn't show. His face remained stoic. She would go. No further discussion. She looked at Alex and wanted to challenge his negativity. He avoided eye contact. No matter. She'd go.

"Now, about the other little situation." Gregory Balogh glanced from Elena to Alex and back again.

"What little situation?" Elena asked.

"The matter about your marriage to Alexander."

Alex stiffened, and a shadow of annoyance crossed his face. He turned, refusing to look at her. He'd just confirmed Marina's observations. Alex had no intention of marriage.

"There will be no marriage between Alex and myself," Elena said. "It was a wish our families made a long time ago, and it doesn't fit into today's present situation. Alex and I lead separate lives. We have not seen each other for at least ten years. We don't even know each other anymore."

Alex drew back as though she'd sucker-punched him.

Pangs of guilt formed, and she lowered her head. She'd come on too strong.

"Ah well, too bad." Gregory looked at his watch. "I must be on my way—a plane to catch."

As Gregory rose to leave, Alex did the same. "I think it's time for me to go as well. Good night ladies." He beat Gregory out the door.

CHAPTER 6

DREAM: BUCHAREST, ROMANIA

DKANY HOME: EVANSTON, ILLINOIS

The apartment door burst open. A man charged into the living room. Splotches of sunlight pouring through the dormers covered his military uniform.

Startled, Elena shouted, and Janek Ivanov rushed from the bedroom, tripped, and almost fell when his socks slipped on the tiles. Jan yelled something in Romanian she didn't understand. The man's focus shot toward Jan.

"Klaus!" The two men argued so fast, Elena couldn't pick out the words, except for "bastard" and "traitor." The man drew a knife from his inside pocket.

"No!" Elena picked up a lamp, and as the man lunged into Jan, she hit him over the head. Klaus spun around and, for a split second, locked eyes with her, his expression dark and lethal. Then he turned and sprang at Jan. Elena got between them, and instead of the knife cutting Jan, it sliced into her side.

Elena screamed as she dropped to the floor.

Jan grimaced in horror, but he didn't have time to react. Eyes narrowed, face contorted, Klaus lunged.

Jan swerved away, then came back and slammed into Klaus with his side, almost knocking him off balance.

Klaus threw a punch, and the impact sent Jan crashing into the table. Klaus dove after him and pressed the knife inches from Jan's throat. Jan's hand on the blade deflected the blade from severing his windpipe.

"Ticalos!" Klaus yelled. He swore first in Romanian, then screamed "bastard" louder in English.

Jan took advantage of the outburst. He regained his balance and shook Klaus's wrist with dog-like persistence. Klaus jerked loose and reached back to strike. Jan caught his wrist and toppled him backward, falling with him. They rolled, each seeking control. The blade alternated between Jan's stomach and Klaus's throat. They rolled one more time, the blade wavering between the men, but this time Jan's luck ran out. The blade sliced into his stomach. Jan cried out and stopped moving.

Recovering from the initial shock, Elena took advantage. She grabbed the knife from Jan's side and plunged it into the man's ribs, producing a thud and cracking of bone. Warm, sticky liquid poured through his uniform and onto the floor. Klaus gasped, surprise mingling with pain. He fell, bringing her down with him. She lay on top of him staring into open eyes as he lay face up in a pool of blood.

The taste of rusty copper landed on her tongue, and sweat-soaked into her nostrils. "Lena, help me . . ." Jan's voice, weak and raspy, trailed off.

Elena tore off her shirt and covered the wound, trying to cradle him from his own mortality. The shirt turned red.

Jan reached up and touched her cheeks smudged with crimson fingers. He was dying. "Lena . . ." He lingered on her name as he rose to his elbows and whispered, "Take the baby. Leave Romania."

"Jan."

Jan tried to lift his hand, but the effort appeared too much for him. He slipped back, his breathing shallowed, one last sigh, and he was gone.

Then, a new and frightening awareness. Stabbing pains from her wounds made it difficult to breathe.

The door opened and several men with blank faces stormed inside. Everything went dark.

Elena jerked awake, disoriented. For a minute, she seemed lost. The room felt cold, damp, and dark, devoid of the streetlights that generally provided illumination. The wind forced sheets of rain sideways against the house.

The years of passing time had almost driven away the nightmare. But, tonight, it came back. This new memory brought pain too agonizing to endure.

A movement shifted beside the bed, but when she turned, nothing was there. At first, Elena thought the rain might be blowing in through an open window. But the wind wasn't blowing in that direction. Her skin was soaked from perspiration. A chill took her.

"Janek? Jan? Are you here?"

She received an answer in the rotation of the ceiling fan and the sound of thunder echoing through the swooshing sounds. She sat still and closed her eyes. *Who are you? If not Jan, then who?*

Elena snapped on the bedside lava lamp. Blobs of yellow light turned her blue nightgown green. She tucked her legs underneath her and waited for something—*anything*—to happen. The Victorian mirror across from the bed mimicked every move. She closed her eyes and allowed external influences to evaporate. The sounds in the room became more apparent and more distinct.

Her mind's astral body floated out into the air, trying to connect. Trying . . .

When the summons received no answer, she opened her eyes.

Looking back at her was a man with blond hair, young—maybe twenty-one. Around his neck hung a plain silver cross with three red chips down its center, the cross she'd given Jan on their wedding day. The cross she wore around her neck.

He hadn't changed in death. His expression painted him heartbroken. Elena yearned to pass through the mirror and console him. She held her breath, afraid he might disappear.

"Jan."

The figure didn't reply.

Elena tried again. She started to say, "What do you want?" but instead asked, "What can I do for you? How can I relieve your pain?"

The ghost moaned, and Elena thought he called her name as the image began to disappear. She got off the bed and went to the mirror to investigate, but there was nothing to indicate he'd ever been present.

Panic-stricken and desolate, Elena began to cry. She didn't stop until she'd grabbed the photo album and opened it to a picture of her, Jan, and Freddy.

"Oh, Jan," she whispered. "If you're here, please tell me you're happy. I couldn't bear to find you'd go through eternity in some unresolved misery."

The moan came from behind her. Elena whirled. Nothing. Just yellow globs of lava lamp hitting the floor.

Unnerved, she glanced back into the mirror. The apparition returned. All movement ceased. Vapors escaped her body and moved her forward in a trance. She was in her room, but she wasn't. She was floating through the mirror. Jan held out his hand, and they glided down a path of clouds.

"Lena." He whispered, *"Danger for you. Many trials will come your way."*

A blurry shadow followed them.

"Who's with you?"

"Peril surrounds him."

"My son? Where?" She turned to look at Jan, but her hand was holding the post of the bed, the clouds replaced by the hardwood floor. No shadow, no Jan.

"No!"

Now another image floated inside the mirror. This one was of a young boy with dark brown hair and a featureless face, wearing that same cross. Then, he, too, began to disappear. Elena ran to catch up— to float into the mirror—but she bumped her head on the glass. "No! Is this my son? Please!"

"Elena?" Marina's voice echoed from the hall. Footsteps grew louder, and the door opened.

"I had a nightmare," Elena said, staring into Marina's horrified face. "I guess I drank too much." Her mouth offered a weak smile. The squeak in her voice didn't convince even herself.

Marina frowned but nodded and turned to go back down the hall. Elena closed the door.

The beating in her head resounded over and over. *Go to them. They love you. Nobody else will ever love you as they do.* No. Yes. The answer resonated in her heart. She'd never be free of this nightmare. Never.

A streak of lightning illuminated the bedroom to a glimpse of a woman in the mirror. Death covered the face, and dark sockets appeared where eyes should have been. She gasped, her mind trying to grasp this new horror. The woman held a gun to her head.

Oh my God. It's me!

The phone rang, awakening her from her stupor.

Elena's heart almost stopped. She bolted toward the dresser, where she kept her gun and checked the chamber. Empty. Strange, when she had range practice, she always replaced the clip. If she'd gotten the gun and pulled the trigger . . . She wasn't meant to die this day.

Who was this spirit in the mirror? Jan? It looked and sounded like him. Why did he want her? For that matter, why did her grandmother come back to her before she crossed over? Could they be communicating that her son was alive? Peace descended over her. She knew what she had to do. She would be going on a journey, and it wouldn't be an easy one.

She gazed through the open window and felt a blast of rain. The name 'Elena' echoed into the storm until the scream of her name interrupted the wild night.

Running footsteps echoed down the hall, then her door burst open.

Chapter 7

Briar Hill College

Evanston, Illinois

The sign above Alex's office door warned, *Abandon Hope All Ye Who Enter Here.*

Stacks of paper piled high on his desk; books lay on top of meeting agendas. Anything left on Dr. Alexander Brancusi's desktop might never be found again, at least not during this century.

But Alex wasn't looking at the disaster piles. He was looking into copied records of Briar Hill College's financial records from three years ago. Frustrated, he wasn't finding the evidence he was looking for. Maybe it didn't exist.

Alex looked up and saw invaders about to enter his inner sanctuary. He stiffened as two jean-clad ladies in sandals and tank tops, perspiration dribbling from their foreheads, strolled into his office.

Elena and Marina. *Hell and Damnation.* Immediately, he shoved the records into his top draw, rose from his chair, and folded his arms.

He wanted to say, "What the hell are you doing here?" But refrained.

His memory still burned from humiliation. Last night a faceless boy invaded his dreams and woke him to a flash of Elena holding a gun to her head. He didn't believe in premonitions, but this had been too scary to ignore. He'd swallowed his skepticism and called. Marina had dropped the phone and ran. When she'd gotten back, her reply stung. Elena was not about to shoot herself—was he nuts? She was asleep.

Damn it, if they were all asleep, why had she sounded scared out of her wits? No, Alex was *not* prone to prophetic visions, but something had happened.

Experiencing the image of Elena holding a gun to her head, desperation filling her tear-streaked face, hit him harder than he could have imagined. If she was living in some sort of horror— oh, the hell with it, the phony smile he'd been about to offer became an honest frown.

"Find a chair and tell me why you're here."

Marina scooped papers off a chair, set them on the floor, and sat. Then she spoke with quiet firmness. "We came to talk to you about what you think you saw last night."

"What I *thought* I saw?" He placed both hands on his desk to steady his resentment. How dare she question his integrity?

But when a shadow of apprehension appeared in Marina's eyes, Alex's anger melted into the soft spot he held for his sister. He sat back in his swivel office chair.

"About why you called my house at three in the morning," Elena replied.

"I called to see if you were all right." Alex focused on her and immediately lowered his eyes from the swell of her breast that peeked out from her tank top. Ten years ago, she'd allowed him to explore their beauty.

No, dammit! Mind off body. Alex's eyes followed as she moved by the window that allowed in a view of Lake Michigan.

"I just want to know what you saw," Elena replied.

"I told you—"

"It's important. Last night I saw Jan's ghost."

Queasiness coated his stomach. "Let's stick to the facts. Ghosts don't exist. You had too much to drink and imagined you saw your husband. Obviously, you aren't over him yet, or maybe the stress of Magda's death caused your hallucination. Maybe you picked up a pistol and thought about . . ."

"What?" Elena looked like he'd slapped her in the face.

He was instantly sorry but continued anyway. "Look, I probably just dreamed that you saw the ghost of your husband in the mirror. *Were* you contemplating suicide? You never answered me. *Did* you have too much to—?"

"I did not have too much to drink," Elena replied. She removed a dark pink shirt she wore over a lighter pink tank top. "And, even if I did, I wouldn't see ghostly visions in a mirror, and I sure as *hell* wouldn't shoot myself. When I get drunk, I fall asleep."

A regatta, sailing the lake, peeked through the trees. But Alex barely noticed anything but the swell in her tank top and the intensity in her eyes.

"You must be a fun date," Marina said.

Alex jerked his attention away from Elena.

He eyed a book of Poe's tales on his desk and covered it with papers. No use anyone thinking he had nothing to do but read morbid poetry.

Sweat trickled down his back. He leaned against his chair and rested his sandal-covered feet on the metal edge of a pulled-out file cabinet. He wore a devil-may-care expression he didn't feel.

"Look, you're taking this ghost thing way too seriously," Alex said. "Maybe it was me who drank too much. I thought you were in trouble. I called. I promise I won't do that again. I'll leave you alone." The woman he used to love was having dreams about her ex-husband. He didn't need to hear this.

"Good," Elena replied. "I wouldn't want you to think I was crazy or anything."

He swiveled his chair toward her, but when she didn't acknowledge him, he turned back to his sister. "Mari, this is carrying things a bit too far. I don't think Elena saw anything in the mirror at all. I think she must have been dreaming. A nightmare, nothing more."

"I do not imagine things," Elena said. The sharpness in her voice stunned him. Her eyes had grown cold and stony.

"No," he said. "I think *you* believe it. I just don't think you saw what you think you did." He reached down for a cooler by his desk to promote goodwill by offering them a soda.

"Okay. Tell me, Professor, if I'm hallucinating and didn't see my husband in the mirror, then who was that little boy?"

Alex came up so quickly, he bumped his head on the edge of the desk. The mirror on the opposite wall showed his blood-drained face.

The boy. Who was that boy?

"Hit a nerve, did it?" Elena asked, lifting her chin and meeting his astonished gaze with narrowed eyes.

"You saw him?" Alex asked before he'd gotten a chance to rationalize—to change his story.

"You saw him. And, if we *both* saw him, you didn't dream me," Elena said. "Otherwise, it means I don't have the psychic gifts I believe I have." Those cobalt eyes turned to a blue inky black as she met his stare. Elena turned away, dismissing any reply he might offer.

"Bunk, I don't believe in the occult, especially ghosts." Alex lied as coolly as he could under the circumstance.

"Since when?" Marina asked. "You have psychic gifts yourself. You always seemed to know what's going to happen before anyone else does."

"When I was a kid." If he did have this so-called gift of foresight, it had deserted him when he'd needed it the most. *Before* Elena had gone to Romania.

"I see," Elena said, crossing one leg over the other and rotating clear polished toes sticking out of her sandals. "So, you think I imagined things."

"Alex," Marina said, "Just admit Elena wasn't hallucinating. Don't drive this poor girl crazy. You weren't there. I was. She was terrified."

Alex glared at the two women, angry they were ganging up on him. They'd lied in the first place. "What are you, Elena, some kind of psychic nut who conjures up tragedies of the past in visions to a present you'd like to exist but doesn't?"

That seemed to hit a nerve. Elena stood up and looked at him, a deep frown crossing her face, hurt reflected in her eyes.

Confusion slammed into guilt somewhere inside Alex. Why did she have this effect on him? He could intimidate the hell out of his students, and they left him in peace.

"Maybe," Elena said slowly, "I am a 'psychic nut,' as you put it. But, if you're not honest with me, I'll never know, will I?"

So, there it was. Magda had not spoken about Elena until after she'd come back and was safely tucked away at the University of Indiana. Then, she'd avoided the details.

Marina picked up a paperweight statue of a horse from Alex's desk and played with it. "It couldn't hurt to go to Romania to help Elena sort out the truth. Maybe there is a boy that—"

Emotional blackmail. "Oh, is that what this is all about? You want me to find somebody who doesn't exist? Elena, you could have been dreaming. Maybe you'd seen the boy somewhere before."

"But I didn't." Elena walked over to Marina and stood by her side in solidarity. "There's absolutely no reason for me to lie about this. And I'm not the one trying to manipulate you. You're the one lying to me. I just want you to know I'm not prone to hallucinations. If you didn't see a faceless boy with brown hair, wearing a cross, then, damn it, tell me, and I won't bring it up again."

But he couldn't because the boy looked exactly like Elena's description. Elena glared at him with burning, reproachful eyes full of intelligence and passion. He allowed himself one full second to admire her fortitude, her smooth ivory skin, and the black braid that fell just at the tip of one pink breast.

And he couldn't take much more of this possessed girl being trapped inside her world of nightmares. In a controlled tone, he said, "Ladies, if we're about done with this nonsense, I'd really like to get finished with this project before fall."

"Okay," Marina said, obviously irritated. "But, Alex, we *will* talk about this later." Marina marched out of his office, followed by Elena.

Alex sat back at his desk, barely glancing up as they left. Had Elena seen a ghost? In despair, had she stuck a pistol to her head? And who was that boy?

Park, Evanston, Illinois

Hadean Petrov walked around the park, wearing jeans, sandals, hair hanging down his back in a ponytail, and a philosophy book tucked under his arm. He settled on a park bench, facing the street, and opened a text. A man preparing an assignment—a student who belonged. He wasn't somebody anyone from a college campus town would notice.

In truth, Hadean was no stranger to his surroundings. Just under two weeks ago, he'd parked his car under the shadows of the trees waiting for the old woman to finish her evening walk. She hadn't even made it to the middle of the street before he'd started his engine and excelled from 0 to 60. She'd been dead before she'd hit the pavement.

Once again, he waited. Hadean had done his homework on Elena Dkany. She was, his informers told him, an academic type, slim and willowy, a weak girl who wouldn't provide any trouble. He planned for a routine burglary gone wrong.

Too bad. Poor girl. Death comes to all. He laughed, watched female college students, and killed time.

Dkany home, Evanston, Illinois

Elena's house seemed as forlorn as her mood, and she felt as sorry for it as she did for herself and her grandmother.

The grand entrance hall, dedicated to family portraits, colorful wallpaper, and gleaming, polished oak wood, supported a stained glass Tiffany lamp. They provided a false sense of cheer. She could almost hear her grandmother's voice when she entered.

She opened the glass doors into the living room, and again family history confronted her. Elena spent endless hours playing with friends on the player piano lit by the corner lamp. The mantel always displayed Christmas cards during the holidays. They'd decorated the floor-to-ceiling Christmas tree with antique ornaments dating back before Magda had been born.

Alex's picture stood on the mantel. Magda had invited Alex over at every chance when they were young. Alex's mother, Nadia, suggested Alex take Elena to school dances and shuttled them there until Alex got his own car.

Even after she'd recovered from the black cloud of Romania, Magda mentioned Alex would be teaching at Briar Hill College. She told Elena he'd grown into a very handsome man and might make some woman a great husband. Magda suggested Elena should apply to Briar Hill for her doctorate.

Her grandmother was getting old and frail and needed someone. Elena decided to transfer to Briar Hill, a decision she was beginning to regret. She should have known her grandmother had a separate agenda. Husband indeed, the man couldn't look her in the eye without grimacing, and in truth, Elena carried too much guilt to be comfortable around him. Someday, Alex would have to know the truth, but there was no way she could tell him now. Emptiness swirled around her like her adopted spirits.

She picked up the phone, pressed the talk button, and dialed the Brancusi's number, unsure of how she'd even start the conversation. Maybe, "Hi Alex. Get your project done? You might want to try Poe's 'Annabelle Lee' for self-indulgent wallowing. By the way, sorry I see ghosts. Want to come over for some wine? We can view them together."

Instead, she left a message for Marina to call her back, fighting off morbid feelings of loneliness and something else she couldn't quite put her finger on.

The study nearly suffocated her. The room reeked of musty books and non-circulated air. Elena had tried to persuade Magda to install central air. Still, her grandmother had steadfastly refused to change her old ways.

Elena opened the double windows in the room, letting the hot afternoon sun pour onto the desk. The light was almost blinding. She would have closed the shades, but the breeze blowing in from the lake surrounded her with fresh air laced with scents from the rose garden.

She sat in the office chair, the one piece of modern equipment besides her laptop in the room, and rolled the chair closer to the fan. Pulling up her ponytail, the combination of air currents caught the back of her neck. She didn't want to move—ever.

Mrs. Rice popped up above the picket fence next door, took off her straw hat, wiped her brow of perspiration, and put her hat back on her head. The older woman waved with a sad but friendly smile before lowering again out of sight, back to her flowerbeds. She, too, had loved Magda.

Elena opened her laptop and checked her e-mail. The usual tons of spam, one e-mail from a friend in summer school at the University of Indiana, a joke from Marina, and correspondence from Gregory Balogh, now back in Romania, filled her inbox.

My dearest Elena,

Again, I cannot offer you enough condolences on the death of your grandmother. Magda was a special lady, and we will all suffer her loss.

I appreciate your insistence on coming to Romania, although I would understand if you should change your mind. Have you decided on a date?

I have mentioned your coming to several prominent Dkany citizens. They are pleased to extend an offer to show you around the city and give you a special tour of Transylvania (it is very lovely this time of year). Mrs. Demidis, the housekeeper of the castle, has instructions to offer you every amenity available.

You may wish to sleep in Bella Dkany's room. Bella, my dear Elena, was the wife of your illustrious fifteenth-century ancestor, Viktor. It is the most historic and beautiful bedroom in the small but habitable section of the castle. I must warn you, however, even in July, the rooms are damp and exceedingly cold at night. You might prefer to live in the caretaker's cottage, where your brother resided.

I shall be here for a portion of the summer, and I offer you the hospitality of my own home.

I realize I am old-fashioned, but again, I want to advise you about marriage to Alexander. You are the last of the Dkany's, my dear. If something happened to you, there would be no family to inherit, and the castle would be forfeit to the town of Dkany. If your wish is to sell, I am confident of getting an excellent price for your "Legacy of Danger" once again. (That, my dear, was a joke, but also a caution.)

With fondest regard, your uncle by friendship,

Gregory Balogh.

Elena wrote back telling him she would be coming sometime during the summer and appreciated his hospitality advice and offer.

She gazed out on Magda's garden. Her neighbor rose to stretch and wave before disappearing again. Beautifully landscaped. She could never be that clever.

Elena thought about Alex as the young man she remembered before she'd gone to Romania. How they'd fallen in love over ice cream sodas and wrestling matches. How she'd allowed him to make love to her for the first time. How she'd—No. No more. It didn't matter anyway.

The stillness in the house became more and more obtrusive until she started imagining she heard a thumping noise coming from upstairs. An involuntary shiver passed through her, then disappeared. Nothing. Just a figment of an overly active imagination after a week of intolerable stress.

Focusing back on her computer, she doused her unease with research on castles in Romania. Dkany Castle showed the same photos she'd already seen and pictured drawings of the castle as it once had been during its illustrious past. Elena turned off her computer and shut the top.

A *kerplunk* echoed from the rooftop. Elena jumped. Only an apple falling from the tree that bounced off her roof and onto the patio. She let out a long audible breath. Everything was unnaturally quiet. The least creak or groan appeared exaggerated. Another noise came from the roof. Outside, the shutters in her grandmother's room banged on the side of the house. She'd have to adjust them. Elena closed and locked the patio door and headed toward the front of the house.

The broad staircase squeaked against her shoes as she ascended the steps. Halfway up, she stopped and listened—nothing—all quiet. A few birds chirped, but no thumping noise and no fruit falling from the trees. Elena climbed the rest of the steps.

Entering her grandmother's room, a sudden disturbance in the air hit her consciousness—nothing out of place, but something not quite right. A quick and unsettling thought entered her mind. Did anyone else know about her ruby and its value? Relief swept over her as she remembered they'd deposited the stone in the bank vault. Even if someone broke in, they wouldn't get it.

The shutters continued to bang outside. Elena leaned outside the window and hooked them into the side of the house. She gazed at the garden and basked in the breeze.

Her neighbor, Mrs. Rice, was looking up at her house, then darted across her backyard and went inside, slamming her screen door behind her. What was that all about?

Elena sat on her grandmother's bed and picked up a starched white pillowcase, stroking the eyelets around the edges. She was sitting on the quilt Magda made by hand as a girl. The patchwork material brought back happy memories—her grandmother recalling her artistic father and mother's past family accomplishments—their secrets and dreams for herself and Freddy. All gone. She swallowed hard and bit back tears.

The nagging inclination of danger hit again, this time stronger than before, interrupting remembrances. The phone shattered the peaceful atmosphere Elena was beginning to absorb.

"Hello?"

"Elena." Her neighbor. "Look, I don't want to worry you, but I saw a shadow crawling around your house just a bit ago. It might not be anything, but, look dear, why don't you come over for a drink. I'm calling the police just in case."

"You don't have to. I . . ."

Elena realized what had been troubling her when she entered the room. The bathroom door had been closed. She never left the door closed, and neither had Magda.

"Maybe you should," Elena said, her stomach suddenly clenching into a knot. Her palms began to sweat, and the phone almost slipped from her hand.

"Quickly!"

Chapter 8

Alex arrived home with his laptop and a load of guilt. This sudden deluge of Elena's prolonged nightmare about an event that happened ten years ago unnerved him. His image of her reflection in the mirror with a gun to her head freaked him out. He'd never had an out-of-body experience in his life, but someone had been trying to convey something to him. Was Elena so troubled she'd contemplate suicide? He didn't think she would ever do such a thing—he thought her too strong for that, but his dream showed otherwise. He didn't know what to think.

He flung his laptop case on the living room sofa and stared out the window.

Last night, he'd thought he was going crazy. When Elena came in with the tales of seeing ghosts, he'd thought *she* was going crazy. But when she'd shared the story about a vaguely familiar boy neither knew, he decided this was all too real. Elena kept her feet planted firmly on the ground.

Okay, so Elena's life since he'd last seen her had been hell. Well, she'd asked for it. She went off and married the first guy who'd come along after Alex told her not to worry about him and have a good time in Bucharest. He didn't think she'd actually marry someone. The swift rise in anger every time the thought bombarded him now hit hard. He still had an old ax to grind. She needed compassion, but he couldn't feel any. In fact, he hadn't been able to feel anything for a very long time. To hell with Elena's ghost. He had one of his own to shake loose. He grabbed the case and headed for his office.

Flashing red lights from the answering machine greeted him on his desk. He hit the play button as he set down his laptop.

"Marina? Call me."

The harmonious velvet flow of Elena's voice crawled under his skin and refused to let go. His anger melted into his usual melancholy. To hell with all women. He started to walk out of the room when the phone rang again. Maybe Elena calling back.

"Hello?" A woman's voice pierced through the receiver, shrill . . . panicky.

"Hello, is this Alex Brancusi?" The woman didn't give him time to answer. "Your number is on Dkany's emergency phone list."

"Yeah?" Fear knotted inside. Disturbing thoughts of last night came back.

"Listen, I think there's an intruder in Elena's house. I called the police."

"You called the police?" He repeated, struggling for something else to say. Icy fear twisted his insides as he remembered Magda's hit-and-run death that he'd suspected was no accident. Right across from the house. Dear God.

"Yes, but I thought you should know. I'm worried. She's alone in the house."

"I'm on my way." He ran out the door and raced to the car.

Elena's disaster antennae arrived a split second before the bathroom door opened. A solid shadow rushed out with something in its hand. Instinctively she swerved. Magda's walking stick just missed smashing her skull.

Elena screamed and leaped off the bed. Her feet slipped from under her, and she bent her knees and twisted her body to keep balance.

Only a clear head and the sharp realization she'd already killed someone once before fought off the sheer magnitude of the black fright that threatened to paralyze her.

The attacker grabbed a handful of her braid and pulled her back onto the bed. She rallied and fought for the cane in his hand. But, instead of a fight, he flung the stick across the room. A broad sickly, insane grin covered his face as he reached for Magda's pillow.

Elena gasped, panting in terror, the pillow with the white eyelets she loved now an instrument of death. She choked back a panicked cry and shoved upward, pushing him to the side.

He grabbed her neck and moved to pin her chest between his legs.

Elena moved quickly. She twisted her body and slammed against him. He grunted a reaction and let go but didn't back down. He grabbed for her wrists, caught one, and held on. With the other, Elena went for his face. Fingernails made contact and sliced through his skin.

He grabbed for her arms, but she wiggled out of his grasp. She jerked away and tried to maneuver off the bed.

I won't let him win. I will survive.

He hissed, his eyes narrowed between fury and enjoyment. "So, they were wrong about you. You are a little hellcat. I'll enjoy the *challenge.*" He gritted his teeth and yanked her back down.

He liked hellcat? She'd give him hellcat and more, glad she'd taken self-defense courses. She breathed in quick gasps as she slacked against his weight. The moment he relaxed, Elena freed two fingers and poked at his eyes as hard as she could. She missed the eyeballs but still got a sensitive spot.

He cried out, let go, swore, and put his hands to his face.

She bought herself only seconds. Elena scrambled out from under him and off the bed. No matter what, this man was *not* going to kill her.

The few feet to the door were miles as she slid, fought to keep her footing, and ran out of the room. So did the attacker. She staggered into the hall as his rough fingers snagged the back of her shirt, yanked it tight against her chest, and snatched her backward onto the floor.

When he came down on top of her, Elena didn't have to think about the next move. She jerked her head around and chomped down hard on his arm.

"You *bitch.*" He let go for an instant and punched.

Elena rolled away, and the man's hand smashed onto the hardwood floor with a thud and crack.

"Jesus!" He grabbed his hand. Scalding fury boiled behind his pain-widened eyes.

Elena came to a stop at the top of the stairs.

The corner of the man's mouth turned upward, eyes focusing on the steps behind her in malevolent triumph. Damn. The man intended to kick her down the staircase.

He approached in slow motion. If Elena wanted to get away from him, she'd have to roll. If she didn't do anything, he'd win their battle. Either way, she'd probably break her neck.

A sudden frost in the air spread through the hall.

Bang.

Elena spun around. Her grandmother's open-door had shut.

Bang. Bang. Bang.

If she'd thought there had been a mistake, there wasn't. All the bedroom doors closed.

The area was now freezing.

The man swerved, long enough for Elena to dive ahead of him, two steps at a time, her heart racing so fast she thought it might stop from sheer fright.

Halfway down, arctic air blasted past, knocking her off her feet. She rolled the last few steps and waited for the attack she was sure would follow. But the wind swirled into a tornado and flew up the staircase.

Elena scrambled to her feet, her back against the door. The man's face had fueled with such insane murderous determination now paled gray. His eyes bulged out from dark sockets looking as if the damnation of the devil was about to cast him into hell. The angry air lifted the man off his feet and spun him around, a carousel out of control. Round and round, they spun, tornado and executioner, banging into the walls on each rotation, his shrieks deafened by the roar of the cyclone. He rose higher and higher into the vortex, moving so fast now, Elena could hardly see his solid form lift up to the ceiling. Then, with one more massive energy explosion, the air hurled him to the bottom. He lay motionless two feet away from where she stood.

Stunned, unable to move, Elena stared at the man who, moments ago, had been so lethal. Now, his neck twisted almost entirely behind him. Stark fear glazed over unseeing eyes as though the last thing he'd seen on earth was the Angel of Death.

Time stood still. She couldn't move—didn't *dare* move, didn't dare breathe. When she finally gasped in the air she needed to survive, she screamed. Then screamed until she could make no more sound.

Faint sounds of sirens wailing and people yelling filtered through her ears into consciousness, then sub-conscious, as the foyer started to spin. She could have sworn she heard the words *'you're welcome'* before the cuckoo bird clucked two, and she dropped into blackness.

She woke only briefly and looked up into the concerned eyes of Alex Brancusi, who held her. Then she passed out again.

Chapter 9

Park in

Evanston, Illinois

The evening slipped into nightfall. Alex sat on a rock at the edge of the park, his eyes fixated on a lake of many colors. He'd never seen a body in that position. How had it happened, and why had the man attacked Elena right on the heels of Magda's death?

The surf splashed and tossed foam against the shoreline before receding and scattering beach stones. An occasional breaking wave sprayed the bottom of his jeans.

He shook his head. How had Elena gotten away from him? Had the man really tripped down those stairs, as Elena claimed?

Alex had known Elena from the time she was little and had always been able to catch her in a lie. Now, he'd spotted the same evasiveness in Elena's tone. He didn't believe her story entirely.

Seagulls squawked overhead. One landed about three feet from Alex, surveyed him, and cocked his head one way then another. When Alex didn't throw food in his direction, the bird flew away to join the disappearing flock. One of the summer's classical music concerts played from a nearby pavilion and provided a bizarre contrast to the violent afternoon.

His cell phone rang at around eight-o-clock. Alex pulled it out from his jacket pocket. "Tony."

"Alex." Tony sounded out of breath. A muted murmur of voices chattered in the background.

"Where the hell are you?" Alex asked.

"In another pub outside of Bucharest. What's going on?"

Alex drew a long breath. "Someone attacked Elena this afternoon."

The raucous laughter coming from the other end of the phone almost drowned out Alex's comment, and static followed.

"Come again. You said Elena was attacked?"

"You heard me right," Alex replied. Oh yeah, murder and Mozart all in one day.

"How is she?"

Alex sighed. "She'll be okay. She's got a nasty black eye and some bruises. Wish I could say the same for the suspect."

"Huh?"

"He was found lying at the foot of the steps with his head twisted completely around. Think *Exorcist*." He lost the struggle to keep the anger out of his voice and wished he'd been the one to push the bastard down the stairs.

Tony cleared his throat. "Give me the entire story, Alex." Tony's ordinarily friendly voice changed to cold professionalism.

Alex shared Elena's account, which ended with her lying at the foot of the stairs in a dead faint.

"How long was she out?" In a far-away voice, Tony said, "Check please," in a Romanian dialect more reminiscent of Greek.

Alex continued, "Only a few minutes. When Elena came to, she was in shock. Then that bully of an officer tried to implicate her in a lie. Jerk."

"So, she said he hid and attacked from the bathroom, and she got away. He chased her down the stairs and tripped?"

"That's what she said."

"Hmm. Did anyone recognize the guy?"

"What do you mean, *hmm?* No." Alex wished the man had been still alive. He would have loved ten minutes alone with the bastard to beat the crap out of him and maybe get the truth in the process.

"The police still there?"

"No."

"Did you tell them who you are?"

"No, I told them I'm a professor at Briar Hill College."

"Good," Tony breathed a sigh. "If they come back again, keep your identity to yourself."

"Of course."

"They took her to the ER, I take it?"

"Yeah. The paramedics insisted." Alex suggested the ER. Elena flatly refused. The charm issued by one of the police officers finally convinced her to go. Alex flushed from the humiliation of feeling irrelevant. Even though she'd clung to him when she'd been scared out of her mind. He still didn't think Elena liked him much.

"The cops took down her statement at the hospital. One bastard asked if she'd pushed *him* down the stairs."

"You're not thinking clearly. You only have Elena's word for it that she was even attacked."

"Only hers, her neighbor's, and cuts and bruises on her arms and face."

Alex thought for a moment. "Oh yeah, and he must have pushed her against the walls. The paintings were all over the steps, all oil paintings with heavy frames."

"So, they both fell down the steps, his neck was broken, and she didn't even get a concussion."

"No. And apparently, she ripped his face to shreds because he had three fresh scratches running down the length of his face." Alex chuckled at the imagery. Good for her.

An evening fireball met the skyline as flashes of orange water rippled over the lake. The water splashed harder, chased by a cool breeze, and the scent of freshly mowed park lawn caused Alex to sneeze as he stood and zipped up his jacket.

Tony became suddenly quiet, and a moment of silence passed between them. "Alex . . ."

"Yes?"

"Look, could this have been a robbery attack? Someone looking for the ruby?"

"Possibly, but I doubt it. If someone wanted it, they could have taken it long before it arrived in the States, even before Elena knew its existence. Something else. Most thieves wait until the house is empty. This guy waited *until* she got home."

"Look, if robbery wasn't the motive, then what else could it be?"

"I don't know. She's not aware of any enemies." Who could not like Elena? She was beautiful and perfect—except for two minor flaws. She saw ghosts, and she didn't care for him.

"So, then the only other possible connection would have to be the castle. So, let me get this straight. The heir to the Dkany Castle dies last month of a heroin overdose. When Magda's out socializing with some of her Briar Hill board member friends, she tells them she plans to take Elena to Romania this summer. The next evening she's run down and killed. And now, a week later, as the only remaining heir, Elena's attacked."

"So, what is it, Tony? Why would someone want to kill over a broken-down old castle?" Panicked beads of perspiration started to form on Alex's forehead. "Someone's killed her whole family, piece by piece, and now they're going for her. Will Elena be the next victim? Is somebody trying to prevent her from taking over the castle? Why? It's just a broken-down castle. Those things are a dime a dozen in Romania."

A rogue wave soaked his athletic shoes and the bottom of his pants. The chill started in his legs and worked its way up to his heart and down through his bones.

"Who told you that? The back may be uninhabitable, but the front doesn't look bad, and Freddie lived in the cottage for years." Tony's voice prickled.

Alex digested what Tony said. "Gregory Balogh said the castle was in ruins, and the cost of rehabbing would be prohibitive. Now, maybe he meant completely restoring it to its former days, but Balogh showed us pictures. I checked the Internet, and all it shows is a pile of rubble and a façade with a waterless moat."

"I don't know who might have the kind of money to restore the castle, Alex. But I have another theory and not a nice one."

Alex didn't want to say what was going through his head but said it anyway.

"You think this has something to do with our operation, don't you? This just might be the holding pen for the heroin we're looking for?"

"I don't know for sure. It's a possibility. I've had men watching the castle on and off for a while but in several locations. Nobody has noticed any gang activity or transfers."

Static from the other end of the line grated into his ear. Two kids on bicycles with wheels covered with cut grass rode down the sidewalk. Two young men wove their way from the opposite direction and nearly ran into the boys. They swore at the kids and passed by Alex, not paying attention to him, probably stoned. Alex thought about what he'd like to do to them, then got back to Tony.

The laughing in the background suddenly ceased. "Tony, you still there?"

"Yeah, sorry. Is Elena still insisting on going to the castle?"

"As of this morning, she was."

Tony didn't hesitate. "Look. Bring Elena to the castle. It should be relatively easy. She's determined to go, and she has her brother's business to settle."

Tony's plan irked Alex. "I *should* be trying to talk her out of going."

"I doubt anyone can stop her if she wants to bad enough, and we can keep an eye on her. I don't think she's safe at home now. She'll be dead unless someone plays bodyguard, and we find out the truth."

Something about Tony's tone gnawed at Alex. They'd been friends for a long time. "Tony, what exactly is going on?"

Tony lowered his voice. "When I see you. For now, don't let on why we really want her to go. Just say she's not safe at home."

"Why do we—" His phone clicked off. Why did they *really* want her to go?

An uncomfortable chill passed over him. Tony was still investigating the Dkany's. Now he'd directed his focus on Elena. Like Elena would ever be involved with this scum of society.

Alex put away his cell phone and watched the Chicago skyline turn orange and dark blue-black. Mosquitoes swarmed, and one bit him on the cheek. He swatted at it and started across the park toward the house.

A middle-aged couple walked arm-and-arm toward the pavilion. Every now and again, the man would stop, kiss the woman, and she would bump him with her hip. Alex got an idea and smiled. He thought Elena would hate it.

Chapter 10

Dkany Home, Romanian Orthodox Church
Evanston, Illinois

Elena curled up on the sofa, swirled brandy in a paper cup, and nursed a bruised body. Her face swelled around her eye, throbbed, and the pain wouldn't let go. Stiffness struck her back and shoulders.

"You shouldn't drink and take drugs." Marina rocked in a chair with needlepoint cushions and round, carved wooden arms, a mainstay from the Victorian era.

"Maybe I'll pass out sooner," Elena mumbled.

"How's your face?"

Elena shifted and groaned. "My entire body aches, but at least I won't hurt so much when the painkillers start to work."

Marina sighed. "Hopefully, soon."

A form appeared, rapping on the patio door glass. Marina opened the slider.

Alex stood outside with wet shoes, socks, and a soaked bottom of his pants.

"Been out swimming?" Elena flashed a sardonic grin his way.

"Yeah, right," he almost smirked. "But, no, not exactly." He removed his shoes and socks, grabbed the towel Marina threw at him, then sauntered into the living room, where he sat on a leather chair, perching his feet on the coffee table.

Where had he been, in Lake Michigan?

He thumbed through the editorial page, periodically glancing at Elena as though something was on his mind. Probably how pathetic she looked with a swollen purple eye and a colorful bruise on her cheek.

"Look," Alex said, "This may have been a bungled robbery, but from my perspective, if the guy had not fallen down those stairs, Elena might be the one lying on a slab."

"Knock it off," Marina said, stepping over her brother's legs and easing back into the rocking chair. "She's been through enough. She does *not* need to hear that."

"I need to hit you with a bit of reality. You need to be aware of what's happening."

Pain shot through Elena's hip as she eased her legs down. A wince pinched her face. In a soft but pained voice, she said, "They think I pushed that man down the stairs and broke his damned neck. I thought they were going to charge me with homicide."

Alex gave her a "don't be ridiculous" look.

The fragrance of vanilla candles scented the room and blended with the roses floating in from outside. It mixed well with the conversation. "Look," she said, maneuvering to a more comfortable position. "The man's dead. He won't be coming back unless he decides to join in the spirit fest."

"As ghosts don't exist, I doubt it." Alex's eyes narrowed, sending an imaginary icicle her way. "But somebody might want to come back and finish the job, and I don't mean a robbery. I mean *you*."

Elena's eyes widened in horror. "Why would they want *me*?"

Marina leaned over and punched her brother's shoulder. "Stop it. You're scaring her."

"I meant to."

"Why? What are you hoping to accomplish?"

"Why did someone want to kill your grandmother?" He moved his legs off the table and sat straight up, looking at her.

"The police said it was a drunk driver."

"You don't believe that. You thought it deliberate. Why?"

Elena exhaled softly, not wanting to relive the nightmare. "The police found no evidence, but now, I don't know."

Anger clouded Alex's already tense expression. He said through clenched teeth, "So, who would want to kill an old lady?"

"Someone who knew she was giving the ruby to Elena," Marina said. "Mr. Balogh knew."

Elena put down her ice pack. Water dripped down the back of her T-shirt and onto her sweatpants. "No. He brought the ruby here. He could have pocketed it. I wouldn't have known."

"You would have found out, eventually," Alex said.

"No. Mr. Balogh emailed me from Romania this morning. He couldn't have had anything to do with it."

"Are you sure he emailed you from Romania?" His question was met by silence. Both women stared at him.

"Who gets the ruby if you . . . if something happens to you?" Alex asked.

"It goes to whoever I designate as my heir. I have no relatives. If I left the face of the earth, it would be as if the Dkanys' never existed."

She turned away, not wanting Alex to see her tears. His austere façade would never show the emotional rawness of her present life.

Alex cleared his throat, and Elena turned. His dark eyes softened and captured hers. Glancing at Marina, he said, "Would you excuse us for a minute?"

"Huh?" Marina raised her eyebrows. "Why?"

"Please, just . . ."

Marina stood. "Okay. I'll make us some hamburgers if anyone's hungry after this."

Elena watched Marina leave. The atmosphere tensed. What would he say to her now?

"I want to discuss something with you."

"What's so important your sister can't hear?"

"Because this is between you and me," he replied softly.

She flashed him a slow blink and sighed. "Are you going to lecture me about what a kook I am for seeing ghosts? Or maybe you think I'm taking LSD, and you know of a good counselor?"

Alex raised his eyebrows, and his eyes widened. A grin spread across his face. "I wasn't thinking that at all."

A happy twin seemed to have replaced the irritating one. The shadow disappeared from his former self. The fun-loving kid still lived inside him somewhere. Maybe.

Alex came over and sat on the coffee table inches away from her. Elena caught his scent of dampened musk, sweat, and sexuality. She scooted up and away from the man too damned attractive for his or her own good.

The patio.

Alex followed and closed in as she leaned against the railing.

"Trying to run from me?" He stood close to her, bumping elbows.

"Yes, I was. I did not succeed. And I'm in too much pain to try again." She narrowed her eyes at him. "You can discuss ghosts in front of Mari. She believes in them, too. So, what is it you really want?"

Elena didn't much want to hear what Alex might have to say, but the patio lights focused on dark eyes that held hers, and a twinkle of moonlight mesmerized her, so she couldn't move.

"I'm sorry. You didn't ask for any of this." Alex broke eye contact.

Elena breathed easier. "You're right. I didn't. So, what else?"

Alex finally looked back at her. "I have a proposition for you." His gaze clung to hers as though analyzing what her reaction might be.

"Oh great. Like I don't have men propositioning me all the time."

"Good. Glad you have such an active social life." His face faltered, and the lightness left his eyes. He stood silent for a moment. "Is there someone special in your life?"

Elena shook her head slowly. She wanted to say 'yes,' but a weak 'no' came out.

The warmth of a smile echoed in his voice. "Let me take you to Romania."

"Are you playing gallant hero to damsel in distress? If so, Alex, I'm not in distress."

"No?" He eyed her bruises until she became uncomfortable. "You sure could have fooled me."

That's when Elena laughed, and pain rubbed her ribs. The laughter turned to brief tears she brushed aside. She faced the garden, putting her back to him.

"No. I might put you in danger by way of association."

"I can handle *me*, but I'm not sure you can protect yourself right now."

Elena was about to mention her karate chop when Alex moved too close behind her. She wanted to move, but something compelled her to stay. His breath warmed neck. His body stood inches away, his sexuality invading her comfort zone.

"Alex, you're too close. Move over." She stepped out of his encroaching presence.

He sighed. "Sorry, I'll respect your space. I have another suggestion, although you might not appreciate it."

"Well then?" Elena tilted her head and stared.

"You were saying before about being without relatives?"

"Don't rub it in." His insensitivity to her loss and tendency to hover began to annoy her.

"You need a family. So, this is what I propose."

"You want to adopt me?" Elena asked off the top of her head.

"No," he said, not missing a beat. "I thought I'd marry you."

A soft gasp escaped her lips when he took her hand. She tried to pull away. He held tighter. She swallowed before a hot spasm spun into the lower portion of her belly and made her yearn for the love she'd only tasted once.

The evening after the prom. The back seat of his Chevy on a deserted dirt road by the lake. Alex kissed Elena in his usual gentlemanly fashion. But this evening, something magical seemed to happen. One soft kissed became harder and hotter. The heat between them became unbearable. She wanted him—all of him. She wanted his hands on her, on her bare skin. Him unzipping the back of her gown, so it fell to her waist, her sitting half-naked, letting him do amazing things to her. They'd gotten so hot, her prom dress and his tuxedo trousers fell into a heap on the floor. He'd carried her outside under the pines and took her in the moonlight. The night she'd fallen in love. She'd never gotten over that night or him.

Alex said, "Elena."

Elena pulled the curtain down on memories of the night she'd lost her virginity. She hoped he hadn't caught a glimpse into her imagination.

He kept talking. "I know we haven't gotten along so well. This would strictly be a temporary marriage. I wouldn't expect you to sleep with me or anything."

Oh no. She wouldn't want to have to *sleep* with him.

"I mean," he continued, "unless you want to." He grinned and gave her his infamous bedroom eyes look. "If someone wants to kill for your castle, they'd have to go through me before it could become eligible for sale."

"I appreciate your offer, but we don't even know the castle was the motive."

"No, but it makes sense. Look, if you want, once this is over, we can dissolve the marriage. You can pursue your own life."

Elena lost sight of herself. Earlier, she'd wanted to hit Alex with a cast iron frying pan. Now, she was mad because she wouldn't get to sleep with him.

"We'll honeymoon in Romania. It'll be a great cover. I promise I'll be the perfect gentleman."

What I don't want on my honeymoon is a perfect gentleman.

She'd had a perfect gentleman on her first honeymoon. She didn't need more of the same on her second. She turned to her knight in shining but tarnished armor, and the resentfulness she'd felt dissipated. Tears stung her eyes. "Alex, thank you."

"For what?"

She sighed. "For caring. For giving up part of your life to protect me. Just thank you."

Alex stood in front of a woman who took his breath away. Hell, he almost had to insult her just to keep his emotions under control. His hand shook when he placed a small gold band on her left finger.

Gardenias and crisp white cotton lace enhanced the shampoo's scent on her silky black hair hung loosely over her shoulders. She was the essence of sweet innocence, beautiful and seductive, a fantasy. Elena was no saint. That he knew from bitter experience. But she was intricately involved in his life now, whether she wanted him or not.

Father Christofides wore black robes and a black cap that covered a steel gray head of hair, a match to his long beard. He presided over the wedding in the small chapel alcove at the side of St. Stefan's Cathedral. Three-stained glass slits filtered light onto Elena's light beige dress and turned it into a kaleidoscope of color.

Stiff wooden chairs with blue seat cushions accommodated Marina and a few close neighbors.

Fortunately, the priest was available to perform the ceremony on short notice, probably because the Brancusi's and the Dkany's were lifelong parishioners and friends. He was delighted to be of service. Alex didn't tell him they planned to annul the marriage as soon as their extended honeymoon in Romania was over.

Alex daydreamed about taking her in his arms and giving her a most passionate kiss. But when the priest told him he could kiss the bride, he blanked. Nerves shattered his resolve into the splinters the size of the pattern of colors flickering on the floor. When he finally came to himself, her eyes focused downward.

One fact Alex learned during his lifetime of experiences is timing is everything. He lifted her chin to kiss her. Startled, she turned her head, and his lips ended up on her cheek. So much for the sophisticated James Bond style.

The priest's eyes widened, and he broke into a grin. Marina's eyes had no right to gleam, but they did, and Alex desired to wipe the smirk right off her face.

Elena colored fiercely.

About to pull a 007 kissing maneuver, Alex stopped when he spotted a flash of shadow outside the chapel. Except for the small wedding party, the cathedral had been empty.

"Wait," he whispered.

"Can I help you?" Another priest stood outside the open chapel door.

A voice echoed across the walls in the cathedral. A male voice answered, "No, I was just looking at the windows of your beautiful church. I'm just leaving."

"You may stay."

Alex moved down the aisle. By the time he got there, the back of a tall blond man was shutting the heavy iron doors behind him.

The priest shrugged and walked with Alex back into the sanctuary.

Father Spaneas, the dedicated sidekick for some forty years, turned to him with a broad smile. "Ah, the wedding is over? Congratulations to the both of you."

Alex tried to sound nonchalant. "Thank you." He motioned toward the door. "Who was that?"

"Just a visitor investigating our cathedral. People come from all over to visit St. Stefan's."

"Did he ask about the wedding?"

The old man slowly nodded. "Yes. He wanted to know if we did marriages on short notice. He mentioned he had a fiancé."

"Thank you, Father." Of course, the man had a fiancé. That's what he would say, and Alex didn't believe it for a minute. Paranoia hit him. Spies appeared to be everywhere.

The wedding party filtered into the main cathedral with puzzled expressions. Elena huddled close to Marina, her face pale, her eyes darting in all directions. Alex took her hand and gave it a reassuring squeeze. She let out a long sigh, and he mouthed, "It's okay," before turning to the two priests.

"Thank you both. You don't know how much this means to us." He had trouble controlling the apprehension in his voice. Nobody seemed to notice.

"Ah, it is a pleasure." Father Christofides nodded to Elena. "Your grandmother, may she rest in peace, would have been so proud. And, Alex, your mother too."

Yes, they would have, but not for the reasons they were marrying.

Elena and Marina, life-long friends, now sisters-in-law. A perfect family. Too bad he wasn't the forever husband.

Damn. He'd just married the woman he'd loved and lost a long time ago, and he couldn't even touch her. Life was full of irony.

Marina said, "Let's go into the parish hall and have some cake."

A phone call from Washington D.C. to Amsterdam, The Netherlands.

In the heart of Washington D.C., a man sat in his luxury apartment, his jaws clenched in angry frustration. He wanted someone to pay for this. But the man who deserved to die was already dead. Besides, Hadean Petrov had been the most efficient hitman they'd ever employed.

"What the hell happened?" He kept the cell phone glued to his ear as though maybe he hadn't heard the conversation right.

"Herr Petrov fell down the stairs and broke his neck. I do not know what happened. The young Dkany could not have overpowered somebody as well trained as Petrov. We told him the young lady would be no trouble. Maybe he was not prepared."

The man smacked his gums. "Apparently *she* was."

Hadean Petrov had taken on a half a team of FBI agents in Columbia. He'd ambushed and killed most of them and got a significant shipment of cocaine out of the country on schedule. How does this one little girl kill him?

"Indeed. And there is more bad news."

"What?" the man growled. What more could go wrong to get rid of the meddlesome heir to the Dkany Castle?

"She has married."

"Married?" The man sputtered out the word as if he'd just spit out fire. "Who?"

"Alexander Brancusi."

"When?" His tone became shrill.

"Today. I was at the church."

"I see—I see. This is a reason for celebration, is it not?" Suddenly, the man's heartbeat a little slower, everything around him seemed a little brighter. Satisfaction tapered his anger. So, the young woman had finally wed Alexander Brancusi. He hadn't thought that possible. But this wasn't bad. Not at all.

"Why is that? It means if they die, there will be more heirs."

"Not necessarily," the man said. "We can keep a closer eye on her, and the castle will still go to the nearest relative. That will be good for us. Meanwhile, I will see our contact in DC. I'll find out about their next move. It would be my guess they will come to Romania, and probably soon. I want to know when they come and where they stay, then I will contact you."

"Right away."

The man clicked off the phone. He stared out at the night.

Chapter 11

Flight to Romania: Part One

Immmense power surged beneath KLM Royal Dutch Airlines. Elena closed her eyes as the plane rose over O'Hare Airport. Her stomach flipped, and she dug her hand into something nearby and held on tight.

Alex grunted and coughed. "We're in the air. I think you can let go now." His lips twitched into a smile. "You're cutting off my circulation."

"Oh, sorry." She removed the death grip on his arm.

"Planes make you nervous?" he asked.

"A bit."

The 'fasten your seatbelt' light went off. Elena unstrapped herself as the plane leveled and flew over the lake. She looked down at the orange sun reflected off Lake Michigan, and uneasiness stirred within her. Romania, her land of romance, castles, death, and despair. What was the old Romanian proverb? *Do not speak badly of the Devil because you cannot know to whom you will belong.*

Maybe she could find out the truth about why someone had decimated her family—Jan, her baby, Freddie, and Magda all snuffed out by some evil being. And now they wanted her.

She was paying a high personal price to go. She married the last man on earth she needed as a husband. His aura was as gray as the color of the plane. Few colorful lines drew happiness around him, and he'd turned into a first-class jerk—a womanizer who used women then discarded them when he lost interest. Elena heard about his reputation and not just from Marina. Her grandmother mentioned how worried she'd become about his lifestyle.

He'd done something decent for her, though. Because he felt he had to? Probably—loyalty and commitment to family. Still . . .

"Alex." She wanted to kick her animosity toward him into the outer atmosphere. She wasn't one of his women. So why should she resent him? She set her chin into a stubborn line.

"I think not taking luggage was a stupid idea, but since it's done, I assume we're not going to spend our entire trip in what we're wearing."

Alex tilted his head and stared until she became uncomfortable and looked down. He shook his head. "I didn't want anyone to know we were going away."

Elena managed a shrug. She didn't hide the smirk at her overbearing bodyguard of a new husband. "You're awfully over-protective for someone who obviously loathes me, aren't you?" There, she'd said it. Let's see what he'd do with it.

Alex said with quiet emphasis, "Overprotective? Oh, I hope so. We're family. And families take care of each other."

So, he thought of her as his wife, did he? She cocked her head toward him. "At least temporary family."

"Touché," he replied. "And I don't dislike you. I've never disliked you." Softer, he continued, "You, of all people, should know that."

"Alex, you were the one who suggested we . . ."

"Stop," he said, holding up his hand. "It's all right."

She dropped the subject—*for now.*

Alex made her even more uncomfortable by scrutinizing her face. "God, you're pretty banged up. You're turning colors." He checked a tender spot on her cheekbone.

Elena winced and pulled back. She *hated* it when people touched sore places just to see if it still hurt. She wanted to smack him.

"For God's sakes, don't touch it."

"Sorry. Still hurts, I take it?" His tone stated compassion. She almost liked him.

"It's getting better." Elena reached into her travel bag for a mirror and was shocked. She noticed her makeup hadn't covered all the marks. The black and blue smudge around her eye blended into a murky green.

A couple sitting in the seats across the aisle looked from her to him. The wife's mouth dipped into a deep frown.

"They think I beat you up," Alex said. He hunched in his seat a little, turning from their stares.

Irked at their unsubstantiated assumptions, Elena said in a loud voice, "It would be a cold day in hell before I'd let *any* man hit me."

The woman shook her head and went back to reading her Kindle.

Elena lowered her voice and leaned into him. "The police never contacted me after the other night. Do they know who he was? I can't stand not knowing."

Alex glanced out the window, away from her.

Elena poked him in the arm. "Come on, Alex, tell me. You know, don't you?"

Alex sighed and looked back. "Yes. I do."

"Damn it, you weren't going to tell me, were you?"

He shook his head. "No. I didn't think you needed to know."

"I'm not the same girl you knew back in high school, who lived to go to your wrestling matches and basketball games. Give me a break. A lot has happened. I have a right to know who attacked me."

"You're right. You do have a right to know. And, yes, I know you've changed." His gaze dropped from her eyes to her shoulders to her breasts. "A lot."

Elena felt the color rise in her cheeks.

The corner of Alex's mouth turned up into a smirk.

"Cut it out, Alex, and tell me what you know."

He sighed and let go of his act. "The FBI cross-checked their files with Interpol and discovered he was a professional hitman named Hadean Petrov."

Her stomach threatened to let go of her lunch. She wanted to know, but . . .

She studied the horizon as the sun was setting. Where the sky and the water met, its rays turned into ribbons of color. It didn't seem fair the water was so calm while her life was in such turmoil.

"A professional hitman? Did they need international help to erase me from the earth?"

Alex almost smiled.

"He appeared as any other rebellious college student," she said, remembering his face before the coroner removed the body. "Kind of cute. The kind of guy I might have dated."

Alex frowned. "I doubt you date murderers."

His remark chilled, and she cringed. "I'm not so sure."

He shot her a look, then softened. "It's just fortunate your neighbor noticed him hanging around your house. How did you get away from him? I never figured that out."

Elena remained quiet, reliving past events. Scalding fury had triggered her to turn and attack. But anger turned to terror when she saw the malevolent vision of her husband whirling up the stairs. She kept that to herself and said, "I kicked him between his legs and ran like hell. How else could I have gotten away?"

"Indeed." An expression of disbelief crossed his face. "Then, somehow, he tripped running down the stairs."

"Yeah, that's how it happened." He wouldn't have believed the truth.

Alex almost smiled. "Unbelievable. You . . ." He shook his head. "Sent him flying down the staircase?"

Elena glanced back through the window and smirked. "Sort of."

He coughed. "I'm not sure I believe this. But, until you're ready to tell me, you'll be in good hands." Alex patted her arm.

He was patronizing her? She pushed his hand away. *Oh please*. She'd have enough trouble just to keep him away from anything in a skirt.

Her attention turned toward the couple across the aisle. Apparently, the woman overheard his remark and tried to stare him down. The flight attendant who pushed the drink cart was even less help. He asked Elena if she was all right, did she need anything, and if he could punch someone out for her.

She laughed. "Not just now, but thanks, I'll keep you in mind." Hah, she thought. *Just hah.*

Alex leaned over her, brushing her shoulder. He gazed at the moon against the backdrop of a now dark gray sky. Constellations were starting to form, and the passengers' loud voices diminished into a steady drone.

She didn't want to move away from the beauty of the night sky, his scent, and the way he looked in his navy slacks, beige shirt, and leather jacket. Wait a minute. You're not actually supposed to fall for him, remember?

Maybe she didn't care for the way he'd turned out, but she couldn't deny Alex was a handsome, sexy, and intriguing man. The female flight attendants made more stops by them than anyone else in the cabin.

Then a word sprang to attention. Elena was sitting next to her *husband*. And she had the quickest and lousiest wedding in history.

Something old, something new, something borrowed, something blue. She *borrowed* Marina's white lace dress with blue piping on the jacket. Something *new and old* was the concept of marriage to her *former* boyfriend.

She thought Alex had fallen asleep, but his eyes were wide open, staring. Elena touched his arm, "Alex, where are you? What's wrong?"

Alex started, his eyes wild, before letting out his breath.

She noticed a woman leading a young boy down the aisle. He resembled the boy in her dream.

"Damn, Elena," he said.

"Damn Elena?" she answered, now royally ticked off. "Alex, you know every detail of my family's secrets, ghosts and all. If we're going to be together, at least talk to me."

"About what?" He sounded curt, abstracted. Wanting to do anything but talk. At least, not to her. "And it was damn, comma, Elena. Not damn Elena."

Oh, for God's sakes. "Never mind. It doesn't matter." Irritation crept into her voice, and she gave him a terse smile. "Go back to whatever planet you were on."

Enough of this animosity. His moods changed by the minute. *I am not going to walk on eggshells around him.*

Elena stared out the window, watching his reflection against the glass. Alex embarrassed her this afternoon. When he realized he needed to kiss her, he'd missed and caught her cheek. *Idiot.*

She dozed to the hum of the engine, and images of killers in ski masks haunted her dreams, forcing her awake. She huddled into her arms.

"Wait." Alex rose and stepped out into the aisle. Reaching into the overhead compartment, he helped a blanket fall into his arms and into her lap.

Elena raised her forehead, and Alex kissed her once lightly on her uninjured cheek. He turned away from her and put his laptop under the seat.

Why did he do that? Elena placed her hand over her cheek where he'd kissed her. He'd have to stop it, or she'd be forced to kiss him back—or get him to seduce her. Yeah, when hell freezes over.

Dark storm clouds loomed in the sky, covering the moon and stars. Thunder clapped. It appeared they might be in for a bumpy ride.

Alex watched as Elena slept curled against the window, her hair half out of her braid, the clip, nowhere in sight. Something inside him stirred. She reminded him of the home he'd dreamed of having—hot chocolate in winter, lemonade in summer, Christmas trees in December, and on Thanksgiving, turkey with all the trimmings.

The blanket fell across her lap. Black jeans hugged her hips, and the white jersey now rode halfway up her back. His heart skipped a beat, and sadness overpowered his insides. This was his beautiful young wife who didn't want him and was professionally off limits anyway.

Can't anything work out?

Elena moaned in her sleep and turned over until her head reached his chest.

Elena, no, I don't dislike you. I hated you once, but now? Do you really think I married you just to protect you? Yes, of course, you do. The truth is . . .

Alex shook his head and sighed. He picked up the blanket from her lap, placed it over both of them, and curled up. At least he could have this. The vibrations coming from the engine acted as a sedative.

For the first time in two nights, he slept.

And dreamed.

A black-haired gypsy girl ran through a thick dark forest partly hidden by dense underbrush and outlined by a full silver moon. She pulled the hand of a young dark-haired boy, stumbling over tree roots. Bramble bushes scratched her face, and tree limbs flew out at them as if they were living, breathing, thinking barriers.

Federal agents with no faces closed in behind. Frantic, the woman and boy ran up a steep riverbank, a castle looming across the river. She ran in a stupor, slower and slower until she reached the top. The Feds' pace accelerated until they were almost on top of them. She turned, her face white with terror.

An agent grabbed the woman's wrist. Terrified, she scratched him in the face and pushed. For a brief second, he let go, and she sprang into action. In her frenzy, she followed the boy to the edge of a precipice high above the river. The Feds closed in again and yelled for them to stop, then fired a warning shot.

Yelling in panic, the boy took one quick look back, lost his balance, and fell over the edge.

The woman screamed, "No!" and scrambled not to topple after him. The Fed cocked his gun. She yelled, "You bastard!" As she tried to jump, the man caught her.

"No, you don't!"

"No!" The woman grabbed for the gun, and it went off, shooting her in the stomach.

Her face changed. No longer was she a nondescript, unknown woman but Elena, tears floating down her cheeks, gasping for air as he placed her on the ground.

The Federal agent was him.

"We've got you, now. You're wanted in connection with bringing heroin into the United States. I'm going to—"

"No, stop," she gasped. "The boy you just killed."

"The boy who just leaped off the cliff?" The agent said, pinning her arms to the ground. The wound made a gaping hole, and blood ran over her and onto brambles. Her face grimaced, and her breaths became short.

She whispered, "He was your son!"

His face contorted, and he started to laugh as Elena struggled for her life. As the boy turned from the murky river, he turned into Gregory Balogh, hovered over them, called to him as if he was his last lifeline, and disappeared.

The dream jolted him awake. There were no dead bodies, no spirits hovering in the air. Elena was fast asleep against his shoulder. Where did that dream come from? He shuddered the omen away and fell asleep again.

He woke with a jolt, and the pilot's voice over the loudspeaker told them to fasten their seatbelts. Nasty weather ahead. Great—just great.

There was more than one kind of bad weather, however.

Rain beat against the roof of the plane and smacked against the side. Streaks of lightning flashed around them, and thunder rumbled. The aircraft bounced up and down as if it was maneuvering twenty-foot waves on the high seas. Concerned passengers looked out their windows. Some vomited into their sickness bags.

The plane plummeted toward earth. In reality, the craft descended into Schiphol Airport, Amsterdam.

"Oh my God." Elena sat up and fought nausea. She managed to hold herself together, despite turning pale and green at the same time.

"It'll be okay, *Papusa*." He said, stroking her hair.

"Papusa?"

Elena turned into the gentleness of his fingers, and he regarded her with pleasurable surprise.

He tried to divert her attention away from the weather. "It means—"

"Little doll." Elena smiled.

Alex shrugged.

"That was sweet of you. Thank you." The softer side of Elena Dkany had overcome her acerbic wit.

"Oh, you're welcome. It's what I used to call you in high school, remember?"

She smiled and a feeling of contentment enveloped her. She took Alex's hand and rubbed his palm with her thumb. "I remember."

Elena settled back until the plane jostled its already hassled passengers again. The pain had subsided with the painkillers her doctor had given her. The medication was wearing down, and her muscles started to hurt again. She downed another pill.

Once again, the captain reassured his passengers they'd land safe, despite the bumps in the atmosphere.

They were ten minutes away from Amsterdam, and the time was six-forty A.M.

"Ten minutes, and we'll be free of this flying torture machine," Alex said over the captain's pep talk.

"Ladies and Gentlemen, your connecting flight to Bucharest will leave promptly at eleven o'clock. You may enjoy shopping at *Schiphol Airport* Mall. Thank you for flying KLM Royal Dutch Airlines."

"Thanks, indeed." Alex removed his seatbelt as they taxied down the runway.

"So, what happens now?" Elena rose and reached for her purse as the doors opened and passengers started to leave the aircraft.

"I've been doing research. We're going shopping." He grinned, took her hand, and they headed down the aisle with the departing crowd.

CHAPTER 12

SCHIPHOL AIRPORT, THE NETHERLANDS

Airport City Schiphol, or *Luchthaven Schiphol,* as it's known in Dutch, was precisely what the name suggested—a city unto itself. Aviation might be its heartbeat, but a vast shopping mall seemed to be at its center. They sold everything from duty-free clothing, furs, perfume, and liquor, to electronic equipment. Someone could shop at seven in the morning, buy an entire wardrobe, stop for lunch, and gamble at the casino. Then finish the day by dining in one of the many restaurants or lounges the plaza had to offer. They could pack their purchases in a suitcase or backpack bought at one of the finer tax-free stores. Just as Alex planned.

They walked from the arrival hall to the concourse, stopping along the way to admire the airport's modern and clean appearance. Dutch flag banners hung on walls decorated with drawings by Amsterdam's schoolchildren. There wasn't a speck of dirt anywhere on floors that looked like tiles of polished marble.

The waiting areas offered panoramic views of aircraft taking off and landing even as the steady downpour barraged the tarmac where planes taxied down the runway. Airport City was a place that never slept.

Alex barely looked at Elena as he pulled her through the checkpoint into the mall. His hand felt clammy-cold. Something had happened to him on the plane. He might have a fever, but Elena wasn't

81

sure of what. He couldn't have gotten sick that fast. When she'd asked him what was wrong, he'd replied, "Nothing." This was not "nothing."

Brewing coffee and fresh pasty aromas seeped into their space, and they went through the counter line of the Terrace Cafe.

They sat at a table viewing the pedestrians who window shopped and moved around in and out of stores. Elena munched a roll and drank cappuccino while Alex's black coffee sat untouched. They scanned their shopping lists.

She regarded him intensely. Maybe her troubles had finally caught up with him, and he was sorry he'd come. She couldn't get him to talk about it, so she couldn't possibly help.

They arranged a buying marathon, two new wardrobes in three hours, which left enough time for lunch. Racing through the stores in record time was sort of like a shopping game show.

Alex mapped out the whole itinerary, where to shop and find items in each store. Only one catch. They had to buy luggage first, and they couldn't buy more than one suitcase could carry. Fair enough. She'd buy a trolley case on rollers.

Elena had a wonderful time exploring the shops. After a while, she didn't even mind Alex's company. She watched him try on clothes, offered her opinion, and then modeled clothes for him. People turned up repeatedly in the same stores.

In one of the shops, Elena found a gauzy peasant blouse, which she wore for Alex. The sales clerk got into the swing of things, located a short black skirt and open-toed sandals that made the perfect outfit.

A black sequined evening gown caught her eye. She envisioned a romantic dinner for two by candlelight. An emptiness in her heart expanded into an intense longing for romance. She found herself staring at Alex, and as his gaze met hers, her heart turned over. She spun in another direction.

In the men's department, she found blue jeans she guessed were just Alex's size. When he put them on, they accented all his best features. He had a tight rear end for a language professor. He must work out a lot.

Despite her former animosity, she enjoyed his company. He could be fun when he wanted and find humor in just about everything.

Alex accompanied her to a lingerie shop with mannequins in the window that appeared to wear stripper's costumes. She balked when Alex insisted he wanted to come in.

Panties and bras Elena never dared to wear lay on black marble counters. She picked out several sets of black and white lace satin and lace bikinis and demi-bras. Okay, so she'd never owned anything so refined, but there was no time like the present to start.

Did Alex prefer women who wore black underwear? She stiffened momentarily, abashed at the thought. Who cared what color underwear Alex liked? It was unlikely he'd ever see her in them. And as far as nightwear, she bought an Irish flannel nightshirt for cool Romanian nights. She might need something for hot weather too. A low-cut white cotton nightgown with lace trim and straps showed off her figure to perfection.

Again, she seemed to run into the same people. One elegantly dressed man she'd seen at the restaurant showed up in almost every store. He appeared to be Dutch—blond hair, blue eyes, high cheekbones, and forehead.

Hmm, the man must be shopping for his wife or mistress.

The word mistress made her feel suddenly felt very sexy. The fact she and Alex wouldn't ever have that kind of relationship started to bother her. *Why?* Alex was one of the most handsome men she knew, but she didn't want to stay married to him. He was far too moody and a constant reminder of a past better left alone. No, the lure of the lingerie-induced thoughts better pushed far from her mind.

But she bought it anyway.

She paid the clerk at the counter. The man whom she'd determined had a mistress waited behind her. She glanced back at him as he followed her out of the store.

Where was Alex?

Elena found him at a wrought-iron patio table close to the door of The Little Bistro. The café stood across from the shop, not far from the stairs that led to departures.

"Elena!"

He stood and waved. His dark intensity spoke volumes of silent thoughts and psychically pulled Elena toward him.

"So, what did you buy in there" He grabbed her bag and peered inside. She grabbed it back, but not in time.

He'd pulled out the negligee and felt the lace, looking from it to her. A vaguely sensuous light passed from his eyes before it disappeared. Her face grew heated, and the warmth spiraled downward. Oh no!

He coughed and put the garment back in the bag. Elena looked down and pulled out her list. Everything bought and accounted for, nothing left out. She glanced at her watch.

At first, she thought she'd read it wrong. The time had flown by so fast.

"Alex, we're going to have to get back to the plane soon."

Alex touched her wrist. "Wait. I have something for you." He pulled out a small box from his inner jacket pocket and pushed it in front of her.

Elena sat back on the seat cushion. Another gift? She remembered what happened the last time he'd given her a present. Still . . . The box was not new but dog-eared at the corners. When she pulled the small top off, she stared, mouth wide open, unsuspecting, unbelieving.

A ring embedded with a ruby surrounded by diamond chips sat on a white velvet backing. "Oh my God," Elena whispered. "Your mother's ring."

"Try it on," Alex said.

"But . . ."

"You and Marina used to go through Nadia's jewelry when you were kids. You said if you ever got married, that was the ring you'd want."

"You remembered that?" Elena stared at him, stunned. "But it's your mother's ring. Marina should have it."

"She thought it was a great idea."

"But, Alex," Elena thought forward to the day when they'd separate, their marriage annulled or divorced.

Alex seemed to anticipate her concern. "If we separate, I'd want you to keep it."

If?

Suddenly, Elena was a mass of contradiction. The thought of leaving him hurt so much, it became a physical pain, and tears welled in her eyes.

"Hey, I didn't mean to make you cry," Alex said, handing her a napkin.

Elena broke out laughing. She reached over and planted a kiss on his cheek. "Thank you," she said. "Of all the rings in the world I could choose, this would be the one I'd pick. I love you for this."

Alex drank his coffee in silence. When he'd given her his mother's ring, Elena's delight and gratitude stunned him. The shadows that appeared after Magda's funeral suddenly disappeared. Had such a simple gesture created so much happiness in her?

And the panic in her face when he'd mentioned splitting up as if the idea upset her.

Bell tones coated her laughter. Her hair hung loosely over her shoulders, the way it had during their wedding. The black jeans, white shirt, and black blazer seemed to blend into her hair. Black, white, black over white, very pale skin, a photographer's delight.

He caught her eye and held fast, not about to let go. She swallowed and tried to look away, but he held on even stronger, forcing her to look back at him. Her breathing rate increased, and she saw a spark of the old desire Elena had shown the night they'd danced that last song at the prom. He'd known then they'd give themselves to each other that evening.

A shadow darted between them, breaking his hold. Stunned, he followed the darkened outline and, he saw him. A man sat a few tables away, his back to the glass wall. Every inch a business executive, he held an Amsterdam newspaper partially in front of his face. He seemed self-assured, almost cocky, until the specter sat across from him. The man dropped the paper and pulled back his chair. The image faded.

But Alex noticed the bulge inside his well-tailored jacket pocket. A gun.

"Alex."

Alex focused back on Elena.

"You see that man over there?" Elena started to point, but Alex grabbed her hand and shook his head. "Don't look at him."

She nodded and whispered. "He's been in every store I've entered. He followed me into the ladies' lingerie shop and didn't buy anything. Now he's here," she said almost under her breath.

"Yes, that's what I mean," Alex whispered. "It's maybe a coincidence, but I doubt it. Let's get out of here."

Elena nodded and stuffed her purchases into the trolley.

"Just pick up our stuff slowly and walk out of here, as though we didn't notice. Gaston's Men's Store is to our right. According to the mall map, there's a back door leading to the departure area. Just follow my direction. We'll make a run for it. Say yes."

"Yes." They stood up.

"Say yes, darling."

"Yes, darling."

"Give me a big kiss, like you mean it." He wondered what she'd do.

Elena's lips parted.

He thought she might turn and walk away. Instead, she offered a crooked smile, threw her arms around him, and kissed him firmly, her nose touching his. Then, picking up the handle of her luggage, she turned on her heels, walking nonchalantly out of the bistro.

Weak in the knees and still tasting Cappuccino on his lips, Alex followed and didn't know where he was going for a few seconds. They entered Gaston's. A crowd of shoppers was taking advantage of the fifty percent off sale. They walked down the aisles, pretending to look at the products displayed in glass cases. Luck was with them. Several women grabbed items at a polo shirt display, coming between the guy in the cafe and Elena and Alex. He had to maneuver in and out to keep up with them.

Mixing themselves into a small mob, they let the rambling flow maneuver them toward the back of the store. But the crowd shifted into several directions when the aisles split. Once again, their tail still shadowed them.

Alex pulled Elena to the other side of the aisle and behind a few shoppers. The man would have to turn back if he wanted to stay with them. Alex didn't think so. He wouldn't blow his cover. He stood looking at gloves that were way too small for him. Alex chuckled.

They walked into another group of women, and Elena struck up a conversation with one of them. "You're an American?" she asked the woman.

The woman nodded.

"We're looking for a gift for a friend back home, and I'm not sure where we'd find something appropriate. Something from Amsterdam." The lady grabbed her hand and pulled them down another aisle in the opposite direction of their shadow.

As they got past the pants rack, Alex's heart leapt into his throat. There the man stood thumbing through short-size men's jeans. He was tall. The look he gave Alex hit him deep in the gut. If he'd had even an inkling, the man was another tourist it went with that glance. Alex placed his arm around Elena's back and pushed her into another crowd toward designer suits.

Their stalker kept to the back of a group of women shoving from their rear. When they hit the suit department, a salesman asked if he could help them.

"Yes. My husband needs a suit for an impromptu dinner tonight. We're in a hurry. Could you help us?" Elena said in perfect Dutch.

Alex acted as a shield between the man who'd wandered into the suit department and Elena, who explained her needs to the salesman.

As the man stood going through the rack in the back, another salesman came up to provide just enough diversion for them to make a getaway. Alex grabbed her hand and pulled her out of the department to the surprised look on the salesman's face.

They stumbled into several burly employees lifting cartons from a cart. Another group of shoppers poured in from the back entrance. They glanced back and saw the man outside the men's clothing department, looking in both directions. He spotted them and moved toward them. Clearly more agitated and annoyed, he was now at the edge of a crowd that blocked his way. He jostled into the center, pushing people out of the way with his elbows.

Now their pursuer was in the same crowd that protected Elena and Alex, and they no longer had a buffer. He moved in and out and was close—too close. Alex heard a scream and a commotion coming from the center.

A dark shadow closed over the crowd.

As everyone's eyes turned toward the cry, Alex grabbed Elena's hand and pulled her up a flight of stairs into the main hallway, where he turned.

The man tangled with the cartons, and employees disengaged himself and rushed forward, the workers yelling at him in Dutch. The shadow vanished.

They wasted no time while racing up the steps to the departure area. Behind them, their stalker struggled in the crowds to gain ground.

Alex pushed Elena into the waiting arms of the security patrol as they made it to the checkpoint.

"That man, over there." Alex pointed him out to the guard. "He's been following us since we got off the plane."

The guard turned and glared at him, and he made no move to go through the checkpoint. He just pulled out his cell phone.

"Damn," Alex said to Elena, "We're going to miss our flight." Dashing toward the plane, they raced down the ramp and into the cabin as the doors shut behind them.

Back in their seats, seatbelts fastened, Alex still wasn't comfortable until the plane started to taxi down the runway. He let out a sigh and settled back.

"Doesn't look as though we can run away from them, no matter what we do. How did he know where we were?" Fear mingled with tears in her eyes.

"I don't know." He didn't dare state what was foremost in his mind. Their stalker seemed to know their every move. Who was he, and why was he doing this? And what was the shadow that hovered over the crowd? He couldn't admit what he thought. Then, another thought. He didn't believe in ghosts. Did he? So, what was that shadow?

Alex put his arm around Elena and pulled her close.

Elena stiffened and wiped the tears off her cheeks with a tissue. "I'm okay, thanks. I think I pulled a muscle again. I don't think I'm supposed to be running around."

True enough. She wasn't. She was hurting, but it could have been a reminder this trip was strictly business. Damn. Strictly business. Yeah right. And the ring looked beautiful on her finger. Overwhelming loneliness hit Alex as he watched his hands-off bride braid her hair down to the tip of her breast.

He let go a groan.

Schiphol Airport

The would-be assassin turned the corner out of sight of the security check, took out his cell phone, and punched buttons. He waited for the other end to pick up.

The other end said, "Yes. So?"

"So, the two got away. Here's how . . ."

A low grumble came through the other end of the phone along with static. "And why should I care *how*? You are trained for this. You should know how to deal with any situation you run across. Is that not so?"

"Well, sir."

"Is that not so?" The voice grew louder—more threatening.

"Not if they're protected by ghosts."

"Protected by what? There is static on the other end of this line. Did you say ghosts? You are perhaps verruckt? Crazy man?"

"No, sir. I just report what I see. I myself . . . One planted itself across from me at a café, then hovered over the department store. Indeed, I did kill someone, but it was not the Dkany or Brancusi."

"You killed somebody else?" His voice grew soft—through the teeth—a long pause. "I did not plan that. This will cause us much grief. You will go to your Amsterdam hotel and wait. Somebody will be there to meet you. There cannot be any complications in this plan. Do you understand?"

The phone clicked before he could reply.

That evening, a room attendant found an unidentified body in a hotel suite.

CHAPTER 13

RUSALKA INN, SOMEWHERE IN ROMANIA

Elena dreamed about plunging airplanes and plunging negligee necklines until she hit her head on the roof of their rented Dacia. Alex drove through a dark tunnel on a brick road full of potholes. That woke her. "Ow!"

"You all right?" They hit another, and she banged her head again—rocks scattering against the broken stone walls. The pain was enough to guarantee her a major headache later on.

"No, I'm not. I think I just got a concussion."

The tunnel opened onto a cobblestone road in front of a rustic pine lodge. A hand-painted wooden sign, *Rusalka*, had small engravings of wood nymphs hanging over the door. A perfect name for the forest setting that covered the landscape and hid the base of the Carpathian Mountains.

Alex stopped the car in front of the walkway leading to wooden porch steps.

A rumble of thunder echoed in the distance. The sky was blue with a few wispy clouds and no hint of an approaching storm, except for the muggy, humid air.

A teenage boy opened the passenger door. "You Americaners?"

Alex nodded.

"My name . . . Christian. Welcome to Rusalka." He pointed to the sky. Might rain. I take car to garage, yes?" He had his hand out.

Alex grinned and raised an eyebrow at him, then reached into his pocket for change. "*Da,*" he said. "*Multumesc.*"

Christian pocketed the coins and said, "Please, I speak the English. So, you are welcome." He flashed a big grin toward Elena.

She rubbed her eyes and was instantly charmed by this boy.

Alex slid out of the Dacia and tossed him the keys.

The kid jingled the key ring.

Christian's happy-go-lucky warmth sent an odd flurry of happiness through Elena. This place possessed a cheerful vibe.

Christian seemed a happy boy.

Alex helped Elena out of the car. She yawned and rubbed her eyes. "*Mindra.* Pretty lady?"

"Oh, thank you." *Well, somebody thinks I'm attractive.*

Christian jumped into the sputtering Dacia and took off down the road disappearing behind the lodge.

She'd slept most of the way from the airport, plagued with dreams of killers, ghosts, Alex, and the dark-haired boy she couldn't get out of her mind.

Elena slid a sideward glance toward Alex. Intense and handsome as the devil, that he attracted her was no lie. Even though she didn't care for him half the time, she still wanted to run her fingers through his hair and kiss him on the spot just behind his ear lobe. What would he do if she just did? As her left hand brushed against Alex's side, she remembered the look on his face when he'd handed her his mother's ring. The man still had a soul.

Before they opened the wooden door with a brass doorknob embedded with the face of a wood-fairy, she turned and looked at the view. It would have been the most glorious honeymoon spot in the world if their marriage had been forever after. Her heart suddenly felt empty.

But, no, keep it real. A real marriage could never happen between them. Alex's relationships never lasted more than a few dates. This dark, morose, and troubled man might be a great lover but would probably make a terrible husband. In any case, she doubted any woman would get him to the altar unless she were in dire distress. And even then, not for keeps. Anyway, when he learned the truth, he wouldn't want her—ever again.

Alex planted his hand firmly on the back of her jacket and ushered her inside.

An elderly woman smiled a greeting from behind a desk and ambled up to them. "*Salut*! I am *Doamna* Malik. Welcome guests to Rusalka Inn."

Within two minutes, they'd learned Mrs. Malik was a widow and that the lodge had been in her family for generations. The boy, who'd driven their car into the garage, was her mechanic and nephew. Then she boasted of having the best cook in Transylvania.

The aroma of roast beef and baking apple strudel wafted through the lobby and settled in her stomach, making it growl. As she looked for the source, a man sitting in the corner of the room near a brick fireplace caught her eye. He was dressed all in black and wore a goatee with a smattering of salt and pepper hair. A newspaper covered his face, but she sensed he wasn't reading the paper. She shuddered and shifted her eyes from him to the restaurant.

Elena poked Alex, her stomach reacting to the first smell of food since Amsterdam.

"Sorry," Alex whispered. "We're going to the cabin. Food is provided."

How did he know that? No way. She was starving. "If you want to find our cabin, go ahead. I'm staying here and having dinner. You do what you want."

Alex stepped in front of her to block her path.

"Excuse me." She tried to step around him.

"No." He took her elbow.

Surprised and slightly hostile at his sudden authoritative attitude, she shook her elbow loose and started around him.

The solitary figure got up and headed toward them. He smelled of sweat and miles of Romanian earth, and his hair plastered against his head as though shampoo and water hadn't touched it in a month. Dark circles surrounded his eyes, making them look sunken. "The restaurant is not opened yet," he said, in a local Romanian dialect. "You may be more comfortable in your cabin."

Aggravated and hungry, she almost snapped at him. However, something about the harsh coldness in his tone stopped her. It stirred a sudden angst that took away her appetite and attitude. Was it imagination or reality? Impressions hit Elena hard. She decided it best to follow Alex to the cabin.

"You understand we would like complete privacy while we're here," Alex said as Mrs. Malik led them down a pine-needled path through a grove of spruces. "We'll take no calls. Should anyone ask, we changed our reservations."

Mrs. Malik smiled. "Your cabin waits for you. Is open." They came to the tree line and saw the row of cabins.

"She is pretty, your little bride," the landlady said.

Elena acknowledged her with a smile and looked down.

"You make the beautiful couple."

Alex grinned back and winked, but Elena saw no light behind his expression.

Vast fields and distant mountains provided the setting for a row of cabins made of knotty pine. Picnic tables and chairs decked the porches, offering a panoramic view of the countryside.

Mrs. Malik walked onto the porch with them, opened the screen door, and peered in. "Is good. I go," she said. Her gray bun started to unravel on the back of her head as she stiffly walked back down the path toward the lodge.

Alex stopped to stare at Elena.

She stood transfixed, looking at a church perched high on a mountain, topped by a massive cross.

For an instant, he couldn't imagine the place without her. She was lovely against the background of the mountains. Feisty and stubborn, but pretty. Her black braid hung over her shoulder, and a smile of delighted enchantment highlighted her pale features and cobalt eyes. She was an ideal blend to a perfect landscape.

He moved next to her and leaned on the railing. "It's something, isn't it? Mysterious and wild. She'll snag you if you're not careful, and you'll never want to leave."

"She?" Elena turned. Their arms brushed. Her perfume tantalized. Alex tried to fight his body's response to her and gave up. He allowed himself to want her.

"I've always thought of the Carpathians as a lovely, untamed woman, waiting for the right lover to come along. Always waiting, never quite finding the right one."

Elena peered into his face, and her vitality fed him. "Are you talking about the mountains?" she asked.

"Of course." He gazed intently into her eyes. "What else could be so lovely?" His meaning didn't appear lost on her. She blushed and glanced away like she was grappling with what to say next.

Alex hadn't planned to seduce her, but if she kept looking at him like that, he might not have a choice.

Her smile echoed in her voice, making him even warmer inside. "I could get lost in the beauty of those mountains," Elena said. "But, I think that was just a metaphor, Alex."

"For what?" He faced her to get her full reaction.

Elena ignored the question. She just stared out at the mountains.

"You managed to escape her beauty once. You never went back."

Her body stiffened, and her expression of delight retreated so fast, he wondered if he'd imagined she'd ever worn it. She backed up a few paces, apprehension filling her face. He lost his ability to continue.

"Alex." Her voice was low and raspy.

He turned away. "I'm sorry, Elena. I don't know everything that happened to you here in Romania, just that you lost your husband and baby. Maybe it's a subject we should just leave alone."

"Leave it alone?" Elena almost exploded, the lashes that shadowed her cheeks flew up, and she tightened her lips.

He froze.

"How can I?" She raised her voice even higher, "When he won't leave *me* alone. When he's contacting me from beyond." She stopped short of telling him she saw ghosts.

"Damn it." Alex didn't know whether he'd rather smack her or hold her. "Elena."

"No." She swallowed hard, lifted her chin, and boldly met his gaze.

"Just forget this ghost nonsense. They don't . . . *he* doesn't exist. You might want him to, but he doesn't. He's dead, Elena." He found his voice rising, trying to bring her back to reality, but causing a rift with every word.

She answered in a rush of words that decked him. "Just forget it." She spun on her heels and almost caught her jacket when she charged into the cabin and slammed the screen door.

Alex stared at a disappearing whirlwind.

Oh no. What the hell did I do? I . . .

But the cabin door opened again, and Elena walked down the porch steps and stood by his side. Puzzled, he waited for her to make a move.

"Alex," she said in a quiet tone. "Sorry, I overreacted." She looked away from him, gazing out over the horizon. "You have been so good to my grandmother and me. You didn't have to come here to protect me from these monsters. You didn't have to marry me, but you did."

He didn't move.

"You couldn't know what happened in Bucharest, maybe just what my grandmother told you. I doubted whether she mentioned it to anybody, not even you." She put her arm around his waist.

Alex faced her. "She wouldn't tell me anything. One minute you were married the next, you were at the University of Indiana. I'd heard your husband and child were dead. I can't think of a worse thing to happen to anybody."

He looked down into her eyes. A tear fell down her cheek. "I don't want to bring up a painful past, Elena. I really don't. When you're ready to tell me, you will."

She nodded, then seemed to lighten. "I guess I gave you the fatal flaw in my personality—walking away to avoid anything unpleasant," she said.

Her smile warmed him—the beauty of a shining face.

"Again, I'm sorry."

"Oh, Elena . . ." he said. They gazed at the mountains, and Alex pointed. "Look at the cross on top of the peak, over there." He'd noticed it when they first arrived.

"The Romanian church. God will protect us," Elena said. "He has so far."

She believed. Alex wasn't sure he still did. When had he lost his faith?

She turned, and glancing back at him, she walked back into the cabin.

Elena knelt on her bed and gazed out the window. Alex hung over the rail and continued to stare at the mountains.

He thought she mourned Janek Ivanov. But it wasn't his death slowly chipping away at her sanity. It was Michael's—not Michael Ivanov, as the birth certificate claimed, but Michael Brancusi.

Elena kept a dark secret all those years. Michael had been Alex's child, not Jan's. To mention this would have been too cruel. Alex chose to remain on the porch and not come in to bother her. Relief filled her. She finished unpacking the trolley's essentials. When she came upon her small photo album with Jan, herself, and her baby. Not wanting to go into a deep depression, she stuffed it back into her handbag.

"The Carpathians." A new voice boomed from outside.

Who was that? As sad as her memories were, she wanted to be alone with them for a while, but heavy footsteps crunched the gravel.

"No mountain range is more beautiful, nor can conjure up such tales of intrigue and horror," the voice said.

"Well, hello," Alex said from the porch. "Figured I might run into you some time or other. You're a little late to be our bodyguard. We've already been stalked."

Bodyguard? Might run into you? Who was this man, Alex knew?

Curious, Elena came out of the front bedroom and looked out the screen door.

"Hello," the man said. He stood between the two rails on the top step looking through the screen at Elena.

The man in the lobby. Elena studied him. Before he appeared as a refugee from the streets, now, in a split second, he emerged as someone she might meet at a Gold Coast singles' bar. One minute they were in the Rusalka Inn lobby, and he'd looked like a bum. Now he was clean, pressed, combed hair and goatee, still dressed in black, though a *dressy* black.

Elena stepped out onto the porch to greet this new, unwelcome addition. Alex strolled over and put his arm around her. She glanced sideways at him and raised an eyebrow. Why had he not told her they were expecting company?

The man said, "A perfect place to honeymoon." The inner pocket of his sports jacket bulged.

The man's got a gun. Why does he have a gun?

"I'd leave you alone, except you seem to be my only neighbor. Everyone else is up at the lodge." He crossed over and sat on the railing as if he planned to stay.

"Welcome to the neighborhood—if there was one," Elena said. "But there isn't. We prefer to be alone."

The man stared through her, and she glared back until his eyes finally flicked and lowered. She took a deep breath and felt good. She'd won a battle.

"I doubt it." A grin spread over his face. "I believe you were arguing when I reached my cabin."

Who is this jerk?

"No, not at all," Alex replied, between clenched teeth. "We were playing metaphor games with the mountains."

"We didn't see you," Elena said. She unleashed herself from Alex and took a step toward the stranger. "Why is that?"

"Maybe because I came up through the back." The man turned to Alex. "You really should stake out your territory better. But now, you two look like you could use some dinner. I stocked your refrigerator with food and wine. The conversation will be *very* welcome."

What did he mean, he'd provided the food and wine?

"Who, exactly, are you?" Elena asked.

"I'm Tony Donatelli, and you'll want to know me." He fished something from his jacket pocket and threw it to Elena.

She caught a U.S. Government FBI identification card.

"You're with the FBI?" Elena asked, wide-eyed. "Vacationing in the mountains like . . ."

"A bum?" he answered cheerfully. "Sometimes I sleep in my car for nights on end. This is my first real bed and shower in a week."

"Why are you here?" Elena asked. "I thought the FBI handled national interests." She fingered the ID and handed it back.

"When domestic and international problems threaten our home-land security, we work with governments to bring criminals to justice. The CIA and FBI can work hand in hand when needed."

She took another step forward toward Tony. Her eyes never left his face. "What problem brings you to where we are?"

Without missing a beat, Tony said, "You."

That kicked-punched her in the gut. "The FBI is interested *in me?* What in God's name did I do wrong?" She put both hands to her mouth. "So, you *caught* me."

Tony frowned.

Alex's eyebrows went straight up.

"You're here because I smoked pot in my dorm two years ago. Why did it take you so long to find out?"

"Oh my God," he said, folding his arms in front of him. "A confession. Think I should take you back to the states in handcuffs. No Elena Dkany . . . er . . . Brancusi. I doubt you did anything wrong, except what many college kids try at least once in their lives." Tony put away his ID and smiled.

"And, you know my name too. Why doesn't *that* surprise me?" She glanced at Alex, who looked away, over the mountains. Tony kissed her hand, and Alex frowned. "I think we're all starved. I know Elena is."

Elena's face warmed with the memory. She'd really been an impulsive fool at the lodge.

"I—" Elena started to say.

Tony topped her. "There's a picnic table, food and wine, and late afternoon sun. So, let's break bread together. People who eat and drink together have to be friends."

They do? Not necessarily.

They sat on the picnic table drinking the Romanian national pastime, some excellent Tuica. The smooth, warm plum brandy slid down her throat before she realized how tired she'd grown.

"I want to apologize for the way I acted toward you in the lodge," Elena said. "I had a splitting headache from our car. and the journey over here was, to say the least, adventuresome."

Tony nodded. "Don't think about it. I looked scuzzy, and you were tired. It's reasonable. But I understand you're having some problems," Tony said to Elena. "You were attacked?"

"How did . . . ?"

"I know someone's trying to kill you as they did your grandmother and perhaps your brother, and probably because you inherited Dkany Castle."

Jolted, Elena replied, "How do you know so much? And why do you believe my brother's death wasn't accidental?" She glanced at Alex. "And what does Dkany Castle have to do with this?"

Alex remained stoic.

Tony ignored her question. "Mrs. Brancusi—"

"Elena, please."

"Elena, why does someone want you and your family dead?"

Elena sought support from Alex. He had one foot on the bench watching a farmer bring his cows home from the fields. The lead cow wore a bell which clanged as she moved.

The Carpathian Mountains, an old farmer and a herd of cows, one that clanged as she walked. What a contrast to the horrors of life.

Elena sighed. She knew nothing about her brother's death. Still, She told Tony what she knew about the castle, her grandmother, and her attack by a professional hitman.

"Hadean Petrov. I know the bastard," Tony said. "You *should* be commended for killing him."

"I didn't kill—" Elena started.

"If not you," Tony said, "then who?"

"He tripped down the stairs."

Tony's hands went up. "Whatever you did, ma'am, you did us all a favor."

"Elena. My grandmother was ma'am."

"Okay, Elena. With Hadean Petrov out of the way, the world will be a safer and happier place."

"Okay. So why did he want me off the face of the earth, and why is the FBI interested in me and my castle?"

Tony raised his glass at her in a salute. "You don't mince words. Good, I'll lay it out for you."

Alex sat on the picnic table, feet on the bench. He kept quiet.

"Romania has never been a major drug player. Heroin usually comes from the poppy fields in Asia. About ten years ago, my agency got word the supply of heroin was escalating in New York City and moving onto the Chicago streets. Our agents penetrated the lower ranks of the drug ring. They were looking for a link between the origin of the drugs and New York. We thought one of our people knew, but her body washed up on a beach off the Black Sea."

"Oh, no." Elena looked down into her glass.

"She was my partner. She went out on a hunch without backup—without me." He glanced away to the last of the cows milling into the barn.

A hint of tear grazed his eye. Not such a toughie, after all.

"I'm sorry."

"They found out about our infiltration and shipped the drugs somewhere for storage until they felt it safe to smuggle them into Europe and the United States. Some time ago, we raided a warehouse in Afghanistan. We caught one of the runners and persuaded him to tell us where the shipments went. He mentioned Romania. Then, before the officers could get him out of the warehouse, a sniper killed him. So went our only viable link. My boss in D.C. asked me to create a new task force to check into it. We've combed Transylvania from one end to the other, and the trail always seems to go cold. About a month ago, your brother died of a heroin overdose, virtually unheard of in a small town like Dkany. We started watching the castle and Gregory Balogh."

"My Uncle Gregory?"

"He's your uncle?" Tony raised his eyebrows. "I didn't know."

"He's an old family friend and Magda's Romanian solicitor, but not a real relation," Alex replied. "Go on."

Elena opened her mouth to say something but remained silent.

"Ah. I see. Anyway, it provided fodder for investigation. We've found out a lot about the activities of Mr. Balogh, but nothing could tie him into the operation. Then, when Magda died after she decided to go to the castle, and when you were attacked, well, why would anyone want to kill you over a castle? They're a dime a dozen in Romania. Someone wanted to keep you away, maybe to get control—ownership. And you're the last surviving link."

Elena frowned. "You think I'm involved."

"I highly doubt that. Although . . . Tony stroked a shadow of a beard. "A possibility. But, unless the Dkanys were making some sort of power play or getting in the way, the organization wouldn't have a reason to kill you. You don't have children who would inherit."

"I . . . uh . . . borrowed Alex, who was already a professor at Briar Hill, to look into the financial aspects of the college and to get to know the staff."

"Alex?"

Alex turned away as though he wanted no part of this.

Elena took in his information and caught her breath. A slow chill ran down her back.

"Oh my God, Alex. You're working as a plant at Briar Hill?"

Elena couldn't speak for a moment.

Neither did the two men.

Elena regrouped and continued. "So, what about my family? Did you discover anything?"

"No," Alex replied.

"Well, thank God," she said softly. "So," she continued, turning to Tony, "Are you going to cart *me* off in handcuffs?"

Tony's eyes widened, and the corners of his mouth blossomed into a grin. "Not today."

"Tony, I own the castle, my brother died of a heroin overdose, and my family's being eliminated one-by-one. You must suspect somebody wants my castle for some reason. If you're involved with capturing drug traffickers, you must suspect the castle is where they're storing the drugs."

"Now that, my dear girl, is a distinct possibility."

"How does Alex fit into all of this?" She caught their glances and waited.

Alex opened his mouth, and Tony cut him off. "I was Alex's criminal justice instructor at Georgetown. When he got a position at Briar Hill, he helped me check some information. He came with you to act as a bodyguard, and I understand, married you to keep you from being the only heir, right? A marriage of convenience?"

Elena's stomach turned over with the barrage of reality. "A noble gesture." A sour taste filled her mouth.

Alex tilted his head at her.

"So, Alex, what did you find out about my family? Did Magda run drugs out of her rose garden tea parties? Did my grandfather smuggle drugs in the textbooks?" Elena felt the knot of betrayal. He wasn't there for her protection. He was keeping track of her. She wanted to throw Alex's ring back in his face.

Alex frowned and stared hard at her. "Elena . . ." Tony said, "No. Let's eat, and then we'll talk."

Washington D.C. and Romania

"You know where they are?" The voice registered through mountain static.

"I do," the other voice said. "The information came from Washington. They stay at the Rusalka Inn. I know what needs to be done."

"That is good," the first man said. "But not a task most pleasant for you."

"No, but still, it must be done."

They clicked off.

Chapter 14

Rusalka Inn, Romania

Thunder echoed over the mountains. The red ball of setting sun faded behind a storm cloud and disappeared as if someone had thrown a rock at a streetlight. A mountain thundercloud took shape overhead. Yet another storm approached.

Elena went into the cabin, took out her cell phone from her handbag, and checked the batteries. Good. Then she took out her laptop and checked her email.

Marina.

Lena,

Just wondering how you're getting on. Got a call from Alex about your near attack in Amsterdam. Am worried about the two of you. It seems, well, we've known all along, someone's out to get you. Take care of yourself. You're my best friend and now sister-in-law. (I know in name only, but it wouldn't surprise me if this were a forever thing. I have a feeling about the two of you. You were meant to be together from the start.) I have a few things I'd like to share with you about Alex but can't do it now. Am rushing off to discuss my internship at Northwestern. I hope you won't be too disappointed if I change my direction. You won't believe it, but it's Criminal Psych. But that's for another time. Nothing's been decided. Take care of yourself and that unruly brother of mine.

By the way, just wondering, have you told Alex yet? Just don't want to open up my big mouth by mistake. I promised I will keep silent, and I will.

Love you.
Mari

Elena started to respond but changed her mind when she heard voices coming from the porch. She caught a few words. "Alex, I didn't know . . ." and "Do you really think Magda . . ."

She needed to put them out of her mind. She put on headphones and turned on a new song she'd downloaded to drown their conversation.

Everything came too fast. First, she and her family were victims. Now, it seemed, the United States Government considered them *suspects.* Unbelievable. It didn't take a doctorate to figure out those two wanted something from her. She just wasn't sure what, except maybe a confession.

Despite what Mari thought, she'd gotten married for the worst possible reason, to the worst possible man. So, what did Mari want to share about her brother? He was a complicated man, but to what extent?

Tony wanted to catch the culprits who smuggled drugs into the U.S. Not Alex. He was just a language professor at Briar Hill. Wasn't he? What did Alex really want? To help her? Really? This put him in a new light. She wasn't so sure now.

The artist sang about a dead lover who resided in heaven. Loneliness and depression swallowed and threatened to consume her. When she went away to school, her grandmother had insisted she have long conversations with a grief counselor. She went and thought the woman had helped her put everything in perspective. She and Marina had many heart-to-heart talks, and they'd gathered other young women who'd lost loved ones to share their stories. Had they helped? She'd thought so at the time, but she still felt empty inside. And with Alex, there was so much unfinished business between them. Only when this all came out could she hope to open her heart to him.

When Alex came in, he stopped in front of her as if he wanted to talk. When she turned her head away, he left, and she heard the second bedroom door slam. The good news—she'd have no illusions as to consummating their would-be marriage vows.

Instead, she picked up a book of popular Romanian sites that lay on the cocktail table and flipped through the pages. Finally, she came upon a pamphlet of Dkany and leafed through the pages.

Inns: A Ramada Inn in the new part of the city, a couple of bed and breakfasts, and the Sandor Inn featured in the old part of town. That seemed a place for tourists. She wondered where they would be staying. She thought he'd mentioned the Ramada. She'd rather stay in the old section of Dkany. There was something about the Sandor though, she wasn't sure what. It looked lovely and not as expensive as some of the more modern places. Probably a haven for sightseers.

Thoroughly unsatisfied, the book fell off her lap and onto the sofa next to her. She closed her eyes, blocking all but the song.

The drizzling rain came down harder until it settled into a steady downpour. The room festered in hot and humid air rather than cold and chilly. Still, she shivered.

Someone's walking over my grave. A premonition? A hollowness in her stomach and goosebumps appeared from something more than cold.

She sensed a hovering presence. The movie line "I see dead people" came to mind. How could anyone take her seriously when she casually mentioned she saw ghosts? No one could know her grandmother's specter told her to find a killer in Romania—a killer and a little boy.

Alex's lack of belief tortured her. Once, he'd *almost* admitted to seeing the visions in the mirror. Still, Elena thought he'd been trying to gather her sympathy. He'd really thought it was a trick of his imagination.

Elena knew better. Jan was not finished with them. In fact, the ghost hadn't begun to erupt into his real reason for being. He came back to set right a wrong, to save a life—maybe hers, maybe someone else's.

Blackness swirled around her mind. Her muscles relaxed, starting from her head, then continuing down her neck and shoulders all the way to her toes.

Memories of Alex at seventeen, the reflection of Janek who stared back at her in the mirror. His murder. Her despair. Where was Jan leading them? Who was the man, Klaus, she'd killed to defend her family? Always back to her failure to save her child and husband. The emptiness in her stomach almost matched the physical pain she'd suffered from the attack.

The features of Alex entwined with the melody as their romance enfolded inside her head. Holding hands, kissing—making love.

An image flashed so quickly through her mind she gasped and nearly broke from her semi-trance. *The blond-haired youth holding the bloody knife, plunging it into Jan.* Then, nothing. What had the killer wanted?

Now mountains—a church—a chapel, a monk holding a gun pointed at a woman's head. A faint sneer from an anonymous man. A shot—so much blood. The faceless boy standing there. Elena cried out and tore off her headphones.

The boy was her son. She felt it with every bone in her body. *But why couldn't she get his description? What did he look like? Was he alive, or was this just another ghost?*

A crash came from the other room. Footsteps. A door slammed. Sweat poured from her face and through her pink and blue seersucker shirt. She was soaking wet, and Alex stood over her.

"Elena?"

She barely heard his voice, barely saw his face.

Jan, the castle, the boy, and Freddie floated around her background. And someone else. Someone who hovered over them all. It wasn't Jan. It wasn't Gregory. *So, who was he?*

"Elena!"

The visions disappeared. Something other than her nerves shook her—Alex.

"What happened? What's the matter?"

Elena blinked back into reality. Alex crouched in front of her, his fierce dark eyes boring a hole into her mind. She tried to glance away, but he took her face with both hands, forcing her to look at him.

"What happened?" he repeated.

"I . . ." He wouldn't understand. Elena jerked away from the claustrophobia around her, ducked under his arms, and jumped from the sofa. "Nothing I fell asleep—a bad dream." Bad dream. *Was that all it was?*

Alex didn't seem to believe her. He pulled her up as he rose. "Your scream didn't sound like nothing."

"I screamed?"

"Yes, you did. So, what happened?"

She shook her head. "I . . . was listening to music and fell asleep. I must have dreamt something. But it's gone out of my head. Thanks for caring, but please, Alex, I'm fine."

She removed his hand from her arm and saw the concern in his eyes. "I don't know what happened."

When Alex didn't appear to believe her, she said, "Really, I don't know why I screamed, but I need some space now. I'm going to take a shower. I need to clear my head."

She walked into her bedroom to get her robe.

Close on her heels, he slammed his hand on the dresser, making her jump and turn.

"You saw him, didn't you?"

Backing up from his violent outburst, she caught the significance of his question.

Her feet stopped moving. She turned and stared. "Saw who?"

"Don't play with me, Elena. You saw that boy." His voice filled with severe authority. His attitude and demeanor were disconcerting.

Not a hint of the gentleman who'd almost seduced her while they gazed at the mountains existed. But at least he'd finally admitted what he'd seen. She wanted to smile but couldn't.

"So, you do believe I've seen him."

He opened his mouth, and nothing came out. Then, slouching like someone stuck a pin into him, he said, "Yes."

Elena's eyes stung. She wiped the tears away with her arm.

"Why wouldn't you talk to me about it?"

Alex seemed to be trying for chilly anger and almost managed to pull it off. Instead, he stood with his arms folded as if he would talk to a failing student.

Exasperated, she bore her eyes into his. "I did, but you refused to listen. So, I don't know who the boy is."

His defiant silence set her teeth on edge.

"All right," she said, "Hold it all in—to hell with you. I need to take a shower. I need to wash away my present existence. *And that includes you.*"

Elena grabbed the first thing lying on top of her suitcase, her cotton negligee. As Elena walked past him out the doorway headed toward later on, Elena's negligee is cotton.

"I don't know," she yelled back. But the words floated in her head, starting with a roar, gradually fading. *He is my son. My son. My son.*

But this was impossible.

Alex watched Elena go and banged his fist into his palm. He shook his head in frustration. Elena wasn't intimidated, especially by him. She knew he'd never hurt her, and anyway, she was too furious to care. She would give as good as she got. He almost smiled.

He loved her temperament. He felt a deep love for her, he'd never get over and something he'd never want her to find out. Eventually, he'd have to let her go. The thought made him nauseous.

The water streamed down in the bathroom, echoing the downpour outside. Alex needed to walk off his love, his lust, whatever it was.

What had Tony been thinking trying to associate her with these drug runners? They'd never find anything on the Dkanys. How Elena's brother had gotten involved with the ring—if he *had* been involved, might never have come to light. Just because Freddy died of an overdose didn't make him a criminal mastermind. And as for Elena and her grandmother, Alex had known them too long, knew their morals, their ethics. He'd told Tony they were wasting their time at Briar Hill, and he'd been right. What about Gregory Balogh? Longtime solicitor and keeper of the castle. Elena adored him. They all had high regard for the man. Why would Tony think he was involved in this?

Alex plunked down on the sofa, pulled out his laptop, and went to email.

Marina.

Alex,

Just wrote to Elena. A short note to you. Take care of her, Alex. Take care of you. I'm worried to death. I'm coming out to Dkany just as soon as I can get away. Even if it means giving up my internship at North-western. You're my family. You're more important than—well, I may change career directions, after all. You suggested I'd be a great shrink. Well, maybe I will.

Later. Love you.
Mari

Oh no. He didn't want Marina coming out to Dkany.

Mari,

Becoming a psychiatrist would be an excellent fit for you. However, coming to Dkany is not—I repeat—not a good idea. It's too dangerous.

Love you back.
Alex

He'd finally admitted he'd seen the same visions. Could that little boy be Elena's son? Could that be possible? She wouldn't admit it but . . . He went back into the saved Dkany obituaries—births and deaths and checked. Found nothing different. Nothing about Elena or her child at all. He'd never even asked Elena her baby's name. Finally, they discovered the truth buried in birth records at a hospital in Bucharest: *baby boy to Elena and Janek Ivanov; Michael Alexander Ivanov.*

A cold chill ran up his spine. Why the hell had Elena named her son's middle name Alexander? Had she been thumbing her nose at him? Then he read the birth date. March. Then he noticed a blackout. The birth date is handwritten in. What was crossed out?

She hadn't met Jan until her brother introduced them shortly after she'd arrived in Bucharest. They must have gotten married suddenly or at least started an affair. Elena never struck Alex as being promiscuous.

He was still thinking when the water stopped and the bathroom door opened. Elena came out wearing her cream cotton nightgown with a matching robe, toweling her hair. The light shining from the lamp behind her showed off some parts of her he'd remembered well from the night of the prom. He gulped and glanced away, frowning. It would be a long night.

Elena had to walk past Alex to get to her bedroom. She was self-conscious, but Alex didn't seem to be paying attention anyway. He sat on the sofa with his feet propped up on the pine-knotted coffee table that almost matched the cabin walls, typing on his laptop. When he glanced up, shivers chilled her spine. Alex's eyes lacked expression. His handsome face frowned an interminable sadness.

He knows. On some level, Alex knows that the baby was his. Oh my God. How did we both come to this place of living hell?

Elena sat on her bed blow-drying her hair, feeling like a tragic heroine in a romance novel. How had she screwed up so badly and end up with a man who might very well be her enemy? She started to brush out her hair, saw a shadow, and abruptly looked up, nearly twisting her neck.

Alex stood in the doorway, in his socks. Although still edgy, his expression held a little more of the old one she'd grown to love in high school. His shirt was open, the hairs on his chest formed a 'V' near his belt. When he forced a smile, he made a seven on her sensual scale of one to ten.

"My bed fell apart. The sides are flat on the floor. The springs are shot and . . ." His sensual scale moved up a notch.

He stopped, raising his eyebrows like he'd seen her for the first time. His glance slid downward, and he stared, photographing her with his eyes.

Elena glanced down to where his gaze seemed glued to the low-cut nightgown she'd bought in Amsterdam. The light material showed off her figure to its best advantage. When Elena bought the ensemble in the lingerie shop, she'd prayed for the precise reaction he gave her now. But, unfortunately, any relationship wouldn't work now. Maddening, her nipples pressed against the material. She'd have to bump him up to an eight-plus for those eyes.

"Um . . ." he said, his eyes still planted, "The springs poked through the mattress."

His choice of words slammed her mind shut. She opened her mouth but couldn't utter one syllable. Her thoughts ran rampant.

Sorry, my bed fell apart. Oh yeah. Now I'll have to sleep with you because the sofa is too small for me. By the way, love your breasts.

She couldn't help it. She laughed.

Alex blinked, swallowed, and raised his eyes back to her face. "What's so funny?"

Elena stifled the chuckle, "You."

Something in his hostile eyes broke. The hardness around the edges disappeared, and his brittle features broke into an ever-so-slight smile.

"I'm sorry, Elena. I had no right to act like that toward you."

Elena nodded. "I'm not the enemy, Alex." Elena started to resume brushing her hair to give her something to do. Keep her hands busy, her mind away from him.

"No? Perhaps not. But . . ." His voice faded to a hushed stillness, and he seemed to soften, change to the boy she'd once known and loved.

Two strides and Alex sat next to her.

"Remember when you were little? I used to brush your hair when you came over to stay with Marina."

She nodded and smiled. "We used to race into the bedroom to see who could get her hair brushed first."

"You always won," he said, chuckling. "May I?" He took the brush from her hand and started brushing.

Hardly able to breathe, Elena sat still, mesmerized by his methodical movements that made her hair fly and land against her neck. A soft purr finally involuntarily emerged through her vocal cords as he stroked a gently growing fire within her. When she arched her back, her head met the bristles. He climbed the Elena scale to a solid nine. Something was missing, though. His anticipation bled through with each stroke. This wasn't about romance. He wanted information. He bumped down to a seven.

She thought she'd counteract his question before it arose. "Alex, Jan saved my life." Her voice whispered as gentle as the caress of the brush. She dared not to look at him.

The brush stopped in mid-stroke. Then, strangely, he started again. "Oh yeah? He saved your life? Please explain. Is that why you decided to marry him?" His voice didn't express anger, but his brushing suddenly got harsh, and he pulled her hair.

"Alex, stop. You're hurting me." Damn. He'd pulled down to a two on the sensuality scale—no zero. She grabbed her hair and pulled away. "I don't mean in Romania."

"No?"

"No. You wanted to know about the attack. So, I'll tell you, if you don't make a mockery or get mad at what I say. If you do, I'll never tell you anything again. I mean it."

Alex raised his eyebrows and opened his mouth briefly, let out a sigh, and nodded. "Okay. So, tell me this is about a ghost."

"It's about a ghost."

He put down the brush and faced her. They stared each other down like warriors squaring off on a field of battle. He, the interrogator; she, the interrogated.

"Start from the beginning, just tell me. How did an apparition save your life?"

Slowly, deliberately, Elena explained what happened during the attack, about how she'd disabled the man and ran down the stairs. A whirlwind of frost rushed up the stairs, knocked her off her feet, and hurled the guy down the steps. When he reached the bottom, he was dead.

Alex didn't say anything for a minute, just stared down at the brush. Elena thought he didn't believe her. But, when he glanced back, his eyes were full of questions.

"Elena, about the other day." His voice became husky, filled with emotion. "Okay, I'll admit, I did see you in my mirror. That's why I called you. I really did think you were about to . . . uh . . ." He drummed his fingers on the bed. "I'm sorry. I'm usually pretty honest, brutally so, sometimes. Lying doesn't come easy."

No? Elena thought lying came very easy for Alex.

"I never would have shot myself. Never."

"Yeah, I know. But I didn't know that then."

He continued. "Can we discuss that young boy you saw in the mirror?"

He might as well have slapped her. Instead, she pushed away and faced him, breathing so hard she could hardly control the air going in and out.

"No. Please, Alex. Let's not."

"Why?"

She blew out a sigh and nodded. "I'm sorry. I wasn't expecting . . . I can't."

"I couldn't see his face, but he seemed vaguely familiar." *You saw it in your own mirror when you were nine years old.*

And that shook her up, as bad as any attempted assassination.

Alex had just discovered her darkest secret. He'd seen the presence of his own son. Alex appeared haunted by something *he didn't—couldn't fathom.*

A sensation of intense desolation swept over her. The image of the boy came back again, and a sob nearly strangled her as it struggled to come out.

They'd sworn eternal love when she left for Bucharest. Then the letters came. The first from her grandmother telling her to have fun, study hard but warned her to stay a virgin. Nice men like Alex didn't want easy girls.

She laughed it off until she got Alex's letter stating they should date other people while they were away at college. The underlying message—he'd found someone else. After all, Alex came from the same background. She'd given herself to him, and he no longer respected her. The same day she received his letter, the doctor told her she was pregnant. Heartbreak, ruin, in an old-fashion society.

Freddie's friend Jan encouraged her to marry him. Then, the birth of Michael Alexander. She'd died of loneliness for Alex every time she saw her baby. Elena's memories twisted into visions of death floating around her.

First, Hadean Petrov—depraved madness in his eyes. The visions in the mirror. The man at the airport. Now, apparitions of soldiers who wore fatigues and stood in front of a weapon's arsenal. Those visions came fast and furious—within seconds. She was scaring herself. Something pointed the barrel of a gun at her, and Elena screamed.

Alex grabbed her as she started to go down. Now he held her, tight in his arms, his cheek drawn against hers. His hand stroked the back of her head.

Elena relaxed in his arms. Alex pulled back and gazed into her eyes. In them, he saw the desire, the want, and most surprising of all, the love. She still loved him as sure as he was alive and breathing.

Slow down, take a deep breath. Then, Elena kissed him.

Everything became still. It seemed as though all life stopped, except for the sound of her heart crushed against Alex's chest. No rustling of the pines, no life outside. The rain ceased hitting the roof. The room's temperature grew colder, and Elena shivered in his arms. A sudden draft of vapors swept around them, starting from a slow rotation and then gradually turning into a faster whirlwind.

Elena gave a cry and saw Alex's shocked disbelief. He saw the vapors. Felt its chill.

"Elena!"

All hell broke loose.

"Jesus!" The sheer, strong intensity nearly ripped Elena out of Alex's arms. Wide-eyed, Alex kept a frantic hold on her. Fierce wind fingers tried to pull her away as he tried to hold on. Then, the force let go of Elena so abruptly it pushed her and Alex back against the headboard.

The wind rushed around with such ferocity Elena could hardly catch her breath. Maps and pamphlets flew around the room, narrowly avoiding her head, clothes scattered. A guidebook of Transylvania landed opened to the City of Dkany. The brush left the bed and slammed into the mirror, leaving a crack before it swept across the dresser, scattering brochures all over the floor.

As fast as it came was as fast as it left. Finally, the temperature came back to normal, the trees whistled through the wind, and the rain pattered onto the roof.

A boy of around nine stared into Elena's eyes. She bolted off the bed. The boy started to fade. She screamed. "No, don't go!"

"Who?" Alex jumped onto the floor.

The voice inside her head. *He's in danger. Find him!*

"Who?" Elena yelled. "Don't leave! Who's in danger?" But she knew who.

The voice and the vision faded, and Elena broke down and collapsed against Alex.

Chapter 15

Rusalka Inn, Romania

An old man wearing faded jeans, and a moth-eaten, gray wool sweater covered by a stained black sheepskin vest, wandered into the Rusalka courtyard. The sudden onslaught of rain poured down his face, and two pairs of socks and boots squished from the leaks in their soles. A flood of water seeped out over their tops. He carried a knapsack on his back and appeared to be one of the homeless, common in those parts of Romania.

Always the soft touch for a stranger with a hungry stomach, Doamna Malik saw the man from her window and beckoned him to come around back to the kitchen. She offered him the leftovers from the day's dinner. He was long and lanky with a head that seemed twice the height as its width. Sitting at a wooden table with its paint peeling and blistering, the old man's bony knees came up to its underside. It wasn't clear which looked more beaten down, the old man or the table.

He ate her humble offerings and heaped upon her the compliments a gentleman from highborn society might bestow. When finished, he polished off a glass of a superb *Dealau Mare* and started to talk. The man wasn't forthcoming about his name or where he was from, but he acted grateful and courteous for her kindness.

He talked about growing up in a small village in the northern parts of Transylvania, where his parents owned an inn, almost like this one.

Doamna Malik appeared in her glory. She talked about her Inn and her youth when her father converted their old barn into a "fine" garage. She mentioned with pride the building that still stood on the other side of the courtyard and had a mechanic's shop, now run by her nephew, a graduate apprentice from the shop in the village. During slow times, the shop managed to keep them solvent. Finally she talked about her marriage and her husband's death not three years ago.

Speaking tenderly with great sympathy and compassion as only a man in his circumstances could, he shared her loss. His people lost their inn under the reign of the communist government. The soldiers forced them from their homes and placed them in a housing development in Bucharest. It broke their hearts and their spirits, and he deteriorated into the condition she saw him, right now.

The old man smiled in a haggard kind of way. He took the old woman back to his youth when he first married. They'd come to a place like this on their honeymoon, stayed for three days, never coming out of their cabin. He chuckled. "A sad waste of missing such glorious scenery." *Doamna* Malik laughed too. A newlywed couple staying there now hadn't been out much either. She stopped, blushing at the gleam in the old gentleman's eyes.

He retreated to a more comfortable topic for *Doamna* Malik. Her historical garage. "Yes," she said, all her guests stabled their cars in the old converted barn. It was part of the Inn's charm.

The man thanked her with graciousness and took his leave. He didn't tell her where he was going, as he hadn't told her where he'd been. Instead, he walked out and disappeared into the driving rain.

He withdrew to the back of the garage and stole in the back door. Making sure no one was inside, he pulled out some items from his knapsack. Sliding underneath the blue Dacia, he connected four waiting wires from a metal box to a sensor device that activated dynamite to explode when the engine started. Chuckling, he limped out of the garage, still maintaining his downtrodden demeanor.

He climbed the fence and headed across the pasture. He met no one. At the far end of the field, he walked up to a waiting chauffeur-driven, black Mercedes and hopped into the back. Shaking off his hat and drying himself with the towel already provided for his comfort, he no longer appeared destitute and downtrodden. He directed his driver to Dkany.

Elena lay on the bed in a pool of pamphlets and clothes. Only a Sandor Inn brochure remained on the dresser, with everything else flown to the room's four corners.

"Do you believe me now?" she whispered, trying to catch her breath. "I see things—visions. I—"

"Have a ghost chasing you. I know you do." Alex pulled her closer into his arms. "Shhh. It's all right. If it really wanted to hurt us, it would have."

From Alex's limited knowledge of ghosts, Jan, or whoever it was, must have had some powerful unfinished business because he was as tenacious as a bulldog. He carried an agenda, and it included his wife and a non-descript dark-haired boy wearing a cross. Although Alex couldn't make out the boy's features, there was a familiarity about him. He couldn't quite make the connection.

A cold chill spread through Alex's heart as he pulled her away to study her face. "Could your baby be alive?"

"Impossible, Alex. He was killed. I was there."

Her expression stilled, grew even more serious. "What if he didn't die? Did you see your baby's . . . ?" He couldn't speak the word *corpse.*

"No. I saw nothing. Some men entered the room, and everything went blank. I don't even remember seeing their faces."

"They left you for dead." The words spilled out of his mouth, chilling implications almost closing off his windpipe. "What if the baby didn't die? What if he was taken?"

"Kidnapped? Why? Why would anyone want to kidnap my child?"

Alex contemplated the possibilities. Babies brought big bucks on the black market. Was that why someone attacked Elena and Jan?

Or had it to do with the castle ownership someone didn't want to be passed down?

She seemed to be thinking the same thing because she'd turned green. "They brought me to a Bucharest hospital. I never saw their bodies. By the time I was out of danger, Uncle Gregory had said he'd taken care of their burials. He got me out of the country as soon as possible. My grandmother and I flew home together, and she never mentioned the subject again. I don't know what she or Gregory knew, but she refused to let me ask questions."

Hot rage flared toward Magda and Gregory, who hadn't given Elena the closure to heal, but then his own anger toward her took over. He had to get out of there before it showed. "Look. This belongs to you. I don't want to intrude." He moved to rise off the bed.

Something grabbed him by his shirt and pulled him back.

Hard.

Was there no end to her re-infecting this wound?

"I have news for you, buddy," Elena said. "You're already up to your handsome neck in my business when we married and when Jan included *you* in his world."

Alex narrowed his eyes and tried to look severe. She stared right back, and he forced a calm, rational tone. "Elena, the only logical conclusion I can come to is the child wasn't killed. Maybe, Jan's parents took him."

"Jan's parents were dead. Jan had a stepfather somewhere in Transylvania he didn't speak about. All he had was Freddy and me."

The possibility gnawed at his conscious. Could she have a son? Growing up with whom?

He turned into his own private hurt. This child wasn't his but belonged to a ghost named Jan. He scrutinized the tension in her face, her eyes—her soul. She was holding back. "What else?"

Her gaze darted up at the ceiling, toward the window, at the far wall, until they rested back on him. "I saw something else."

Alex looked up at her sharply. "What?"

"After Magda's funeral, I saw a girl executed."

"When?" Alex almost gasped out the question. "Where?"

"In the ruby."

So, that's what the ruby showed her. But was the dream on the plane connected? How could they both be dreaming the same thing?

"Yes," he said. "And the girl was you."

"You knew? How?"

"Because I saw it in a dream, too. On the plane."

"Oh, my God." Elena looked at him, anger and disappointment raging inside. "You've been experiencing this all along? You wouldn't admit to seeing the vision in the mirror? And you saw this in a dream? My God, Alex, why make me think I was crazy?" She jabbed a finger in his chest. "What *else?*"

A warning voice instantly flickered inside his head. *Don't make me ask anything else. Don't pursue this.*

"I don't know anything more. What else is there to know?"

An unreadable emotion darkened her expression as she stood up and looked down at him. There was more. Much more. She didn't want him to know. What the hell was it?

"Elena?"

She let out a long sigh, got off the bed, and walked to the other side of the room. "No," she said.

He got off the bed and followed her. "Hey."

Elena turned, and whatever had been bothering her seemed to evaporate. Either there wasn't anything more to know, or she was a good actress.

She touched his arm. "It's getting late. Don't sleep on the floor. Sleep here with me. Don't worry, I'll stay on the opposite side of the bed so you don't have to touch me or anything."

He didn't have to touch her or anything? Like he could lie beside her and not make contact?

"I don't think . . ." But where was he going to sleep? Outside in the rain? On the floor? On a stunted sofa? "Yeah, okay. But first, I want to know something."

"Like what?"

"Like what part's missing. I know you're not telling me everything. I want—I *need*—to know."

Her face clouded. She shook her head and spun away from him. Elena turned back toward him, ready to speak, but she clammed up again.

Alex grabbed her hand and pulled her back to the bed. "Elena, what's the matter?"

Elena's face went chalk-white, and she looked at the ground. Alex picked up her chin and looked into her eyes. He saw a different kind of heartbreak. And it caught him off guard.

Alex waited for the other shoe to drop. What could she possibly tell him she hadn't slammed him with already?

"The boy in your vision, Alex . . . he's . . ." She stopped in the middle of the sentence.

Oh no. "Go on. He's what?"

She was looking away from him, tears blinding her eyes. The rain had let up a bit, but the continuing thunder promised more. They sat on the pamphlets spread over the bed.

His gaze met hers, and his heart turned over. He couldn't keep badgering.

"Look, never mind. We'll talk about this another time."

He touched her hand but wasn't prepared for the electricity passing between them. He tried to pull away, but she held on. A shiver caused his pulse to quicken while his heart pounded out an erratic rhythm. What the hell was this? Her nearness, her scent, shampoo, the essence of Elena kindled feelings of fire he hadn't had since the night after the prom. A rush of pink stained Elena's cheeks as her eyes implored him.

"What is this? What are we doing?" He rasped out the question as a hot ache grew in his throat. His eyes dropped to where the swell of her breasts met the blue ribbon holding together her cotton robe. As though she knew what he was thinking, she untied the knot and let the robe fall open. The blood coursed through his veins like a gorging river, settling in his groin. The pain and wanting were unbearable. Unable to control himself any longer, Alex swept her into his arms and kissed her hard.

She couldn't pull away from him. She desired the man as much as she disliked him.

No. He could hate her tomorrow. Tonight, she wanted to belong to him. Wanted his hands to touch, his mouth to kiss, and his body against hers. She gently pulled away and let the robe cascade down onto the bed. Alex's eyes slowly moved down to her breasts. In a swift movement, he pulled the straps of her nightgown down over her shoulders, taking the bodice with them. Goosebumps covered her flesh, her nipples seemed to react to the appreciation his eyes gave them.

"My God, Alex. Touch me. Please." Elena took his hands in hers and covered her breasts with them.

He whispered, "If we keep this up, we'll have no choice but to make love." *And something bad will happen between us.* His mouth went dry. Something already had occurred between them. What could be worse?

"Please," she whispered. "Take me away from these ghosts."

He wanted to say this was not a good idea. But instead, he crushed Elena into him. He held her closer, tasting her tears, her hair, smelling her shampoo, caressing her back, rubbing her breasts against his chest.

In a moment, the earth moved under his feet, and rockets zoomed in his brain. But it wasn't love. An explosion nearly rocked the cabin off its foundation.

Chapter 16

Rusalka Inn, Romania

Shockwaves hurled Elena and Alex onto the floor. He hit his head against the leg of the dresser, scrambled to his feet, and grabbed Elena.

"What is it, an earthquake?" Elena asked.

"Hell no, not with that sound." He felt around his forehead for damage and decided there wasn't any, except a possible lump in the near future. He didn't take more time to consider.

They bolted.

Briefly, they caught in the door before he pushed her in front of him onto the porch.

They froze.

A blaze of light filled the gaps between pine trees that formed a barrier between the lodge and the cabins. "My God!" Elena said.

"Shit," Alex repeated. "No, no, no. This isn't happening." But it was.

Streaks of fire haloed the trees and reached high into the night skies. Diminishing rains didn't stop the blaze, and the wind propelled it in all directions calling attention to its hellish magnetism.

Elena couldn't tell whether it was the lodge itself or one of the other surrounding buildings that exploded.

"Clothes," Alex yelled.

They ran back into the cabin. Elena pulled on her jeans and a sweatshirt and met Alex coming out of his room, one athletic shoe on and untied. He nearly tripped, trying to cram his foot into the other.

They sprinted out of the cabin, grabbing jackets that refused to cooperate while their owners struggled with sleeves.

Alex seized Elena's hand, and her legs automatically seemed to propel out from under her.

As they got closer to the inferno, they ran into Tony, who darted between pieces of wood that acted as burning missiles. Briefly, the horror diminished when she realized it wasn't the inn but the garage.

Some of the lodgers were already dragging a hose across the concrete. Once considered an eyesore, the parking lot surrounding the entire garage was now a Godsend barrier that prevented the fire from extending its flaming fingers over to the inn. But the hose barely reached the garage.

The lodgers poured water over rivers of puddles while the raindrops dripped down their faces. Even God's own tears couldn't seem to extinguish the blaze. Then the really bad news began. Billowy blackish gray smoke poured from the blasted-out garage door opening and through broken windows.

Elena entertained a bizarre thought. If you went in, instead of burning alive, you'd suffocate—quickly. A cloud of asphyxiating ash blew in her direction, and she tasted the smoke before it went up her nostrils. She gagged.

"Garage!" Doamna Malik, still in her nightgown and threadbare terrycloth robe, grabbed onto Alex's arm. She turned away from the scene, its horror all too real.

"Did you call the fire department?" Elena asked with a take-charge attitude. Sobbing, the woman nodded as Tony left them to help the other villagers' futile attempt to put out the flames before the whole garage went.

An uneasy feeling came over her. In an out-of-the-way rural area such as this, it would take them at least twenty minutes to arrive from the village. By that time, all they could hope to accomplish would be to prevent the neighboring buildings and trees from catching fire. She doubted any amount of water and help could squelch the inferno incinerating the structure in front of them.

"Was there anyone in there?" Alex spoke to her quietly, putting his hand on her shoulder.

"No. I don't think . . ." But Elena's eyes grew wide as another unimaginable horror seemed to strike her. Her eyes shot up toward the top of the building, where black smokestacks poured out of the small windows.

The rain turned into drizzle, then stopped as though blocked by the insurmountable barrier of fire, and the wind let up for a respite. Elena focused on the second story.

"Where is Christian? The boy—my nephew. Where is he? He live above garage."

Hysterical, the woman pulled away from Alex and ran toward the building like a wild woman. Tony grabbed for her as she flew by him but missed. Alex sprinted behind as she broke through the force of workers and gained entrance.

Horrified, Elena ran after them, catching a last glimpse as they crashed through the door, Alex and Tony on the heels of *Doamna* Malik. Heat seared the area, provoking a fresh smell of burning wood. An explosion shattered the other side of the building, and a group scrambled out of the way of a hurling car seat.

"*No!*" The force of the blast rocked her mind with the realization Alex was in the building.

Blindly, she ran as though her presence could get them out before another explosion killed all of them. She collided into a solid wall of men who prevented her from following.

"*Alex!*"

Struggling, she managed to free herself until burning debris of car metal and scalding tin cans stopped her altogether.

The men once again pulled her back. She resisted, but they were too strong. She watched with her horrified captors until the three human forms dodged angry flames that threatened to cover them as they retreated out of the building.

Alex and Tony half-carried, half-dragged the screaming innkeeper across the parking lot toward the lodge's back porch.

"No! My boy. My boy!"

Alex caught Elena's eye. *"Alex!"* Elena screamed.

The men let her go. Her first instinct was to run to Alex, but flaming timber crashed down around her, preventing her from moving in his direction.

Sirens from the local fire department sounded around the lodge toward the garage.

Elena darted around the flaming missiles, barely feeling Alex grab her arm. He pushed her away to avoid another onslaught of scorching stones propelled by another small blast. The realization hit with sickening reality. She was in a war zone, and the enemy was after *her.*

"Nu!"

Inside the lodge, *Doamna* Malik's English abandoned her as she sobbed. Her nephew came home late from town and wanted to fix their car's knocking.

"Was going to make sure car work right for *you*." Her voice shook with accusation.

"What could have caused the explosion?" Tony sat questioning her, ruling out how it started. The possibilities—anything other than what Alex already knew. This was no accident.

Had anyone been in the garage that afternoon? Anyone suspicious? She'd been entertaining a homeless man who'd come to her for food. They'd talked about . . .

That got Alex's attention.

Doamna Malik, confused by Alex and Tony's interrogation, threw one question after another at her, got muddled, and started to cry again.

Alex stood by the window, half watching Mrs. Malik speaking with Tony and Elena taking coffee to the fire personnel. They doused the last smoldering remnants of flames that still steamed and bubbled with enraged agony until the fire died.

Turning his attention for the moment on Elena, something struck him. She'd tried to follow him into the building. Those men blocked her. They'd only let go when she screamed his name after he'd come out. Stupid, stupid girl, he fumed. Why had she risked her life like that?

Alex softened when the realization hit that she cared enough about him that she'd forgotten about her own safety.

Elena helped the lodgers pass out coffee to the firefighters who investigated the perimeter of the lodge. Cautiously, they surveyed the burned-out building. She joined a small group gathered around an object lying on the ground. One woman passed out, and two men carried her from the site. Others pointed to a reminder of the boy's presence—a severed hand lying on the ground.

A firefighter leaped from a door frame, away from parts of the garage roof that collapsed after him, nearly landing on top of Elena and spilling a portion of the coffee she held out to him.

His hands shook, and his body nearly collapsed. He took the remains and gulped it down as though the boiling liquid had no effect on his insides.

"In there . . ." he started.

Elena put her arm around him when his legs began to weaken.

"The boy . . . not here."

A fireman carried something smoldering in a blanket. "It . . . him. Oh, God!" He started crying, shaking with convulsions.

Elena held on to him, sobbing right along with him. A woman's leathery face wrapped in sorrow removed the fireman from Elena's arms and led him toward the lodge.

Elena stood alone amidst the screams, commotion, residue of smoke, and charred remains. Her teeth chattered, and she hugged herself to prevent an entire breakdown.

There had been another attempt to exterminate them, and this time an innocent boy died.

Chapter 17

Rusalka Inn, Romania

Dawn looked out of place. The sun tried its best to crash through recalcitrant clouds and finally succeeded, claiming the horizon as its exclusive territory.

Two medical personnel helped *Doamna* Malik into an ambulance. They'd transported her to a hospital in the city of *Cluj* for observation. She hadn't stopped crying, and her heartbreak threatened to tear apart her already shattered mental state.

An overwhelming fear shadowed every move they made, every word they uttered, and every breath they took. Whenever anyone said anything, Elena envisioned someone popping out of the trees to attack them.

They traipsed back to Tony's cabin, where Elena huddled against the headrest of the bed, her arms encircling her knees. The two men sat in pine knotted chairs surrounding a small table.

"This was our fault," Elena said. "We brought our danger here, and it killed a boy who had his whole life ahead of him."

"Yeah," Tony replied without emotion, staring out a crack in the pulled curtain, not moving his head. His gun lay on the table in front of him.

"You still expecting company?" Alex asked, his eyes dark, angry, and Elena thought frightened.

"I doubt whoever pulled this off will return with all the police and commotion around here. I think it was a hit and run. Like my grandmother. Only with explosives," Elena said.

"No," Tony replied quietly. He pulled apart the curtain, shook his head, and pulled them together again. "It was deliberately set and well planned. But, yes, I think they will try again, and soon."

"An infestation of rats," Alex said.

"So, do we at least still have your car?" Elena dreaded the answer.

He shook his head. "Afraid not. My Renault was in the garage too." He pulled out a cell phone. Hang on. I'm calling Washington."

"Isn't this a little exposed for you to be doing this?" she asked.

He shook his head. "The messages are scrambled. No one can key into my conversations on this phone." He held up his hand. "Lucille? Tony. I need Larry Simmons, immediately."

Elena closed her mind while Tony explained the events of the evening. She woke when he raised his eyebrows and frowned.

"Shit. No." He listened again. "Well, can we at least have a car? We're stranded." His grimace explained the news wasn't altogether great. "Damn it, it wasn't our fault they found us." He clicked off. "They're sending us another Dacia from town. They issued a warning about trying not to destroy this one. Anyway, it'll be here shortly. Hope it's not booby-trapped."

"No!" Elena responded nervously.

Alex shot a glance at Tony that said, 'shut up.'

Tony nodded and whispered, "Sorry, Elena. I was trying to make light of a nasty situation. Bad choice."

"It's okay, Tony. I understand. But how do they know we're here?" Elena asked, blinded by tears. "How do they keep finding us, no matter where we go?"

"Don't know," Tony answered, "But a tramp came round this afternoon. Mrs. Malik gave him dinner. He was here for quite a while. Turns out he was asking questions about the garage, vehicles, and people who were staying at the lodge."

"Is it too much to ask if he gave her a name?" Alex asked.

"He didn't."

"Did she give us away?"

"Probably—without knowing it. That means they knew where to look for us." Alex's eyes turned to cold and angry slits.

Elena broke in with a cracked whisper. "Too bad they've abolished executions in Romania. Maybe we could just walk up and shoot these people."

"Let's try to figure this out." Tony tightened his jaw with determination. His eyes squinted. "Who knew you were coming?"

Elena blew out a breath. "When Magda was alive, she didn't make our plans a secret. I mentioned it to Gregory when he was here for her funeral. He didn't encourage me, but he didn't try to stop me either. I never mentioned when I planned on leaving."

"What about your neighbor?"

"Mrs. Rice knew, but not where we were going. I asked her to watch the house. Anyway, she probably saved my life. If she were involved, she wouldn't have called the police. She'd have helped the guy climb in the window."

"There were some that knew," Alex said. "Our office in D.C.," Alex said. "I told my department chair I was leaving on my honeymoon and wouldn't be back until September. I didn't say where we were going." He looked at Elena. "That is what we wanted, wasn't it?"

Elena nodded.

Alex said, "The only ones who knew were the college staff, our office, you, Marina, and the police."

"That's all?" Tony glanced at Elena.

Elena gave up a nod.

Alex's expression still held the suspicion she'd noticed from the instant she'd told him about the boy in the mirror. That this was her son, she had little doubt, but now she thought Alex might question her further. He wasn't outright asking, but doubt lay in his eyes. She suspected this child meant more to him—to *them*—than either one knew.

Her body still hadn't completely recovered from Alex, even after the events of the night. But then what? To bed—and slam-bam-thank you, ma'am? Our marriage was the best. See you around?

Then another dread hit her. If they did find her son and if Alex did find out, would he want to divorce her and claim custody? She observed him looking out the window. He might find a reason to put her in jail and throw away the key. Would he really do this? No, she didn't think he would. But he'd resent her.

She tried to concentrate on the immediate disaster in front of her and failed. She remembered Marina saying her brother had a reputation as being 'hard to get.' A love 'em and leave 'em type of guy. She focused back on the conversation.

"There are other professors and teachers affected by my absence," Alex said. "My chair had to cover my summer seminars and had several instructors to choose from. In addition, some of the faculty are from Eastern Europe."

"Could there be information lying around your house? Maybe someone broke in?" Tony asked.

"I haven't been back there since the night of the attack," Elena said. "People *are* watching the house. They would have texted or phoned me."

"What about Gregory Balogh?" Tony asked, narrowing his eyes. "What exactly does he know?"

"Gregory? That we'd gotten married," Elena said. "He emailed back congratulations, and if we decided to come, he'd make us feel welcome and introduce us. That's all. He didn't know when we were coming, did he, Alex?"

"Not that I know of."

"I don't think it was Gregory," Elena said. "He's been a central part of our family for a very long time. He saved my life in Bucharest, brought my grandmother here to see me in the hospital, and then got us out again. If he wanted us out of the way, he could have done it there. No. I don't think he's involved. He could have stolen the ruby, and I'd never had known." *And he could have stolen my child, and I wouldn't have known.* Elena put that out of her thoughts.

"And your sister, Alex? What did she know?"

"Marina wouldn't do anything to hurt either one of us," Elena said. "Of that, I'm sure. In fact, she might come out to Romania after next month to join us. Depends on her job."

"Okay," Tony nodded. Still, his expression held reservations.

Alex focused on Tony, his eyes still cold but now hard and questioning. "Tony, who in the office knew?"

"Larry's office?"

"Yeah, the Team Office Bureau in Washington. Could there be a leak there? All your directives and decisions come from there, don't they? They've discussed the possibility Elena's castle is the headquarters of this drug gang, haven't they?"

Tony's eyebrows shot up in surprise. "Yes," then said slowly, "So? They suspected several of the castles and monasteries." He scratched his head and ran his fingers through his hair. "But. . ." He shook his head, then nodded as though recognizing the possibility. "If it came from my office, that would be a disaster. I can't imagine the consequences." He shook his head. "Shit."

Elena said, "Look, right now, it seems Gregory Balogh, possibly my grandmother, maybe my brother, and I are your chief suspects because we own or have an interest in the castle. I'm not sure whether you're here to protect me or to arrest me, Tony. Which is it? You're trying to find out if I'm involved? If I managed to run over my grandmother and to attack myself?" Her temper flared. "I wasn't even in Romania when my brother died."

"Uh—" Tony said, astonishment clouding his eyes.

"Tony," Elena said, trying to hide a growing resentment. "When we were attacked in Bucharest, I killed the attacker. He was a student. Someone Jan knew."

"What?" Astonishment broke out on Tony's face. He raised an eyebrow. "So, you've killed two men then, Elena. Quite a record, wouldn't you say?"

Elena's felt her face drain.

"Two assassins, Tony," Alex said. "One a student with a grudge, the other, as you pointed out, a trained assassin. They were both in self-defense. And one was ten years ago. Also, she had another name, then."

"Not when she first went to Romania." Tony blew air between his lips. "But, yes, it was self-defense."

"If you wish to put it that way," Elena replied. "He'd just stuck a knife into my husband. I grabbed it away and caught him off guard. He wasn't paying attention to me. When he figured out what I was up to, he grabbed my wrist, nearly broke it, before he finally stabbed me."

The agony of those memories—rehashed over and over.

"Leave her alone, Tony," Alex said.

"When I finally got him, he died, pulling me on top of him." Elena finished. "So, in Romania, I'm probably a murderer. Lucky, I'm officially declared dead."

"Oh yeah, lucky, that," Tony said.

"You don't think Elena would kill just anyone, do you?" Alex asked.

"Obviously, if she's protecting her family, she would." Tony softened. "I wish I had someone who loved me that much."

Before, she was scum. Now? A hero.

"Maybe someone at your university knew, Alex. Briar Hill is full of people who have Eastern European backgrounds."

"It doesn't have to be someone with a foreign background," Alex responded.

"Anything's possible," Tony admitted.

"Or maybe pigs fly," Alex said. "My guess? There's a mole in your office."

Tony said, "That's why we're leaving as soon as the car arrives. I'm cutting off communication with Washington until we get to Dkany. We'll be staying at the . . ."

Elena, who'd been lying with her head against the pillow, sat up.

"Sandor Inn," she said. "We'll be staying at the Sandor."

"No, Elena. We have reservations at The Ramada."

"I don't care, Tony. It'll put them off. If there's a leak in your office, they'll know what's on our itinerary. Forget it. Don't let them know where we are. Besides, I have another reason to stay at the

Sandor."

"And that is?"

"The Sandor lies at the heart of the mystery."

Alex and Tony both sprung to attention.

"What the hell do you mean?" Tony asked.

"I'll just say, I think we were meant to stay there."

She didn't mention the brochure left on the dresser when all the others scattered with the wind.

Elena picked up her cell phone and dialed the Inn. "Stefan Baklanov, please."

But Alex and Tony were no longer paying attention. Alex opened the curtains and watched a man walk up the stoop onto the cottage front porch. He didn't need to bang on the door. Tony picked up the gun, signaled to Alex, who opened it.

The man's sad and angry eyes stared at—through them. When he stepped into the cabin, he saw the gun and raised his eyebrows but didn't move away. Instead, he said in dialect Romanian, "You seem like good people, despite your guns, but you brought great sorrow and tragedy into our midst and our hearts. I will not hurt you, so you may put your guns away. That is not our way. Now, your car is in front of the lodge."

Elena said, "I'm very, very sorry about Christian. I liked him."

"Christian was my son." The man bit his lip and tried to keep his tears from flowing. He didn't quite succeed.

"Now, goodbye. As I said, your car is in front of the lodge." His eyes said, 'good riddance.'

Lucille Robinson's Apartment, Watergate, Washington D.C.

"Mr. Thomas Smith," obviously not his real name, knocked on the door to Lucille Robinson's apartment at the Chesapeake Apartments . He waited with anticipation. What she would be wearing and not wearing underneath.

It has been a long flight, and he was tired but ready for a few days of rest and relaxation—and steady, kinky sex.

Their affair had gone along smoothly. She'd done everything he'd asked, and if she hadn't particularly liked the tied-up role play, nor the spankings or the rope around her neck when in the throes of passion, well, she never let on. After all, she'd never been this flush or secure.

She came to the door. The blue see-through negligee he'd bought her showed everything underneath. He licked his lips, and his mouth turned upward into a grin. The nightie would be off her before she'd gotten halfway across the living room floor.

"Yes," he said. "That is exactly the way I like it, Miss Robinson." He brought his tone down into a sexy, raspy tone. "I think maybe the fuzzy cuffs to play with today?"

She didn't answer but led him into the bedroom. Comforter turned down, cuffs attached to the bedpost. Just the way he liked.

But first— "The information I requested. Where are they?"

Lucille pulled her negligee over her head and stood in front of him naked. She unclipped her hair, so it fell into her face, and she let his hands explore her breasts. Although he squeezed a bit too hard and pinched her nipples, so she cried out. After all—first things first.

"You tell me first, then we play, yes?"

She sat on the bed propped up against the pillows. Legs spread as he'd taught her. Still—he waited.

"Mr. Donatelli called into the office with a request for a new car. Apparently, his old one got blown up."

"Indeed. They sent him another one?"

"They did. I have the number over there." She pointed to the chest. Mr. Smith turned and took a sheet of paper off the dresser. On it was the description of the car, its license plate number, everything."

"And where will they be staying?"

"Uh . . ." She slowed down avoiding his eyes.

"Come, come," Mr. Smith said. "You agreed. You will tell, no? Nothing unpleasant happens to those who obey me." He implied what would happen if she didn't obey.

"They are scheduled to go to the Dkany Ramada, but I discovered they canceled their reservations there. I'm not sure where they'll go. They wouldn't say."

Mr. Smith scratched his chin. "I see. So, they suspect they are being watched. I will know what to do."

He turned his attention to Lucille. "Now, Lucille, you were a bad girl today. You didn't get me all my information. You know what I do with bad little girls, don't you?"

Lucille paled.

"But first, you stay there, just like that. Do not move. I will return." He walked into the living room, pulled out his cell phone. "The Dkany and Brancusi are on their way. There is only one main route into Dkany through the mountains. Here is a description of the black Dacia." He provided the license. "It should not be hard to waylay them and send them into a ditch or shoot them if the job is not bungled like the other attempts." He chuckled and clicked off.

He peered out over the D.C. skyline. So this was the life he was meant to live. A high-priced apartment in The Chesapeake Apartments, A villa on the Riviera, an apartment in New York City's Central Park, a limousine, a ticket to any sport's event, show, or opera anywhere in the world. And beautiful women for him to escort.

Life took him from a poverty-filled childhood, with a mother who neglected then deserted him, a father who beat him consistently until he left him on the streets. Then that woman who'd taken him in and used him. Yes, this is how great men fell. If he wasn't so intelligent, he could have fallen there too. If it weren't for the Gods, he would still be there, but he wasn't. He wouldn't—didn't let that happen. He'd maneuvered himself into the right hands, played the game, and now . . . now, look where he was. Number Two in The Hierarchy. He was smarter than all of them. He'd never get caught, and he'd be Number One before Number One even knew what he wanted.

Lucille. He chuckled. He'd leave her with not too many bruises that showed. He, himself, felt good. That's all that mattered. Let the games begin.

Chapter 18

On the Road to Dkany, Romania

The rented Dacia waited in front of the inn.

Alex bumped Elena's trolley down the wooden steps, carrying his backpack on his shoulders. Tony followed, glancing around at the inn's employees and guests. Their tight lips and angry postures emphasized they wanted them out—now. They reminded Elena of the old Frankenstein movies, and who could blame them? Christian's father stood in front, his eyes red, his lips tight, and his heartbroken. He'd never be the same. Never.

"Elena, you and Alex sit in the back," Tony said as he slid in the driver's seat. Alex held the door for her, and they got in.

"Well," she said, "the Rusalka is one place we can't go back to." A shiver rattled her spine.

Tony and Alex looked at her.

"Yeah. We make some exit, don't we?" Tony asked as he turned the engine over and over and over. Finally, it started. The three exhaled when the car didn't blow up.

"Don't we?" Elena asked. "I was just thinking about how we can never go back there and how those employees in the department store hope we don't shop there again. We just seem to make an impression wherever we go."

"Yeah," Alex said with a wry grin. "And, I don't think the Evanston Police Department will soon forget us, either."

Tony laughed. "Well, cheer up. Something unpleasant is bound to happen again soon. It always does."

Elena became silent. *Yes, true.*

"However," Alex said, taking her hand, "that is why I'm here. I'm going to protect you."

Yes, but who's going to protect me from you? Elena's attitude softened. Out loud, she said, "You've kept me alive. If it weren't for you, I might not have been. I'm grateful for that, Alex."

Tony turned stone silent. All the way into the mountains, he negotiated a two-lane highway, not saying a word. He drove around rocks fallen from the surrounding mountains and swerved around a slow-moving hay wagon pulled by a draft horse that looked as though he'd seen better days. The highways in Romania left something to be desired.

"So, I need to recap. Sorry, I know this is sore to you, Elena."

"Go on. I don't mind if it will help you."

Tony rehashed all the events that had passed before them. She almost tuned him out until he said, "Next comes the airport where someone in a business suit stalked you before he killed an innocent woman in that department store. Who was *he* working for?"

Elena inhaled too much air and gasped. "What?"

"You didn't know?" Tony asked.

"I didn't tell her," Alex said. "She's had enough trouble without knowing . . ." He tightened his grasp on her hand.

Elena pulled away from him. "You didn't think I needed to know? Alex!" She leaned forward toward Tony's seat. "How was she killed?"

Tony didn't reply.

"Please. Tell me."

"A knife. She was in a group of shoppers pouring over sale items."

Involuntary tears formed in her eyes and started to trickle down her cheek. "Oh no. I'm responsible for the death of that woman." She pounded her fist on the back of Tony's seat. "No!"

"None of this is your fault, Elena. None of it," Tony replied, his voice softening to almost a whisper.

Elena said, "We seem to leave death and destruction wherever we go."

"We still don't know who's behind this. We only have one suspect so far. No one has volunteered their participation. They usually do if it's a political attack."

Silence engulfed the car as they passed the white-capped mountains on one side and tree-filled ravines on the other.

"So, do you have any ideas, Elena? Enemies of Magda?"

"Magda didn't have enemies, only friends."

"Okay, but what about Janek's killer? Was he familiar to you?"

"I didn't know him at all. His name was Klaus Groscu. He went to the university and knew Jan from school. Klaus called Jan a traitor. When I came to, I was in the hospital with Magda, Freddie, and Gregory. My Grandmother flew home with me. You know the rest."

Tony removed his sunglasses and glanced back into his rearview mirror, locking eyes with her.

"Did you ever Google anything about the attack or ask Magda or Freddy?"

"Yes, I did. Magda remained silent. I tried to pry it out of Freddy. He didn't know Klaus Groscu at all. He wished he had. Marina and I discussed it and even talked to the chairman in my department. He said there was political infighting going on at the University. But Jan never spoke about politics when he was in school. Klaus was never part of his circle of friends. I searched on the Internet. There was nothing. *Nothing.*" She shook her head. "Really, that's all I know. So after that, I escaped into my books."

"How about you, Alex? What else do you know?"

Tony's tone appeared much sharper when he spoke to Alex. She thought she saw his eyes narrow a bit through the mirror. *Perhaps just an impression. I can't really see up into that glass, can I?*

Alex shrugged and looked away. "Magda refused to say anything. She said it was better to leave the past alone. I respected that. Instead, I heard all about Elena's activities at the University of Indiana."

She composed herself and gazed out at the rising mountains and thought about Tony, an FBI agent stationed in Romania, searching for drugs going to America. What about Alex? Was he just the professor he claimed to be? She didn't think so. As much as she thought she knew him, she didn't. There was more to him—much more. He was doing some investigating for Tony that much she did know. What else was there?

She shifted her attention to Tony. She liked the way he managed to talk, keep his eye on the road, and watch the rearview mirror all at the same time.

The dark blue Dacia sped its way continuing on the two-lane highway heading north, now a smoother road than before.

Elena wasn't too sure about this trip. She had a bad feeling. Were Alex and Tony enemies or friends? She wished she could have driven by herself.

Still, they were good traveling companions. Romania was something they had in common. She loved the scenery. They mentioned little tidbits about medieval towns with ancient legends, historical battles, terrorizing princes, and patriarchs who ruled the country.

Elena blanched when Alex mentioned the Ceausescu reign of terror. Nicolae Ceausescu had been the General Secretary of the Romanian Communist Party from 1965 and only stopped with the rebellion and the execution of him and his wife in 1989. She'd heard the stories of massive police raids and genocide across Romania, even into the outback regions of Transylvania.

"I remember hearing about it from Magda years ago. She knew people who were killed during that time."

"I did too," Tony responded, a cloud shading his voice.

"I believe there was an uprising in Dkany, wasn't there?" Elena prompted.

"Just before the president 's execution," Tony replied, surprising her. "There were a lot of killings by the secret police before he and his wife finally got it." His voice turned brittle, his tone bitter. Alex kept silent as though struggling with something. He finally sighed, and she thought, decided to let it go, until Tony said, "Elena, you sound like you know something about that time. Do you?"

"No, I didn't come to Romania until much later, but some of my brother's friend's relatives and friends were there. Many were killed during the Dkany massacre."

Elena struggled to turn the conversation. She chatted about regional wines, foods, museums, and monasteries, especially the Transylvanian treasure, the Dkany Monastery.

"I hope you can visit there while you're in Dkany, Elena. It's almost a fortress. The outside is surrounded by tall stone walls.

You'll love the intricate details, *especially* the painting on the outside of their church. And the tunnels go underground. They were created centuries ago to provide a refuge and an escape route from the police.

They discussed the National Opera in Bucharest, how the season ran from September to June. Wasn't it a shame they'd missed the performances, the summer festivals, and concerts in Transylvania? Finally, she told them about the Dracula Castle in Bran. Another tourist attraction.

Meanwhile, they managed to avoid the topic of conversation on everybody's mind, who was trying to kill them and why?

The Bran Castle took their conversation to the Bram Stoker novel, *Dracula*, a source of infinite fascination for Elena. Until her grandmother died, she felt distinguished by being part of a family blessed with such a rich, historical tradition. Their conversation got more and more interesting as they discussed Romanian history that would shape its people. The mountains towered ahead, revealing colorful, rolling hills all around them. They were climbing.

Even though providing stimulating conversation, Tony's eyes alternated between the road and his rear-view mirror.

Elena sat close to Alex. His shoulders and his arms stiffened, seeming to anticipate some unforeseen danger. The car took sharp turns and curves as the road ascended a ridge, revealing breathtaking mountains around each corner. Each time they swerved, she smashed into Alex.

"Too bad we won't see The Borgo Pass," Alex said. "Too far north."

Tony steered the car sharply to the right to avoid a passing Audi. But, instead of speeding ahead of them, the vehicle slowed down to their speed, keeping abreast of their car.

Alex noticed the vehicle, too close for comfort, and shoved Elena onto the floor.

Elena jerked her head to the left and pinched a nerve. "Alex, what the—"

"Tony, watch out!" Alex leaned forward over the seat and reached for a blue bag, but the momentum of the car jerked him out of reach.

Tony needed no coaxing. He floored the engine under the ongoing protest of shrieking tires. Elena didn't have to see anything to know they were under attack. A shot rang out.

Alex managed to straighten himself back into the back seat. "Damn!" he said.

Elena watched Tony reach into that same blue bag on the floor through the crack of the seats. He threw a .45 Glock into Alex's waiting hand.

"Take this," he said. "It's loaded."

Tony drove with his right hand and fired a semiautomatic with his left. He had a job concentrating on staying on the road and not veering off into the drop-offs on the side. Elena sat up and watched the Audi pushing at the Dacia, inch by inch. Tony pushed back harder.

Bullets ricocheted off the side, just missing the window.

Alex rolled his window down halfway and aimed the pistol, waiting for another approach. The vehicle slowed, then sped up again. It dropped behind their car then sped up enough to whack it in the rear.

Elena stood about all she could before saying, "Tony, do you have another gun?"

"What?" he asked, almost turning around, thus avoiding a bullet that passed into the seat cushion. He breathed a sigh of relief. "That was close." He reached down under his seat. "Sure thing, sweetheart."

"What?" Seeing her touting the pistol, Alex's shock almost made her laugh, except the situation was so serious. She ignored him. "Hell no, Elena."

"You know how to shoot a gun?" Tony asked, fumbling in his bag, his hand still on the wheel while dodging more bullets.

"You bet I do," she responded. "I'm not quite the helpless little waif you all seem to think I am."

"What the . . . ?" Alex didn't take his eyes off her. Elena, Alex, and Tony had the opportunity to provide an army of three against what seemed like four men in military fatigues. She couldn't be sure of any more detailed description, except two of them had beards. She sent out prayers that their persuers were less intelligent than they appeared.

The Audi slowed down and came up behind them, rear-ending them again. Elena reached up with her other hand and placed the gun between shards of glass, waiting for an opportunity.

"I wish you had automatic windows in here, Tony," she yelled, over the whooshing noises, coming from the outside.

"Me too," he called back, tense but trying to sound cheerful. It wasn't working. "Hell, beggars can't be choosers."

Elena got her chance. The Audi made a mistake and tried to clip them on the right side. The maneuver proved fatal. Just as the driver attempted to shoot into their car, Elena raised her pistol. For an instant, she saw steely eyes of hate above a cold metallic black object, its barrel aimed right between her eyes. She shifted her target to the tire and pulled the trigger. A tire discharged a loud *bang*, and the car swerved, rocked, and spun out of control before it slid sideways and plunged into the valley below.

As Elena tried frantically not to lose self-control, Tony pulled the Dacia to the side of the road. They got out just in time to see the Audi explode into a myriad of flames.

Alex removed his cell phone from his pocket. He turned away from the wind blowing down the mountain, fanning already growing flames, and reported the accident. Fortunately, the fire blew itself over a river and didn't hit the trees. No sign of human life exited from the car. No one could have escaped that inferno.

"Oh my God," Elena said, trembling.

In her self-defense class, they'd talked about what it felt like to kill another human being. The police who gave testimonials stated it was the most awful thing they'd ever had to do. Even though it was a necessary evil attached to the job, they never got over it. Elena knew what that felt like. She'd experienced it.

"I killed those people. I killed them as sure as if I'd shot them in the head. I had no choice. That could have been us."

Alex took her in his arms and turned her away from the ravine. Wobbly on her feet, she allowed him to lead her to the car, too numb, almost, to breathe. She barely knew where she was anymore and fell to her knees.

The concrete highway could hardly be called smooth at that juncture. Rocks fell off the mountains and cascaded onto the road, causing the sharp objects to cut into her knees through her jeans. It almost felt good. She hardly felt Alex's arms around her, supporting her, and didn't hear Tony until he was crouched down in front of her. She couldn't catch her breath, and panic rolled around her. She pushed Alex away and stumbled, trying to get up and away from them, attempting to breathe in the mountain air.

"Elena, don't try so hard," Tony ordered. "Relax. Just breathe shallow for a minute. You just had a panic attack. You'll be okay."

She shut herself down and took in a minimum of air, as much as her body would allow. She forced herself to relax, and gradually her intake increased.

After brushing the glass off the seat with his jacket, Alex helped her inside.

She handed Tony his gun back, but he waved it aside. "Keep it," he said. "It fits you, and you use it well. I'm assuming you know about storing a pistol safely?"

"Yeah, I do. I won't ever use it . . ."

"Don't be so sure," he said.

Tony drove off toward Dkany, and Alex held her close.

Elena's breathing returned to normal, her heartbeat at a regular pulse.

She kissed Alex on the cheek. "Thank you."

He blinked and gave her a surprised look. "You're welcome. But you were the one who demolished their car."

"I mean, the both of you-helping . . . protecting me. I didn't understand how dangerous this would be. I never would have let you . . ."

"You're welcome." Alex's voice came as barely a whisper.

Elena turned her attention outside the shattered window. *Who are these people? Why do they want me dead so badly?*

Chapter 19

On the Road to Sandor Inn

Dkany, Romania

Life was not pleasant for anyone the rest of the way to Dkany. Alex moved to the front, and Elena stretched out in the back. For a while, she rested her eyes, trying not to relive the past hour.

When her name came up in conversation, Elena sat up. Tony's delving into her personal life annoyed her. Knowledge of the castle, things her grandmother might have told her, what Alex knew of her grandmother's hit-and-run accident, her own attack, chewed over and over. Is that what FBI agents did?

She sat up and coughed. She didn't want this conversation to continue.

"Tony, if you want to know about me, ask me. But not now. You're making my headache."

"Okay, Elena. However, I need to know as much as possible."

"You know as much as Alex or even I do. Probably more."

Elena figured Tony might be in his late forties, maybe early fifties. His eyes were dark with circles and age lines. But he was sharp and didn't miss a thing. He was like a pit bull. Once he got onto something, he wouldn't shake it loose.

She perched in her seat, never taking her eyes off Tony.

Tony shot her a look and concentrated on the road. He said, "All the information you got from Alex, you knew already."

"Yeah, I guess I did."

"So, are you searching for, oh maybe, discrepancies? Lies we may have told you?" Alex smirked.

Tony peered back again and touched his tongue to his cheek.

He appeared to be about to say something, then shrugged. "No, Elena, not really. We haven't told you any lies. But I would like to know more about your marriage to Jan Ivanov. I think he plays a key part in this, don't you?"

"No, I don't, so just shut up, Tony." She huddled against the passenger side door, her arms folded, curled up into as much of a ball as she could get.

Elena wanted to grab Tony's neck and shake the stuffing out of his brains.

"Leave her alone. She doesn't want to talk about this now." Alex's expression stated, *neither do I.*

Tony grunted.

They passed through the gates of the great wall fortressing Dkany.

She stared out into the town. Nothing in the old city appeared different from medieval times. They'd gone from a modern to an ancient city in the shadow of a castle on the hill.

"Where the hell is this hotel?" Tony growled. He was in a mood. Apparently, Elena's unwillingness to continue his interrogation had spoiled his humor.

Elena knew the town's intricacies. She told him to go around the clock tower and follow it out of town.

"What clock tower?" Tony asked.

"She knows where she is," Alex said. "Her husband probably gave her directions."

"No," Elena said. "I've never been here before. I looked up Dkany in a brochure. It included a map. That's all."

The clock tower appeared as if by magic, towering in the town's center square surrounded by a bakery, grocery, hair salon, boutique, and pub. People milled around the square, talking. Some young folk singers gathered under the clock, strumming guitars. Girls sunned themselves in bikini tops and shorts, and the boys whistled and flirted.

They passed houses whose facades looked like they'd survived for hundreds of years, a medieval haven. The road curved down a hill, and in the distance, a wooden bridge crossed a river. About a mile down stood the Dkany fortress wall, leading to the road out of town. Off to the right, a path led to a castle that shadowed the landscape.

When the road forked, Alex saw another walled complex. "What is that?" he asked.

"The Dkany Monastery," Elena said without hesitation.

"How the hell did you know that?" Tony muttered.

"I told you, she's been there before," Alex said in a deceptively calm tone, even for him.

Elena shrugged. "Gentlemen, do you ever listen? I told you I've read about it."

"If you say so," Alex said.

"Alex, please, just stop it." Elena turned to look upfront at Alex and winced, the pain shooting up her neck. She worked a rough massage in the spot. "Damn, that hurt," she said. "What is wrong with you two?" Elena asked.

Tony opened his mouth as if to say something but shut it again.

Their car climbed a hill up to the Sandor Inn, which backed the Dkany River nestled in the castle's shadow. Built almost entirely of logs, the inn's structure was a mastery of steps up a hill, wrap-around porch, and huge windows that gave guests a perfect view of the mountains.

It would be hard to stay mad at anyone in such exquisite surroundings, but Elena thought they all managed to do their best.

Tony was the only one talking when they entered the foyer created with cathedral ceilings and maple floors varnished with a rich fruit-wood stain.

Tourists, visiting one of the local early summer festivals, filled the lobby, talking and laughing, adding a bizarre kind of gaiety to Elena's morose mood. At the desk, the man in front of them spoke Greek. The hotel manager addressed him in the same language.

When the man walked away with his room key and Alex faced him, he changed to English with a hint of Romanian accent.

"You're multi-lingual," Alex said. "At the turn of a customer."

"*Multumesc* . . . I thank you," the manager replied. "Yes, language is a hobby of mine, and that is a good thing, being in the tourist business. We receive visitors from all over the world. And who might you be?"

"We called this morning with a reservation for two rooms. The names are Brancusi and Donatelli."

The man raised his eyebrows and stared from him to Elena for a minute. "An honorable name in Romania. We have a famous sculptor named Brancusi. Are you related?"

"Not that I know of," Alex said. "Possible. I suppose Brancusi isn't a real common name."

"But *you* look familiar," Stefan said, smiling broadly at Elena. "I do not think we have met, have we?"

"No. I doubt it. I'm Elena Brancusi."

"Stefan Baklanov at your service. The guests have not yet checked out of your room, although they were supposed to leave by noon. The room next door is ready. They have a lovely view of our castle, a local piece of Transylvanian history."

Alex nodded and smiled. If the man only knew.

"Mister Baklanov," Alex said, responding to his gesture.

"Call me Stefan,"

"Baklanov is not a Romanian name. Are you Russian, then?" Alex asked.

"Very good. You're a student of names?"

"Kind of, I'm a professor of Romanian studies in the States."

"Ah, you must come back to my office while we wait for the room and talk to me. I have a great interest in such things. We have long wanted a language academy in Dkany." He looked around the room and called a tall, thin woman across from a group of tourists, headed for the elevator.

"My sister, Mrs. Demidis, will take over for me."

The woman didn't speak but nodded as Stefan moved from behind the counter.

A tall boy with wavy dark hair and brown eyes that flashed with self-importance jumped out from nowhere. "I speak English too," he said.

"Oh, hello," Alex said. "Yes, you do. Who are you?"

"This is my grandson, Mikhail," Stefan answered.

"I give tour around city and show you castle?" he asked, grinning.

"Do not mind him," Stefan said, rumpling the boy's hair. "He tries to take all guests for tours around Dkany. He makes extra money."

The boy looked about nine or ten.

"He *drives?*" Alex asked. "I thought you had to be eighteen."

"No," the boy said, his eyes shining as though he did something far more significant. "I drive a horse and carriage."

"Oh! Silly me!" Alex grinned.

Elena suddenly felt a shiver running down her spine. She didn't know where it came from. It left as quickly as it arrived.

"Would you, Mr. and Mrs. Brancusi, be so kind as to wait in my office? Mikhail will show you the way."

Mikhail suddenly took a shine to Elena, grabbed her hand, and pulled her along. "See, she . . . My *Doamna.* My Lady."

"Go ahead, Alex," Tony said. I'll get our bags up to the room, somehow."

"No," Stefan said, shaking his head. "We have an attendant. No guest may carry his own luggage. Not at the Sandor." He rang the small bell on the desk.

An attendant appeared from nowhere, bringing a luggage rack to the desk. The man helped Tony and many other guests roll their bags into a terminally waiting elevator.

Alex and Elena followed Mikhail down a winding hall that outlined a pictorial history of Dkany in photographs. When they got into the room, it was more living room than office. Furnished with classic Romanian hardwood antiques, the only thing modern were two computers standing side by side on a large, sturdy oak desk. A printer lay on the bottom shelf of a wall bookcase, appearing like an afterthought against such a time-honored backdrop.

"Neat, huh?" Mikhail led Alex over to the desk and showed off his computer. "This is mine. Want to see Internet?" His enthusiasm ran rampant.

Alex soon got caught up in the boy's zest for cyberspace. While they waited for his grandfather to appear, they searched for places unseen, people unknown, and anything without advertisements. Elena hung over Mikhail's shoulder, helping him to find all things American.

In addition to his love of life, something else struck Alex about this boy. Something reminding him of . . . The feeling came and went so fast it disappeared, leaving him disturbingly unfulfilled. He couldn't put his finger on this unsettling sensation. Mikhail, however, didn't give him time to dwell before he entered a new website.

Alex felt Elena behind him and turned. Her attention focused on Mikhail shifted to Alex and back again.

She appeared tired, her face almost sallow.

"Mikhail means Michael in English, doesn't it?" Alex asked.

Mikhail nodded and turned his head, grinning. "How old are you Mikhail?" Elena asked.

"How old do I look?" Mikhail asked her back.

Alex chuckled.

"Well, maybe about ten?" Elena smiled at him through those star-tling blue eyes, those eyes that endeared her to everyone whom she'd ever met. Except for *him*, Alex thought. She enchanted Mikhail. She charmed his age right out of him.

"Not right! I am nine." He offered a big grin and puffed out his chest. "I speak English like American?"

Elena laughed. "You're very good."

Alex's throat constricted at seeing her light up for one of the few times since he'd met her. She astounded him. How could anyone love someone yet cause such indifference at the same time? Alex could. Love and hate seemed to parallel each other.

"Mr. Brancusi,"

"Call me . . ."

"Alexander. Yes, Alex Brancusi. We can talk now." Stefan appeared unexpectedly from the lobby entrance.

"Your grandson has been showing us his favorite places," Alex explained.

"Yes. A favorite pastime. Smart boy."

"If you don't mind," Elena said, "I'd like to go to the available room and lie down. It's been a harrowing . . . uh, a long trip."

Alex looked at Elena and sympathized. She appeared as if she'd been through a war, and he probably didn't look much better. But the thought of her left alone with Tony in the interrogative mood he was in left him cold. "You sure?" he asked.

She nodded. "Don't worry. I won't let Tony bully me."

"Mikhail, you will, please take Miss Elena to her room?" Stefan asked. It was a direct order.

"Uh . . ." Alex started. No offense to these good people, but he didn't want anyone other than Tony or himself taking her anywhere.

Mikhail let out a huff and a sigh, denoting he didn't want anyone to leave but rather have everyone play computer games with him.

"Mikhail," Elena said, "Why don't you lead the way? You can show me around."

That seemed satisfactory, and Mikhail walked off with his new friend.

Stefan broke out into a laugh and put Alex into a much better frame of mind.

"Now," Stefan said, "Vodka and tonic?" Alex nodded.

"That boy. He has the intelligence of his father. God, rest his soul." He raised his glass in the air to someone unseen.

"I'm sorry. Your son?"

"My step-son. All too soon." They respected a moment's solemn pause and went back to normal conversation. "So, you and your charming wife are honeymooning in our beautiful mountains?"

"Yes, my wife has always wanted to come here."

"And you have been here before?" Stefan poured vodka into two glasses.

"In Romania, yes. When I was a kid," Alex replied. "I've never been to Dkany."

"You are in for a treat. And you have brought someone along as a chaperone on your honeymoon?" Stefan asked, grinning, as he handed Alex a glass. "Please . . ." He motioned for Alex to sit on a leather office chair.

Alex offered a smooth smile. "No. A simple coincidence, really. We met a friend I haven't seen since college. We thought we'd travel together for a while before going our separate ways." *Good thinking, Alex.*

"Ah," Stefan said, raising his glass. "And, you'll be going to our castle, no?"

Alex looked up into Stefan's gleaming eyes full of mischief, and with his grin, thought the game might be up. He tried for a recovery. "Doesn't everyone?"

"Come, come, Mr. Brancusi. Your wife has the Dkany stamped all over. She can be no one other than the young castle heiress, Elena Dkany." He nodded in the direction she'd walked with Mikhail. "Yes, she fits in Dkany."

"So, you know?"

"Of course. She looks like her brother, Frederick Dkany. Everyone knows about the succession. Gregory Balogh told me you would be coming to visit this summer. He was filled with joy you and Magda's granddaughter married. I am honored you chose to stay with us.

"It would have been my greatest pleasure to have provided you with the wedding reception right here in our hotel. But, then, there was some trouble, no? An accident, then a break-in at your wife's home?"

"You're right. You seem to know everything," Alex said. "I don't know the reason for any of this."

Alex considered his next move. Should he bombard Uncle Gregory with their presence and get it over with? Or should they take a more cautious approach?

"Is Mister Balogh here?"

"No, Mister Balogh is gone for a couple of days. Or, at least, so I've heard. The lady in charge, Mrs. Demidis, should have that information."

"Stefan, we'd like to get into the castle."

"But Miss Elena can go into her castle anytime she wishes, no?"

"Yes, but we'd like to be given a tour by someone who knows the castle, personally. What parts are safe, what might be hazardous? I've heard about the ruins. We'd like to keep it as secret as possible. Any chance?"

"Ah. I see. Yes, always. The good woman, who takes care of the castle, she is my sister. She speaks some English, and she and Mikhail can give you the tour."

"You have handy relatives."

"Everyone in Dkany has handy relatives. We're a small population."

Alex considered this statement for a minute. Maybe Stefan might know about Jan. "Stefan, maybe you can clear up a mystery for me."

"Yes?"

Alex considered, then changed his mind. "It was some time ago. I want to know what happened to a friend of mine."

"A friend? What was . . ."

Stefan didn't get a chance to finish his question. A hotel clerk came through the front entrance with a summons for his help.

"My friend, I will be back right away," Stefan said as he scurried out with his employee. A slight commotion came from the lobby, then quiet again.

Alex focused on Stefan's office. Photos and paintings of the castle, Dkany scenes in summer and winter, portraits of monasteries, the mountains, lakes, and streams hung in a collage on the walls. A world map with pins—possibly of places traveled—hung on the wall. Next to it hung a blue and yellow cuckoo clock crowned by the Transylvanian coat of arms, symbolized by a golden eagle, a symbol of Romanian courage, determination, power, and soaring to grand heights. He'd need all that and then some to get through this nightmare.

What he noticed wasn't so much what filled the room but what was absent. No family photographs. Not one picture of anyone. He wondered why.

The cuckoo broke the silence of the room. Alex thought some things never change. Wherever they went, a cuckoo clock livened up the place—a stamp of old European culture.

Stefan came back rubbing his hands together, as though to say, "And that takes care of that." He raised on the side of his lip and pushed back his thinning hair. "Tsk-tsk. Good help is hard to find these days. I am so sorry I cannot stay and talk longer. I have some employee matters to deal with." Then, as though finalizing his conversation with Alex, he asked, "You said you want to go to the castle in secret?"

"Yes, I do."

"What about tomorrow morning? I will arrange to have Mikhail take you there. So you can leave before dawn when no one would notice. And we will talk another time."

And Alex was dismissed. His unanswered question would have to wait until another time.

At least something was going right. They were going to the castle.

Chapter 20

Dkany Castle

At five the next morning, Elena, Alex, and Tony waited on a picnic bench near the back entrance for Mikhail to arrive with his horse and carriage.

Tony turned toward the mountains, pointed at the castle, and said, "Tourists out on a sight-seeing tour driving in a horse and carriage and looking at the sunrise. Romantic and good cover for us."

"It's not going to be a cover for long when it gets around the Dkany heiress is in town," Elena said.

"Stefan already figured it out," Alex said.

"If you don't start to act like you're actually in love," Tony said, frowning, "the whole town will know this is a sham." He said it so softly Elena almost missed it. "And I wouldn't discuss annulment in a public place like the restaurant, if you don't mind, Alex."

"Je . . ."

"Stop it," Elena commanded. "No squabbles."

Tony grinned and turned toward the stables.

"Tony's right," Elena said. "I'm sure we can handle our relationship. Can't we?"

Alex nodded slowly.

Mikhail drove a white carriage pulled by a bay mare wearing a straw hat with a feather between her ears.

"So, you drive a horse." Elena patted the horse's neck and giggled when the mare bumped her pockets looking for—

"Treats. Her name Bear. She like sugar," Mikhail said. He took out a cube from his pocket and jumped off the carriage.

The horse nudged him.

"See, you hold your hand like this." The boy flattened Elena's hand and put the sugar in the middle. The horse used her lips to gently pick up the cube in her mouth.

"She's really a lady, isn't she?" She giggled. "Her name is Bear?" Elena looked at him and tilted her head.

Mikhail grinned. "Like, Go Bears—American football team."

"You like football?" Alex asked.

"I watch on Internet." He tossed Elena a couple more lumps of sugar. The mare picked up the cubes. "I also like soccer, basketball, and watching horses race around a track."

"He watches football," Alex said. "On the internet."

Tony chuckled and hopped into the carriage.

"I drive cars, too," Mikhail said.

"I don't believe you," Elena said. She laughed—teased.

Tony moved to help Elena hop onto the running board, but Alex stood and took her hand. He pulled her next to him. "My bride," he affirmed.

Elena thought Tony had tried to sit down beside her deliberately. She wasn't exactly sure why. Maybe it stemmed from Alex's reaffirmation during breakfast that they'd dissolve the marriage once they returned to the states. Why he'd said it and why he'd said it in front of Tony, she wasn't sure. She hadn't seen the verbal punch coming, and it caught her between the eyes. At least, they'd better not say anything in front of the boy.

"Go, Bear," Mikhail said. The horse jerked the carriage forward.

"Go, Bear," Elena said softly. "What a creative kid."

"Here we are," Alex said, looking out at the landscape, at the mountains. "This is actual Romania."

Elena looked at the mountains, then focused back on Alex. An emotional roller coaster, last night he'd slept on a pull-out sofa so small, his legs dangled over the end. She thought he might fall over the side and almost wished he had. At least, it would have provided some entertainment.

"I tell you story about history of castle?" Mikhail said as his horse clopped along.

"Sure," Alex said. "I'd love to know her history. He knows Dkany Castle better than I do."

Elena turned her head and watched the sun blazing its way up and over the distant high peaks.

"You know story of Dracula?" the boy asked.

"Sure, we do," Alex said.

"He was real person, you know?"

"Yes, I know."

"Oh," Mikhail appeared crestfallen.

"But go on. We all know the vampire tales. So what's the true story?"

Mikhail looked back and grinned. "Okay, I tell story. Our Prince Vlad-Tepes rule in Transylvania. Bad Turks come and try to take country. Our prince kill thousands of them. He impale." He turned back again. "You know impale?"

"Yes," Elena shivered. "Oh yes, we know what that means."

"It means you stake someone and takes them *long* time to . . ."

"We know, Mikhail. Go on with the story," Alex said.

"Nothing too much, but he hero in my country. They write books about him. They claim him monster. No monster. Real live prince. People think him hero. He keep country safe. But other people do not like. They kill him."

"Who killed him?" Elena asked, not wanted to burst his historical bubble.

"*The Legion of the Silver Cross*, of course," Mikhail said. "Led by *our* Viktor Dkany, head of Dkany family. You hear about Dkany family? Our town named after family. Our pride. My hero.

"Legion of Silver Cross. We all wear cross in Dkany. He close friend of prince until prince become crazy and kill many *good* people.

In battle with bad Turks in *1476*, Viktor kill prince. We play games. Take sides. Sometimes I play Vlad, sometimes I play Count Dkany."

"You even know the dates," Elena said. "Smart kid."

Mikhail turned his head and grinned at her. "Yes, I am smart."

"Interesting tale, that," Tony said. "I wonder what happened to the cross."

"I know," Mikhail said.

"You do?" Elena asked. "What?"

"It destroyed in earthquake long time ago. No longer exist."

"Oh, that's a shame," Elena said. "Such a valuable cross."

Mikhail turned to them. "But *I* think cross still exist. Not destroyed."

"What?" All three stared at him.

"Yes. I know where cross hides." "Where?" Alex asked.

Mikhail shook his head. "Secret. I no tell."

Mikhail believed the cross still existed? Was that possible?

The mare trotted over winding roads that alternated between dirt and concrete and maneuvered around the rocks that fell from the mountainside. They passed through a scented forest of pine and fresh mountain air.

Christmas in June.

Elena pictured a bouncing boy on Alex's knees in front of a decorated tree. Sadly, she thought they'd missed the joy and challenges of raising a child.

I would have married you, Elena. Would he have?

If she didn't look at him, Elena could dream. She pictured him as he was in high school. Funny, intelligent, and loving. She could escape into his arms and not even be close to him—to her husband. But how could she love someone who seemed so indifferent, even hateful at times, but so tender and loving at others? She thought of the Rusalka. If it hadn't been for that explosion, there might have been an explosion of another kind.

Probably just as well. She might be in love with him, but she no longer liked him very much. Like this morning, he could be so hurtful.

A lump caught in her throat. The word wasn't *he*. *It* was *they*. They'd been horrible to each other. Maybe it was sleeping in the same room and not being able to be together. Elena tried to shrug off those feelings, but it didn't work.

They were climbing. A drop of hundreds of feet stood inches from the carriage wheels. Mikhail and his horse seemed to know what they were doing, and he didn't seem concerned. He and Bear looked as confident as if they were taking a Sunday drive in the park.

Alex stared at her. Those expressionless eyes caught and held hers before they looked away again.

She felt the chill of being silently humiliated. What the heck was wrong with him now?

If she hadn't been so sheltered from life's experiences, she might not have gotten into the trouble she had. Even more, she wished Magda was alive so she could tell her the truth. Beg her to understand. Magda had been an excellent role model and companion, but they'd been generations apart. Old world traditions and morals. A world that would never understand a young seventeen-year-old girl getting pregnant.

As Elena daydreamed, Mikhail pointed out all the unusual places of interest. While he droned on, Alex and Tony made comments and laughed with him. Elena kept quiet, not wanting to be in the same world as any of them.

In the distance, Elena saw a castle that reminded her of the ones she'd seen in pictures and books. Like a massive skyscraper, the castle loomed ahead as fifty-foot walls connected four guard towers strategically surrounding the fortress.

Wow, and this is mine?

"Dkany Castle," Mikhail said as they approached. He looked back at her and gave her a big smile. "She is beautiful, no?"

"My God," Elena said, a slight quiver reinforced her awe. She'd never imagined anything like this. Not even her grandmother or Gregory prepared her for this. "*This* is Dkany Castle?"

The air felt chillier now that the trees no longer buffered the breezes floating across the mountains. In the distance, the river wound through the countryside, then disappeared, hiding behind the castle. It circumvented the inn and flowed beyond view. This couldn't be the same castle as Gregory described. The photos on the castle's website were mainly of ruins with a few rustic front door shots. A primitive drawbridge once covered a moat filled with ten feet of water to dissuade enemies from attacking. Now, a permanent concrete bridge crossed an empty ditch.

The horse and carriage passed into the enclosed courtyard. A Romanian peasant, who looked to be about ninety, sported baggy jeans and a brown cardigan sweater covered by a vest. He wore a brown hat weathered, like his face, by time. He stooped when he led the horse and carriage away, both ambling into the stables across the yard. Mikhail banged on the door by pulling a bronze clapper. The clang resonated through an echo chamber of sorts.

The noise made Elena jump. She asked Mikhail about the echo.

"It's so they can hear you if they're on the other side of the castle," Mikhail said.

"It's that big?" She asked.

"That big," he replied, holding his hands out past his waist. His eyes shimmered from the light of the red ball of the dawning sun.

Alex took her arm, leading her to the threshold.

Elena gently removed his arm, shook her head, and turned away, so her braid flipped over her right shoulder.

Alex raised an eyebrow. "What's wrong?"

You're antagonistic, unforgiving, bull-headed, and you're always mad at me. And you confuse me.

"Nothing," she said. "What could possibly be wrong? You're the perfect gentleman." She detected a discouraged sigh. "I don't like you much," just came out. She hadn't planned it.

"You don't like . . . ?"

A woman, a taller version of Stefan, opened the door and cut off Alex's remark.

Elena recognized her as the woman who'd taken over the desk for Stefan. Besides their differences in height, she looked like her brother. Astounding, in a way, because the woman also seemed a bit like Jan. She shook it off. Everyone in Dkany resembled each other. Jan had come from Dkany.

"Mikhail." The woman grabbed the boy and hugged the stuffing out of him. Elena thought she'd crush the poor kid to death. However, he seemed to come out of it unscathed and happy.

"I am Zsophia Demitis. You new owner? Mikhail and I give you tour."

Astonished, Elena said, "Your brother said you don't speak English. But that's not true. You speak it very well."

The woman looked down at the ground, then smiled at Elena. "I thank you, Mrs. Brancusi. I not speak well—not like brother. But some. We all speak some English in Dkany."

Mikhail raised his eyebrows. His expression looked puzzled with new thoughts. "You own Dkany Castle? Really?"

"Really," Elena said.

"Then," he said, squinting his eyes, glowing with happiness, "you are Miss Elena Dkany?"

Elena smiled. "I am—though I wouldn't want that to get around if you don't mind," Elena said. "Can you keep a secret?"

"I am good with secrets." Mikhail crossed his heart. "Cross my heart and hope to die. That is expression, no?" He skipped on ahead, leading the way, touching and playing with everything he could find.

Alex and Tony maintained stoic faces.

Chapter 21

Dkany Castle

Mrs. Dimidis made no comments and asked no questions. She gave Elena her arm while the two men trailed behind. "Mrs. Dimidis . . ."

"Zsophia, please."

"Zsophia, you're very kind to meet us," Elena said in Romanian.

Mrs. Demidis' face lit up, and she relaxed into Romanian. "Call me Zsophia. And you may speak English. I enjoy—" She stopped abruptly. "You do not want anyone to know you are here, yes?"

"Yes," Elena replied. "We can trust you, can't we?"

"You can trust me," Zsophia said. A conspiratorial closeness swept over Elena.

The woman led the way up the stone steps and into a large hall. Elena stared at the vastness of the interior.

"My God. Is this the run-down castle Gregory told us about?" She whispered, half to herself, half to Alex, who stood nearby. His eyes widened with surprise. "This is magnificent."

"Yes, is it not?" Zsophia said.

"How do you take care of all this?" Elena asked, looking around, trying to figure out how someone could get up high enough to clean the windows and polish the wooden beams. Certainly not Zsophia Demidis.

"Most of the house cleaning chores I do. But Mister Balogh hires a cleaning crew to do the heavy cleaning. "They come with big trucks, and I get the day off. That is good for me."

"So, Mrs. Dimidis . . ."

"Zsophia."

"Excuse me. How often does the cleaning crew come in here to keep it this nice?"

"Will depend. I do not make arrangements. Mr. Balogh, he does that."

"Does it always look this nice?"

Zsophia nodded, then shrugged. "Most of time, yes. That would depend on how many people come. Sometimes many, sometimes not. But, as you see," Mrs. Demidis said. "The windows are spotless, the ceilings immaculate, and they are due to come again soon."

"Oh yeah?" Tony asked. "When?"

Mrs. Demidis shook her head. "I do not know. End of this week, maybe." With a vague hint of disapproval, she puckered her lips. "Why? You do not like?"

Elena shot Alex and Tony a harsh glance. "No, Zsophia. It's lovely. We just wanted to know how you keep it up so nice."

The woman smiled. "Ah. So now you know."

Elena looked up so long, surveying old and sturdy fixtures, she crimped her neck, and her muscles tightened with the strain. Breathtaking, awesome and mind-boggling, were only some adjectives she could think of that described her astonishment at the brilliance of carved wood beams, Baroque furniture, and stain-glass windows. Oriental carpets Elena had never seen in stores graced highly polished oak floors. Some, she thought, were original planks.

Zsophia walked them out into a hall, with passages leading in several directions. One way went to the council hall. With a hint of yellow, freshly painted white walls caught the sunlight from the wooden framed windows hiding in alcoves. Elena walked into one of these recesses and peered out. An outdoor courtyard lay in the center of the castle. Directly across, she saw the remnants of a building and the ruins.

"Oh!"

"What?" Alex said, coming up behind her.

"Gregory was right about one thing."

"Yeah?"

"The castle does have ruins, look."

The perimeter tower bisected the walls with piles of rubble, stones, and cement bricks. The site, where castle rooms connected, overlapped the turret with debris. They saw significant gaps in the structure. It looked like a disaster site. Sad, she thought, for an earthquake to demolish such a historical treasure. She couldn't say the same about this side of the building. This was amazing. How could one part of a building sustain such destruction while the other remains untouched? One of nature's amazing tricks.

"Look, Elena." Alex pointed. Peering from behind brick and mortar stood a cottage not far from the river that wound behind the castle.

"That's where Freddie lived."

Tony spoke up. "Yeah, but who's paying for all of this?" Elena and Alex turned to hear him. "This . . ." he pointed to the surrounding area, "is no ruin."

Elena said, "Probably why he didn't want me here. Maybe we have a lot more money than recorded in the will's financial statements."

"Or maybe he's spent it all trying to keep it up," Alex said. "Maybe he doesn't want anyone to know how long he's been pilfering the family assets."

"Why?" Elena asked. "My grandmother wouldn't have denied him the funds to keep this place running if she had the money."

"How about land? How many acres are really attached to this castle?" Tony asked.

"I think the will mentioned a hundred," Elena answered. "But he's been wrong about other things."

"How much is still yours?" Tony asked.

"I'm not sure, but I think everything in the will is still intact. The question is, how much of the will is accurate? Isn't it true, the more usual places of this caliber had more land attached?"

"You mean, besides the town?"

"I don't think we own the town, at least not anymore." Elena sighed. "I think that's true for most castle and mansion owners these days." She could just see herself, owner of a town. Queen Elena of Dkany. Boy, would that give the guys back at the college something to talk about.

"It doesn't seem the Dkany cash flow amounted to this much," Alex said.

"Maybe he's found another source of income," Tony said, brushing off a passing spider who'd mistaken him for part of the wall. Alex and Elena turned to him.

"Yes," Elena said, lost in thought. "Possibly." Or maybe her family had been the victim of some kind of swindle? A nagging feeling kept plaguing her. An eyesore to sell to the government? Never. Maybe Gregory sold parcels of land to keep it up. No. There wouldn't have been any reason he'd hide the sale from Magda. And Magda would have had to sign papers.

"So, Alex, do you think he planned on sending us money and claim it came from the sale of this place? To keep us happy?" she asked.

"And in the dark," Alex responded.

"No," Tony replied. "I doubt you were the victim of fraud. I believe the upkeep is coming from an entirely different source than your family funds."

She'd been avoiding this. As Tony predicted, someone had an enormous amount of money. Drug trafficking was the first thing that came to mind. So, where did they store the drugs? She thought of a place she'd ask about later.

Mikhail scooted around the corner and came to a sliding stop. "You want to see where the family lived? We take you there."

Zsophia and Mikhail escorted Elena around the living quarters. On the first floor, they explored the hunting room filled with trophies of both the heads of victims and the cups honoring their executioners. The heavy furniture combined with leather sofas and suede lounge chairs made a sophisticated and elegant eclectic appearance.

When they got to the library, Elena reminded herself to breathe. First editions filled the bookcases from ceiling to floor across three walls. The fourth wall accommodated a myriad of original paintings by famous artists. A large, gold-framed manuscript hung over a solid, sturdy, and highly polished wooden desk. It was a parchment, old and delicate, hand-scribed with black and red ink embossed in a frame of silver. It read, 'League of the Silver Cross.' A small, exquisite ornate silver cross with rubies down the center stood alone in the corner of the frame. A treasure in its own right—a duplicate of the one Elena wore around her neck.

"My God. So, it really did exist, then?"

"The League of the Silver Cross," Alex said. "It wasn't a legend."

"Mikhail is . . . ?"

Mikhail had dashed out of the room and was running down the corridor. His footsteps grew dimmer.

"He sure is a feisty one, isn't he?" Alex said with a crooked smile. "Reminds me of me when I was a kid."

Elena regarded him, trying to remember something. It went out of her head. But there was something about Mikhail.

She focused back on history and legends; her eyes clouded with visions of the past. "No. The stories are no mere legends. This is history." She could picture Viktor and his men sitting around the table, planning strategies to take down the prince who'd caused so much bloodshed and heartbreak.

"But remember," Elena said, "in Romania, Prince Vlad was and is a hero. No matter who he impaled."

"True," Alex said.

Tony wandered through the room, scrutinizing the books, fingering wooden frames of original paintings, and looking at engraved carvings.

"Elena," Alex said. "Do you know how much treasure is in here? I've never seen anything like this."

Elena nodded. "Yes, there are some priceless assets here."

Alex moved on to a glass-enclosed book stand. "Tony, look at this." He pointed to a Romanian bible dating back to the eighteenth century.

"Where did he get this stuff?" Alex asked.

"Look here, this is original. This belongs to the castle—to you, Elena." Tony fingered the glass encasement.

"But back to Gregory," Tony replied. "I wonder where Gregory and his men are storing . . ."

Before Tony could finish, Elena said, "Look at this, Alex." Elena stood in front of one of the paintings.

"What?"

She pointed to a young girl's painting, long raven hair, and blue eyes—skin, milk-white. She wore Romania's peasant costume, but her bodice opened to the waist, exposing her breasts. Her expression showed no hint of embarrassment or shame. Elena reached up and touched the flesh.

"It's me, Alex," she whispered. "It's me. Who painted me?"

"Ana Dkany," he said, looking at the bottom of the frame.

"This is my mother," she said, fingering the gold lettering. "Look, Alex, she's inviting someone to come and touch her. To love her."

"I wonder who she was seducing."

"Seducing?"

"That's how I see her. See those eyes, full of fun and mischief."

"She's saying 'touch me . . . love me.'" Elena reached up, touched the creamy face on tiptoes, and stroked the garment as she would the real material. "That's my mother. What a beautiful woman."

Lowering herself down, she spoke half to herself, half to Alex. "Who painted her? Who was the artist? Was he also her lover?"

"Why do you ask?" Alex questioned.

"Because no one could have captured the expression of sheer joy and sexuality if he wasn't in love with her."

Alex took a step back and scrutinized her until she felt her cheeks turned warm.

She let go of a nervous cough and refocused on the canvas. "Is his name on the painting, someplace?"

"Must be," Alex said, examining the bottom right corner. "Here it is." He looked closer. "Your father painted her." His finger tapped the signature. Robert Dkany.

"Magda told me my father was an artist. My God, Alex, he painted beautifully. I wonder if he painted that before . . . before they got married."

A thought came to her. "I never saw his work. Magda didn't keep it." Elena felt her whole life enfold in one sentence. She didn't even know what her father did. Why hadn't she asked? Magda never volunteered any information about her parents.

"When did she die?" Tony asked, coming to her rescue.

"When I was a year old—of pneumonia. Strange circumstances. They planned on taking me to Romania to visit the castle, and before they could go, Ana developed walking pneumonia. She'd been recovering at home. They'd given her a regime of antibiotics. When she died, the gossip circles blamed my father for neglecting her. He committed suicide shortly after. Magda said he died of a broken heart. She never quite got over it."

"Their deaths probably broke her heart. That's why she couldn't bring herself to take out his paintings and show you."

"Yes. You're right." A heaviness centered in her chest. Tears well up in her eyes, she forced to control.

"I'm sorry, Elena." Alex put his hand on her shoulder. A comforting move, but somehow, she didn't want his hand on her just now.

Gently, she took it off her shoulder and held it tightly in her own before releasing it.

He looked at her, turned his back, and started to walk away.

"Alex, over here."

Tony was looking at a painting stacked against others, leaning against one of the bookcases. He pulled out another picture, a small but exquisitely painted landscape.

"Original Monet," he said.

"No kidding?" Alex responded. "From the estate?"

"No," Tony said. "There's a sale tag." Elena and Alex huddled in to get a closer look. "Purchased last year for a hundred thousand dollars. Damn!"

"Where would a caretaker of a castle, even if he is a lawyer, get the money to buy that caliber of original art?" Elena whispered. "What has Gregory been up to?"

"I could take a good guess. He has reason to want to hang onto this place."

Elena wanted to continue the conversation but noticed Zsophia standing quietly by the door, watching. This benign old lady seemed to grow in stature, her eyes narrow and her lips turning down into a frown. The severe middle part of wiry gray hair pulled back into a harsh bun.

Elena glanced at the title of a book on the bottom shelf next to the woman. *Rebecca.* That's it. She's Mrs. Danvers in the flesh. What's she got to do with all of this?

"Zsophia, is something wrong? You look, well, displeased."

"You question the character of Mr. Balogh. That is not right."

"Oh, dear. I'm sorry. We're just wondering where all this came from. My grandmother never told me about this."

"Oh, I see."

Still, she didn't want to discuss this while the woman was in the room.

But Zsophia's frown flashed back into a smile. Addressing Elena, she asked, "You want to see the castle ruins?"

"Yes, please," Elena replied. Before she allowed herself to be ushered out, she turned and looked one more time at the portrait. She was her mother's daughter.

She turned and caught Alex watching her, his eyes flickering to the portrait and back to her. He turned away when she noticed him staring.

The Mrs. Danvers of the Romanian castle coughed and gave them a slight bow. "This way, please."

CHAPTER 22

DKANY CASTLE

Something nagged at Elena as they crossed over rubble and through the archway into a large stone structure. The outside was severely damaged, but the inside was, besides being neglected, intact. High on a wall that formed the end peak of the roof stood a stained-glass window. They'd found the chapel, complete with rotting pews, an empty altar, and a choir loft that still held a decaying pipe organ.

In awe of this piece of history and heritage, Elena said, "This is where the greatest musicians of the Renaissance came to play for the Court. Guillaum Dfay, Gilles Binchois, Josquin Des Pres—all of them." She stared at the upstairs crumbling pews. "All the nobility attended the performances. The earthquake destroyed most of the structure, but Viktor and his family were already dead by then. I'm glad they didn't live to see this."

Mikhail pointed to the altar. "You ask about silver cross? That is where silver cross stood."

Mrs. Dimidis said, "You don't know that Mikhail. That is where monks thought it stood. Nobody knows for certain. So, we leave story in past."

They reached the ruins on the opposite side of the chapel. The section once housed the Dkany estate offices. The grounds' financial business and the surrounding territories kept estate managers and staff busy. The fifteenth-century earthquake hit this section the hardest and left the rubble still residing on cold slab floors. Only hints remained of the rich wood flooring long since lost to the weathering of time.

The cottage functioned as both business office and Freddie's house, where so many events happened—births, deaths, and friendships. All the fears and uncertainties uncovered and unmasked. The old insecurities of Freddie's life and death made her cold all over. Still, she needed to get into the cottage. There were things inside she wanted no one to see. Things better destroyed.

They stumbled along the footing on a path that once had been the outside wall.

Elena tripped on a rock and went over. Her hands reached hard rubble on the ground before her knees landed. Alex caught her around the waist and pulled her up. Her back fell against him. His warmth and sexuality caught her off guard, and she pressed against him.

Alex's face was warm. His lips brushed her hair as he steadied her.

"Okay?" Alex said.

"Um . . ." Elena took a step and decided she hadn't sprained anything and could go on. "Yeah, I think so."

Alex let go of her and brushed past without looking back. She stared after him, then moved on. The rejection bruised. Oh well, she didn't care anyway, did she?

They reached the side entrance. Pine trees lined a path that seemed to end at a log-built cottage.

Zsophia bowed formally to them. "I beg pardon. I take leave. Much to do. Feel free to come and go. Mikhail will show you around."

Elena searched. No Mikhail. And soon, Zsophia disappeared. She tried to get her bearings.

"Tony," she said, "Ruins or not, there's no way this castle could have been kept up like this with Dkany funds. Do you really think they're doing it with drug money, and how do you think they bring the drugs in without anyone seeing them?" She circled around, looking for various avenues of hiding places. "Where do you think they hide it?"

To her surprise, he showed no reaction. "I have no idea."

She did, though. "I wonder where the dungeons are. I wonder if they're held in one of the cells down there."

"You have to know where to look," Mikhail said with a grin. He'd finally caught up to them and was playing 'kick the stone.' The three looked at each other, then back at him.

"You're ten years old. And you know about this?" Tony asked.

Mikhail threw back his head and put his hands on his hips. "I come every day with Zsophia to help with chores. I clean in the cottage and find a drawing of map. You want to find something in castle? You look at map. And . . ." He grinned. "I am nine years old, and I know lots for my age."

Alex and Tony shared a brief, sharp glance. Alex exhaled a visible sigh of relief.

Elena wondered if they really thought the kid knew what they were talking about—a nine-year-old kid with a map that showed the location of heroin. Did Mikhail even know what heroin was? What about Zsophia and Stefan? Did they know? If so, why would they let Mikhail explore the castle on his own? No, none of this made sense. It was too bizarre.

"Okay, so there's a map of the castle," Tony said, his eyes resting on Mikhail with a thoughtful pause. "Though I doubt what we're looking for will show on it."

"Yeah," Alex agreed. "But there may be obvious places where they might hide the stuff."

Then something else flashed before Elena's eye. Alex had his hand on Mikhail's shoulders. Elena's jaw dropped. Whatever she'd seen left as fast as it came. She'd seen it before. But, again, it was gone, and she couldn't get it back.

Mikhail grinned. "I think stuff locked in cottage."

"What do you mean by stuff?" Tony asked.

"You know, map. Locked in desk drawer. I investigate. I see."

"God, you didn't," Alex said.

"Yes, safe."

They walked past the nine-foot-thick castle wall entrance and down the path toward the cottage.

"Cottage locked," Mikhail said as he picked up a stick and threw it as hard as he could. He hit the middle branch of a pine tree.

Alex whistled and gave Elena a sidelong glance of disbelief.

"Where the heck did you learn to throw like that?"

"Is good, yes? I practice American baseball."

"Hmm. I think the Cubs could use you right about now," Alex said. "But, back to the cottage. You said it was locked? Where's the key?"

Elena fully expected Mikhail to know precisely where the key was.

"No. I do not know where is key." Mikhail looked apologetic and unhappy.

They all stopped dead in their tracks.

"We can't get in," Tony said, his hands on his hips, eyes narrowing. "So, what the hell are we . . . ?"

"You follow me, please." Mikhail grinned at them, then ran up ahead. He rounded the corner of the cottage. Several windows provided light to its interior, but Mikhail stopped at one in particular.

Squashed between the bottom window frame and the ledge was a stick.

He looked at the others, satisfaction glowing in his eyes. He grinned as he heaved the window open, sprang up, and into the cottage.

Alex stared wide-eyed. Then crawled in after him. When he got into the room, he held his arms out for Elena and helped her through the window. They roamed through a bedroom and into the living room.

It appeared it hadn't changed much since Freddie lived there.

The inside looked as rustic as the outside. Paintings of the Transylvanian landscape done by her brother still hung on the walls.

He took after our father. Elena thought. *Talented and creative.*

Freddy was a neat freak when he lived at home. But this looked like it hadn't been kept up for a long time. Clutter scattered everywhere. Newspapers from Dkany and Bucharest were strewn on the coffee table, spilling onto the floor. Paper cups once filled with coffee lay around the floor next to squashed beer cans and broken bottles. Dust collected on sheepskin lampshades with dirt-encrusted bears at the base. It could be a beautiful home for someone, but Freddie chose a mess instead. Shame. Without thinking, she picked up a stack of magazines lying on the floor and piled them back onto the round table. They slid off again, and ants ran in many directions. Elena jumped back.

"My God!" Elena sighed. "You would have thought somebody would have cleaned up this mess."

"I come in here, but Mr. Gregory, he does not want things touched." Why not?

As Tony surveyed the room, he seemed lost in thought. "A druggie's delight. Look here." He picked up something just visible from under the couch—a syringe.

"Dear God, no," Elena said. Something inside of her was on the verge of breaking. Her brother who'd saved her when she was in trouble. Her brother, with whom she'd played and climbed trees as a kid, and her brother, whom she'd loved dearly. How could this have happened to him? And why had Gregory not discarded the paraphernalia?

Alex tripped over something on the floor and fell into the chair. As Elena's gaze rested on him, she looked behind him. On the wall was a photograph of Jan with her holding the baby. Next to it was a painting of her and her child. The caption *Mother and Child*. The photo painted by her brother.

Alex glared at the painting, then at Elena. Her deceit captured in his eyes. It wasn't his anger that made her eyes start to burn with tears. It was the baby shoes that hung next to the photographs.

Something inside broke. A piece of her died right there, and she knew it. Blood rushed into her head. She forced the dizziness away and ran into the office away from everyone. Something was choking her, making it hard to breathe. Internal sobs stopped the airflow. Tears flowed down her cheeks. When she was alone, she covered her face and cried.

Then footsteps followed her inside, and she quickly wiped her face with her sleeve and swallowed the remaining despair. She turned.

Alex was watching her, frowning. He said nothing.

"Couldn't you have left me alone for even a minute?" she asked.

She was silenced by his dark, sad expression.

Shrugging at her, he turned away toward one of the two walls of bookshelves.

Mikhail pranced in, a bundle of energy and happiness contrasting the gross despair engrained in her and Alex.

He made his way straight to the desk started opening desk drawers one after another.

Elena forced herself out of her misery. She had to find the letters she'd set out to recover. She stood, hands on her hips, staring at each bookshelf, at each book, wondering where in the world Freddie would have put them. He was great at hiding things in books.

Alex pulled out books one by one, looking at titles, blowing dust off the jackets, and putting them back. Some were in English, some in Romanian, some in German.

Another book nut. Alex and Freddie always had books in common from the time they were young.

Freddie had been a quiet kid, his nose in a book the same as Elena, Marina, and Alex. Intellectual families. No, Elena had been the one whose nose had always been in a book.

She peered inside a closet filled with clothes she'd worn in high school. Clothes she had dated in, the evening gown she'd worn to the prom. She turned and saw Alex watching her. Her heart took another beating.

Alex stood watching her holding her prom dress. The memories flashed back like unfulfilled dreams.

He crossed the room and fingered the dress. "You remember?" he said, the hurt rising up inside him. "Do. You. Remember?" He clipped his words short, anger on the tip of each syllable.

Elena pulled out of his grasp, put the dress back, and slammed the door. She brushed by him then stood by Mikhail, who rummaged through desk drawers. But while he continued to try and pry open one particular drawer, Elena seemed to be looking for something else. So, what was it that she wanted—a birth certificate, instructions for when the drugs were coming, and where they were going? Was she trying to find evidence to get rid of? His heart told him they were nothing of the kind, but he was suddenly feeling evil.

Elena came up empty-handed and proceeded to an end table, pulling out papers from the bottom's small drawer. A cloud covered her face.

Whatever it is, she's not finding it. There was some satisfaction there.

"What are you looking for?" Alex asked.

Elena shook her head. "I don't know. Not sure. Nothing in particular."

"Yes, you are, Elena. Tell me, and we can help you find it."

"No. I'm not sure what I'm looking for, so how could you help?"

"Okay, have it your way." He shrugged and pulled out a collection of Edgar Allan Poe works, his favorite author. Flipping through the pages, several packets of, what appeared to be letters wrapped in a blue ribbon, floated onto the ground. He stooped to pick them up, but Elena scooped them into her hands and shoved them into her purse before he could take a breath.

Alex raised his eyebrows and opened his mouth, confused. Elena's blue eyes met his as though analyzing his reaction. "Thank you for finding these," she said. "You've done me a favor." She peered at the book title and murmured. "I should have known they'd be in a Poe collection."

Love letters from Jan? Had Freddy been a fan of Edgar Alan Poe too?

Or had it to do with Jan's child? A child he now wasn't convinced was Jan's. He glared at her.

"What are they, Elena?" he asked.

"Nothing," she said, spinning away from him and helping Mikhail sort through papers on the desk.

Tony hadn't missed the exchange. He, too, stared at her, his eyes finding Alex's, then when nothing was forthcoming, he turned back to her. Yep. As soon as they got the chance, they'd be searching her purse.

"Found it!" Mikhail held up the map in a triumphal wave.

Tony cleared a table and lay the map flat. They all came and stared down at it. The castle was a maze of floors, hallways, rooms, secret passages, dungeons, and catacombs. The only problem was most of it lay under a rubble of ruins. *Now what?*

Chapter 23

Sandor Hotel

The sun streamed through the window of Elena's hotel room. The mountains weren't able to stifle the humidity, and the air conditioning didn't work to full capacity.

Elena tucked her legs underneath her on a blue, yellow, and red quilted bed, the colors of Romania's flag. She scrutinized a detailed map of Dkany, then moved her head toward the corner of the patio. She caught a glimpse of the church steeple towering over the Dkany monastery.

The afternoon sun blasted in through the open patio, which created an uncomfortable mixture of sizzling, sticky air. Perspiration soaked through her light cotton shirt. Removing her top and bra gave her sudden comfort. The only thing better would be a shower, so she reached for her robe and froze.

The door swung inward, and Alex crossed the threshold, stopping dead when he saw her. He opened his mouth, and it hung motionless. A quickening of the light in his eyes, a conveyed desire inflamed the longing in her belly.

Still, as a statute, Alex sucked in the air, his hands dangling at his sides. His eyes stared, didn't blink, never left her. Those sensitive fingers she would have to stroke her, now clenched into a fist. Those dark eyes reflected what he'd avoided last night—a smoldering flame.

He wanted her.

Unfortunately, Alex would never admit it to her or even himself. Just watching his turmoil was an erotic experience. She swallowed and hit the reality button.

"Alex." Her voice reflected a suffocated whisper. Not a muscle in her body moved. "So, you couldn't knock first?"

"I'm . . . I'm sorry. I should have warned you. I'll wait outside until you put something on."

His ears turned red, and the awkwardness made him actually charming.

Elena willed him to come to her, and his eyes locked into hers. He made a move, and Elena held her breath.

Please, Alex, please come over here. Please kiss me, touch me—make love to me.

She tried to speak from her heart to touch his. Her thoughts seemed to connect, and he took another step forward. For one brief happy moment, she thought he would, but he didn't.

Abruptly, he started to leave, but as an afterthought, he turned back. His gaze left her body and jerked up to her face. Then came a forced cooling of desire.

"Elena," he said, his voice shaky, not quite able to disguise his nervousness, "you're a beautiful woman. Some man is going to be incredibly lucky, someday."

She gritted her teeth and balled her fist. "I am not beautiful, so don't bullshit me, Alex. I'd rather you get lucky right now." She lowered her eyes onto the bedspread, afraid to look at his response. Tears welled, anticipating rejection. A sharp intake of breath caught her attention, and her head jerked up. He took still one more step forward.

His body turned stiff, his expression mocked, giving Elena shivers and not the erotic kind.

"Elena." His voice turned severe, intimidating. "I'm here to protect you, not have sex with you." He abruptly spun around and, with his back to her, said, "And, if I were to screw you, our relationship wouldn't last. I don't want to get serious with anyone." *Especially with you,* went unsaid.

"Is that because you're a government agent, Alex? You're working undercover with Tony? Don't pretend I don't know. Because I do."

Alex flew over to the bed in one split second before she had time to become frightened. He grabbed her shoulders, and his gaze pierced through her eyes. "So, you know. All right. But it better not leave this room, Elena. If it does, I swear I'll know for sure that you're involved with them."

"You think I am already." She jerked her shoulders away from him.

He eyed her for a minute. "What was in those papers you grabbed from me this morning?"

"I told you, nothing that concerns you."

"What did you do with them?" His tone blistered—scalded.

"I ate them, you jerk. Damn it. I'm half-naked, so get your hands off me." Elena grabbed her robe and put it on. "Get out of here. You've humiliated me enough."

Alex shot off the bed and clenched his jaw. His face turned pale. "Shit," he said softly. "When I think what we could have had together." He shook his head and gazed up at the ceiling. But his eyes were damp.

Shock hit her. Alex didn't hate her at all. He still loved her. As though he'd heard her thoughts, he pulled her up off the bed, grabbed her, and crushed her into his chest. He claimed her lips with a punishing and angry kiss, setting a fire burning in her lower body, then pulled away.

"What are you, Elena, a witch? What kind of power do you hold over men? Did you seduce Jan?"

Elena slapped him—hard.

Alex's hand flew to his cheek like someone had thrown a torch at him.

"You don't know *anything* about Jan or me—or our relationship." She shot back, waiting for repercussions, but none came.

A knock invaded the tense, quiet atmosphere. "Dinner!" Tony shouted but didn't knock again. Footsteps faded outside the door.

Alex swallowed hard. His voice softened. "I'm sorry, Elena. I was hard on you."

Elena's tone became gentle. "I'm sorry I slapped you. You just made me so mad."

Alex put his hand over his cheek. "I hope I don't make you mad again." He shook his head as though fighting a battle within himself, and without responding again, he opened the door, stepped over the threshold, and left the room.

Breathing hard, Elena jumped off the bed and started for the door—and stopped. Alex said he hated her. No, that was passion and, she thought, love. He said if he screwed her, he'd leave her—that he only had one-night stands with his women. What made him such a bastard?

Me?

"Scusa-ma."

Still dazed, Alex nearly plowed into a waiter carrying a tray of drinks. He wove around white linen-covered tables centered with a fresh single red rose and a candle. He couldn't get his mind off the image of Elena's naked beauty, nor her temper. The lady knew what she wanted, but that wasn't going to get *him*.

Her eyes had beckoned him over to the bed to make love to her. And why not? He was her husband, though this wasn't a real marriage. They just couldn't, even if he wanted to—badly.

Guilt battered his stomach. He'd been rotten to Elena. He'd hauled all his emotional hang-ups out on his sleeve and called her a witch.

He'd brought her down to the level of a one-night stand. Made himself out to be the worst possible type of man. And, somehow, he'd blown his cover.

He found Tony's booth and slid onto the bench across from him, moving the damned rose to the end of the table.

"So, where's the fair, Elena, and why isn't she with you?" Tony frowned, looking over into the crowd of diners.

"She'll be down." Alex looked away from Tony's probing eyes. No way was he going to explain anything.

"You left her alone?"

"It's a long story."

Tony stared hard. "Shit, Alex. How stupid. Does it have something to do with the red mark on your cheek?" One side of his lip almost turned up into a smile. Alex wanted to knock it off.

"Kind of, and I'd rather not go into it. It has nothing to do with the case."

"I see." Tony didn't believe him for a minute—his expression told him so.

"She knows, Tony."

Tony raised his eyebrows and tilted his head. "Knows what?" He took a swig of whiskey and sat back. "What exactly does she know?

"Elena knows I'm an agent. I don't know how she figured it out, but she did."

"Un-huh. And that surprised you?" Tony was usually decked out in black T-shirts, black slacks, a black silk shirt, and a black jacket. He always managed to appear to be mourning something. "I practically told her when we were at the Rusalka."

"No, you told her I was doing some investigating into the financial affairs of Briar Hill. Not that I was a special agent." Alex said.

"I see. I stand corrected." Tony didn't seem like he stood corrected about anything.

The place came alive with tourists back from seeing the nearby medieval town of Sighisoara and the Bran Castle or exploring the region's monasteries and breathtaking views. Ladies wore everything from designer jeans with sequined blouses to fancy dresses.

Several well-endowed girls at the next table stared at them with greedy, lustful eyes. They raised their glasses.

Alex ignored them.

Tony smiled, raised his glass, and went back to his conversation.

"Elena's one smart lady." Tony smiled into his glass. "She saw through your act because she loves you. If you can't see it, you're blind. So, now what are you going to do about it?"

Alex reached for the drink the waiter put down and took a swig. He needed one to face her again. He hadn't even remembered what he'd ordered. Conflict choked him, two alter egos battling for control.

But Alex didn't listen to the rest of the conversation. He blurted, "Okay, okay. I'll go back up to the room and—"

"Forget it. Here she is now."

Elena stood at the entrance with Mikhail, every male eye turned in her direction. Her movement full of elegance and grace, and, Alex thought, her head held a little higher than usual. She'd recovered fast.

Mikhail escorted Elena over to their table, grinned, and bowed in his white pants and white shirt covered with a tunic vest, the Transylvania's traditional male costume.

Alex couldn't take his eyes off Elena. Suddenly, he noticed all kinds of things about this lady whom, years ago, he'd dated, loved, and then hated.

"*Buna seara*, Miss Elena is beautiful, no?" Mikhail bowed, smiled, and skipped off to search for other ladies he could escort.

Kid's going to be a heartbreaker when he grows up. Alex thought about his own behavior towards women and suddenly didn't feel too proud of himself. *Like me.*

"Hi, Tony," Elena said. The two men stood. She nodded to Alex, sat, and then turned her attention to Tony.

Gone was the trademark braid. Her hair glistened. She'd pulled back the front and fastened it with a silver clip, tendrils curled around her ears, and framed silver hoop earrings. The rest of her black hair hung loosely down her back. She rested her left hand on the table, her ring showing off beautiful long, sensitive fingers. A sterling chain encircled her neck, while a silver cross with three ruby chips nestled just above her neckline. Alex had never noticed it before.

He felt flush and grew weak in her presence. He should have stayed in his room.

Elena and Tony were so full of chitchat and small talk, they didn't appear to notice his sudden discomfort or the beat of sweat starting to form on his forehead.

The familiar scent of gardenias hovered over the table. Elena's blue sultry enchantress's eyes lit her face as she discussed the Dkany Monastery pamphlet. Her smile radiated youth, vitality, and—God, help him—the sexuality he'd just rejected. No, this would never do. He pulled himself together and found her and Tony staring at him.

"Alex?" They asked in one voice.

"Oh, sorry." His gaze wandered from their prying eyes and focused onto a strolling troop of musicians playing Romanian folk tunes with their violins and guitars. They stopped at the table and appeared to be playing just for Elena. Their eyes never left her.

Eşti tu honeymooners?" One musician asked, shifting his gaze from Elena to Alex.

Elena nodded and replied in Romanian. *"I dragoste al tău muzică."*

The man gave her a broad smile, winked, and moved off to the ladies across the way.

A group of businessmen walked between the booth and the table, nodded, and preceded to another table close by. They, too, seemed to stare at Elena. Okay, okay. The girl was gorgeous. But every man in the place? Ridiculous.

Elena seemed not to notice.

When they finally got around to ordering dinner, Alex tried to give Elena advice about the Romanian food selections. Still, she knew more about the Romanian menu than he did. When the waiter stopped at their table to take their order, Alex became aware of the long time he lingered over Elena waiting for her to choose her entrée.

You don't even realize what you can do to a man.

His thoughts obsessed him. And as he stared, he thought he saw a shadow hovering over her. Not even a split second later, it vanished. He'd imagined the whole thing.

The overwhelming sense of loss and sadness blanketed him, which was becoming more and more a common occurrence since she'd walked back into his life. The wine swirled in his glass.

Alex shook off his demons and decided to enter the conversation. They chatted about the country, the mountains, and the Transylvanian people. Alex and Tony laughed about Mikhail and his way of having all the correct information at the right time, his ability to drive a horse, and his fantastic grasp of different languages. Quite a feat for a nine-year-old boy.

A nine-year-old boy—the sense of disquiet came over him again. Elena, he noticed, didn't laugh along with them. She watched Mikhail play the guitar with the musicians. "My grandfather played the guitar," Elena said. "Magda and I used to listen to him when I was little."

"Played classical guitar, didn't he?" Alex asked, remembering the evening soirees as kids when their families got together, played cards, and entertained.

Elena nodded without turning her head. "That boy is amazing."

Two waiters dressed like Mikhail brought their food.

A paprikash hendl, plump, tender, and right from the oven, complemented a steamy bed of wild rice and warm, dark Romanian black bread with a cheddar cheese spread. Local, regional wine provided an excellent accompaniment. Then came the Tuica wine tasting of warm and tangy rich plumes. Its smoothness soothed their palates. He wondered how she would taste if he kissed her right now. He didn't want the evening to end.

In reality, Alex was afraid to go back to the room and be alone with her. He'd have to take back everything he'd said.

Elena sat opposite Alex, listening to the words that came out of his mouth but sensing they meant nothing to him. They were up for a rough night. She'd thrown herself at him, a grave misjudgment. The longing still resided in his eyes when he didn't think she noticed, but he'd never admit it to her—*never.*

For the first time in her life, her feelings for a man truly frightened her. She probably should apologize for her behavior and go back to the sweats—or better yet, get her own room. No, they wouldn't let her be on her own.

Except for small talk at the beginning of dinner, Tony said relatively little to enhance the conversation. As the meal progressed, they'd said less and less. Tony hadn't looked directly at her, but he'd been glancing from her to Alex out of the corner of his eye. The restaurant was closing, and the bar started its nightly momentum when they got up to leave.

Visitors there for the summer festival gathered at the bar. Women flirted, men tried to score.

One person stood out by his absence. Stefan. The evening lost a certain amount of vitality without his quick wit and tales of Dkany. Several of the men turned in her direction as Elena walked by. Alex took her arm and held on.

Elena stood between Tony and Alex, waiting for the elevator as the businessmen from the other table approached. When she looked at them, they turned their heads, seemingly engrossed in their own conversation. Business talk. They weren't trying to flirt with her, far from it.

Still, the hairs on the back of her neck stood on end, and her body crushed closer to Alex.

Startled, he turned to look at her, then glanced at the men. His body seemed to tighten.

They were foreigners, two maybe came from the Middle East somewhere, one was . . . Chinese? The third, perhaps the Netherlands. They were dressed in expensive business suits and talked about the Romanian landscape. They made small talk about the small towns they would hit next.

They stared at her in such a way, Elena was sure they knew her. They spoke in a Mid-Eastern dialect, nodded to them, and pivoted toward the bar. Elena breathed a sigh of relief when they left.

"Everything is making us nervous, isn't it?" Tony asked on the way up. "Watching our backs, waiting for the moment when a member of this organization will recognize us. It's sick, living like this."

"I'll . . ." Elena replied. The sensation of the alarm at the root of her spine still hadn't left, and Elena edged backward against the elevator wall, tried to catch her breath, but it wouldn't come. Suddenly, hands pushed her head down, slapping pats on her back. Air seeped back into her lungs.

Then, someone said to get her into her room, and the next thing Elena knew, she lay on the bed looking up at Alex and Tony. She tried to rise.

Alex gripped her shoulders and held her in place.

"Hey, easy . . . come on now. It's going to be all right," Alex said. She wasn't sure he believed that, but she was glad he'd said it anyway.

"Those men, in the elevator . . ." she began.

"Yes?" Tony sat on the edge of the bed. "Did you recognize them?"

"No." Once more, she struggled to get off the bed.

Tony put up a hand. "Elena, don't get up yet. Tell me more."

"They kept staring at me through dinner. I think those men recognized me."

"*Everyone* was looking at you tonight, love," Tony said. "You look beautiful."

Elena blinked away Tony's remark. "No. You don't understand." She glared at them, hands on her hips. "It was the way one of them looked at me like I was a piece of live meat ready to be slaughtered." She shivered.

Tony's mouth opened, then shut. "That was graphic," he said. A frown crossed his face. His voice held a more authoritative tone and sounded more like a cop. "I think we should stay close tonight."

Elena caught the insinuation, and by the way Alex's mouth took on an unpleasant twist, he had too.

She saved Alex from escalating his already fragile emotional center.

"We're supposed to be married. We've got a gun, and neither of us is afraid to use it. Besides, there's only one bed in here, and I'm not sleeping between two snoring men. I'll . . . *we'll* be fine. Thanks for the thought."

Alex's fixed his eyes on her and held the gaze, then slowly nodded. There was more than an ability to shoot a gun in his glance.

Tony coughed and rose.

She felt the heat in her face and looked away. She said, "No, we'll be all right. Really."

Tony stared down at Alex as though he wanted a piece of him for breakfast. "Well, okay, but if you run into any trouble, you just come knocking." He shook his head as he got up to leave.

"Alex, don't you think—?" He stopped. "I don't think this is healthy."

His expression took on a mask of stone.

"What do you mean by that?" Alex asked.

"You know what I mean, Alex. I know you. I know your past." "What the hell?"

Alex looked back at Elena and dragged Tony out the door, leaving Elena puzzled.

"Explain yourself," Alex said, his mood veered sharply with anger.

Tony said, "I mean, Alex, don't do to Elena what you do to your other girlfriends. Play the love 'em and leave 'em, playboy. She does *not* need that. You're here to protect her, not mess with her head." Or her body went unsaid.

Alex clenched his teeth. "I know why I'm here, Tony. She is my wife. If we want to sleep together, nobody has the right to interfere. I'm not messing with her head." No. That role went to Elena.

"You're wrong, Alex. It is my business. I don't need any emotional complications that could lead to disaster. Nor does she need a broken heart."

Elena's heart doesn't break. She breaks others instead. Instead, he asked, "You really think I'd break her heart?" His white-hot anger smoldered into startled hurt.

"In a heartbeat. I've seen you do it. Without looking back at the damage. And let me tell you, you hurt Elena Dkany Brancusi, and I'll come after you."

"Tony, Elena might *be* involved. She grabbed a stack of letters that fell out of a book I was holding and stuffed it into her purse before I had the chance to see it."

"Yeah. So? Did you ask her about it?"

"This afternoon. I demanded to see it. She said she ate it."

Tony chuckled. "Maybe, Alex, it was personal. Had to do with things from when she lived in Bucharest. Something she doesn't want *you* to see."

"I think we need to investigate it further, though."

"So, go ahead. But you don't have to screw the lady to do it."

Alex was ready to pounce, but Tony had already turned his back on him and walked across the hall, opened the door to his room, and closed it without looking back. Alex watched the door slam, contemplating what Tony said. Had he really hurt that many women? He'd pick girls who were as footloose and fancy-free as himself. Women who wanted nothing more from him than a pleasant evening or two. The thought he'd actually hurt anyone by this had never, ever *occurred* to him.

Chapter 24

Elena's Bedroom, Sandor Inn

Dkany, Romania

Elena flopped on the bed after she'd showered and changed into a red cotton nightgown she'd purchased in Amsterdam. Pretty, but in a non-sexy sort of way. The only problem was the heat, and the ceiling fan couldn't circulate enough air.

She opened the sliding glass door that led onto the balcony. The mountains and trees formed shadows now. Lights twinkled from below and in the distance. A lovely evening. An evening for romance, but not for her. She turned back into the room.

This passing out thing was becoming a bit humiliating, as was the way he was treating her.

He was still attracted to her, but he didn't like her much. Yet he gave her his mother's ring. Well, he could just have that back along with his freedom once this was over. She took out an emery board and started to file her nails. Where had Alex gone when he'd shoved Tony out of the room? He didn't tell her when he returned. Probably discussing the letters, she reportedly ate. Now, she bet they thought she was a spy for the drug runners.

She checked her purse, just in case. Yeah. Still there.

She shut her bag as Alex came out of the bathroom, now in tight-fitting jeans, shirt open and flapping behind his broad chest. This was the Alex she'd known in high school. He reflected hair-roughened, almost olive skin, possibly due to lengthy periods in the sun. His muscular frame fascinated her. Did they all look like Alex and Tony? And how could Alex look so darn sensual and be such a jerk?

She scrutinized him. *Oh, man!* She had to admit the boy had a body that didn't quit. She'd have to remember how angry she was so she wouldn't try to get her hands on him again. No problem, she reasoned. He wouldn't allow himself within three feet of her.

Elena needed air—now. She slid off the bed, went back to the balcony, and stepped out into a hot, muggy evening to look over the darkening mountains and into the courtyard. The evening drizzle had already dissipated, but the skies promised more rain. Outside, everything was still. Deathlike. No voices, no chirping of birds, not even a cricket—why?

She thought she spied a shadow dart across the lawn, but no figure seemed attached to it. Her ghost?

The cotton rubbed against her nipples, shooting a warm sensation that ran straight down into her belly and gave her a sense of need she could never satisfy by herself. She didn't think the clown back there would either. All she really needed was a good cry.

The shot shattered her peace. A sudden icy fear knotted inside, and hands grabbed her from behind, pulling her backward and onto the floor. Pain stabbed her somewhere in her neck.

Grabbing the pistol from the nightstand, Alex looked her way, once, mouthing "keep down." He inched out onto the balcony, kept low, and stayed close to the opening. When he moved out of her sightline, she found herself holding her breath for what seemed an eternity. Finally, remembering to breathe and gasping for air, her heart started to pound, and her hands went clammy. A back spasm sent pain signals to her brain.

Alex edged back into the room, closed, and locked the balcony door. He laid the pistol on a wooden nightstand and blew out a puff of air. "Just a backfire. It's all right. I suggest we stay *inside*, though." He eyed the interior of the room. "Away from the door."

A silly and stupid move. She should have known better than to go out there when danger seemed to threaten from all sides. She waited for sharp criticism.

"Come on, let me help you up."

He grabbed both her hands and pulled her to her feet—a little too hard. She bumped up against him, her chest colliding with his. She had to grab his shoulders to steady her balance. His reaction was like he'd been thrown in a vat of boiling oil. His face went white, and he abruptly turned and walked away. Damn.

"Just out of curiosity," he said, "Why did you decide to go out on the balcony? You could have gotten ambushed."

There, it came. The self-justified scold. *Doggone it.*

"You said it was just a car backfiring," she replied. A muscle spasm hit her neck and intensified. She reached back and fingered an oncoming lump.

"Elena?"

Tears washed down her face in an involuntary movement, and now her hip felt like someone had punched it with boxing gloves. She limped back to the bed.

"You're hurt." He sat next to her.

"Yes. The fall, I think."

"Where?"

"Neck and hip mostly." So far. She circled the sore area of her neck. "You pack quite a wallop when you push someone over."

"It was only a car, but it might not have been. It could have been a trigger-happy killer."

"But it wasn't."

"No, it wasn't."

She turned to look at him, but the pain settled into the muscle, and she winced.

"Elena?" A gentle softness covered his tone. "Are you okay?"

"Yes. No, I think I just aggravated the spot where I got slammed the other night. And yes, it does hurt."

His brows drew down into a frown. "Sorry, I reacted without thinking." He surveyed the damage. "I shoved you pretty good, I guess," he said as he touched the back of her neck.

"You might have saved my life if it had been a bullet," she said.

"Thank God it wasn't. Please be more careful." He probed her neck gently with his fingers.

Elena pulled away from him and slid off the bed.

Alex raised his eyebrows, and his mouth turned upward into a smile. He patted the bed. "Please don't be afraid of me. I won't hurt you. I promise." His voice changed to a more reassuring, unaffected manner. Back to their school days again.

She sat back on the side of the bed. The throbbing acted as a catalyst through which all pressure, tension, and pain melted into one big cauldron. She began to cry. She hoped he thought it was the pain, but it wasn't. She'd lost everything she held dear and made an enemy of the man she loved. Too much for anyone to handle.

"Elena." He held on a little tighter. "I'm sorry for the things I said to you before. I don't know what got into me. I'm not usually this insensitive. I do care for you, you know?"

No, she didn't know. But she'd accept it.

"Thank you." She raised her hands slightly.

"Hang on, I'll be right back." He walked into the bathroom and came out moments later, carrying a hot and steamy washcloth. "This always worked for me when I wrenched my neck wrestling." He placed it on the back of her neck.

The warmth of the cloth flowed downward and started to relax the rest of her body if that were possible.

"Oh!"

"Good?"

She reacted. "Yes, very good. Thank you."

"Here?" He touched the back of her neck at the hairline.

She shook her head and pointed down, trying to bring her hand across her shoulders but couldn't succeed.

He moved his fingers around her neck to the affected muscles, massaging in tiny circles. This time he reached the tormented area.

When he touched her, her body jumped. "Alex, stop!"

"Shhh. It'll only hurt for a moment."

"Easy for you to say," Elena said, a glint of humor returning.

But Alex didn't reply. He kept on massaging, holding her firmly as he rubbed. She felt strong hands and fingers on her shoulders and back, and her body responded to his touch.

"You're so tense."

Yes, Alex, and you're the one who's making me that way. Damn, she'd hoped he wouldn't have noticed. Maybe he'd think it was just the pain.

"Hang on." He tried to get his fingers under the top of the robe, not enough room. "Elena," he said softly, almost a whisper in her ear, "Take off your robe so I can reach your muscles."

"You're sure you want me to do that?" Without waiting for a reply, she did. The robe floated behind her onto the bed. He sat so near, and his scent made her want to lean back into him, her hair caressing his cheek.

"I'm not going to do anything or touch anything I shouldn't," he said.

"I didn't say you couldn't."

He dug his fingers into her shoulder a bit harder than he should have.

"Ow!"

"Oops, sorry, too rough, I guess."

As the tension left her, his stiffness and hostility seemed to lift.

She wasn't looking at him, but she felt his energy. There was love left in the core of this man. She even detected a chuckle and relaxed.

Alex pushed the straps over her shoulder. His thumb dug deep into the muscles of her shoulders and back. While he dug, Elena pulled the straps down and off her arms. Being this intimate with him, Elena was hardly able to inhale. Her breathing flowed unsteady, erratic, shallow, and fast. Too close. His breath warmed her neck.

He massaged harder, banging on her back until she couldn't help stifling a laugh.

"What's so funny?" he asked, turning her to face him with a broad boyish grin. But the smile froze as he looked at her.

"Well," she said, her glance moving away from his, "You told me to take off . . ." She stopped in mid-sentence.

"Oh," Alex whispered, half to her, half to himself.

His reaction incited one in her. Shivers, causing goosebumps, careened down her spine and collided with smoldering heat rising from his flesh, sending desire down into her belly and below. She needed him . . . prayed he'd respond. Their eyes connected, and she knew he understood what she wanted from him.

"We can't." He whispered. But his eyes spoke the words his voice couldn't. They searched, asking her to tell him what to do. It was his moment of conscience—conflicting, emotional. He bit the bottom of his lip as though trying to take control, and she knew she had assessed him correctly. He needed her every bit as much as she needed him.

Alex took both her shoulders in his hands, then brushed the side of his hand against her cheek. She kissed his fingertip and held her breath—waiting.

"Baby girl." He took a strand of her hair and twirled it between his fingers before he touched it to his lips and let go. "We can't make love, Elena . . . we *can't*."

"I do want you, Alex. I can't help it. Whatever it is between us, whether it's love or just plain lust, I can't help the way I feel."

"Are you really sure you know what you're doing? Baby, there will be no turning back. Everything will be different. We'll never look at each other in the same way again."

His hands rubbed her arms from the shoulders down to her wrists, raising goosebumps on her skin. His eyes never left hers, like he was trying to probe unanswerable truths from deep down inside her, and maybe even himself.

"Do you really want me?" He whispered, so softly it sounded like his breath.

"God, help me, I really do," she whispered, her voice trailing off. Her breath came in a short and unsteady rhythm. She loved Alex Brancusi with every fiber in her body. And tonight, she'd let him love her. Damn tomorrow. She blinked away the dark shadow in the corner of the room.

Still looking at her with questioning eyes, he finally decided. He pulled the nightgown down to her waist, exposing her breasts to him, making her feel shy and vulnerable. Like she had in the back of his Chevy that June night. She made a move to do something—anything. He stopped her.

"Wait, I want to look at you for a moment." When Elena looked down and blushed, he took her chin and lifted her face, so they looked eye to eye.

"Elena, you don't have anything to be shy about. You're breathtaking. You've grown to be so lovely." He touched her breast gently with his fingertip. "But . . ." He stopped and shook his head.

Elena almost smiled, but Alex didn't give her a chance to answer. He moved in and claimed her lips, gently pushing her against his bare chest.

She gasped at the sensation and started to pull away.

"I hurt you."

"No," she murmured back to him. "You surprised me."

She thought Alex looked a bit taken aback, but the impression passed. First, running his hands through her hair, he kissed her. He tasted from an intoxicating tinge of fruity Tuica. She wanted more of it, more of him. She'd ached with longing and desire for him for so long, and she held on as long as she could before she came up for air.

"Alex . . ." She stroked his cheek lightly, allowing her heart to use her fingers as its medium.

"Alex, do you want to make love to me?"

He lowered his eyelids and slowly nodded. "You know I do."

There, at least he'd said it. That's all she needed to hear.

She allowed him to kiss her, part her teeth with his tongue, circle, probe, and examine her mouth before pulling back. He possessed her with dark, caressing eyes.

"Alex . . ." She needed to say his name, to watch his eyes love her.

"Are you sure? It's not too late to back off."

"Alex, I've never been so sure about anything in my life." Her voice cracked into a hoarse whisper.

She crushed her body against him, throwing both arms around his neck. She didn't want him to see her tears. She'd take what she could tonight, and if she lost him in the morning, so be it. But she didn't want to lose what little she could have.

"Elena. What's wrong?"

"Nothing, Alex. Not a thing."

She hadn't fooled him, though. Elena diverted his attention by placing his hand hard against her breast, holding it down.

Alex responded. This time, there was no gentleness about him. He removed his hands and pulled her roughly against him, kissing her so hard, it took the wind out of her. She gasped, and he released her. "There. I've wanted such a long time to do that."

"How did you like it?" She tried to sound light, and Alex caught on. He moved with her mood, quip for quip.

"I'd have to try again, just to make sure." He kissed her again. He nodded. "Better than the first."

Smiles locked again and vanished like a comedy turned drama. Alex took her hand and pulled her off the bed, kissing her on the cheek. Then, in a swift, exciting movement, he lifted her into his arms. She clasped her hands around his neck and kissed him before gently laying her back. He sat beside her, taking off his shirt and dumping it on the floor.

She felt more exposed and vulnerable and strangely excited when his hand caressed her cheek with his knuckle and turned it over. The tip of his finger skimmed the top of her neck down to her waist and back up again. His hands gravitated back to her breasts, teasing them, then finally moving away to find other ways to drive her crazy. She moaned from sensations never before experienced.

"Move over, love." His erotic, whispering tone sent a delightful shiver of wanting through her.

He sat next to her, bent over, kissed her, and pulled her nightgown over her head. Alex didn't move for a while but stroked her with his eyes, sending primitive spasms throughout her body.

"Elena . . ." The name floated in the air, a soft breeze in a garden of flowers, and she was the most delicate and beautiful flower of them all.

He exchanged fingers for lips and tongue, starting with her forehead, and moving slowly down to her neck and shoulder, then finally easing down again to her breast. The caressing movements of his lips as he captured her nipples and gently circled them with his tongue sent electrical vibrations through her. She could hardly breathe. He finally grasped the elastic of her lace white bikinis and pulled them down over her hips and off. As he gazed at her body, she thought she might die from the spasms of desire exploding within her.

His fingers started to explore those parts he'd missed. Alex appeared a master at the art of lovemaking, and she didn't feel she could ever live up to his expectations.

Alex, though, didn't seem to have expectations. He slowly undressed piece by piece. She started to sit up to help—to touch him. He shook his head, and she lay down again, watching him. As the last remnant of his outer shell came off, he turned down the wall lights, leaving only the small bed lamp and a dull yellow blaze, which flickered onto the walls, then dropped and danced on her body.

He lay beside her and ran his fingers through her hair and gently onto her cheeks. He shaped out the outline of her cheekbone with his fingers, then down to her lips, where he delineated their fullness and removed her remaining lipstick onto his finger. His lips sought out her neck and, for a brief second, Elena thought maybe he would bite down. An appropriate gesture in the heart of Transylvania.

Thank God she was lightening up. She was also losing her shyness as she reached for him and copied the manipulation of his fingertips. She fingered the hairs on his chest and lightly ran her fingertips around his chest and onto his nipples until she produced goosebumps on him.

Alex reversed his position, so he could move his hands directly onto her breasts, where they lingered, massaged, pressed, and squeezed her nipples so hard, her body shook. His handling of her was more aggressive and more demanding. He seemed to know exactly what he wanted to do and where he wanted to do it. Moving further down, he grazed only the very top of her skin until her body arched to him, reaching up for more. His hands stroked her belly, down the side of her legs, and over to her inner thighs. When he reached the warmth between her legs, there was no going back.

His finger entered her. One became two, and she arched her back to thrust him even deeper. But he pulled out and let go. She thought he was going to stop—to retreat.

Elena took control. She took his lips to her own, roughly pulling him on top of her. Together they rolled off to the side, Alex nearly fell off the bed. Elena grabbed him as he was about to go overboard.

He grinned and stopped. "Just a minute. I need something. Poking around in his bag, he produced a condom. Good, God. He was ready for anything.

"Where in the world? Did you think . . . ?"

"No. I didn't think we'd make love, Elena. But I hoped. I got this downstairs in the drug store."

Good. She was glad he'd taken precautions. She hadn't thought it would come to this, either.

Her hands sought him, tentative at first, then boldly down to feel the fullness of his arousal, she helped him put it on. She remembered the first time he'd entered her, how it felt. Tight, a pinch, then heaven as he'd plunged into her, and they'd fulfilled a driving need they'd had for a long time.

Alex maneuvered himself above her. "Wrap your legs around my waist when I go in," he whispered in her ear. "Ready?" He pushed her hair back from her eyes with his fingertips and bent over and kissed her eyes. He pushed his legs between hers, and she moved her knees apart to make way for him.

He entered her with a driving force, and she involuntarily cried out.

Without coming out all the way, he pushed back.

"God." He pushed her hair out of her eyes and kissed her.

She whispered, "It's been a while, but please, don't stop."

Yeah, it had been a while. The first and last time had been Alex. Jan had loved her, taken care of, and protected her. They'd even slept in the same bed together, but they'd never made love. Jan and Freddie had been lovers. No, she wouldn't tell that to Alex, either.

Alex started to protest, but she drew him back inside. In a few seconds, the pleasure obliterated any thought of pain. The rhythm of their movements fell right in time with the beating of their hearts. Each climaxed at different times, and each allowed their pleasure to ripple into the other. She'd never experienced anything like this before and probably wouldn't again—with anyone else.

She turned over on her side, away from him, not wanting him to see her tears—tears of joy, love, and memories of childhood and the baby they'd made nine years ago.

Chapter 25

Sandor Inn

Dkany, Romania

Alex hung onto her for dear life. He thought if he let go, he'd lose his lifeline. "Elena." He whispered her name and stroked her hair. For a budding moment, he thought—he knew he loved her.

"Alex." She snuggled closer.

The love in her eyes broke his heart, made him feel like the bastard he was. He hadn't expected this. Elena wanted him, yes, this he knew. But *loved* him? Now? After all these years? Had they both been in love forever and never gotten over it? Or was it mere words after tremendous passion?

His finger caressed the softness of her breast, the silver cross with ruby chips around her neck. Where had she gotten that? Better he didn't know.

He'd ached for this gorgeous, sensuous creature, whom he'd loved for so long. Now, he'd finally made love to her, and once again, his heart burst with animosity.

Why is that? He wondered. Why in the hell should we not make love? She's a beautiful, passionate, hot-blooded woman who's in love with me—and I'm *married* to her.

It made him even madder at himself that he couldn't think of any reason he shouldn't love her back. Just because nine years ago, she'd fallen for someone and married him instead? Why couldn't they make a life together now?

Because Elena challenged his unyielding pursuit for a life without love. A lifestyle caused by her in the first place.

Something else bothered him. Why had she grabbed those letters and not let him see them? Her secrecy tormented him again.

And professionally, he was wrong—dead wrong to have sex with a woman he was charged to protect.

Alex had lost his head and control over his feelings. Dear God. This was going badly. This whole thing was wrong, a betrayal of the job he had to do and a betrayal of her trust.

"Alex . . . ?" She reached up and touched his shoulder. Her scent and the sheer electricity rising from her rocked him to his core, and he felt aroused once more. He couldn't do this again.

With an inward sigh of regret, he got up and retrieved a sweat-suit from his backpack. He retreated into the bathroom, where he sat on the closed toilet seat, his head in his hands. God, did he need to regroup? Shaking off the last vestiges of remorse, he turned on the shower knob, as hot as he could, and plunged into the tub. Gradually, he rotated the dial over to the cold side as though he could purge himself from guilt until his body protested under the shock.

Elena wore her sweats and looked like a college girl rather than a siren from *The Odyssey*.

He didn't have a clue as to what to say next. "I shouldn't have let this happened." What a stupid remark. It had happened, and they'd both been willing participants.

She gave him a look of utter disbelief. "Alex. What do you mean, this shouldn't have happened? It just did. You must have feelings for me, with that much passion in your body."

Passion, girl. You're the only love of my life and my heart.

"Elena," he said, "you're an amazing woman. You know how to drive a man wild. That's not love. That's sex. There's a difference." He didn't want to say that old cliché. Elena knew very well the difference between raw sex and love. She'd chosen love.

He tried to touch her face, but she pulled away like he'd struck her.

"I know the difference," she said. "What we did wasn't just sex."

With a gentler, less harsh tone in his voice, he said, "Perhaps I thought it was something else. But it can't be for us. Elena, do you understand? It was a moment of mutual desperation." Why the hell did that come out of him?

The answer came as if she'd slapped him. "I've never been that desperate in my life, you *bastard.*" She spat out the words that resounded in hurt and anger. They stung and cut right through the middle of his self-righteous halo.

The knot in her stomach choked up through her throat into a sob. She felt a flood of tears flow down her cheeks.

"Elena?" Alex gently turned her around to face him. Elena jerked her head away, but her neck reacted with shooting pains.

"Damn it." She tried to pull off the bed and walk away, but he held her back.

"I'm not trying to hurt you," he whispered.

"Yes, you are. That's why you're here." The words flooded out of her mouth. "You and Tony are both trying to incriminate me from the beginning. But, one thing I know about you, Alex. That's your way with women. You use them to get information. Is that what you're doing to me?"

"Why do you think I'd . . . ?"

"If I'm so guilty of being a terrorist or drug mastermind, why is someone trying to kill me? Answer me that!" She pulled out of his arms and shot off the bed.

"I don't think you're a terrorist," Alex protested. His eyebrows furrowed into a frown, and he looked down. "I know you better than that."

"You were once my best friend. I know I hurt you. I'm sorry—please believe I had my reasons. Reasons I can't discuss with you." She struggled off the bed.

"Elena, damn it, then why can't you show me those letters?"

She turned on him. "So that was the reason you seduced me? Because you did. Nothing less. You wanted to get those letters out of me." Her eyes narrowed, and her lips tightened. "There's a place in hell for people like you."

Elena grabbed a handful of clothes, stormed into the bathroom, and slammed the door. Turning the knob toward hot and not getting a response, she realized the hotel had turned the hot water off. She needed that anyway and flung off her sweats, flopping on the floor of the tub. Water poured down from the top of her head, splashing off in layers, finding its way down the rest of her body. The noise from the shower muffled the sounds of her frustrated sobs. She let herself go until she didn't think she could force out anymore hurt.

While she braided her hair, she tried to decide what to do. Staying in this room would be impossible. She couldn't sleep with him, not now, not ever. She put on black jeans and a crewneck tee and pulled on two pairs of socks and hiking boots. He'd never let her out without following her, so she had to think of some diversion.

The letters. He wanted them so bad. They were her ticket out of the room. He'd needed sex and wanted information. She'd handed him sex on a platter. Well, now, she'd give him the letters too. No one could be hurt by them anymore—except him. Let him deal with *that*. She laced up the boots and got ready to face him.

When she finally came out, Alex was lying on his back, looking miserable, his head turned up toward the ceiling.

Alex's head snapped toward her. "Where do you think you're going?" His authoritative tone fueled her anger. She grabbed a blazer and stopped.

"Out. I'm not sleeping in the same bed—same room—no, the same country with you." She grabbed her jacket.

"Oh no, you're not." Alex shot off the bed.

Elena held up her hand, and he stopped. "You're going to stop me? Go ahead and try. I'm probably as good at karate as you are, and if you lay a hand on me, I promise I'll make sure you never have children again."

Alex's face paled. *Again? What did she mean by that?*

She thought more of the imagery. Alex could stop her in a second. She continued, "If you shoot me, you'll have to shoot me in the back because I'm leaving right now."

"Elena, wait," Alex said, softening his tone considerably. "Don't be stupid. You can sleep on the bed. I'll take the couch. You don't have to leave."

"No, I can't. I won't. Good night, Alex. I don't want to be around you anymore." She put her hand on the doorknob, stopped, and faced him. "For a while, I thought we were in this together fighting the good fight to find justice for the deaths of some very wonderful people. I believed you really wanted to protect me from these fiends—maybe you even *cared* about me. Loved me." Her voice cut the dead silence deafening the room. "But . . ." she banged her fist against her head. "Stupid me. All you wanted was to gather intelligence that would incriminate my family and me. Oh, yeah, and help yourself to another one-night stand. You're damned good at that." She gasped for breath. "I actually *fell* for it."

When he didn't answer, she reached into her purse. For a minute, his expression turned wary, like maybe she was planning to shoot him with a gun she didn't possess. No matter. She had a weapon a lot more deadly. She grabbed the letters from her purse. "You really want those letters? You deserve to see them."

Alex raised an eyebrow, then blinked. Yeah, he was confused—bewildered. Good.

"These only contain the letters of a young pregnant girl, who was dumped by the boy she loved. She couldn't tell him because he was already dating someone else. She wanted to protect her family from old-world shame, so she didn't tell them, either. She married a boy who cared enough to protect her and her child—instead of the father, who'd abandoned her like he's doing right now. You shit."

The anger and bitterness took hold more than any time she could remember. She aimed the pack at his head and pitched. After slamming into his face, they scattered onto the bed.

She had her hand on the door and turned to him, virtually spitting out her following, most vehement line. "You've really turned into a bastard. I hate you, Alex, more than I've ever hated anyone."

She opened the door and gave him one last parting shot. "Don't follow me. I'm going to sleep in Tony's room." She flipped a "drop dead" as she slammed the door.

"Elena!"

Elena walked down the hall. Out of the corner of her eye, she saw Alex open the door, stand in the doorway, and wait until she got to Tony's room. Blinded by tears, she didn't look back at him, somehow managing to make it to Tony's door. She heard the creak and click of the door lock. Elena breathed a sigh of relief.

Instead of knocking, she turned and walked straight to the elevator. She waited for a second in case Alex should come out again.

When he didn't, she swore. *What a pompous ass!*

Chapter 26

Sandor Inn

Dkany, Romania

Elena pushed the elevator button and, when it didn't respond, assaulted it until she heard its gears protest below.

Damn it, hurry up!

She kept her eyes fastened down the hall, waiting for the traitor to open the door, but he didn't—probably too busy reading her letters.

Now, he'd know the truth, the whole truth, and nothing but the truth, so help her God. She'd never wanted him to find out this way. She should have told him long ago, but it would have devastated him. There would be no point.

It wasn't as though he didn't deserve every bit of hurt the letters gave him. First off, he hadn't wanted her. His interest in their contents proved it. Second, he'd pried into her most personal life with the belief somehow, the information would incriminate her and her family as drug lords. She wasn't even sure what heroin looked like. How could she possibly sell the stuff?

And how could Alex have not told her he was a special agent who'd been working with Tony all along and not just a language professor. What a stupid pretense. Instead of protecting her, they'd been trying to uncover evidence to arrest her. She stifled a sob from his betrayal.

The elevator screeched to a halt, and the door creaked opened. Elena stayed rooted to the spot for another second before she shook her head, brushed the tears away from her face, and stepped inside.

When she hit the down button, the elevator jerked and descended, once again groaning until it slowly opened.

Tentatively, Elena stepped outside. Stefan stood by the elevator door.

"Miss Elena?" He frowned, and worry lines formed around his eyes. "What is the matter? You look like you have been crying? Is that the case?"

"Hi, Stefan. Yes . . ." She stifled a laugh. "I must look dreadful. I'm going to the lounge for a drink."

"No Alex? No Tony? Where are the gentlemen?" he asked.

"In their rooms, probably. In any case, I don't care where they are or what they're doing."

"Come, you need a hug," Stefan said.

"Thank you, but I don't feel like one just now," Elena said. She actually pulled off a smile.

"I understand. You need some time alone, I think. If you should need to talk, please feel free to come into my living room. I shall be there."

"You are very kind, thank you."

Elena stepped into an empty lobby. Oak and iron chandeliers dropped over seating arrangements set in front of two stone fireplaces on either side of the room. A sudden shadow spooked her until she realized it was the head of a moose displayed over the front desk. She forced herself to relax and walked into the bar.

As she entered through the swinging doors, loud, raucous laughter assailed her sadness that demanded solitude. There was such a thing as safety in numbers. Nobody would be as likely to attack while others stood around watching. The only empty booth resided at the far end, close to the corner. She grabbed it and sat.

She waited for a young waitress dressed in a Transylvanian peasant costume, not unlike the one that had unleashed her ghost.

How could Alex have made love to her? Made her think he loved her, then purposely betray her trust? She'd known what he was about. Marina had told her. Damn it. She'd wanted him to *love her*.

Did he honestly suspect Magda and her grandfather of being terrorists or drug kingpins? Had he returned to uncover evidence against his family's closest friends? Of course, he had. Tony said as much.

Another thought hit her. Could her family have worked for a mob organization? Or even worse, headed it? *If* the castle was used as a drug operation, then her family was indeed suspect. Freddie and Jan lived in the cottage. Heroin had killed Freddie. Her stomach lurched. Her family had never flaunted money, but she'd been left very well off. So, was it from the proceeds of drug money? No. Too bizarre. Now she was turning against her own—dead—family.

The waitress came with a pad and a puzzled, empathetic expression. Tears formed on Elena's cheeks again. She wiped them away with her fingers, tried to smile, and ordered a gin and tonic with a slice of lime.

The crowd swarmed the bar until it was invisible. Loud, cheerful voices filled the air with jokes and accounts of someone's hunting expedition.

Suddenly, the hairs on the back of her head rose straight up, and prickles as sharp as needles ran through her arms. The men she'd seen earlier in the evening stood with their backs to the bar staring at her. Her reaction to them made no sense. They hadn't done anything other than flirt. But something was different.

The gin and tonic with a slice of lime climbing over a goblet arrived on a napkin with the Romanian flag's blue, red, and yellow striped colors. Stefan certainly knew how to promote the ambiance of his inn.

As she sipped, she focused on the entrance. Part of her hoped Alex would have finished reading the letters by now and would come looking for her. The other part didn't ever want to see him again. Besides, he thought she was tucked away in Tony's room for the night. He wouldn't think about talking to her until morning.

Would he think she was sleeping in Tony's bed? *With* Tony?

That brought her to another question. Where *would* she sleep? Maybe the inn had a spare room somewhere, but she hadn't wanted to ask Stefan, so she wasn't sure who to ask.

"Maybe I sit?" The voice sprung from behind.

Elena's heart nearly burst out of her chest. She put both hands on her chest and blew out a sharp breath of air.

"Mikhail, don't do that! You scared the daylights out of me."

Mikhail didn't wait for an invitation. He laughed and bounced on the seat across from her.

"He-lo, my fair Princess Elena."

His what? He was nine. "What in the world are you doing here? It's eleven o'clock. Does your grandfather know you're awake? You're too young to be in here."

The grin never left his face. "I help. Now, my grandfather asks me to come to talk to you—keep you company. So, here I am."

"Does that include scaring me half to death?"

Mikhail's beaming face changed into a partial chagrin, then creases developed over the bridge of his nose. "Princess Elena, are you sad?"

Startled, Elena felt the residue of tears on her cheeks. She took her napkin, dunked it in a glass of water, and wiped off her face.

"Where is Mr. Alex?"

Elena shook her head. She was not going to have this conversation. "He's upstairs in his room. I came down alone."

"Did Mr. Alex make you sad?" Mikhail focused every bit of attention on her face. "If he not nice, I go yell at him." He grinned.

"Mikhail, I don't want to . . ."

"Sometimes I unhappy too." Mikhail placed one short leg on the bench and reached both arms around it. "I know about sad."

Curious, Elena looked closely at him. "What makes you sad, Mikhail?"

Mikhail bumped his forehead on his knee before looking back up. "I no have mother or father. Only my grandfather and aunt."

"What happened to your parents, Mikhail?"

Mikhail shook his head. "I do not know. They die when I was . . . baby."

"I'm sorry. That's tough." She knew how he felt. She brushed away newly formed tears for the loss of both their families.

Mikhail searched through his pocket. He pulled out a small pocketbook of American phrases, a long piece of string, a dead beetle, a flashlight, and a cell phone. From the other pocket, he produced a packet of tissues and pushed them over to Elena.

Elena suddenly got a case of giggles. She laughed until she almost cried again. The boy was adorable. She wanted to take him home.

"I make you laugh, yes? This is good?" He didn't sound too sure.

"I'm not laughing at you, honey. Just something about the way . . ." The way what? What was it about him that made her feel warm and fuzzy, made her want to laugh and cry at the same time? "Mikhail, where did your parents come from? Did they live here?"

He shook his head. "No. They come from Bucharesti. When they die, my grandfather takes me here."

Elena leaned over to take his hand, but her arm brushed against her drink. It started to fall. Mikhail leaned over and straightened it. As he did, a silver cross fell out from under his shirt—a silver cross with three red rubies running down the front. Jan's cross.

Oh my God.

Elena flew back against the seat, eyes wide. There he'd been all this time. The dark hair, dark eyes, familiar smile, and humor that made her laugh until she wanted to cry. The curiosity and native intelligence enabled him to speak many languages. She'd had her baby nine years ago.

She was peering into the eyes of her nine-year-old childhood friend, Alexander Brancusi—Mikhail was her *son.*

And that's what Jan's ghost had been trying to tell her all along. Mikhail was her child, and he was here.

"Oh my God, Mikhail. That cross." Elena dug out her own cross. Both the same—the same silver, the same ruby chips.

Mikhail's eyes widened. "How did you get . . . ?"

"I got this the same place as you did, Mikhail. This came from your . . . no, it came from your stepfather. Baby, you have to know, I'm your mother."

Mikhail's eyes got as wide as saucers. "No, not tell me this if it not true. Please, is true?"

Elena nodded. "Yes, it's true, Mikhail, and I'm happy it's you."

Mikhail leaned forward. "And you lady I saw in my dream."

That stopped Elena dead. She and Alex had seen this boy in their dreams. Now, Mikhail tells her he saw her in his dream. What the heck was going on?"

Chapter 27

Sandor Inn

Dkany, Romania

Alex stepped back into the room and slammed the door as though he could force out the guilt that wouldn't let go. His chest tightened as he looked at the letters strewn on the bed. He wasn't sure he wanted to read them anymore. He'd tried to humiliate Elena, and she'd turned the tables. And some tables they were. *Oh my God.*

Well, he'd see what those letters said. Maybe he'd pick up a clue to her feelings back then. Perhaps even his.

He sat on the bed and picked up the first letter.

Magda's handwriting.

Dear Elena,

I was so proud of you when you got that scholarship to the University of Bucharest. I will miss you tremendously, but Uncle Gregory's generous subsidy to the university couldn't be ignored. Living in Romania and going to the University of Bucharest will be an experience you will never forget.

I don't think a year apart from Alex will hurt either one of you. I noticed you two getting a bit closer than maybe is good for you. You came home very late from the prom. I fully expect you are still a virgin.

I am hopeful that someday you and he might marry. You must know Alex was raised in a strict, old-fashioned family. He'd never marry anyone with loose morals. His father was like that. Call me old-fashioned. I am and proud of it—and of Marina and Alex for their purity of spirit. And, especially of yours.

Love
Magda

Oh, Lord. The old guilt trip. He sat back on the bed and opened the second. His own handwriting shot into his line of vision. With trembling fingers, he read:

Dearest Elena,

I'm glad you got to Bucharest and are settling in. I miss you but have come to understand that it would be best for both of us if we were free to date others and go on with our separate lives. Who knows? You may want to stay in Romania and finish your education at the University of Bucharest. As for me, I'll probably go to Washington. Georgetown offered me a scholarship. I'll probably take it.

I've found a friend who's nice—not like you, but she'll have to do, I guess. You'll find someone else too, I'm sure. And, we'll always have our childhood and the prom. The night we both grew up.

I love you, Elena. Always have, always will. But this is best, at least for now. All my love Alex.

His heart stopped as he read the letter he'd sent to the girl he loved. He hadn't meant a word of it, and he'd lied about seeing anyone else. He'd thought he wanted the best for Elena, but not like this. His eyes burned as he pulled out the third letter—this one from Freddie.

Dearest Elena,

I'm so glad Jan and I can help you.

Help her? Had she just told him the truth?

Maybe we can all help each other. I realize Jan is not a replacement for Alex. Why he did what he did is, well, who knows? Maybe he figured it was better to be free than to be tied to someone living halfway across the world.

Know that you will always have Alex in the eyes of your child.

"No!" His voice echoed around the room before it came to a sudden stop.

He swallowed, and his hands turned clammy. The letter fell into his lap. Elena's baby *had* been his, not Jan's. She hadn't told him, but he'd known it, somehow. The sudden loss of a child he didn't even know produced a sudden misery that turned into physical pain.

He thought back to the birth certificate on the Dkany web page. What had been crossed out? The actual birth date? The baby had been born nine months after they'd made love in the back seat of his Chevy.

How could he have been so stupid?

He read on, angry at Freddie but more upset at himself.

If you were to go home now, Magda probably would accept you and the baby with open arms. She loves you. But the shock and disappointment of reality creeping into her ultra-Victorian world might break her already shaky heart. Your sacrifice for our grandmother's well-being must be heart-wrenching.

Her sacrifice for her grandmother's well-being?

As far as Alex, that's an even worse scenario. I have no doubt he'd marry you, but there would always be the realization he only did the "right thing." Married you out of honor. It would ruin his life and yours. If you stay here, you can have everything you need. If you went home, both of you would lose.

Alex looked away.

Elena's brother had convinced her to stay in Bucharest and not tell him Elena was pregnant. Damn Freddie. But deep down somewhere, Alex knew he'd been the cause. His letter had severed their ties so she could be free. No, so *he* could be free to date someone else. He finished reading.

Just know, Jan and I love you and will always accept you. You are the sweetest girl in the world. So, you made a mistake and got pregnant. Alex should have known better and worn decent protection. But that's over and done with.

As long as you don't make any physical demands on Jan, he'll be the best husband in the world, and I'll be Uncle Fred. You and Jan will come to live in the cottage, finish your education and be whatever you want. Suppose someday, you might want to marry someone else. In that case, I know Jan will let you go with his blessings and a little nostalgia that he couldn't be the husband you'll eventually want and need.

So, take care, baby sister. You will hurt for a little while. Better that than a lifetime of misery for the both of you.

Love
Freddie

Cold sweat swam out from Alex's internal emotional center. He picked up the next one and held his breath, almost turning blue before a spurt of air let loose—a reply from Elena.

Dearest Freddie,

Thank God for you being my brother. Magda now knows about the marriage. She was disappointed that I hadn't married Alex (if she only knew the truth). Still, she was ecstatic that I'd married a fellow Romanian in the Orthodox Church and would now produce a new generation of Dkanys. (Brancusi's—but let's not split hairs) She said she'd break the news to Alex. I should be the one to do that, but I'm glad I'm not. I couldn't handle saying the words my heart would deny, and if Alex heard my voice, he'd never believe me.

Oh, Elena. My God. He had to blink a few times before his eyes cleared. Then the words blurred. A tear landed on the page. He didn't want to, but his eyes were glued to the paper. He read on.

Jan's really understanding. He sat up almost three nights with me while I got sick and cried my eyes out. I'm not sure there's a tear left in my body. I miss Alex so badly, I can't even see straight. He was my best friend, and I loved, no love him. I will always love him to the day I die.

Jan misses you. We'll be moving to Dkany as soon as the baby's born and the semester is over. You're my brothers, as far as I'm concerned, and I love you both.

Elena.

My God! Jan and Freddie were lovers. That's why Elena didn't want him to see the letters. She was protecting Magda and him from Freddie and Jan's homosexuality and to safeguard his future.

If Alex had known about the baby, he would have moved heaven and earth to marry her, attend a local college, maybe even go to work. He wouldn't have thought twice about turning down Georgetown.

He'd cared so much about her; he'd freed her to pursue her dreams. Elena had been a passionate girl who'd given her heart and body to the boy she trusted more than anyone or anything. And instead of freedom, he'd given her hurt and rejection. And now they'd come full circle. A few minutes ago, he'd taken advantage of her love, reinforcing the antiquated ideas Magda imposed on her for years. Now she thought he'd made love to her so he could get the letters. And the only one who'd been hurt by them was him. She'd known and had tried to spare him.

Bile rose into the bottom of his throat.

The agony of truth hit him full force in the gut. Tony's assessment of him wasn't entirely wrong. He'd taken any willing girl to bed and moved on when he'd finished with her.

But Elena was wrong about one thing. He loved her. As much, if not more than when they'd been children in the backseat of his car. One thing he knew for sure. He had responsibility for her heart and her being.

Alex shot out of bed, scattering the letters. He grabbed jeans, boots, and a flannel shirt then called Tony's room.

Tony greeted him with, "What the hell?"

"Is Elena there? I really need to see her. Wake her if she's asleep." His breath came heavy, labored. He paced the floor.

"Hold on. Elena's not here." A deep intake of breath came through the other end of the room phone. "She's not with you? Why the hell not?"

"Maybe she went down to the bar. I've got to find her."

"What happened?"

"Later."

He grabbed the letters and stuffed them into his shirt pocket and ran.

Tony dashed out of his room, hopping on one foot to get into his shoe, and was on Alex's heels.

Chapter 28

Sandor Inn

Dkany, Romania

Mikhail relived the words he'd wanted to hear all his life. "Mikhail, I'm your mother." Stephan had told him his mother and father were dead, but here she was.

He didn't know how or why this wonderful lady happened to be staying at his grandfather's inn. Still, his Princess Elena, as he liked to imagine her, had just made him a prince.

He had a lot of questions, but his mother hadn't been able to hear them, let alone answer. She'd choked and couldn't continue.

"Please, Mikhail, let me be alone for just a minute while I think this through." His Princess-mother squeezed his hand before saying, "Please don't tell a soul about this, okay? We need to keep it a secret."

"But . . ."

"No. Dear Mikhail, I shouldn't have told you this. But, for now, do not tell a soul unless it's . . ." Elena furrowed her brow, trying to figure out if he understood. "Mikhail, *e o urgenta*. Do you understand?"

"Emergency?"

"Yes, good! Emergency, and then only tell Alex or Tony. Please promise me."

"My grandfather, too?"

"Only in an emergency. Now, please, honey, please wait here. I'll be right back."

Elena rose to leave. He didn't want to let go of her hand. She squeezed gently, and she felt like home.

Mikhail watched her go. Although he loved secrets, this was the biggest he'd ever had to keep. Nonetheless, when Elena went off alone, he followed her outside and skipped off the long wraparound porch. An immediate scent of pines and mountain air filled his nostrils.

His first thought was he hoped he didn't have to leave his beautiful mountains. His second, why had his mother left him? The third, what would his grandfather say when he found out? Who then was his father? How did this American lady know him? Had his dead father *really* been his father? This was a bit much for his nine-year-old brain to comprehend. His grandfather told him he was killed. But death was a new concept for Mikhail, one which he'd never had to handle. He'd seen a man shot, but he'd been taken away from the scene and never knew what became of him. He couldn't remember when he'd been a baby. His first memories were of his first birthday with Stefan, his aunt, and the hotel guests. The white cake and a frosted Romanian flag. He'd had one every year since.

Now that he found his mother, he wasn't about to let her go—ever. He would be her champion, her defender and protector against sad thoughts and bad people. When Elena insisted she needed to be alone, Mikhail clung to her hand, almost pulling her back.

He followed at a distance, watching his mother stop in the grove of pines where picnic tables faced the mountains and the river. There she sat with her head buried in her hands.

Ducks from the river waddled to her feet and investigated. When she didn't throw them breadcrumbs, they shuffled back to the river and swam off.

As Mikhail came closer, he noticed a black Mercedes hidden among the trees. Two men snuck up behind her, but she didn't seem to notice. He wanted to cry out, but the words froze in his mouth.

One of the men pulled out a cloth from a bag he carried and covered her nose and mouth. Elena reacted too late, and she slumped into the man's arms.

Mikhail ducked under the porch, watched them carry Elena into the car, and silently backed out of the grove.

Mikhail remembered a TV movie where the bad guys knocked someone out with a cloth just like the one they had. Now Mikhail was in the middle of a real adventure, where his mother, the Princess Elena, was in the villains' hands. It was up to him to inform the King and to help rescue her.

He dashed up the porch steps into the inn and through the office, looking for his grandfather. In the living room, the cuckoo clock clucked eleven o'clock—stupid bird. No grandfather.

He pushed the elevator button but got no response. Somebody was probably holding the dumb thing.

He dashed up the stairs full force looking at the steps until something stopped him, and he nearly fell back down the stairs. Two hands grabbed his shoulders and broke his fall.

"Mikhail! What the . . . ?" The men he needed to see, his mother's prince—Mr. Brancusi and his sidekick Mr. Donatelli.

"Mikhail, what's wrong? Why are you in such a hurry?" Alex asked.

It took a moment for Mikhail to catch his breath, and when he did, his body shook, and he started to cry from the shock of discovering his new mother. All he could utter was, "I lose her."

"Huh?" Alex said. "Who have you lost?"

"My *mother* and now she gone. She cannot go away again."

"Lost your . . . ? What are you talking about, Mikhail? You said your mother was dead."

"I thought she was, but she is not." Mikhail stamped his foot.

"Princess Elena is my mother, and somebody grab her."

Alex's reaction was a bit much for Mikhail. He turned white and backed into the wall.

"Your . . . Elena is your *mother?*" Alex took him by the shoulders and said, "How do you know this?"

Alex's reaction shocked Mikhail into backing away from him and into Tony. He jumped forward. "She tell me. We have matching crosses. See?" He pulled out his cross.

"Oh my God!" Alex said.

Tony's jaw dropped open. "Holy shit," he said.

Alex took Mikhail by the hand. "Shhh, son. Come on upstairs." He motioned to Tony. "We're going to your room," Alex whispered, pushing Mikhail ahead of him.

Tony opened his mouth, shut it again, and followed.

The hallway was deserted, but the laughter from the bar still made its way up three flights. The sound ceased altogether as the door shut. When Tony flipped the light switch, he put his fingers to his lips.

Alex walked to the window and peeked through the curtain. Nothing. Just shadows from the porch light and outside lanterns. He turned back to face Tony and Mikhail, his insides bristling with fear.

"Tony, you said Elena was not in your room. Then where the hell is she?"

"That's what I was hoping you'd tell me."

Mikhail pulled on Alex's sleeve. "I know." He slapped both cheeks with his hands. "Oh no!"

"Oh no! What?" Alex asked.

"I promise not to tell anybody. I promise . . . but somebody take her—she gone." Mikhail paced the room.

The two men looked at each other and shrugged.

"Mikhail, you just said Elena is your *mother*?" Alex stopped Mikhail's walking and put his hands on his shoulders. "Is that true?"

Mikhail raised his eyebrows and nodded. "She think is true, then I think is true." He pulled out his cross again. "See?"

"Yes, I see," Alex whispered. "Oh my God, I see." He remembered seeing the same cross around Elena's neck and wondering where she'd gotten it. "That's the same as Elena wore."

If Mikhail claimed Elena was his mother, then the vision, dreams, and letters were true.

Elena had been pregnant when he'd sent her that letter of good-bye. A stupid kid trick trying to make her feel guilty about leaving. It backfired—big time. But that also meant Mikhail Baklanov was his son. The thought filled him with a keen sense of joy and overwhelming responsibility.

Tony shouted, shattering Alex's revelations. "Damn It, Alex—" He stopped when he looked at Mikhail, who'd fallen onto the bed, his mouth wide open.

He softened. "Sorry, Mikhail. I didn't mean to scare you. We need to know where she went."

Mikhail began to talk, and Tony turned his back on Alex and listened. And while Mikhail told his story, Alex couldn't take his eyes off the boy and his reflection in the mirror. His eyes, his hair, even his expression. Him, when he was nine. Why hadn't he noticed this before?

He suddenly became nervous as hell. If anything had happened to Elena . . . He winced as Mikhail mentioned how unhappy Elena had been. She'd told him she was too upset to talk. She needed to step away, to clear her mind, to think things through. Mikhail said he followed her outside and down the path toward the pine grove, then ducked under the porch when he'd seen two men.

"Two men?" Alex's stomach turned over. "What two men?"

"Men I see at a restaurant tonight."

"Did she appear to go with them willingly?" Tony crouched down at Mikhail's eye level.

"Why would she do that? She just found *me*!"

Tony rose, and Alex noticed an undercurrent shaking inside him.

Mikhail shook his head told the rest of the story.

"Chloroform," Tony said. "The crudest anesthesia outside of knocking someone over the head."

"Damn it," Alex said.

Alex sat on the bed and pulled Mikhail closer to him. He wanted to ask who his father was but decided against it. The boy had been through too much already and probably didn't know. Inside him, his stomach crawled with an emptiness that couldn't be erased. He already knew who fathered Mikhail.

Alex's mind reeled with emotions out of control. He felt the blood drain from his face. He waited until Mikhail ended his story, then watched their faces change as he looked at them.

"What?" Tony asked. "Besides losing Elena to the bad guys, what the hell else is wrong?"

Mikhail bounced off the bed, and the cross dangled out of his shirt.

Alex's glance gravitated back to the cross. Mikhail grabbed it and stuffed it back into his shirt.

"I'm not trying to take it away. I just want to know where you got it."

"I always have it. Since I was little."

"Mikhail, go across the hall and see if Miss Elena is back in the room. Would you do that, please?" Alex asked. He handed Mikhail the key. "I need to talk to Tony."

"Okay."

When Mikhail had left the room, Tony frowned and shot Alex a glance. "What the hell?"

"Tony," Alex said, "Mikhail is my son."

"So I gathered." Tony had one hand on his hip, his other balled into a fist, the usual stance of a one hell-of-an angry Tony Donatelli.

"So, lover boy, talk. How did she get into this mess? Where the hell did she go, and why?"

"Huh?"

Tony pushed Alex down on the chair and put one foot up next to his surprised body.

"Why did Elena walk out on you?"

Alex drew a deep breath and stalled. Explaining wasn't going to be easy. "I'd rather not talk about this. We need to be looking for her, not wasting our time—"

"Wasting our time? Is that what we're doing? I want some information—some stuff *you've* been holding back, and I want it *now*. Maybe then we can get her back." Tony's glare penetrated somewhere through Alex's skull. "What the hell happened?" Tony persisted.

"Elena and I had a disagreement, and she stomped—"

"About what?"

Alex shook his head and avoided Tony's eyes.

"Dammit, Alex. You slept with her." A shadow of annoyance crossed his face, blending with the shades formed from dim light.

Alex's anger started to rise. "It's none of your damned business what I did with my wife tonight," Alex answered.

"Elena is your wife in name only, if I remember the arrangements." Despite Alex's attempt at protesting, Tony went right on. "And yes, it is my business. The United States Government's business. This is a kidnapping investigation. Elena's an American on foreign soil. I put her into this situation as a decoy, and she agreed to help. Damn it. I trusted you to protect her, to act professionally.

"You have somewhat of a reputation with women, Alex, as being something of a shit. I hope you didn't pull out your slam-bam-thankyou ma'am school of romance."

Alex closed his eyes to distance himself from the truth. He'd come across exactly like that. "I've never hurt any of the women I dated. They all knew."

"That you know of. I happen to know differently. I was the one they came crying to after you ditched them. I know you, Alex. You're so scared and frightened of commitment you don't know what's coming out of your mouth half the time."

"Not this time," Alex responded slowly, guilt rising in his conscience. If he'd hurt anyone, it had been because he'd never gotten over the one woman who'd captured his heart and soul a long time ago.

"Elena thought I'd . . . uh . . . wanted to sleep with her to gain access to those letters she found in the cottage. She threw them at me and bolted." Alex sighed, a frown masking the self-contempt he felt. "The letters contained personal family information. Information where I discovered Elena's son was mine, not Jan's. That's why I came banging on your door to find her. But that's between her and me."

"Oh great, just great," Tony said. "No, this isn't just between you and her. Look, five hundred kilos of heroin are scheduled for shipment into New York in the next few days, and I don't know where it's coming from or how it's being shipped. Elena might hold the key, and now she's gone." *Because of you* was left unsaid.

"So, you think she's involved."

"I think nothing of the kind. I think *you* may be involved. You were friends with the Dkany family. They might have pulled you into it. They've had a major stake in the castle, so why not?" Tony yanked him out of his personal catharsis. "So, Alex," he said, "are you secretly working with her family's solicitor trying to get the castle transferred over to yourself?"

"That's a hell of a thing to say, Tony."

"Yes, it is, and if it's true, I think you'd screw Elena to get what you want."

"Son of a bitch!" Alex lurched at Tony, momentarily knocking him off his feet. Still, Alex was no match for Tony's years of combative instincts and training. Alex got off a good blow to his jaw but found himself whirling off balance. A cowboy boot slammed him onto the ground, the heel coming down on his chest. Alex was looking up into the barrel of a pistol.

"So, should I assume you're tied up with this heroin business, Alex?"

"Wait a minute, damn it." Alex struggled to stand up, but Tony wouldn't remove his foot. "Tony, get your damned foot off my chest." Alex tried to move again, but still, the foot was immobile. He struggled for air, and Tony let up, just enough for him to breathe. "I didn't . . . don't think you'll believe one damned word of what I'm going to tell you, this story is so out in left field."

"Try me, Alex. I'd thought you'd trust me by now." Tony removed his foot, and although he didn't holster the gun, at least he pointed it away.

Shaken, Alex got to his feet and stood. He looked out the patio window at the stars struggling from a marauding band of clouds.

"So, tell me," Tony said.

The earth seemed to stand still, and except for the rumbling thunder, Alex heard only his own voice, which came from an echo chamber far away. "You knew about my relationship with Elena in high school."

"Of course."

"I sent her a letter releasing her from our commitment to each other. I wanted her to have fun at school. It backfired."

Alex proceeded to tell him about the sequence of events in the letter and the ghosts of Magda and Janek, including the one he actually saw.

"Ghosts. Jesus, Alex." Tony whispered. Tony's stare washed over Alex until it left and focused on the river. "I don't know whether to believe you or think you and Elena have gone over the edge." Tony shook his head. "When did you start believing her story?"

"I've never been a believer in ghosts, but how can I not believe? I've seen it. Saw the shambles it created in our room, leaving only the Sandor Inn brochure on the dresser. I know he's using Elena as a medium to show us the way. I know something else as well."

"What?"

"Janek Ivonov killed Hadean Petrov."

"What? How? He's dead."

"Elena didn't think anyone would believe her, so she made up the story about him tripping. Jan's ghost threw the bastard down the stairs. She told me at the lodge before he, or it, decided to destroy our room."

"Our room . . ." Tony said, his voice trailing off. "You weren't staying in the other bedroom?"

Alex turned and stared at the man. "Be careful, Tony. My bed broke, there was no other room."

"Yeah, right. So, tell me about tonight." Tony's voice became soft and gentle but candidly to the point. "So, you slept with her tonight. And . . ."

Alex sighed. "What's the use denying it?"

Contempt showed through Tony's eyes as the moon finally broke through the clouds, shining in through the sliding doors. "All right then, go on. Then what happened?"

Alex remained silent, not knowing how much to tell him. What had been the happiest moment in his life was sacred, not exposed like dirty laundry.

"Look, why can't you trust me with the truth? We're supposed to be on the same side."

Alex ignored the question, brushed himself off, and rubbed his bruised knees.

"You pack quite a wallop," Tony said, chuckling and rubbing his jaw.

"I'll never be a match for you," Alex replied, his lips slipping into an almost-smile.

"Yes, you will. I'm old and worn out. You're just beginning. But, Alex, you must learn to trust your partner. The past plays an essential role in this case, and your relationship with Elena is a key component. I wish you'd told me before you were in love with her."

His gaze penetrated through Alex.

"I care about her, but love? I don't think so."

"You just keep telling yourself that. Your feelings for Elena have ruined every relationship you've ever had."

All Alex could do was nod his head. "Okay, okay. You're right. I didn't know myself until tonight. But some things are just not meant to be."

"Love," Tony said. They watched the dark flow of the river and the shadowed outlines of the mountains. "I knew there was more to your involvement with Elena than a simple attempt to help her reach the castle without getting killed."

So, there it was. There had been more to Alex's determination to take Elena to Romania than just helping the United States government. Had he known from the beginning? Maybe so.

Tony said, "I believe Elena is in the castle, and I think her 'Uncle' Gregory Balogh is involved up to his ears. Everything that's happened is tied together in one untidy package we haven't quite figured out. But one thing I'd stake my life on."

"Yeah, what?"

"Elena is there, and Gregory Balogh, if he isn't there now, will be by tomorrow night to help persuade her to sell the castle to them. That's why there are so many non-tourist types descending upon Dkany. They'll be at the castle, too."

Mikhail jumped into the room, grinned, and threw his arms around his father's neck. "I knew you believe me! You are my American *dad!*"

"Oh crap," Alex said. "How much did you hear?"

"Not much. Just something about drugs, castle, bad guys, and my mother. Then you have a fight. Now we get her back, yes?" Mikhail asked.

Tony grinned.

"Yes," Alex said, holding him and rumpling his hair. "Now we get her back."

Where had they taken her, and how to get her back?

Tony pulled out his cell phone.

Chapter 29

Sandor Inn

Dkany, Romania

Alex and Tony hiked down a path toward the grove. Mikhail tugged Alex forward and refused to let go of his hand. Pine needles crunched under their weight.

They stopped under a gas lamp, and Tony's face was grim. He whispered to Alex, "If you and Elena are Mikhail's parents, I wouldn't make this known to anyone. Too dangerous for Mikhail and you. I'm not sure why but trust me. I don't think it's a good idea." Tony's black sweatpants and black T-shirt blended in with the darkened background, revealing him as almost an outline.

"That is what my *mother* said." Mikhail gave a tense nod of consent to the suggestion.

"Hey," Tony said. "You weren't supposed to hear that."

"I know. I promise not to tell anybody . . . except in 'mergency." His lips turned down. "But I tell you."

"You did the right thing," Alex said. "You had no choice. Your mother won't blame you."

"Oh! It 'mergency?"

"Yes, it's an emergency."

His frown turned into a grin. "Then, I . . . happy."

Many small dark-gray clouds floated in from the west and tried to expand themselves into rain clouds. They obliterated the moon, and the sky filled a gray-on-black canvass.

"She go there," Mikhail said, pointing towards a picnic table. Mikhail stumbled over a root and nearly brought Alex down with him. Alex regained his balance, steadied Mikhail, and walked over to the picnic table that dominated the grove's center.

Alex spotted it first. Elena's handbag lay next to the bench. On a neighboring leaf, he found their room key.

Mikhail bent over, picked it up, and handed it to his father. "Look." He showed Alex the key. The printed number read 218.

"Oh crap," Tony said. "So, it's true, then."

"Is true," Mikhail began, "But, I forget to say," Mikhail began, looking from one man to the other. "I know . . ."

"What, Mikhail?" Tony had been checking the ground but stood straight up and addressed Mikhail. "What did you forget to say?"

"I know car."

Tony arched his eyebrows. "Car? What car?"

"From here." Mikhail pointed around him. "Men drive to town in afternoon. They stop for drink, in bar."

"He's allowed in the bar?" Tony asked.

"His grandfather owns the bar," Alex replied. "Mikhail helps around and provides entertainment."

Mikhail beamed. "I make friends with all guests."

"I'll bet you listen in on conversations, too, don't you?" Alex stooped to Mikhail's height.

"Yep." Mikhail nodded as he looked on the ground for further evidence of Elena's presence. "I am not supposed to, but I do." He brushed the leaves. Nothing. Mikhail rose and Alex with him.

"Did you listen in on their discussion?"

"They talk low, so I could not hear everything. They mention castle."

"Mikhail, very *good*." Alex's mouth curved into a widened approval, triggering Mikhail's self-satisfied grin. "What else did you hear?"

"They say nobody could find somebody in castle, even if they look. It so big." He widened his hands.

"So, you think that's where they took your mother?" Alex asked.

Mikhail nodded. "I sure."

"Why are you so sure?" Tony asked.

"Because they say so. I sit in next booth. I hear. These men say something about a lady. She called Bella Dkany. She lived long time ago. She has bedroom in castle."

"Very good, Mikhail. Very good."

"We're going up there. Now." Alex said. "We have to find her."

Tony nodded and thumbed his goatee. "Yeah. We could do that. I'm sure that's what they'd expect. Do you honestly think she'll be having cocktails in the library waiting for us to rescue her? I doubt it. That castle's so big, we'll never find her room without help."

"Stefan and Zsophia know where it is," Alex said.

Mikhail said, "And I know too. I help."

"Wait, Mikhail." Alex sighed, and he gazed at the ground, his heart pounding like a fist slamming into his chest. "Tony, this is my fault. I've got to get her out of this."

"No, *we* have to get her out of this."

"I come help?" Mikhail repeated.

"No, son," Tony said. "I don't think this would be a place for you. These are some bad men."

"Bad dudes?" Mikhail asked.

"Very bad dudes," Alex replied.

"But . . ."

"No buts," Tony said. "You stay here, Mikhail. We'll find her."

"But . . ."

A shadow covered the path, and a sudden flash of light beamed into Alex's face. Stefan.

Stefan glanced from Alex to Tony and demanded to know why Mikhail was out there and what had happened. His light beamed in Alex's face.

Alex had to glance away to avoid the glare.

Mikhail tugged at Stefan's coat sleeve. "Princess Elena has been kidnapped! She missing—just like in movies." Mikhail explained about the kidnapped American lady.

Alex put his hand on Mikhail's shoulder. "Earlier, Elena ran into two men in the elevator she thought recognized her. They'd been in the restaurant, but I don't know who they were. Mikhail said he'd seen a black car here this afternoon and heard two men mention the castle. Could be where they have her."

Stefan frowned and shook his head. "Possible, perhaps, but Gregory hosts gatherings to show off the place for enthusiasts who pay to see the famous castle. He told me the proceeds go for its maintenance. If she were brought there, Zsophia would know. I'd know."

The wind rustled through the trees, and the scent of rain permeated the area. A chill broke through Alex, and he wasn't sure it was the weather or his dread for Elena.

"But kidnappers?" Stefan shook his head. "My sister works at the castle and has never seen evidence of intruders. Gregory Balogh has never mentioned people of the sort you describe. And since he is not there, I doubt there will be such a gathering."

Stefan continued, "And, if they did kidnap Mrs. Brancusi, why would they take her to a place where everyone would look? The *first* place anyone would look."

Stefan turned to Mikhail. "Are you positive they said they took her to the castle?"

"Yes." Mikhail looked at his grandfather and shrugged. "Almost positive," he added and looked at the ground.

Almost positive?

Stefan looked at his grandson, and his lips turned upward into a smile, but a brief hint of mockery shifted in his eyes. It left so quickly, Alex thought he'd imagined it.

"Sometimes Mikhail lives in a world of his own. Such mystery and drama are the histories of Dkany Castle. Mikhail likes to play there, and he makes up stories. There is no reason to believe Mrs. Brancusi was forced to go up there. Maybe she left with somebody she knew?"

"No, she did not want to go with them," Mikhail insisted.

Stefan said, "Mikhail, you do not know this." He turned to Tony and Alex. "I suspect if someone took your wife, they would not bring her to a popular tourist spot."

Alex raised his eyebrows. "Yeah, but it's so big, who could find her?"

"Perhaps. That might be true," Stefan said.

Tony moved further into the grove and appeared to be looking for something.

"You might want this." Stefan handed him his flashlight, and Tony beamed it down on tire tracks.

"If Elena were going with someone she knew, she would have met them in the parking lot, not in the trees." Tony shook his head. "Well, maybe we'd better go up there and look around."

"And me too?" Mikhail asked, stopping Alex in his tracks.

"No," the three men said simultaneously.

"But I know where she kept," Mikhail said.

"No, Mikhail," repeated his grandfather.

"Wait, Alex," Tony said, pulling out his cell phone. "We're going to need additional help. If she's at the castle, there will be guards waiting to ambush us."

"And who are you that you know so much about what might happen?" Stefan spaced his words evenly, cold, and exact.

Tony pulled out his credentials and held them against the gas lamp.

Stefan shone the flashlight beam on them. "I apologize. I did not bring my glasses. Ah. So, you work for the United States Government?" A sternness edged into Stefan's tone.

"Yes, Mr. Baklanov. I've been watching this castle for some time."

"What for?" Stefan asked with increasing impatience. "You think we harbor terrorists here that will threaten your country? You have found evidence of these illegal activities?"

"No," Tony replied. "I have not."

Stefan shook his head. "I do not think you will because I do not think anything illegal takes place there. Gregory Balogh runs . . . how you say . . . a tight ship. No uninvited guests are allowed, unless with a tourist group. Dkany Castle, after all, is a family treasure. What happens to the castle affects all of Dkany."

"Is that why Dkany wants it back so bad?" Alex asked.

"Ah," Stefan offered a polite smile. "Yes, the husband. The new inheritor in case something should happen to Miss Dkany—excuse me, Mrs. Brancusi. Yes. That is the reason. We should not want to see a developer get his hands on this and turn it into something it should not be."

"So, you don't think Gregory Balogh is responsible for her kidnapping?"

Astonishment touched frown lines in his face. "You think Gregory Balogh is responsible for this?" His eyes grew wide, and he appeared stunned at the suggestion. Finally, when he'd gained his composure, he said, "I would doubt Mr. Balogh would do anything to hurt the Dkanys or the castle. He has lived his life protecting it."

"But what if . . ." Alex started to say.

"Should he be involved? I doubt he will kill anyone today. As I said, he is not in Dkany at the moment. He is not expected to return for a few days."

"So, why should anyone be up there? And why kidnap Elena tonight?"

"Nobody should be at the castle tonight. My sister was there this morning, as you know. If anyone came, she would have informed me. She said Mr. Balogh went into Bucharesti. Anyway," Stefan continued, "a black Mercedes was spotted leaving Dkany about an hour ago. Headed out of town. The opposite direction of the castle."

"Oh no," Alex said. He shook his head. "Oh no."

"So, we involve the local police," Tony said. "You do have a police force here in Dkany, don't you?"

Stefan opened his arms in a gesture of frustration. "A police force of four. They usually take a long time to respond."

"I called the American Consulate and the FBI office in Bucharest and a few other people. Maybe we can negotiate to get her back." Tony said.

"We don't . . ." Alex started.

Tony jostled his elbow. Alex shut up.

"Yes. I will call the police now." Stefan put his hands on Mikhail's shoulders. "You make sure Mr. Donatelli's car has gas, yes?" He turned the boy toward the inn's garage.

"But—"

"No buts," his grandfather said, leading the boy in the direction of the garage. "And, then you go to bed."

Mikhail shook his head and mumbled something Alex couldn't hear. His cell phone rang. Alex scrambled to get it out of his jeans pocket, flipped the lid, and answered. "Alex?"

"Mari?"

"I'm coming to Dkany."

"No!" Alex said. "Don't come. Look, Elena is missing, and it would be too dangerous for you."

"Missing? What do you mean missing? Never mind. I'll find out soon enough. I'm already in Romania, and I'm on my way."

Just then, the earth rumbled. Alex fell into a nearby branch, Mikhail went to a legs-apart stance, Stefan fell onto the ground, and Tony fell onto a tree. It lasted only a second, but the tremor caught Alex off guard.

"Wow," he said. "So, this is Dkany's famous earthquakes. Can't imagine it doing much damage."

"No," Stefan said, "But this is only a minor quake. Wait until you face a big one. We all have. It knocked part of the castle down."

"Oh," Alex said with a shudder. He didn't think he'd like it.

"No, you, Mikhail. You go and fill their car with gas, then go to bed!"

"*Ja Bunic*," Mikhail said and trudged his way toward the garage.

Alex became aware of the clouds scurrying off to the west. The light of a full moon engulfed their immediate vicinity. It shone on Tony's expression—his face full of anger and worry.

Stefan greeted the police like family members, which they all were— first or second cousins and one nephew. They discussed the shaking ground for a minute. Earthquakes seemed to be a favorite topic of conversation among the townspeople. Many small quakes had shaken up the town lately and caused more damage to the castle and monastery.

"Stefan," Alex said as they walked around the reception desk and into his living room. "Why is your entire police force related?"

Stefan smiled and almost broke into a laugh. "Most people in Dkany are related." He explained nearly everyone in Dkany was now related because of the decimation of the town's population during Ceausescu's regime. Only those who could convince the authorities they were pro-government and could afford to bribe the officials had been allowed to remain in their town. The others had been forced into government housing units in Bucharest. A long time ago, long time repercussions.

Alex nodded. He understood—had studied the Ceausescu and communist regimes. Dark days for all back then.

Once settled, the police took their statements while sipping on a glass of what one of the cousins described as Uncle Stefan's most excellent Tuica.

Alex was about ready to strangle them when they finally focused on business. One officer took a description of Elena but gave the impression he thought she probably had run away with some boyfriend or other.

"That man there," Tony said, pointing to Alex, "is her husband."

"Ah," the policeman said, with an expression that implied, *So sad. She cheats on him.*

That's all Alex needed to hear. Though furious, he forced himself to show an outward calm, his hope for any competent police help all but shattered. He caught Stefan's eye, but the innkeeper shrugged. The police acted as if they didn't like the Dkanys much and really didn't care what happened to any of them. Alex wondered why. Another mystery unfolding.

As he started to say Elena was in the castle, Tony shook his head and gave him a stern, 'be quiet' look.

Alex wondered about Tony's attitude and why he didn't take charge when Tony pulled out his cell phone and disappeared from the room.

Alex was perplexed. Instead of talking, he kept still, observing. The keystone cops were idiots, so they wouldn't be much help in negotiating her release. Instead, he concentrated on Romania's Coat of Arms that hung over Stefan's computer desk. The golden eagle symbolized Romania's courage, determination, power, and hopes of soaring to new heights. He'd need all of that—and then some—to get her back.

"Alex, the police assure me they will investigate the castle immediately. My own sister will take them around. As I said, I do not think she is there."

Yeah, right, thought Alex. Sure they will. By that time, she could be dead. And do you really think they'd tell you if they found her?

The four-man police force trudged out joking and laughing with Stefan in a hail-fellow-well-met comradeship, as though they had been drinking at a bar. Alex watched them. He thought this did not bode well for her recovery.

Tony stood close to the door, cell phone in hand, until Alex only heard faint voices in the distance. He started to follow, but Tony put his fingers to his lips and ordered him to sit.

Alex didn't. "So why did you let them leave without forming some kind of plan? You know they won't go up there unless we force the issue," Alex said, his nerves getting the better of him. He paced back and forth through the living room until he was sure he was driving Tony crazy.

Tony merely lit up a cigarette that had lain dormant in his pocket.

"You don't smoke," Alex said, surprised.

But Tony's eyes only narrowed further. "Shut up, Alex, sit down and listen to me."

This time, Alex obeyed. He remembered the last confrontation he'd had with Tony.

"Alex, they're probably . . . no, I'm *sure* they're on Gregory's pay-roll. He'd have bribed them to be uncooperative."

"Why?"

"Money talks Alex. They don't have to like the castle owners or representatives to take their money."

Then Alex thought of a new angle. "Then, why the hell are we wasting all this time?"

"First, we're following protocol. We're in a foreign country."

"So? We've been invited into this country." Alex paced. "Protocol be damned. What about Elena? Do we sit here while they murder her?" Alex was ready to storm the castle single-handed if necessary.

Tony took a long drag of his cigarette, looked like he might choke, didn't, and continued. "Let me finish. We're not wasting all this time waiting for them. Look, I've already called in Romania's version of the cavalry, as well as the CIA and other FBI operatives. They work in Romania, my own team. Besides, I've already notified my office. They'll call the State Department and the American Consulate. The people who kidnapped Elena are terrorists who fund their activities through the drug trade.

"So, are our troops going to bomb the castle, with Elena in it?

These are not negotiating people, Tony. And, if you've noticed, there are walls twelve-foot thick surrounding that structure rising some fifty feet high. How are we going to storm that?" Alex got up and paced.

Tony replied. "They're not going to bomb anything. Getting out the storm troopers won't help in this situation. Anyway, you could hide someone in there for centuries and still not find them without a guide. Elena will be safe until Gregory gets back. They want something from her. The Romanian government will make a stink. Hopefully, they will send in the police."

"Hopefully?" Alex stopped and turned to him. He tightened his lips and narrowed his eyes. "How do you know Gregory's even in charge here? He might be part of it, but what if it's someone else who has the authority. What about those goons who kidnapped her? You don't think they might try something with her?" Alex persisted, not content to sit idly by. "What the hell do you have planned to get her back?" Perspiration flowed down Alex's face, got into his eyes, and burned them. Alex brushed the sweat off with his sleeves.

"As I said, Alex, Gregory's not back yet."

"How do we know that?" Alex slapped his hands on Stefan's desk. "How do we know Gregory's even involved? So, he takes care of the castle." He slumped into a chair and buried his face in his hands. "How do we even know for sure she's there? They could have taken her anywhere."

"Relax, Alex. Mikhail took down the plate number of the Mercedes."

Alex's head shot up, wide-eyed. "He what? How do you—?"

"I heard him tell his grandfather."

"His grandfather and not us?"

"Look, Stefan and his sister would know about who comes here. Hell, even Mikhail would know." Tony's voice sounded as if he'd like to raise it, but he kept it even, steady, with short, clipped words, as if talking to a schoolboy. "Anyway, this might be a good thing."

Alex's eyes widened. "A good thing? How?"

"It will bring attention to this drug-running operation and where they're hiding the heroin. It's the proof we need. Now, we have a kidnapped American. The government of Romania doesn't want that kind of publicity, and they want the location of the heroin as much as we do."

"Damn!" Alex huffed. "All this over a castle. Why didn't I sense this would happen?" He shook his head and ran his fingers through his hair, not having anything better to do with them. Sharp chills ran through him from which there was no relief.

Gently, Tony said, "You did. You felt something was wrong from the very beginning, from your reports. You didn't—couldn't see the entire picture."

"Yeah, but . . ."

"Besides, Alex, we suspect everybody." He laughed as a cynical commentary about his business. "Especially the good guys."

"Yeah. I know," Alex replied, instinctively rubbing his bruised knees. "There's something else. You called the office?"

"Yeah, so?"

"No. I mean, just now. Got hold of Larry. How well do you know him?"

"He has a reputation as a skilled administrator, and he's a decent guy. He speaks highly of you, Alex. Why do you ask?"

"Well, because we have a problem—a *big* one."

Alex felt lost. He hadn't the extensive FBI field experience others had. He'd been thrown into left field without a glove, not knowing what or who he was looking for, where the danger would come from next, or how to handle the next blow when it arrived. For the first time, Alex was beyond pleased Tony was there. "We wanted to know how someone knew where we were going and when we were going to be there."

"Yes, we did. And . . . ? Alex, you were the one who first suspected there was a leak in the office," Tony said. "Whenever we called in, the information seemed to go straight back to someone. Maybe Gregory Balogh or someone else. We were set up, and our mission was compromised. Larry is searching now. God help him or her when they're caught." He took a puff on his cigarette, coughed, and said, "These things will kill me one day."

"You don't smoke," Alex repeated.

Tony crushed it out in the ashtray. "But whoever it is *will be caught.*"

"What about Larry Simmons?"

"No. I know Larry very well. He's honest and hard-hitting. The decision for you to go undercover came from him. He thought it would be a good first assignment for you."

"Did he? He secured me the position at Briar Hill? I thought *you* recommended me."

"I confirmed you'd be a good choice," Tony said, stroking his goatee.

Alex, looking at a monastery painting, turned his head and wrenched his neck. He was furious with himself. He considered himself a loser and a danger to ladies in distress. "And I screwed it up."

"Don't be so hard on yourself," Tony said softly. "You're a decent man with a lot of potential but little practical experience. You happen to be standing in the way of a nasty bunch of criminals who've been getting away with a fortune. Besides, you didn't screw up. You found out not who was involved, but who wasn't, and that was important." Tony smiled at him. "The only thing you did wrong was fall in love with the right girl at the wrong time. And, I have no doubts you are very much in love with her, whether you want to admit it or not."

Alex looked at the ground. Yeah. He'd said a mouthful. Elena was the right girl at the wrong time. She'd always been the right girl at the wrong time.

He banged his fist with his knuckles. He'd felt like choking these people with his bare hands. "So, what do you suggest?"

"Stefan's sister is busy cleaning rooms at the castle, cell phone in pocket, ready to call at the first sign of either Gregory or Elena."

Alex started to pace again. "Already? You talked to her? What if she's involved?"

"Calm down, Alex. I don't think she is. But Mikhail can help. He knows the castle."

"The map."

"Yep. The map."

"And then?"

"And then we get the CIA's version of storming the castle walls." Tony got up to leave. "I'm going to call Larry on his private line at home. I want him to check on some information for me, and then I want to check out the resumes and personal files for all the employees that work in the department. We'll get him—or her."

And get Elena back alive remained unsaid.

Tony left by the reception area door as Alex wondered if they shouldn't bring back the death penalty for moles who'd been put in a position of trust. They'd nearly been killed on several occasions. Hell, lethal injections weren't painful enough. How about bringing back hanging? Or better yet, the rack before they arranged a delightful afternoon of fun, frolic, and drawing-and-quartering the bastards on the market square.

As he was thinking pleasant thoughts about hanging the bastards from the nearest tree, a knock came at the door, and in walked Marina Brancusi. A very tired-looking Marina Brancusi.

"Alex," was all she said as she dropped her luggage. She glanced around at Stefan's living room, stared at the cuckoo clock and the Romanian Coat of Arms. "Nice hotel. It's late. I want to go to bed."

"Marina!"

"*You're*—" Tony's eyes opened wide, and he took a step backward. "Alex's sister?"

"Yes," she said, eying Tony.

Tony's mouth dropped open, his gaze fixed.

Alex coughed. He wasn't sure he liked this sudden attraction that seemed to radiate between Tony Donatelli and Marina.

"Alex." She didn't pause. "What's going on over here? I ran halfway around the world because Elena emailed me. Said you were being attacked—set up—wherever you went. You were nearly killed. Then you two had a fight or worst. Had a knock-down-drag-out. She wanted you both to come home. She's furious with you." She paused to pant, then continued. "You were even attacked by a ghost."

Tony's eyebrows shot straight up. "Is there anybody who doesn't know about this?"

"Oh, stop it. You know it's true. I know it's true, so let's not pretend it's not."

Alex sighed. "It gets worse. I'm an ass. Really am. But that's not what's made it worse."

"Oh?" Marina's voice began to get an edge.

"It's a long story, not one I want to share here. Elena's been kidnapped."

"You said she was miss . . . She's been *what?*"

"We're doing all we can to bring her back."

"Oh shit," Marina said. "Oh shit. How can you lose Elena? You were supposed—"

"I didn't want you coming, Marina. It's too dangerous for you."

"You mean for you. You think I care about that when my best friend—no, *my sister-in-law* is in trouble? I think right about now, you need someone with a few *brains.*"

Tony laughed. "You are feisty, aren't you?"

Marina turned to him, put her hands on her hips, and glared. "I've been traveling for the past thousand hours or so. I'm just getting *started.*"

"What about the hospital?" Alex asked, trying for staid calmness but feeling anything but.

"They've already given me a family emergency leave. Plus, I've worked humungous overtime. I can stay a month if I want. And I want to."

"Okay. I can't say any more about what we're going to do, Marina. We're working that out now."

"You do that. And, stay out of trouble, yourself. Damn it, Alex— and you, too, Tony, whatever your name is."

"That would be Donatelli," Tony said.

Alex glowered at him, and he shrugged. But Tony didn't take his eyes off Marina.

Tony pulled Alex aside. "Look," he said. "I think we need to put Marina someplace where it's safe. I'm not sure the Sandor is that place."

Alex nodded. Made sense. He didn't think so either. Where though? The Ramada? Then he remembered. "How about the Monastery?"

"Yeah," Tony said. "Good idea. They take in people, occasionally. I've stayed there myself for a few days. The friars are good people. They'll protect Marina. I'll call them."

Marina eyed Alex with narrowed brows. "*I* need protecting?"

"Hmm." Tony picked up the phone, checked his contact list, and dialed.

Stefan entered the room and started when he saw Marina.

Alex made the introductions. "She'll be staying at the monastery."

Marina didn't look happy. Neither did Stefan.

Chapter 30

Dkany Castle

Elena shivered in the dampness and cold, her first inclination she might be awake and not dead. But where?

The combination of fungus and chloroform left her nauseated with a throbbing head that might split in two. Perhaps if it did, she wouldn't have to put up with this misery any longer. Everything seemed so bizarre—so fantastic. These things didn't happen to your ordinary person. Why couldn't she live an ordinary life?

She stared straight up at a moving carved wooden ceiling which seemingly attached to four-posters. It danced around in a circle, spinning to the right, at first fast, then slowing until it finally stopped altogether. It wasn't the ceiling, after all. It was a wood canopy covering what she thought was a monstrous ornate Baroque bed. The eight posters she saw narrowed until they focused into four. Kind of like the blurry photos she scanned into her computer, then edited.

The bed was huge but minute compared to the stark white room in which it resided. Its top almost reached the wood beams that lowered the original ceiling. Heavy Baroque furniture sprinkled the room, and even their large and cumbersome structures seemed small by comparison. She guessed she was in one of the bedrooms in the castle. She was so cold.

The only decoration on the walls was a silver cross hanging over the bed. Again, that silver cross. Everywhere she went.

Another strange phenomenon hit her. Someone had changed her clothes. Instead of the jeans and sweatshirt she'd stormed out in, she wore a long, thin, white gauze dress. No. Not a dress. Then what? A nightgown? Soft ballet-like slippers covered her feet. Who had changed her clothes? The invasion of privacy hit her hard.

For a day in mid-June, light cotton attire didn't seem to cut it for appropriate castle wear. Even in Romania.

Romania? It was coming back. She was no longer in Evanston, safe and protected. She was halfway around the world. Huddled in a bedsheet, she wondered how the Romanian nobility ever survived the winter.

A thump pounded inside her head again. A groan escaped her lips. Where the heck was an aspirin when she needed one? She wondered if the room had a bathroom and if they stocked it with pain-killers. She stumbled off the bed, and when she became dizzy and nearly passed out, she grabbed one of the bed posters for support and looked around.

Across the room resided a bathroom. No kidding. In a Thirteenth Century castle—a *bathroom*. She hobbled over and peeked inside. This small, outcropped room had not only a toilet but a free-standing tub, medicine cabinet, and sink. Flinging the cabinet doors open, she found a needed bottle of Tylenol. Thank God. She grabbed a few and was about to toss them down when it hit her. Suppose someone laced them with something lethal?

Shaking her head, she didn't care what they did to her. Anything was better than this pain. She tossed a few into her mouth and cupped her hands under the faucet. Good water. River water? Now, if they only had *hot* water. Did castles have . . . ? Of course, they did. She tried the tub, and the water came pouring out—steamy. The soak helped her to feel better and clear her mind.

When she came back into the main room, she searched the closet for her clothes. Empty. Who took them and why?

How about in the antique dresser on the far wall? Maybe they placed her clothes in there? She tried. Empty drawers opened with stark sunlight beaming down in them.

She became aware of one large latticed window on the bed's right side that turned inward.

The light poured in, breaking up as it hit the cold medieval walls and flashing back in lazars into her eyes. Her eyes blinked. Must be daytime. But which day? She'd never been in the position of not knowing the day or the time, and it was a strange and bizarre feeling to her. *The Twilight Zone* came to mind until a more sobering thought hit her—this was real.

No matter. Somebody must be looking for her by now. Alex and Tony certainly would have noticed she was gone, and so would Mikhail. Mikhail—her son. She wondered if he'd already spread the good news. She hoped not. But he was nine, and it was a *'mergency.'*

She'd just found him and now . . . Damn, she wanted her little boy. She'd grown so fond of him.

She thought they'd search the castle. Maybe, but the place was so big, they might never discover her. She'd have found a way out, herself.

She took the necessary steps to get to the window, carefully taking one slow step at a time. She still felt dizzy and nearly fell over but caught herself on one of the posters. The lead frame easily pulled inward, and she crawled onto the ledge, getting into position to jump.

She didn't. Breathing a sigh of relief that she'd looked before she leaped. She stood high up in the castle, and there was at least a fifty-foot drop into the courtyard. A courtyard with rubble—she'd fall on stones.

So much for that thought. Any other bright ideas? She couldn't think of any. Her head still pounded, and she felt sick. Then she thought of something which made her even more nauseated.

Alex.

God, he'd hurt her. Once again, she'd made a fool out of herself over him. And she'd put herself into this situation because of her overwrought emotions and damaged pride.

Damn him—damn her for loving him, and damn him on general principles.

As she stood looking out onto the ruins of the courtyard, she felt like an adolescent in an adult's world. Well, Alex wouldn't have to worry about her again. Unless he was part of this whole scenario.

A light bulb flashed in her brain. Alex inherited the castle after her, and then Mikhail—if anyone knew about their relationship. How vulnerable was she? Were there more nasty insects out there than her mere uncle?

Another thought. Why would those men take her here? Wouldn't this be the first place someone would look? Noises by her door startled her and, she whirled around. A key turned in the lock.

The wooden door opened, and two security guards stood poised, ready to fetch her. Their wide grins made her realize they knew she'd been trying to escape, and the long drop had deterred her. She wondered what the looks on those smug faces would have been like if she'd actually managed.

"Where am I?" she asked, leaning back against the wall, still too close to that open window. No response. "Who wants me?" She repeated in Romanian.

That they understood. Speaking in a Romanian dialect Elena didn't recognize but could understand, the taller, more aggressive guard moved toward her.

"We have been instructed to bring you into the library. You can walk, or we can drag if you wish. It is entirely your choice."

Chivalrous fellows. She thought she'd comply.

Elena walked between them through long, dark corridors that seemed to run in a circle until it ended at a long staircase leading to the first floor. Elena kept tripping on the hem of her dress over rough wooden stairs, nearly falling but held up by the two guards. The muscles escorted her to the library, where she, Tony, and Alex had been just—when? Yesterday? The day before?

Again, she tripped on the skirt coming into the room before she had a chance to observe the characters sitting around a long wooden table.

Around the medieval piece she'd admired so much sat four men who watched her enter. She recognized them from the elevator. The other hid behind a large package lying in the middle of the table. He finally stood and made his presence known.

Gregory Balogh.

Yes, Gregory Balogh. The situation became clear. Stunned, Elena never expected Gregory to be involved, despite Tony's assessment. He'd presented himself as a charming gentleman, a friend of the family, and her rescuer from Romania all those years ago. A bit eccentric, maybe—but a criminal? The look on the old man's face told her a different story. This was a fierce face with a hint of cruelty and intimidation. He narrowed his eyes, then turned away. His expression changed in an instant.

He began talking to the men as though Elena was not in the room. "All right, gentlemen. The rest of the shipment comes in, Friday. All arrangements made, *Domnul Mudani?*"

Domnul Mudani smiled and took a sip from a crystal brandy snifter. "Excellent brandy *Domnul Balogh.* I thank you."

Gregory acknowledged him with a nod, then took a sip from his glass and smiled—a smile that did not extend to his eyes.

They're transporting heroin, and he's smiling. This is a business meeting, and I'm part of the excess baggage. Good, God!

"So, good. We are all here. Now for our product. This is a sample—the rest is locked away. It is pure?" Gregory took a sip from his glass. "Only the best can come through here."

"It is pure," the man said.

"It will arrive on time?"

The man nodded. "I can guarantee its arrival by next Friday."

"Understand, I want to own those poppy fields. No more middlemen. The entire business, ours."

"Then, that's settled," the man said.

"Now to some unfinished business." Gregory Balogh focused on Elena with a more amiable demeanor and his usual charm. He pulled back his chair and stood, his tall frame towering over the table. His smile belied the dark, menacing expression around his eyes. The contrast of the benign and the sinister terrified her. It exuded evil, insanity. This was not the same Gregory Balogh who'd visited her in Evanston.

"*Buna ziua*, Doamna Elena," Gregory said. He made a grand gesture of hospitality.

My God, this is it. This is what I've been protected from. A cold shiver passed over her as the seriousness of her situation slammed with the power of an avalanche. She looked around the room for possible means of escape, should an opportunity present itself. None did. Guards stood by the door. The men at the table would be on her before she got to the threshold.

"Uncle Gregory," she said, in as conversational a tone as she could muster. "Why am I here? Why the chloroform to get me here?"

Get them talking. Stall them. If they're talking, they can't be killing you.

"If you'd asked me to come, I would have without all this," Elena said, looking at Gregory Balogh.

"That was the thoughtless action of a rather crude team of soldiers who work for me. I am sorry," Gregory replied, looking around the room. Then, focusing on Elena, "You are pale, my dear, but not hurt, I hope. A bit shook, and you might not feel well. I trust the bathroom accommodations were sufficient?"

He didn't give her a chance to reply.

"And the bed? How was the bed? Comfortable? That room was the chamber of your illustrious ancestor back in the fourteen century, Bella Dkany."

The man talked as though he were the host at a weekend social in the country. Bizarre.

"You've been trying to prevent me from coming here, but now have you brought me? Why?" Still self-conscious in her white dress, she asked, "And why the change of clothes?"

"Ah, down to the business, is it? Well, my dear, it is a little too late to let you go home. I did try to frighten you away from this venture, if you remember, but here you are."

Gregory tapped the table, maybe thinking of his following sentence. "My dear Miss Dkany, er, Mrs. Brancusi, you don't want this castle. It has been in my possession for years. As you see," he eyed the package on the table. "I have an interest. You do not." He smiled a carnivorous, toothy grin that sent shivers to the back of her neck. She wasn't looking forward to the next line.

"Sign the castle over to me. I let you go. Simple."

Really? He thought she'd buy that lie?

"Why is this castle so important, Gregory? I thought you said it was run-down, uninhabitable."

"Well, if you will look in this section of the castle, it is not neglected. Anyway, I have my means, and I know you were here yesterday. Legally, the castle is yours, as long as you are alive."

She shuddered. Here it comes, Elena thought. Here's where he says he's going to kill me.

"However, I will make a trade."

"A trade? What do you mean?" She became aware of the men seated at the table who stared at her—eyes ogling, mouths smirking. The light must be hitting at such an angle, they could see through the gauze. That's all she needed.

"Sign a transfer of the castle to me, Elena, and I will escort you personally to the airport to fly home. And Alexander . . ."

"Alex? What does he have to do with this?" The fear rose to a new level. "And he inherits, in case I die, anyway, so what's the point?" There. She'd throw *that* in for good measure.

"All in good time." He rubbed his hands together, a reminder of the evil witch, about to throw Hansel into the oven.

A chill ran down her spine, and she felt the gasp before she let it out. *Either* Alex or Mikhail was next to inherit.

Was Alex mixed up in this? Had he set her up? Escorted her to Dkany, so they could kill her? Dear God, please don't let that be true.

But, Gregory, her dear supportive and fatherly figure—now, demeaning, condescending, narcissistic, and evil—spoke again. "You can forget about him, dear. He's mine—all mine and has been for some time. You might as well turn this castle over to me. Then, we— you will be free. Otherwise . . ."

Otherwise?

"What about Mikhail? Does he come with me too?" Would her spark of hope be dashed as well?

Gregory's eyebrows raised. "No, I am afraid the young Mikhail will stay in Dkany. He will not be coming. You will forget he exists." His fist pounded the table and made Elena jump. "*Must* forget he exists. He is dead to you and always has been."

Elena lowered her eyes, thinking. Yes, it made sense. Gregory knew Mikhail was her son. "So, he stays here and becomes a part of this? And his grandfather, does he agree?"

"He will not know—only that you go back to America. He knows nothing else."

Elena waited for the next shoe to drop. It came.

"One more thing. I want that ruby."

"The ruby belongs to the Romanian Church."

"It belonged in a silver cross that is buried in the castle grounds. We will find the cross and put the ruby where it belongs, then sell it to the highest bidder."

"And if I don't agree?" Elena forced herself to glance upward into Gregory's face and keep it fixed there.

"That would be a gross error in judgment, my dear," Gregory said, as though he'd just rejected a pair of ill-fitting shoes. "We have means of persuasion."

Then he laughed. He glanced at Mundane, who hadn't taken his eyes off Elena or her dress for a second.

"What do you think? Maybe that harem of yours?"

Oh, dear God. What was Gregory talking about? Did they even have harems anymore? She breathed out a short, shallow gasp that came without any effort on her part.

"What's the matter, my dear Elena?" Gregory's voice mocked—seeded and disgusting.

The man across the table rose from the table and walked behind her. He grabbed both her breasts with his hands and squeezed—hard.

Surprise, then pain and humiliation, overcame Elena's better sense of judgment. She saw red and attacked. Jerking from his arms, she turned and slapped him across the face.

"Don't you dare touch me," she said, barely managing to get the words out.

Without much effort, the man slapped her hard enough to knock her onto the floor, leaving her dazed and confused.

Gregory laughed. "Big mistake," he said, but his laugh was short-lived.

Out of nowhere, a dark whirlwind emerged and sent the man flying across the room, knocking him onto the floor.

Thank you, Jan.

The man didn't move. Out cold.

Gregory's skin color turned to ash. The look of fear flooded his face. "What was that?" His voice trembled.

The other men's faces paled. They overturned their chairs as they rose and hurried from the room. The cold wind dissipated.

"Elena, I ask again. What was that?"

The tension that had formed on her face relaxed. She now had the upper hand for the time being.

"I don't know what that was. However," Elena said, with more bravado than she felt, "he deserved what he got."

His eyes narrowed, and his face contorted into a black look. Cold like a predator. "I am disappointed in you, Mrs. Brancusi." He looked back at the door. "You do want to die."

The two guards huddled in the corner; fear riddled their faces.

"Take Mrs. Brancusi back to her room. I will decide what to do with her." As he spoke, though, the power in his voice diminished as he looked around for the now non-existent whirlwind. "Be gentle with her, but do not let her escape."

Turning to Elena, he said, "Now, Elena, when you see reason, maybe we can talk more." He coughed. "You do realize what your ancestors did with their prisoners, don't you?"

Dizziness draped over her. She knew what Gregory was about to say.

"Your ancestors impaled their prisoners on stakes. I will have no compunctions of doing the same unless you see reason. A Harem would have been a lifelong luxury by comparison to what awaits you. But it is too late. Maybe your ghost can protect you from the spear. Oh, and nobody will find your body." His piercing gaze locked onto her and wouldn't let go.

Elena glared back and didn't move.

Gregory turned away. "Now, the guards will take you back."

Until you see reason. Gregory's remarks were so casual, as though he was speaking at an after-church Sunday brunch. He'd really enjoyed this. He was—they were all insane.

He snapped his fingers, and the guards moved toward her.

The guards looked at each other, glanced around the room, then shrugged. They came one on each side and took her by the arms.

Panic spread over her like something she'd never experienced before, but she held firm. She was damned if she'd show her fear to them or to Gregory. "No need to force me," she said. "I will come."

Not looking back, she positioned herself between the two and walked out of the room. As she left, she heard the sound of paper hurling across the table. She didn't think it was Jan this time.

Was Alex involved in this? Then she didn't stand a chance. Her mind carried her into dark places.

She stumbled along in a trance, back up the stairs and into the rocky aisle ways with crumbling stones coming out of the walls. The ground seemed to move with her pace. She didn't care if they killed her. It would not be merciful to live after losing Alex and Mikhail a second time.

God, Alex. How could he have done this to her? While Alex escorted her to her doom, he'd played with her, made love to her, made her love him. An even darker thought entered her mind. Had he been responsible for murdering her grandmother on that lonely evening in front of her house?

Gregory Balogh's face when he'd spoke told a different story. His expression said all she needed to know. Almost a smirk resided there. Either he liked that he'd shocked her or . . . No. Gregory played her. Alex wasn't in this any more than she was. It was the tried-and-true technique of divide and conquer.

Alex was probably scared shitless about her disappearance. Were they coming to rescue her? And would Gregory and his men know and lay a trap for him?

Chapter 31

Dkany Castle

Mikhail took Alex's hand as they snuck out the back door of the Inn. Nobody occupied the parking lot or path that led to the small barn near the river.

"Are you sure she's there? Absolutely sure?" Alex asked.

"Yes, I sure. We go on horseback."

Horseback? *Oh great. Just great.* It would take them hours to get there. "I don't ride horses, Mikhail."

Mikhail pierced his lips together. "You will now! I give you gentle horse. He is not problem. Just hang on." He tugged on his Alex's sleeve and pulled him along."

"And we take shorter way than when we go by carriage. And my horses, they go fast." Faster? Oh no. He'd never stay on.

"Okay. Good." Oh yeah, just great.

Mikhail had the horse saddled in five minutes flat. When he put on a wool cover over the saddle, Alex asked: "What's that for?"

"Is Romani custom and helps you stay on."

"Oh! What about that thing?" He pointed to the pom poms on the saddle.

"For decoration. Not help you stay on. His name Smokey because he color of smoke."

"So he is. Okay. I'll ride Smokey."

Mikhail rode the bay mare that pulled the carriage.

The boy helped Alex mount from a two-foot box, then swung into the saddle with one leap. He grinned. "I show you way. We save The Princess Elena."

The Princess Elena? What a creative mind his kid had.

"Wait, Mikhail. Are you *sure* Elena is in there? Absolutely sure? You weren't a little while ago."

"My grandfather, he pinch my shoulder. I do not go against my grandfather. When he get idea, I obey. Most of the time."

Why would Stefan think Elena was not in the castle? Alex shook his head. Then, thought about logistics—the castle. "How do you think we'll get in there without being seen?"

Mikhail crinkled his eyes, and the corner of his mouth turned upward. "I show you tunnel. We go underground."

"Underground?" Alex asked. How come he hadn't heard of a passageway? Though, it made sense. These old castles must have secret ways of sneaking someone out.

Mikhail started his horse at a trot. When Alex found his seat and could stay on, they galloped along a path by the river, occasionally hopping over a small river channel that blocked their way. At one point, Alex nearly fell into the water but hung on to Smokey's mane. Shadows formed from the dense trees along the path. Occasionally, Smokey would jump over one. Alex had to readjust his seat but kept going. They rode to the edge of the field to the backside of the castle.

Mikhail reigned in his horse. "See? Over there!"

An outline emerged from behind the trees. "That's the cottage," Alex said.

"We go there."

"Oh!"

They slid off their horses and brought them over to a small corral under the trees, where he took off their bridles. "Nobody notice them here. Nobody come here."

Their trip took fifteen minutes. Now they were in the shadow of the castle.

They walked on a path that ended at the cottage. Mikhail took out a key. "I take key when we go. In case we need . . ." A childish pride exuded from his voice.

"You sure did. You think fast." An adaptable and adventurous kid.

"I do," Mikhail answered, unlocking the cottage door. He was about to switch on the lights when Alex held him back.

"No lights. Where's your flashlight?"

Mikhail pulled it out from his pocket. "Okay," he said. "You follow."

Everything was as it had been before. Instead of going into the library, Mikhail opened a door at the far end of the kitchen, leading to stairs descending into the basement.

"Cellar," he said.

Could they store the heroin down here?

Alex looked around. The room appeared empty, except for the carpet.

"Were they planning on making this another room?" Alex asked.

Mikhail pressed his lips together and shrugged. "No, I do not think . . ." He pointed. "I show you where we go."

Over in the corner, the carpet had been sliced into a large square. Mikhail moved it and opened a trap door. Rickety wooden stairs led downward.

"Oh!" Alex raised his eyebrows with surprise. But it was black down there. "My God, you can't see down there. Do you suppose there's another flashlight?"

"One for you." Accommodating, Mikhail produced one from the top of the stairs and took the first step down. Stones blocked one of the steps. Alex nearly slipped and fell. He steadied himself on the railing, and it rattled so hard it almost tore out of the ground. Alex slid the rest of the way down.

"Earthquake," Mikhail said, skipping over another step with more rocks.

Alex followed, avoiding debris.

"You play here often . . . ? He stopped. His voice reverberated.

"We need to be quiet," Mikhail whispered. "I come all time. Interesting adventures. I pretend to rescue ladies in distress. I play Count of Monte Cristo." He pointed to himself and grinned. "I Count."

Alex chuckled. "You are creative. I'll give you that."

They descended into a tunnel. "Does anyone come through here anymore?"

Picking up a stick on the path, Mikhail said, "Not too much. Sometimes, maybe. Many paths blocked with stones and bricks."

"What's down here?"

"Rocks, spiders, sometimes snakes," Mikhail replied. "You like?"

Alex gulped. "Not particularly, thank you."

This was more like a cave. The walls were made of old brick and the ground of dirt and rocks. The roof was low, but they could walk, sometimes standing upright, sometimes they had to stoop.

As they walked, rocks and dust fell from the ceiling. Debris scattered over the already stony path. The way narrowed. They crawled over the rubble. Alex bruised his knee, hit his head on sharp rocks above, and gashed his forehead. "Mikhail, what *is* this place?"

"*Shhh,*" Mikhail said. "You make noise. More rocks fall. Not safe place. Nobody comes here."

"I'll say," Alex said.

After crawling through some mud, the path opened up again. The rocks turned into a brick floor, and cells lined the walls.

They came to a fork.

Mikhail looked around and pointed to the flashlight. "Ah-ha! We go this way." They made a right turn.

As they turned, Alex looked back. "Where does the other tunnel go?"

"Old Monastery. But is a long walk," he whispered.

"Really? You mean this tunnel connects the castle to the monastery?"

"Built years ago, during war. Something to do with old government. They would come to arrest, and person could not be found. He go through tunnel to monastery and to freedom."

"Ingenious."

"Ingenious? What that mean?"

"It means your people were clever, Mikhail."

"Oh."

They walked on.

"We underneath castle," Mikhail said, kicking a rock out of his way. Dust churned upward and into Alex's nostrils. He sneezed.

"Shhh," Mikhail said. "We must be quiet. People might hear."

Alex said, "We're underground here. How can anyone hear us?"

"Don't know but might. And falling stones." Mikhail looked upward. His forehead missed the ceiling by inches. Mud dribbled down on his forehead.

A small boulder slid down from above, diving inches from Alex's head.

Okay, he'd better be quiet, he decided. They trudged onward.

On the right wall stood a large open iron door that stopped Alex in his tracks. Inside ancient tortures filled a dark and dusty room.

Deep underground, the room would have no windows. The walls that separated the chamber from the hall were so thick no sound of the screams of victims could be heard outside the room.

Remnants of medieval devices lay strewn around the chamber.

An iron maiden, open with all the knives sticking out for all to see. On one side, a chain, attached to a pully, ran up to the ceiling and down to the ground. This chain attached to the prisoner's hands, and they would be hoisted upward. The executioners jerked the body downward and dislocated the arm sockets. They attached weights to the prisoner's ankles, so when they pulled, it exacerbated the agony. Alex had read about these torture chambers. The rack, the wheel, and the fire were all designed to encourage confessions, many of which were false. He traveled around the perimeter, getting a glimpse of the horrors when he stepped into a separate area.

If the other devices hadn't scared him, this pitiless one did. Holes dug deep into the ground, and lances lined the walls. "Oh my God." Did they actually impale people anymore?

Mikhail seemed immune to it all. He said, "Sometimes I play on metal body. The door swings in and out."

"Mikhail! Do you know what that thing could do to you?"

"The knives are sharp. I cut myself once. I stay away from inside."

"Well, thank God for that." Alex stumbled over a large stone and into the face of a skull. "Crap!"

His stomach lurched, and he tripped out of the room, kept from throwing up, and brushed himself off.

"So, where next?" Alex whispered.

"That way."

They continued on and passed by a cell filled with packages.

"Wait a minute."

Mikhail caught up and pointed. "Oh, these come in with cleaning trucks. Must have stuff that cleans castle," he said.

"I don't think so," Alex said under his breath.

Alex ripped open one of the packages filled with white powder. Heroin. So, that's where they stored the stuff. They were familiar with this underground facility. No wonder nobody caught on to where the drugs were or how they got there.

"Mikhail, don't ever put that stuff in your mouth or sniff it? Do you understand?"

"Eeww." Mikhail put his fingers to his nose. "Who would want—"

"Come on. We have to move along. We may not be alone here."

"No. They not come here much."

"How do you know?"

"See tracks? They old. They *were* here. They not come again."

"Usually."

"Yes."

But, if Elena were here, they would be back, and she might be down here.

He breathed hard. "Where is she, Mikhail? Where is Elena?"

"We go this way." He led Alex up a ramp, opened a steel door, and trotted up a staircase. "You come," he whispered. "Coast is clear. See?" He giggled. "I know American."

He pushed a button, and the wall split into an opening—bookcases on either side—shadows formed in the corners.

The room was huge—a dark bedroom, with the outlines of large and heavy baroque furniture. Light appeared through a window near the bed. No, it couldn't be. Too early. On a bed stand stood a lit candle. Someone had been here and would come again.

"Now," Mikhail said, "we wait." He pushed another button, and the bookcases closed.

Alex pointed to a dark corner, between a dresser and the wall—in the shadows. "Over there."

Alex and Mikhail backed into the darkness, held still, and waited.

Chapter 32

Dkany Castle

Until she sees reason. That's what he said. Gregory's remarks came so casual, as if spoken at a church social. That man really was enjoying himself. Was he crazy? Sadistic? Or was it all just business? Perhaps it was all three. What made him that way? He'd had such a great relationship with her grandparents. Was there ever a hint from her he wasn't normal?

The package she'd seen on the table. Heroin. They stored this drug in her castle. That's why they didn't want any of the Dkanys visiting. It all made sense. Tony mentioned holding facilities in Romania for drugs on their way to the United States and other markets. Tony had even suspected Dkany Castle as being one of those spots.

What was it doing on the table? Obviously, they'd wanted her to see it. Her heart leaped into her mouth. He'd never let her go, not if he allowed her to know what he was doing. No. Gregory had pronounced a death sentence on her.

And that silver cross she'd heard so much about. Was it really here within the ruins? They wanted the proceeds of this priceless object to help monopolize the trade. Who would buy such a thing? The Romanian Government? The Church? She didn't think so.

They half dragged her up the stairs. Her legs kept slipping from under her—was it the ground, or was it her nerves? The guards didn't seem to notice.

Her mind kept moving as well as her feet.

And Gregory tried to implement Alex. She didn't believe it, but she hadn't known him for a long time. Could he be a double agent? Hell no. Alex may be a lot of things, but a traitor to his country, never. So, what would Gregory and his men do to Alex and Mikhail if they caught them? Her mind carried her into dark places.

Her heart dropped to the bottom of her knees, which collapsed onto the ground. The guards yanked her on her feet, and they moved forward. They shoved her from the carpeted hallway onto the rocky path with stone-covered walls.

Her mind floated into a peaceful trance. A place where she didn't care if they killed her. Elena's strength gave out. She stumbled through the rubble that now passed for halls and tripped up the shattered staircase. Sharp debris of stones and jagged rocks cut through the soft pads on her thin slippers. The guards were not gentle, but at least they kept her on her feet.

At the top of the staircase, Elena recognized the hallway, which was smooth and debris-free. At the far end of the dark, concrete hall, the guards pushed Elena into Bella Dkany's bedroom with hardly enough light to illuminate a path to the bed. Shadows seemed to jump off the walls and attack her as she passed through them. Would she be murdered in this medieval chamber where no one would ever know her fate? No, Alex would find her. This seemed to be the ingredients for a Gothic romantic fantasy. However, this was neither romantic nor a fantasy. This was real, and she was in serious trouble.

Perhaps they would give her an easy way out, and one of Gregory's men, maybe Gregory himself, would come and kill her. She'd love to look into his evil eyes and watch as he choked the life out of her. Or would he go ahead and impale her as they did back in the days of the early Dkanys.

A grim possibility entered her mind. Had Gregory been responsible for ordering the hit on her grandmother that lonely evening in front of her house? Did he order Hadrian Petrov to kill her? Yes, she thought that might be a distinct possibility.

She squinted—peered around Bella's chamber. As her eyes adjusted to the darkness, an outline of a full-length bookcase lined the back wall. Was this the same room? Yes, there was the window she nearly fell from, the bathroom, the same furniture. Why hadn't she recognized the bookcase? If she got bored, she could always read in the dark. She looked around at the candle on the nightstand. It was flickering out. Soon there would be no light at all.

The guards stared at her as she got on the bed. One snickered, and the other guard roughly shoved him out the door. Thank God. At least no one else would be touching her for a while.

Elena realized how wrong she was when a black-on-black silhouette emerged from a corner. At first, it appeared to be just another contour merging with other shadows. Fear gripped her when the form took shape, and she clung to the rosewood post on the bed, digging her nails into it as though that might relieve her apprehension. Someone had been ordered to kill her, and they were going to do it now. The figure now glowed a dull yellow against grey shadow, and his illuminated presence approached.

"Elena?"

Alex? Is that you?

But was he a friend or enemy? Elena lost her composure. Frightened out of her wits, her rational mind became a combination of reality, fantasy, and horror. Could Alex really be the one behind all this? Death hadn't frightened her before, but now its harsh reality devastated her.

"You! How did you know I'd be here unless you were the one who brought me?" Her glance defied him. She wasn't going down without a fight.

"Elena?" He performed brilliantly, the voice shaky and insecure, the expression puzzled. Great acting.

"You've won, okay? You can have the damned castle if you want. I don't care anymore."

"Won—won what? Elena, are you all right?" He approached her again.

"Stay away from me, damn you," she said. She inched back on the bed. The more she moved away, the more he approached.

"Tell me what's happened?"

"Boy, you're good. But you always were, weren't you? Right from the very beginning. When did it start, Alex? When did you first decide I would be your sacrifice?" Rebellion struck out of her depths and attacked for a brief moment. Then, she asked softly, "How are you going to do it?"

"Do what?" Astonishment masked his expression. Brilliant.

The act continued, and he had the nerve to continue to look perplexed. *Good Alex.* "Are you going to strangle me with your bare hands or stab me with a knife? Or will you charm me to death and kill me while we make love? Or just plain shoot me. No, I don't suppose you'd use that method. It's not creative enough." She was panting now.

Alex blinked, then reacted. "God, you have a fertile imagination. What the hell are you talking about?"

"How long did you and Gregory plan this?" She tried to hold her voice steady, but she was losing ground fast. She wanted to know—but *didn't* want to know. "You don't have to pretend anymore." Alex made a move toward her, his eyes reflecting disbelief.

Elena picked up the most challenging thing she could find, a pillow, and threw it at him. He caught it.

She wondered when he was going to stop pretending and tell her the truth.

"We don't have time for this. We have to get out of here."

She barely heard what he'd said. "Alex, please. Don't make a fool out of me anymore. Please, if you're going to kill me, just do it. I'll enjoy it. It'll ease my . . . my . . ." Elena was losing it. She was going to fall apart in front of her adversary. She'd just say it, consequences be damned.

"Broken heart."

"What's this all about? Kill you? Why would I want to do that?" He approached further, and she threw another pillow at him. He caught that one too and sat on the bed, holding both in his lap. She rolled over to the other side and hopped to the ground. She backed herself into a corner and tried not to panic.

"I don't want to play a game of cat and mouse with you," he said.

"Okay, this is when you start to change, isn't it? This is when you catch me and—"

Alex did just that. He cornered her between the bed and the wall, so she had no place to go.

Elena tried to decide if she should close her eyes before she died or leave them open. He inched closer until his body pressed up against her. Dirt, sweat, and grime mixed with the scent of musk, and she was intoxicated. *Just kill me now while you're standing so close to me.*

Instead, her would-be nemesis caught her and swept her off her feet. He planted her firmly back on the bed, grasped her arms, and pinned them down. She made a move to get away, but he caught her and held on. "Sorry. Would you please tell me now what is going on?"

"Let go of me," Elena shouted at him and pulled away again, this time managing to free her wrists. Struggling, she crawled out from under him, but he grabbed her by the waist and pulled her back. This time he sat over her and provided no opportunity for escape. She was so scared she shook, beads of perspiration sprinted down her face, and she had a hard time breathing.

"Elena," he said, his voice cracking, "Please give me a chance. We have to get out of here." He tilted his head and infuriated her when she thought he might grin.

He said, "This isn't about my being a stupid bastard in the bedroom, is it?"

Elena couldn't do anything but shake her head. Her handsome prince remained steadfast. At that moment, she wanted him to ravage her. The tears flowed down her cheeks, and she couldn't stop. She choked on them, and Alex finally had to let her up as she gasped for air.

He wrapped his arms around her and held on. Her cries turned into whimpers and eventually stopped altogether.

His hands went to her neck, and she thought maybe, her wish might come true. Instead, he supported her body with the one and ran his hand down against the material of her dress.

"What are you wearing?" He frowned, and he looked worried.

"Why are you concerned about what I'm wearing? I'm sure you had a hand in picking it out, didn't you?"

Alex put up his hand to silence her. "Elena, stop this for a minute. Gregory told you I was part of his organization?"

She nodded.

Alex frowned. "What, the hell else did he tell you?"

"He told me you were involved. A lieutenant, in fact."

"Son-of-a-bitch." He sighed. "And you believed him?"

She'd never seen him so angry. She was relieved it was not directed at her.

"Elaborate, Elena. A Lieutenant in his cartel?"

"Gregory didn't exactly use the term, Lieutenant. Just that you belonged to him."

"And you *bought* that?"

Elena shrugged. "I had no reason not to."

A sharp breath escaped his lips. "Shit, Elena. You have a thousand reasons not to believe his garbage, his *lies*. But we'll discuss that later. What else did he say?"

"You mean about the drug smuggling operation that's going on here?" She moved out of his reach again, relaxing but not completely trusting him. "Their organization produces, markets, and distributes the heroin. *This* is where they keep it. The people who clean the castle bring in the heroin, then when they come back, they take it out again. Gregory also mentioned wanting the ruby and finding the cross to sell it. I don't know how they think they can sell such an heirloom. They want to buy up the poppy fields in Afghanistan."

"They couldn't. First of all, they'll never find that cross? Hah. It's been missing since the sixteenth century. And he could never sell it if he did."

"Tony was right to suspect this castle. We're right in the middle of a hornet's nest. That's why they didn't want us coming," Elena said. "So, you're not involved?"

"For God's sakes, Elena. Hell no, I'm not, but I was sure Gregory was."

"He held the meeting in the library where they tried to force me to transfer the castle over to them. They told me if I signed it over and handed over the ruby, they would allow me to go back to America. I didn't sign. I didn't believe they'd ever let me live, let alone send me back home."

"Smart girl. You know too much."

"Gregory also told me I couldn't take Mikhail with me. He was to remain here, and I was to forget he ever existed."

"You know that Mikhail is our son," Alex said gently.

Elena nodded. "Yes. I noticed him wearing my cross. It's unique. There isn't another one like it, outside of the larger one in the library." Elena fingered the cross around her neck that duplicated Mikhail's.

"He told me, too. And I read your letters."

Elena smiled through her tears. "The ones I threw at you?"

"Yes, those would be them." The warmth of his smile echoed through his voice. "Listen, I do love you. I've always loved you. Hated you, yes, but only because I loved you so much. But now I know the reason behind all this."

"Thank God, because I still love you—even though I think you're a shit."

Alex laughed. "I was. There was no excuse for my behavior." He fingered her face with his knuckle. "Then, let's stay married, shall we?"

She nodded and gave him a gentle smile. "Yes, let's."

A shadow crossed Alex's face. "I need to know everything Gregory said to you. It's important."

Elena didn't hold back. "They had a shipment of heroin on their table. They said it would ship out on Friday." She shook her head and blew out a sigh. With a shudder, she continued. "He also said, unless I agreed, they would impale me like their ancestors."

"Impale? God, how medieval." Alex barely kept his voice under control. "What a load of crap."

"What is today, anyway?" Elena asked.

"Wednesday. We've been out searching for you. We thought you were in the castle but weren't sure where. It's been a nightmare."

"How did you know where to find me?"

"Mikhail told me. He saw you leave. He led me here."

"Yes, he would. He seems to know everything."

"That's probably why they won't let him leave. He knows too much."

"I hope he's not in danger too."

"Sweetie, I think we all are. That's why I didn't want Marina staying at the Sandor."

"Marina? What do you mean?" She grabbed onto Alex's shoulders. "Is she *here?*"

"Well, damn it. You should know. You've been emailing her."

"Of course I have."

"Elena, we have to get out of here—*now.*" Alex fingered her dress, concern etched itself on his face. "Where did you get this dress?"

Elena answered, astonished by his question. "The degenerates put me in it. Why?"

"Honey, what they've put you in, is a death shroud."

"A what?"

"Elena, it's what they've buried the Dkany women in for centuries."

Alex placed a finger under her chin and peered at her face. "Holy shit." He grabbed the candle from the nightstand and shone it onto her face—bruises and a cut on her temple. "Elena, you're hurt. What happened?"

"One of those men touched me, and I slapped him," she said, almost smiling. "Unfortunately, he slapped me back, and I fell onto a chair and rolled over on the floor."

"Son of a bitch." He'd pay for this—eventually. "I'm sorry about one thing, though."

Elena raised her eyebrows. "What?"

"I should have told you I was an FBI agent a long time ago. It would have made things so much easier on you and on me. I've been working for them for seven years. Tony was one of my professors at George Washington University, and he helped me get the position. I was chosen to go underground, so I became a professor at Briar Hill. They thought the Dkanys were the go-betweens. I never thought they were, but it was my job to find out. I tried to prove they weren't. As it turns out, it was their solicitor."

"You could have trusted me, Alex. I could have helped."

"I couldn't. At that time, except for Tony, I was totally alone. I didn't know who I could trust, and Elena, I hadn't seen you in years."

"True."

"I'm sorry for the way I acted toward you. I was a jerk. I didn't mean a word of it."

"Good, now that I know, *now* we can get out of here."

"Alex . . ." she said, putting her hands on his chest and under what was left of his shirt and kissed him until he had to separate just to breathe. Something moved in the shadows. He pulled away.

"What—?" Elena started to ask.

"We have company." Alex pointed.

Elena turned in the direction of the bookcase where shadows melted into the walls. With a smile and glow on his face, Mikhail walked forward toward them.

Alex had forgotten about him.

"Hi," he said. "What does 'being a bastard in the bedroom mean?"

CHAPTER 33

DKANY CASTLE AND RUINS

DKANY, ROMANIA

Mikhail whispered, "But we hurry now. No play fight, okay?" He turned back to the wall and pushed a spot on the bookcase frame. A noise like squeaking brakes escaped from the doorjamb, and the bookcase moved a foot inward, allowing for passage. Alex didn't remember that noise when they'd entered the room. "What the hell was that?"

"Does that sometimes. Come . . . you hurry." Mikhail jumped through the door, followed by Elena and Alex. Stones and sand poured around them. The wall closed and appeared as if it was part of the structure.

"Well, well, well, I thought that only happened in movies." Alex said. "How the heck did they maneuver that back in the fourteen hundreds?"

Alex took Elena's hand and helped her down the rubble stairs to the main tunnel. Elena slipped on a rock and caught herself on the railing. Water dripped down the sides, and stones continued to fall. The floor became muddy and formed into puddles. Alex remembered the ground as dry.

"What the hell?"

Mikhail took his nine-year-old hand and rubbed it against the side. "This not good. We hurry."

"Why isn't it good?" Alex asked.

Mikhail didn't have a chance to answer.

Elena stepped into a hole that went as deep as her ankles, and a rock cut through her shoe. Alex grabbed her by the waist and pulled her out of the mud. Shoes squeaked from sloshing water, and she removed one and tipped it over. At the entrance of a cell, she noticed large bundles filled the room.

Alex stopped—dead. "Yes," he said. "This is where they store the stuff."

He stepped into the cell and gazed around the place. Taking another step over one of the bags, he grabbed a sharp rock and cut the corrugated box. Brown powder spilled out the opening. He sniffed and rubbed it between his fingers. "Come on. Let's get out of here."

Elena held onto one soggy shoe and peered over Alex's shoulder. "So that is what the world's finest agencies are looking for and what half the world would love to get its hands on." She held onto Alex's shoulder and slipped into her slipper.

Mikhail placed two fingers inside and started to lick. Alex grabbed his arm and shook the powder from his fingers. "No, Mikhail. Believe me, that stuff can kill you. Don't *ever* do that."

"Oh! I—" He clamped his mouth shut.

Alex stared. "You what?"

Mikhail shook his head. "I tell later. Now, we go." He turned and ran from the room.

I'm going to have a talk with that kid. His curiosity will get him someday. Instead of addressing the issue, he said, "We're not sure they know we're gone or if they'll figure out *how* we managed it, but they'll figure it out. They know about this place."

Mikhail held the flashlight, but it dimmed, then lit, then covered again. The boy knocked the head against his hand, and it regained steady illumination.

They passed the hall of tortures, and once again, Elena stopped to look.

"No, Elena, don't." Alex tried pushing her along, but she was determined to see what lie inside. The alcove of impalement.

"My God. They would have . . . could have done that to me."

"Come on. We have to hurry."

Alex held Elena by the waist and pushed her forward until she tripped over an abrasive rock and fell. As he picked her up, he noticed blood soaking through her shoes.

"Elena—" That's when they heard the voices.

"Shhh." They stopped.

Mikhail pointed upward. "They in hallway above us. We be quiet. They hear from holes in rock walls."

"Oh crap," Alex said. "Come on. We have to *move*."

They ran like the devil was after them.

The walls guided their way until they came to the fork in the passageway.

"Which way?"

"Outside chapel," Mikhail said. "They not go there. We go *that* way." Mikhail pointed to the left.

But Alex had been wrong about Gregory not knowing about the opening in the wall. He must have. Muffled voices lurked in the background. The sounds got louder as they sprinted down the hall under the castle toward the cabin. Sooner or later, they'd catch them. They started to climb up rocky steps. One stumble, and Alex nearly fell backward. He managed to hang on and flew up the steps with Mikhail on his heels. They turned the corner, and voices shouted after them.

Another turn, and they climbed more stairs. Rocks fell at their heels.

"Put me down," Elena said. "I can still run."

"You're bleeding."

"So what?"

Not so sure, Alex put Elena down anyway and stumbled on a rock. This time he nearly fell to his knees. Elena caught him, and they ran. They didn't dare stop to catch their breath. Lightened shadows formed as they moved. The fresh air of pines and mountains mingled with the bouquet of musk and earth as they ran. Elena's feet and side hurt, but she moved faster.

Elena couldn't hold up anymore and tripped and fell. This time she went down. It seemed where they were headed no longer mattered.

The voices grew louder.

"Damn," Alex said. "They're getting closer. They're coming from all sides."

"No, not them," Mikhail said. "Something else up there."

"What?" Alex looked up at the rumbling her thought might be footsteps.

Mikhail started shaking just before the earth shook beneath them. "We have earthquake," he said. They ran. Stones, rocks, and boulders fell all around them. Mud puddles became deeper, and crevices formed where solid earth once stood. If they'd wanted to go back, they couldn't. A pile of rubble fell off the walls and almost hemmed them in. They jumped clear.

The rumbling grew louder. A crash followed them from the path where they'd been running. The earth shook, and they held onto the side of the walls. But the walls seemed to cave in and pushed her into the center of the pathway. Rocks and dust covered her, and she almost lost consciousness.

Alex dug Elena out of the debris and carried her toward the end of the tunnel walkway. Mikhail tripped and jumped over cracks in the earth, and they both tried to keep their feet. A boom catapulted them out of the tunnel, and they went flying into the castle ruins. They had a hard time catching their breath.

A voice startled Alex from behind. "My dear Brancusis, this is the end. Isn't it fortunate there was an earthquake? Now, there isn't anywhere else for you to go."

They turned to face their captors.

"As you see, I have ten men behind me and quite a few perched on the roof. You cannot get away." Gregory and four of his men were spread out between them and the tunnel entrance.

"So, where are your ten men, Gregory?" Alex asked. "I only count four. Did they come from the tunnel? Perhaps get buried in the earthquake? They couldn't have come after us. The quake blew us out of there."

Gregory glanced behind him, but as Alex made a move toward them, Gregory narrowed his eyes.

Elena pushed Mikhail behind her. "What are you going to do with us?"

"Nothing." A voice came out of nowhere. Tony. "They will do nothing to you." A group of men stalked out of the ruins, from behind rocks, behind doorways and trees.

"Ah, you have brought out the cavalry, I see. The big guns." Gregory laughed. "But, you see, we have the first shots, and they are all aimed at Alexander and Elena." He laughed. "And Mikhail."

Mikhail put his arm around Elena's waist and hung on."

"He didn't do anything to you," Elena said. "Kill me, if you want, but leave him alone."

"I do not think so. If you look around, not all of these men will be on your side. I think?"

Then the shooting started. A Romanian soldier aimed a shot at one of Gregory's men. He fired back and caught the soldier in his stomach. He lurched over and fell.

Alex pushed Elena and Mikhail out of the way. Tony threw him a gun, and he darted behind boulders as Gregory's men opened fire.

Retaliation flattened their attack. Men from all sides assaulted Gregory's men, who retreated back toward the tunnel. Gregory ran after Alex.

Alex aimed at a group firing from the chapel, his back to Gregory.

"Watch out," Elena screamed at him, leaped at Gregory, and tried to shove him off balance, but Gregory pushed her out of the way. He raised his gun to fire at Alex, but a shot rang out from somewhere above. Gregory staggered back. Surprise covered his face as he looked up and fell backward, blood streaming from his mouth. A large red stain covered his shirt, his eyes rolled back in his head—dead, black eyes.

Stefan stood tall with a grin on his face. "I got him," he said.

Gregory's men tried to run back through the tunnel. Tony motioned his men to go after them, but again, Tony stopped them when the ground started to rumble. Elena heard the screams coming from within. Tony's men stopped in front of the entrance; their mouths were wide open.

Another crash came from the stories above. Bella Dkany's bed crashed within inches of Elena.

Elena sighed and grabbed Mikhail and Alex. It was over.

CHAPTER 34

SANDOR INN

DKANY, ROMANIA

Everyone in Dkany loved a good party.

When word had gotten out that Gregory Balogh used their castle to house an international drug ring, the Dkany residents were outraged. They would have loved to hang Balogh and his men off the tallest oak tree in the square, but as that was illegal, and these people were dead anyway, they came out to the Sandor Inn in droves to celebrate.

Waiters wore traditional Romanian costumes, passed around trays of champagne and canapés to the folks jammed in the lobby, restaurant, and bar. Mikhail vaulted from one group of people to another, pointing out his new parents whenever Alex and Elena were in view. The wine flowed freely. Everyone was jovial—some drunk, most not quite.

Elena's eyes riveted on the mayor, congratulating Alex. She thought the town had gone a bit far in viewing them all as some kind of folk heroes. One guest compared their situation with *Clear and Present Danger*. Elena nodded. He'd gotten that right. It had been 'clear and present danger' from the moment her grandmother had been murdered.

Elena's mind—as well as body—was exhausted, and depression settled somewhere deep inside. She wasn't sure why. Everything was perfect—the bad guys were defeated. The earthquake had pretty much destroyed parts of the castle that needed repairs, anyway.

Much had remained stable. An excellent time to build the school Magda wanted so much. Most of the work would be removing the debris from the quakes.

Elena and Alex had gotten closer, physically and emotionally. Both appeared to be happy and in love.

But today, Alex appeared to have something on his mind. She'd notice him staring at her, then turn as soon as she glanced his way. It wasn't a wink and a smile kind of look.

They'd talked about their future. Alex asked her what he could possibly give her as a wedding present. Elena had looked down, feeling blood rush to her head. Alex had raised that quizzical brow of his and said, "Elena, you're blushing."

Elena giggled and answered, "Alex, what I want most in the entire world, besides you and Mikhail, is . . . a little girl."

Alex wobbled a bit, then laughed. "Well, let's go make one." And that was the beginning of the happiest time of her life.

She glanced down at her ring—couldn't imagine it not being on her finger, as she couldn't imagine life without him or Mikhail. But why was she even thinking that way? They were married, had a lifetime commitment, a little boy, and had defeated the bad guys.

They weren't in harm's way anymore, were they? So why this empty, almost frightened feeling inside?

Elena maneuvered out of the crowd and stepped onto the porch. A warm and enticing evening. Moonlight, pine scents, warmth, and miles of twinkling sky. The stars showcased their constellations. Stefan's staff strung lit paper lanterns around the porch. Romance wrapped into one perfect package—the perfect night.

Glancing down the gravel road was another couple engaged in conversation with occasional bursts of laughter. Marina and Tony. She smiled. What an exciting development that would be. Neither one of them had many opportunities for a social life. Maybe . . .

"Elena." Alex strolled onto the porch, hands in his suede jacket pocket. She turned, and he stopped by the porch steps, gazing at her. "How come you're all by yourself?"

Elena smiled and pointed to where Marina and Tony had stopped and faced each other. "I'm not alone. Look."

"Oh!" He stood next to her, regarded the pair, and slowly nodded.

"I'm assuming that meets with your approval?" Elena asked.

"They're a good match." He chuckled. "I haven't had any control over my sister in years. Hell, she's a doctor." He took Elena's hand.

"I haven't had much control over my own life, let alone someone else's. I've had no responsibility for anyone other than myself." He fell silent for a moment. "Now, it seems I'm responsible for the life of two other people." His mouth gaped open. "Oh shit. I'm sorry, Elena. I didn't mean . . ."

Elena stiffened and removed her hand. "And that scares you?" she asked softly.

He sat on the porch railing. "Scares me? I'm not sure I'd put it like that exactly."

Elena's stomach flopped over, and a kind of dizziness overcame her. That wasn't the kind of remark she'd been expecting. "So, we're excess baggage? About to ruin the carefree existence you led?"

She backed from him and walked to the porch steps, suddenly wanting to leave the conversation.

"Why do you always do that, Elena? Walk away from a discussion?"

"Because I think this may turn into an argument. Besides, I don't always walk away." Yes, she did, she thought. And the last time she'd left, she'd gotten into big-time trouble. But that was then. This was now. She needed resolution—confirmation of love, not 'I'm stuck with you.'

She swallowed and took a deep breath before facing him. "When we made love this morning, I thought I was looking deep inside your heart, Alex. And I gave you mine, totally, unconditionally. Now, are you saying you're stuck with me?"

"Hell no! I'm not saying that at all. I love you and Mikhail." He shook his head and shrugged his shoulders. "I'm just honest with you about my life. I've come from a very carefree existence."

"Carefree?" Elena turned on him. "Nearly getting yourself killed for a living is *carefree?* Sleeping with a different bed partner every night is carefree?"

"Elena! That's not what I—"

She didn't look at him. "Isn't it?"

Wasn't it what he meant? He'd been contrasting the life he'd lead before with the one he'd be leading now, and it didn't appear like it pleased him all that much—his Dr. Jekyll-Mr. Hyde persona had returned. Alex didn't want to commit to a life-long relationship. She was sure of it.

A cell phone went off from the direction of the driveway. Tony reached into his pocket.

Marina waved.

Elena wanted to cry. "Damn." Tony was halfway down the steps, and she heard him.

"Now what?" Alex asked. "Elena. I didn't mean it to come out like that. Of course, I love you and Mikhail. You know I want to stay with you. I'm just going to need a little bit of time to make an adjustment." He looked at Tony, then turned back to Elena. "Honey, before he gets here with whatever it is he wants, I want you to know that I do love you and whatever adjustments I—hell, *both* of us make—will be well worth it. Because we'll both have to compromise. We have a son to raise."

But did she? Doubts surfaced like so many bubbles from a drowning woman.

Tony came running up the driveway. "Alex, I need you for a second. Elena, excuse me." He grabbed Alex, and they went inside, Alex glancing back at her and shrugging his shoulders as he went.

Marina came running up, and they stared at the door bewildered. "What was that all about?" Marina asked.

They didn't have time to explore the options. Alex and Tony came out of the inn. Alex stopped but Tony kept going. He ran down the stairs, and headed toward the garage.

Elena hurried up to him. "Alex? What happened?"

He wore a scowl on his face, and his eyes were darker than usual, even with the porch light.

"Elena, I have to leave. That was my director. The Justice Department wants us in our office in Budapest. There's been a development."

Elena shivered. A strong feeling of foreboding fell over her. Something was very wrong. "Can you tell me?"

"I don't know anything, or even when we'll be back."

Elena stiffened and drew a deep breath. Frowning, she asked, "Is that by choice?"

"No!" His eyes widened, and he pinched his lips together. "I had nothing to do with this. Please, Elena. I meant what I said."

Mikhail came out onto the porch, and Alex turned toward him and back again. "Elena, I didn't mean what I said before. Sometimes, I think I can say anything to you, and it doesn't come out the way I mean it to. But believe me, I love you. I need to know that you want to stay married to me. I mean, we have Mikhail and . . . each other."

He mouthed, "Please. I love you."

Stefan walked out and stood behind Mikhail. And, behind Stefan stood . . . *Jan.* Almost solid in form. Angry-eyed, staring at her.

"No!" She said, staring at the ghost. "No."

She hadn't had a chance to recover when Tony's Dacia puttered up to the porch. "Let's go," he yelled. No luggage—no nothing. Just *let's go.*

"Okay. I'll be right there." He spun toward Elena, took her arm, and walked her down the porch stairs out of hearing range of Mikhail and his grandfather.

"Okay. As much as I love you, Elena, I'll let you go if that's what you want. You and Mikhail stay here. You can take care of Freddy's affairs like you'd planned." He drew out a card. "Here's where I'll be.

If you want to divorce me, I won't contest it. It shouldn't be complicated. We'll work out an arrangement as to raising Mikhail. I can't talk about it now."

"Alex!" Elena pleaded with her eyes. "That's not why I said *no!* Please, listen to me. I saw Jan's ghost behind Stefan. I saw him, Alex. I thought he was gone. He's *back!*"

"Alex, hurry," Tony yelled.

"Oh shit, no. I'm sorry, Elena. I thought you meant us. You want . . . ?"

"Of *course* I want you."

"I'm coming, damn it," Alex yelled at Tony. He grabbed Elena and held her so she could hardly breathe.

"I love you. More than you could possibly know." Her tone came out in a whisper.

He turned and looked at her. "We'll keep in touch. I love you too. I don't want us ever to be apart again." He ran down the steps then stopped. "See you soon, take care of yourself and that boy of ours. I love him, too."

And then he was gone. Elena couldn't breathe—couldn't think. Her stomach turned over.

"My God, Elena. What happened? You're as white as your dress," Marina said, hurrying up to her.

She shook her head, turned toward the inn door. Jan had disappeared. "I saw Jan's ghost again, Marina."

"And?"

"I told Alex. Not sure if he believed me or not, but we're staying together."

Marina nodded and cocked her head. "I knew you would. You were destined to be together."

Mikhail ran down the porch and slid up to them. "My American dad just leave in car with his sidekick. Will they come back? I no want them to leave." He ran to the porch steps and ran after the car down the driveway until he tripped on a pothole.

Elena, Marina, and Stefan ran after him. Elena bent over. Mikhail was rubbing his knee, which was bleeding. "Let's put something on that," Elena said.

"No, my dad going away. He not coming back?"

"Where did you get that idea?" Elena asked.

"He say so. I hear him."

"No, honey, we had a small misunderstanding, that's all. He has to go away with Tony on some business. They'll be back. We're a family, Mikhail. A family. We love each other." She hugged him. "All of us."

"Me too?"

"You too, and your Aunt Mari."

He grinned. "You, my aunt? Really?"

Mari laughed. "Yes, really. Your dad is my brother."

"Oh! So, you another princess. Princess Marina, yes?"

"Yes."

A glint formed behind the tears, and a grin broke out. "Okay."

They grabbed each other and hung on. Off in the distance, the sound of the departing Dacia was gradually dimming.

For the next few weeks, Elena sorted through the tons of Freddy's books accumulated throughout the years. Some she boxed, others she left on the shelf. Some, she discovered, Freddy had written himself. A book on death and dying, the grieving process, how to get over a loved one. All written years ago while he was still getting over Jan. She hadn't realized he was such a prolific writer, nor that he had been published. The dust and moldy smells gave way to open air and rose furniture polish. Workmen came in and replaced worn, uneven floorboards that now shone. Elena thought she might like to live in this little cottage forever.

A wave of nausea came over her. She hadn't been feeling well lately. Flu? She hadn't had it in years.

"What's wrong?" Marina stood in the doorway with a handful of jeans.

"Oh, nothing. I've been working too long. I need a break." She leaned on a chair and boosted herself onto her feet.

Dizziness whirled around her. She held on until it passed.

Marina eyed her with a calculating expression and said,

"Honey, do you want some tea? You don't look too hot. Mikhail's in the kitchen making some."

"That would be a good idea."

They wandered into the kitchen and sat at the table.

"I got an email from Alex," Marina said.

Elena's stomach clutched in response. She tried to sound nonchalant when she said, "Oh? What did he have to say?"

Mikhail came over and brought them two mugs of tea, then scampered off to another room.

"First of all, this email is for both of us. Alex is not going to email you directly. He wants to make it clear to you that he loves you." Marina gave Elena a crooked smile. "Just in case you should get the wrong idea." Marina whispered, "They've been in conferences with officials from the Justice Department. FBI, CIA, DEA. Lord, Elena, the reason you were stalked wherever you went was that one of Gregory's accomplices was a plant in their office. She knew every place you went, everything you did."

"She?" Elena lifted her eyebrows in surprise. "She?"

"Why not a she? She's an assistant in the office. Gregory paid rent on a posh apartment and provided her tuition to Georgetown. She'd been turning tricks to earn her tuition before. He offered her stability for information."

"So, what are they going to do with her?"

Marina shook her head. "They haven't caught her yet. She's responsible for the deaths of several innocent people plus other charges. There will be a trial, and it won't be pretty."

"Poor girl."

Marina sat back in her chair, her mouth open before she said,

"Poor girl? You're sympathizing?"

"I'm saying Gregory Balogh could be a very persuasive individual. I'm thinking if he asked her to spy for him, she probably had a choice between taking his money or him taking her life. As it is, she's lost the rest of her life, anyway."

"Yeah, but the problem is, we might have to testify at her trial."

"Ouch! I should have seen *that* coming."

"Alex asked me how long we wanted to stay here. They plan on coming back as soon as this thing in DC is over."

Elena's heart jumped. "They're coming back?"

Marina nodded. "I think so. He just said I should look after you and Mikhail. Said he had to meet with his director in Bucharest. He told me to tell you he loves you and to take care of yourself, and he indicated we might be in danger if she gets away or if it goes to trial."

She swiveled in her chair. "Oh no, not again. Will it never end?"

Marina shook her head. "Now, I'm involved, and even Mikhail will have to be protected."

"Oh no, Mari. I'm so sorry. Maybe that won't happen." Elena breathed out. "I have something else to say, unrelated to all this garbage."

"What's that?"

"Tony."

"Huh?"

"Oh, come on, Mari. You can't tell me you don't like him. The man's sexier than hell."

Marina laughed. "Well, yes, I guess he is, and yes, I do. But I have a job. I can't just up and leave it. I'm going to have to go back home sooner or later. So do you. Your Ph.D."

"Mari, you said you'd given up the internship. You wanted to go in a different direction. Are you changing your mind again?"

"No, I'm not." Marina opened the back door and leaned on the porch railing. "It's so beautiful here. I wish I didn't have to go back." She shifted and faced Elena. "Maybe we could stay here and work on your school? I could get my psychiatrist license in Romania or put it off for a year or so."

Elena said, "I'm concerned about Alex. Something he said. I'm not sure he's let go of his old lifestyle."

"I highly doubt that, Elena. I know my brother. Once he's committed to something, he's tenacious. He doesn't let go. He'd never let go of you."

"I hope not. It's just that I'm . . ."

Marina shook her head. "No. I'll never believe he doesn't want to stay with you."

"I just wish everything were more settled. I . . ." The queasiness returned. Elena felt sicker than she had before. If she got any more nauseous, she'd have to run to the bathroom.

"Ladies!" Stefan peered at the screen door. "I come bearing food for the hungry and the tired."

Mikhail jumped up and ran to the door.

"Ah, Mikhail. I thought you might be here." Stefan smiled and handed Mikhail a tray of cold meats and cheese. A second trip offered them freshly baked bread from the inn, and a dark local beer to wash it down.

Elena nibbled, not too interested in food. She was anxious about Alex and their future. But even a tiny amount of food upset her stomach. She excused herself and ran to the bathroom. She didn't think she had a fever, but God, she felt sick. Her throat burned, and the taste in her mouth made her want to throw up.

When she got back, Marina was looking at her with a peculiar expression.

"What?" Elena asked.

Marina raised her eyebrows and shrugged, glancing at Stefan and Mikhail. Stefan smirked and averted his eyes. Mikhail looked like a typical nine-year-old who hadn't a clue, wanted to be included, but didn't know in what.

Elena sat back at the table, looking away from the food. She knew what Marina was thinking. She thought the same thing. Three-four weeks. She'd missed her period—the night after the drug battle.

They'd made love for several beautiful days and nights before the party when Alex had to go.

What was Alex doing in Bucharest so long? Or had he already flown back to the states?

Well, maybe she wasn't pregnant. She blew out a sigh. She knew better—was pretty sure. Even if she was, she could support another child, and she was married to the baby's father. Alex wanted to stay married. So, there was no reason they shouldn't have another child. Wouldn't it be funny if Alex decided to go back to Briar Hill, and she went for her PhD, with him as her professor? Oh, she could just see that. Her big as a house, sitting in the front row of the classroom. She giggled.

Stefan came in another loaf of bread. "For later."

"Here, please sit with us, Stefan." Elena made room for him at the table. "Thanks for the food. I'm sorry, I'm not really hungry. Maybe later."

Marina and Stefan looked at each other, then back at Elena.

Elena said, "It's nothing. I've just been working too hard. I probably need a break."

Stefan said, "Ah, my dear girl. You need to get *out*. My Mikhail—our Mikhail," he coughed. "He should take you sightseeing. You lock yourself away in this cottage. Too much to do."

"Yes, there is. We'll take Freddy and Jan's clothes to the monastery later today."

"Have you decided what you will do with the castle? Only a portion of it was destroyed."

"I'm considering my options. Magda's idea was a school. I haven't given up on that idea, even with the earthquakes." Elena replied. "One thing Gregory had been right about was its need for renovation and the removal of its ruins." *Maybe find the cross if it's buried in there.*

She walked outside, followed by Stefan. They looked at the spiraling towers set against the mountainous landscape. "It's beautiful, isn't it?" She turned to him. "It's been in our family for centuries. It's a Dkany icon. If an earthquake can't destroy such a piece of historical treasure, neither can I."

"No, my dear girl. That you cannot do. You wish to restore it?"

"It would be a glorious dream," Elena replied.

"And the boy. Will you take him away from here?"

Ah, so that was why he'd followed her out. He wanted to talk about Mikhail.

"My future is so uncertain," Elena explained. "I love it here, love the cottage. I wish I could stay here forever."

"You fit in, Dkany," Stefan said. "You seem to belong to the land."

"Yes. But I'm American. I belong there too. I'm supposed to start my doctorate in the fall. And there's Alex."

Stefan's expression became deadpan. "Yes. Alex—Mikhail's father. I thought Jan was Mikhail's father. Now, I know better. This makes a difference, does it not?"

Yes, she supposed it did. In many ways. "No matter what, Stefan. I promise Mikhail will see you often. If we live here, he can continue to help at the inn and go to school. If we move back to the states, I will make sure he gets back here often. I think we may stay here in the summer and go back to the States in the winter for school."

She noticed the frown settling into his features. "I hope you do not go back to America," he said. "Mikhail has been a son to me. More than he has to Alex."

She nodded. "I know. And he hardly knows me as his mother."

Stefan patted her shoulder. "That is already changing. You are both family to me. I can see the bonding between mother and son every day.

He has not wanted to leave your side since our victory celebration over the dark forces of evil in the castle."

"I'm sorry. The presence of Gregory Balogh brought something vile to this beautiful town."

"No matter. That is over."

"You killed Gregory, didn't you?"

Stefan removed his hands from her shoulders. "I did. He was about to shoot Alex, and probably you and Mikhail. I couldn't let that happen."

"Thank you. You saved our lives." Elena exhaled.

"Elena, my dear Elena."

Elena looked up at him. A serene countenance covered Stefan's face.

"I am a father to Mikhail. You are his mother. If something should happen to Alex, or he no longer wishes to be married, why do you and I not marry and raise Mikhail? You could build your school in the American tradition? I am an old man. I will make no demands on you."

Elena gasped. "Why? Did Alex say something to you?"

Stefan put up his hand. "No, I do not know anything, only that you love Alexander. Love never goes away. But he has a tendency toward the free life, is that not so?"

Elena looked down.

Stefan continued. "And he is an agent for the Federal Bureau of Investigation in the United States. He might never be a good family man for you. Here you have the beautiful mountains, a castle, a school, and my inn. And a man who will care for you. And, you may have another child? Am I not right?"

Elena stared. "You know?"

"It is evident, is it not?"

She looked over the railing at the mountains. "How good you are, Stefan. But this is so overwhelming to me. I don't even know if I am pregnant."

"No? You do not have to make a decision now. It is just something to think about."

Elena sighed. Marriage to Stefan Baklanov? The stepfather to Jan? Good God, this was becoming incestuous. She changed the subject. "I've taken Mikhail away from his duties at the inn. He's been helping me clean up Freddy's things."

Stefan smiled. "That is not a problem. Did you find anything of importance? Anything that sheds light on his heroin addiction?"

"No." Had she? She stared down at the ground, thinking. No traces of heroin or its paraphernalia lay in any recess of the cottage. All she'd found beside his clothes and furniture were health books focusing on eating right, an exercise manual, the art of playing bridge, and the classics of fiction. Not the sort of repertoire one might have if addicted to heroin. She turned back up to Stefan. "Nothing. But it could have been cleaned up long ago. I would never know."

Stefan stared out at the castle, avoiding Elena's eyes. "Nevertheless, Frederick did not come out of his cottage for days on end. My sister brought food when she went to work in the castle. Toward the end, Elena, he was a sick young man."

"Didn't anyone call a doctor?"

"We did not know how serious it had become. I blame myself. I thought Gregory was close to your brother. But now we know. He must have supplied him. A thing most awful."

"Yes, it was. Stefan, I don't believe Freddy was a heroin addict." Stefan regarded her thoughtfully. "No? What then?"

"My family has had a history of tragedy. My husband was murdered nine years ago. My brother died recently, and then my grandmother was run down just before we came. Gregory's associates tried to kill me too. I believe Freddy was murdered."

"Perhaps, there is that possibility, always."

Stefan turned to leave. "But it is over. All is well. Now, I hope you will stay here with Mikhail and the pretty Marina."

Elena strolled out to the back and watched the river water's ripple and the trees swaying in the breeze. Alex, Mikhail, Marina, Tony, Stefan—the people in her life.

But one figure has been missing since the night of the party. Jan. Where is Jan? Somehow, I don't think he is finished with us—with me.

Washington, D.C.

The doorbell rang at Lucille Robinson's apartment. Right on time. Another expectant lover. Now that Gregory Balogh was dead, she no longer feared anything. He'd paid up her rent, and there was enough money for some time to come. Now, with her job and the funds, she could have any number of lovers.

She opened the door wearing her blue negligee, the one Gregory bought for her. But instead of her newest boyfriend, there stood two men in blue suits holding badges. FBI badges.

"Lucille Robinson?" one asked.

She recognized them from her office. "You know who I am. What do you want?"

One of them said, "We need to speak to you. May we come in?"

Lucille attempted to shut the door, but the agent was too quick. He stuck his foot in the crack.

"No!" she yelled and ran to the bedroom, slamming the door in their faces. She locked it just in time.

"Lucille, we have a warrant for your arrest in connection with providing sensitive information to terrorists working against the United

States. That's treason, Miss Robinson. If you cooperate, the department may go easy on you, but you need to come with us."

Lucille rummaged around her underwear drawer and pulled out the Glock 37 she kept loaded and ready. She shot once through the door.

"Shit!" an agent hollered.

A bullet flew through the door in her direction, narrowly missing her arm. She backed toward the balcony window that looked over Washington D.C. As the agents shot out the lock, Lucille took one last look at life and the few weeks she'd lived in the lap of luxury, then jumped.

CHAPTER 35

FBI Office

Bucharest, Romania

"**D**ead!" Director Larry Simmons shouted at Alex and Tony through their secured Skype connection and banged his fist on his conference table. They were 4950 miles from Washington DC, and Alex still thought his eardrums might burst.

"Dammit, Tony. I needed to *talk* to her."

"Sir," Tony said. "Your agents had no control over her movements. She kept a loaded gun in her dresser. She knew the consequences if she got caught."

"That's not the *damned point!*"

Alex had never seen Larry Simmons so mad—on-screen or off.

"Sorry, it happened that way, sir. It really wasn't their fault," Tony replied. "She jumped from her top floor balcony."

Alex and Tony sat in the conference office in Bucharest. Two large, framed paintings decorated the whitewashed walls—one of George Washington crossing the Delaware, and one of Nathan Hale about to be hanged. Otherwise, pictures of the United States president, suspected castles, fugitives from justice home and abroad, things-to-do lists, and take-out menus from local restaurants embellished the whitewashed walls in the FBI foreign office.

It had been four weeks since they arrived. And, it had taken all that time to locate the mole working within their home office and discover the rest of the local drug traffickers. Eventually, they caught some of the lower levels out on the streets.

Larry suspected the leak possibly came from Bucharest, but that wasn't the case. No, the woman responsible for compromising their whereabouts on every leg of their trip to Romania—the lady guilty for the young mechanic's death from the Rusalka and many others. Who would have thought? Alex shifted uneasily in his chair. There would be hell to pay. He was glad he stayed in Romania and not in Washington right now.

Larry Simmons glowered into the Skype screen.

"Sorry?" The director's face was in a rage. "Sorry? There's more than just Gregory Balogh behind this. Lucille Robinson was a credible source of information that might have led us further up the ranks. And you're *sorry?*"

Alex raised an eyebrow, instantly awake. He'd been sure Gregory had been the top dog. "What do you mean to the top? I thought Gregory Balogh *was* the top," Alex said.

"No. Not quite. This organization is run like a multi-billion-dollar corporation. President, Vice-Presidents, then the generals, colonials, lieutenants going on down the line. Organized like our own military structure. We only got one of the leaders." Larry rose from the table, pulled down a screen, and moved the computer closer so they could see. It read like a corporate organization chart. "There," he pointed with a long stick. "See?"

Tony's mouth twitched as though stifling a smirk, and he turned away and coughed.

"Don't you laugh, Donatelli," the director shouted. "Okay, okay. I'm preaching to the choir. I know it. You're not responsible, and neither were those agents. They could have anticipated, I suppose. Or better yet, it could have been you two going in and getting her." He banged the stick on the floor. "Enough of the temper tantrum. More news. The Romanian Association basically worked out of the Dkany Castle as the holding point. The bulk of the raw material came from Afghanistan."

Tony shrugged. "Poppy fields. Yeah, tell me something I don't know."

"Okay, I will. You know the heroin was being shipped into New York. What you might not know is that it was held in other locations besides Dkany. From the intelligence gathered, Balogh controlled the Dkany, Romania connection. So, where are those other locations, who are the ones that head them, and who's the master puppeteer behind the whole organization?" He stared blankly at the two men. "We've crippled them, but we haven't disabled them. We get the leader, then maybe we'll put them out of business—at least temporarily."

"That's nice to know. As soon as we get the head, a new group will take over." Alex folded his arms and sat back, waiting for more to fall. Damn. Here they'd just brought in the bad guys, and that wasn't enough? Some smart lawyer will get them out. Shit. He tuned out the world of corruption.

He couldn't get Elena out of his mind. He missed her something terrible and wondered how she was doing. He couldn't forget the look on her and Mikhail's face when he left. She knew he'd come back, but his son didn't. Mikhail ran after their car and tripped, falling on the concrete. That was awful. They couldn't have stopped even for a minute? Shit. What a lousy business. He hated the way he'd talked—

"Alex?"

His director stared at him. "I was talking to you. Where the hell were you?"

Alex moved forward in his seat. "Sorry."

"Never mind. I don't want to know. I want the two of you to look through these surveillance photos taken in Afghanistan through the past years. We have reason to believe Balogh got his supply from a group of warlords who hold control of poppy fields. Central Intelligence found out where they were and that the proceeds have been funding terrorist activities. So, we need to look for familiar faces. Maybe you can come up with something. You might have seen someone hanging around Dkany."

"I was hoping Miss Robinson could have told us *something*. I doubt she knew the ringleader. That would have been a closely guarded secret. But she might have had something to offer—if we could have gotten her to talk."

"Oh, we could have done that," Tony said.

"Oh yeah? Well, you didn't. She's dead." Larry said through gritted teeth. He put his finger on the power button, then said, "Find me something. *Anything.*" He snapped off the Skype, and the screen went blank.

"Well shit," Alex said. "That went well." He checked his laptop screen. "Why couldn't I have done this on my computer in the comfort of the Sandor? So we don't have to be here."

"Security. We don't know who might have hacked in, and we don't know who might still be lurking over there."

"That's a comforting thought. My sister, wife, and son are there."

A startled look crossed Tony's face, and a tense silence lengthened between them. "Marina," he said softly. He clicked on a government surveillance video.

Alex glanced over at Tony. How far had their relationship actually gone? He tested. "I want to get back to my family. Are you coming back to Dkany with me?"

They searched the screens and scrolled.

Tony clicked the next screen and looked back at Alex.

"Of course. When you say family, do you mean Elena and Mikhail, as well as Marina? I mean, as part of your family?"

Alex shot Tony a look. "Of course it does. They are my family."

Tony half grinned and started to pour over the photos.

"If you keep going with Marina, you might end up my brother-in-law." *Hah, so there.*

Tony smirked and went back to what he was reading.

Realizing the conversation he didn't want was over, Alex opened another file.

They poured over them for hours. Alex didn't even look up when sandwiches and coffee were brought in.

Tony, however, did. "Got something stronger?" A grunt receded into the background as the door slammed shut. "We're prisoners," Tony grumbled.

It was way past five o'clock when Alex saw the first person he recognized. He half rose in his seat and sat back down, just staring. Then, he motioned Tony to come over.

Tony bumped into the edge of the table as he almost hurtled himself to Alex's side. He slumped into the nearest chair. Then slowly said, "Okay, so that's Balogh. He looks like he's outfitted in Afghan fatigues or something. Where was this taken?"

"Outside of Kabul. One of their strongholds. The men he's with are terrorists camped in the mountains."

"Hell of a way to live," Alex said.

"Yeah, by our standards." He turned to another photo. "The others behind him are hired guns of the revolutionaries bent on killing off anyone who gets in their way.

"Dangerous bastards. They'll stop at nothing to get what they want, and they'll stop at nothing to get revenge. Okay, what about this photo? Looks like Gregory is in this one, too." Alex pressed enter and went to the next photo.

"Hell, no!" Alex gasped in a breath. He turned his head and bit his lip, tears blinding from the fury that overcame him. When Tony came over, he skipped to another photo.

"Let me see." Tony peered over his shoulder. "You can't hide it, Alex. It is what it is."

Sick with the struggle within, Alex clicked the backspace and forced himself to look at the screen. Stefan Baklanov stood in army fatigues next to Mikhail. Both carried military assault rifles and big grins. Mikhail couldn't have been more than seven-years-old. "Stefan. Oh my God," Alex whispered.

"Jesus," Tony said. "What has Stefan been teaching this kid?"

Alex buzzed Larry's office.

More photos showed Stefan and Mikhail. Others showed Gregory and Stefan coming out of the castle.

"Take a look at these." Alex bombarded Larry with more and more photos before he'd had a chance to look at the first ones. Then, Larry's face appeared on the screen. "Hold on. Hold on. That's Gregory Balogh. You know someone else?"

Alex nodded. Standing with them were Stefan Baklanov and Mikhail.

The three men stared at the photos. Picture after picture. Stefan and Mikhail standing next to each other, the older man's arm around the boy's shoulder. Images showing Mikhail firing a rifle in a range. At tin cans. At a target showing a human heart. Mikhail wore his trademark big grin with each shot.

No, with my big grin, thought Alex grimly. Some kind of prickle indicator forecasting sinister events worked overtime. His kid and the boy's adopted grandfather, working, conspiring with known terrorists.

Larry tapped on one photo. "Who are they, and who's the kid?"

Tony and Larry were now staring at Alex, who wanted the earth to swallow him whole. "The man is Stefan Baklanov, the Sandor Inn owner where Elena and Marina are right now. The kid is my son."

Larry paled a little. He had his own children, two boys and a girl. He went from warrior on the warpath to father just that fast. "Oh shit. I'm sorry, Alex."

"That means Stefan must have known about the baby's kidnapping or hired the assassin. He ended up with the boy," Alex said. "Jan and Elena were gotten out of the way.

"Stefan must have thought with Jan, the father, Mikhail would inherit the castle. As Jan's stepfather, he would be next in line. And Gregory must have felt the same thing. It didn't matter to him if Elena married me. I wasn't next. Mikhail was."

"And trained him to be part of the next generation of thugs." Alex walked away from the computer and across the room, running his hands through his hair. "And something else is nagging me—I can't quite . . ." What *was* it? Something about their escape from the castle. About Gregory and his men meeting them at the entrance. He couldn't see it, could not grasp.

Alex paced the room and stopped. "How did everyone know we'd come out that entrance?"

"What, Alex?" Tony asked.

"How did Gregory know we were coming through the chapel entrance? Why were you there, Tony? It hadn't been used in years."

Tony stared at him, color draining out of his face. "You don't think I—"

"No, hell no. Not *you.* "

"Mikhail was the only one who knew we were there," Alex whispered. "He had to tell Stefan where we were going. Stefan must have told him which way to leave. They knew we were coming to rescue Elena. Alex banged his fist on the table. "He betrayed us. He told Stefan, and Stefan told Gregory."

"He's nine," Larry said. "He would tell his grandfather. But I don't understand something." A look of confusion settled on Larry's face. "Stefan led a group of villagers to rescue you and Elena. He killed Gregory. Why would he have done that if Gregory was in his employ, or if Gregory employed *him?*"

"Maybe because he was afraid Gregory would implicate him. He had to silence him."

"Or because Stefan wanted to take over— so, which is it?"

"Yeah, but there were still others there who—"

"No," Larry replied. "In this type of organization, each player knows the person he reports to. None of them would have known about Stefan. They can't talk about what they don't know. Too many people knew about Gregory. He was the one who set up meetings, instigated the kidnappings, and hired Lucille to spy. Stefan was the only one nobody knew about. Now we must figure out the rest. The hierarchy to the top."

"And we can," Alex said. "Through my son and his grandfather. And, God help us, Elena and Marina are in their care." He pulled out his cell phone.

"Who—?"

Alex gave him a look and spoke on his cell. "Marina?"

"Oh," Tony said. He stroked his goat-tee. "Do you think I'd look better if I shaved this thing off?" He had a faraway look in his eyes.

Alex shrugged him off and spoke into his phone. "Mari! Don't talk, just listen. You and Elena need to leave the cottage. *Now!* I'll have someone pick you up. I'll explain later. This is important. Don't tell Stefan or Mikhail where you're going. Make an excuse. Just get out of there. We'll be there in a few hours. We're leaving now. Take care of yourselves until."

When Alex clicked off, he turned his head toward the door. "Tony, our girls are in trouble. We've got to leave *now!*"

Chapter 36

Castle Cottage

Dkany, Romania

"What happened to Freddy's computer?" Elena asked, walking into the kitchen. "I've combed this whole place and can't find it."

Marina sat a plate of leftovers on the table. "Probably stolen. Taken by the police or Gregory, maybe?" She sat across from Elena and started piling food on her plate. "Elena, eat." She didn't feel particularly hungry.

"What's wrong?"

Well, I'll just lay it on her. Marina's a doctor. Let her practice. "Nothing much. I'm pregnant."

"Nothing much? Really?" The corner of Marina's mouth turned upward with satisfaction—maybe. She put her hands on her hips and nodded. "I kind of figured that's what was going on. You've been looking a bit green lately. Are you sure?"

"Pretty much."

"But that's great! I'm going to be an aunt. I mean an aunt for a second time. Mikhail will have a baby brother or sister to play with. Alex will be the proudest papa this side of—"

The acute sense of loss prickled her insides once again.

Elena smiled. "I hope he takes it as well as you. I worry about his former lifestyle and if he'll want it back. It will be either me or it." She shook her head. "Alex may not want the responsibility of a family." She stood and pushed the chair back from the table.

Marina folded her arms and regarded her. "Come on, Elena. You know damn well Alex wants you and Mikhail. I don't think it went quite like that. My brother asked you if you wanted to stay married, and you said no."

"I was looking at a ghost, for crying out loud."

"Yeah, but he didn't know that."

"I told him, he seemed to understand. Besides, I didn't tell you about the conversation before that." She told her.

"Hmm. So, my brother thought he could talk straight to you about anything. That means he considers you a friend as well as a lover. I don't think it would have been something he couldn't adjust to. I think that the life he led was something he was throwing to the wind to see if he could let go."

Elena leaned against the pine cupboard, moving when the knob caught her back. "Ouch. What if he can't?"

Marina continued, "Alex was not a happy man. He started womanizing after you left him to go to Romania, and he tried to forget you. I don't know why he didn't get seriously involved with anyone for all those years. Probably for the same reason you didn't. Did you think of that?"

"He said he wanted us to be together. But for some reason, when he told me, he looked lost, like I was trapping him." She twisted the ring around on her finger. "If he thinks I was trying to rope him in then, can you imagine how he'll feel once he finds out I'm going to have another child?"

"It takes two to make a baby, Elena. And, despite the fact you're already a mother, he's had a lot more experience in the sexual arena than you have. He knew the risk."

Elena smiled. "He asked me what he could give me as a wedding present. I said a baby girl. He looked excited, happy. There wasn't anything we were planning that would prevent us from having a baby. I loved—*love*—him. I didn't think having another child would ever—" She let go a huff and sat at the table. "Inflict a prison environment on him. Damn. I wanted—*want*—another child. We didn't take precautions. Probably a mistake given everything that's been going on. But that's all over—*over*."

Marina smiled. "Knowing Alex, if he thought you two should wait, he would have told you upfront. Honestly, he would have. But one thing I do know, he loves you. Period. If you are pregnant—"

Marina's face suddenly dazzled with determination. "Why don't we get a home pregnancy test kit?"

"Do they have them here in Dkany?"

"I would imagine. Why not?"

Marina's cell phone rang. "Hello, Alex."

Elena flinched at the sound of his name.

"What? Why?" Marina said, gazing at Elena, frowning. Her eyes went wide.

Panicked, Elena asked, "What's going on?"

"Nobody else is here. Mikhail? He's outside. Why? Don't go to the Sandor? Wait a minute. What's wrong—roach problem? You want us to go where?" Marina nodded. "See you when you get there." She ended the call and said to Elena, "They're leaving Bucharest. He's going to call you in about fifteen minutes."

It didn't even take that long before Elena's cell rang.

"Alex, are you all right? Where are you?"

"Hey, baby girl, I'm fine. We're on the road right now. How are you feeling?"

Elena nearly choked. Did Alex *know?* How? "Uh, fine, why?" She paused and decided to go for it. "How the hell did you *know?*"

"Uh, only wanted to know how you were. Know what?"

"Nothing's wrong. What should be wrong?" Everything was coming out wrong. If Alex didn't know something big was up, he was utterly insane. And that he wasn't.

"Oh yes, there is. So, tell me."

"Can we wait until you get back here?"

"Why? Why can't you tell me now? You haven't fallen in love with some old Romanian farmer, have you?"

"Fallen in—" Elena giggled. "Hell no."

"Good. I'd have to challenge him to a duel."

"A duel?"

"So then, why can't you tell me now?"

"It's a surprise."

"Bullshit."

Elena let out a deep sigh. "Okay, this might not be an ideal time, but here goes."

"Why isn't it an ideal time?"

"Shut up and listen."

"Yes, ma'am."

Elena almost laughed. "I'm pregnant, or I'm almost sure I am."

Silence over the phone. *Oh no. I knew this wasn't a good idea.*

She asked, "Are you still there?"

"Yeah, I'm still here. Did you say you were pregnant?"

"That's what I thought I said. I didn't mention having three heads or anything."

Alex chuckled.

Whew, at least he still had a sense of humor.

"Our little girl, maybe?" he asked softly.

"Either one will suit me just fine," Elena said.

"Me too. This will make it doubly important for you to listen to what Marina has to say. I can't stay on the cell. I'll see you in a couple of hours. Don't tell anybody about this call, okay?"

"But—"

"Promise me."

"Of course."

"Take care of our little girl," Alex said softly and clicked off.

Suppose it was a boy?

Elena was left with a dead cell phone in her hand; a sudden feeling of tired sadness and chills passed over her. It wasn't over.

"What?" Marina asked.

Elena stared at her. "He told me to ask you."

Marina glared at Elena. "Well. It seems something has happened."

"Like what?"

"Like we have to go to the monastery. Now."

"I know that, but *why* do we have to leave?"

Marina gritted her teeth, and her eyes narrowed into slits. "I'm a doctor for God's sakes. You're a scholar. You'd think my brother could have at least told us what was wrong. I am not a child."

"What did he *say?*" Elena felt like choking the truth out of her. Except maybe he hadn't told her. "Okay," she said. "He told us to go to the monastery. In what? We don't have a car."

"Someone will pick us up."

"Why?"

"Because he said so, that's why." Marina stamped across the floor, poured a glass of water, then pitched it out and slammed the glass on the counter. "I need something stronger." She headed for the wine bottle.

"We don't have to do what he tells us," Elena said, "But he did say *please.*"

Marina suddenly looked up and the anger lifted. "Yeah. I know. He's polite if nothing else." A smile filled her face. Then, the smile turned back downward. "But I think we'd better. Oh. There's one more thing."

"What?" Elena came and sat down at the table. "We can't tell Stefan or Mikhail where we're going."

"Why not?"

Marina shrugged. "I have no idea. But . . ." she paused, and this time smiled.

Mikhail peeked his head in the screen door. "I come with you?"

Both women turned and looked at the intruder. It seemed nothing could be kept from Mikhail, even if they'd wanted—needed to keep something secret.

A black limousine pulled up in front of the cottage, and a priest slid out of the driver's seat. "Greetings. I am Brother Tibor, assistant to the

Holy Father of the Dkany Monastery, Father Samuka. I have instructions you will come with me?" He turned to Mikhail and mussed his hair. "Hello, young friend. You will come too?" Mikhail beamed and gave a definitive nod.

"I come too?" He asked, grinning at his mother.

Marina and Elena shook their heads. Marina said, "No. You must go back to the Inn. Stefan expects you." Mikhail's face fell.

Brother Tibor shrugged and said, "Well, next time, yes?" He opened the passenger door, and the women got inside.

Elena said, "Go back to the Inn, honey. We'll see you later."

As Elena looked back, Mikhail put his hands in his pockets, kicked a stone, turned, and with his head down, he walked in the direction of his grazing horse.

A feeling so strong inside her told her to stop. She had no idea where it came from, but something terrible would happen if she kept Mikhail behind. She knew it. The car pulled out toward the road. Elena jumped up in her seat and knocked her hand on the door. Pain shot through her knuckles. "Wait!"

The driver pulled to a sudden stop, and Marina banged her chest into the back of the front seat. "Ouch. Damn." The driver looked back at her.

Elena opened the door and ran in the direction of where Mikhail was petting his horse's head. "Mikhail, you're coming with us. "

"You want me to come, too?"

"You bet I do."

Mikhail hopped into the car, and Marina pulled Elena out of hearing distance. "Why did you do that? Alex said—"

"I know. But look, if we leave Mikhail behind, the first thing he'll do is tell Stefan where we're going. Besides, he's my child, and I won't leave him behind." She started back for the car. "I also know that if we leave him here, something bad will happen to him. I don't know how I just do."

Chapter 37

Dkany Monastery

The unique thing about Dkany Monastery was the reason for its being. Providing protection against foreign invaders, the monastery housed the church, its offices, dormitories, vast library, restaurant, and a clinic for the Dkany townsfolk.

A chain still enacted the clanging of the doorbell inside, as it had for centuries. A gatekeeper dressed in black robes came out of the round guardhouse, opened the gate, and signaled them to pass through to the parking lot. When they drove through the gate, Elena couldn't believe the artwork on the side of the building. The exterior walls were painted with action scenes taken from the bible. They blended into other Transylvanian landscapes, giving the impression bible characters could step from the church into the Carpathian Mountains.

Father Samuka, Patriarchal Father of the monastery, greeted them at the door. Two friars stood behind him.

"Doi Duamna Brancusi's," he said, smiling at them. "Welcome both. *Va rog.* We go to my office to talk and have a glass of wine, but first, you might want to freshen up, yes?"

"That would be nice," Elena said.

Father Samuka smiled. "You are Elena Brancusi? Your husband described you to perfection." He turned to Marina. "You must be Miss Marina Brancusi, Alexander's sister?"

"Yes, I am."

"And you," he said to a restless Mikhail, "I know you well. You will please try to settle yourself down? I know that is hard to do at nine."

"Yes, sir," Mikhail said, looking around, his eyes focusing on one of the painted horse icons on the wall.

"Now, ladies and Mikhail, Brother Timor will escort you to your room. We will meet again in, shall we say, two hours? That will give Alexander a chance to get here from Bucharesti and you a chance to rest, but you have no luggage with you?"

"We left in a hurry," Elena said.

"Ah, yes. We may have some extra women's clothes that might fit. But we take care of that later. Nobody knows where you are. That is how Mr. Brancusi wanted it."

"What about my grandfather?" Mikhail asked. "He might be worried?"

"Ah, not to worry. Stephan will be informed you are safe." Father Samuka took Elena aside out of Mikhail's hearing distance. "Mr. Brancusi said no one should know where you are, not even little Mikhail."

Elena nodded. "Alex did mention that. I was afraid he'd tell Stefan and maybe other people at the inn. Mikhail is nine and doesn't discriminate very well yet. Besides, he is my son. You understand, don't you?"

Father Samuka breathed out and nodded. "Yes, I understand. Keep him close to you, Mrs. Brancusi. Keep him very close. There is danger very close at hand, this I tell you."

"From—?"

"I do not know from where it will come. I only know you are not safe in Dkany. I hope we can offer you protection here until Alexander can get you out of the country."

"Out of the country? I don't understand. Who would want to hurt us now?"

Father Samuka shook his head. "I do not know, only that you must leave Romania."

She started to walk back to Marina and Mikhail when Father Samuka pulled her back again.

"Excuse me, Mrs. Brancusi, you take good care of the child you carry."

Elena's stomach twitched. "How did you know? Did Alex—?"

"No. Alexander said nothing. I do not know how. I just know. You will have much to do later, so it will be good for you and Marina to rest. Forget all the trials you have gone through. There are computer games for Mikhail to play on, but no Internet. He must not make contact with the outside. We will ring for you when it is time for you to come down here."

Elena didn't understand. Why were they still in danger? Why couldn't Mikhail go on the Internet? What was all this? She simply said, "Thank you. Thank you very much, and please call me Elena."

"You are most welcome, Miss Elena, a most admired lady."

Admired? Her?

Father Samuka said no more, and Brother Timor escorted them to the ladies' dormitory.

Two hours later, Brother Timor knocked at their door and accompanied Elena and Marina back to the main sanctuary, where Father Samuka greeted them. "We will go to my office where we can talk. Brother Tibor and Brother Benci, our curator and head of archives, will answer questions. They speak English, and you speak Romanian, so communication should not be a problem."

"Yes. We grew up in Romanian households. My brother lived here in the cottage at the castle," Elena said. The increasingly familiar nausea was returning. *No, not now.* She willed it to stop.

"So we go."

Elena and Marina looked at each other and followed along.

The priests led them down the aisle of the chapel. The interior décor was even more elaborate than the exterior. Stained glass windows formed prism-like roses bouncing off plain white walls from the afternoon sun. A picture of the young Christ stood majestically in the middle window. His face shone down and reflected the light on the white marble floors. On each side of the main chapel were smaller chapels with original religious figures painted by their time's great artists. Elena noticed the artist *Dragosin, a* prominent fixture in the artwork of the Arbore Church in Moldavia. She didn't know much about him, but she did recognize his work.

One thing differed from the traditional Eastern Orthodox Churches. Most did not have pews but rather a few chairs situated around the Nave and Narthex sides. Not so at the Dkany Monastery. Benches lined the interior as in any western church. Elena meant to ask why, but then the thought left her head.

They passed through a door leading to the stairs to a lower floor which housed the church restroom, monastic prayer room, and choir room. At the end of the corridor, they walked into a large office. Elena would have thought the room simple, except for the books and papers neatly stacked in well-organized wall-to-wall bookcases that provided for a dozen or so ornate drawers. The decor reminded her of the castle. Maybe constructed by the same architect? A highly polished rosewood desk and leather chairs sat in the middle of the room. Bibles and books about religious figures were stacked up on a bookshelf with historical documents peering out from the pages.

"As you can see, we have a simple but complete monastery here. We function as a church to serve the needs of our local residents, as well as our order." He spoke slowly and seemed delighted she could understand his English.

A third brother walked up to them. "I am Brother Benci, the keeper of the archives."

"They've come," Father Samuka said to the newcomer, "for protection against those who might hurt them. Am I not correct?"

"Yes," Elena admitted. "My husband told us to come here. He called Father Samuka. I don't know what they said or what threats we face now."

"*Duamna*," Brother Benci said.

"Please call me Elena, and this is my sister-in-law, Marina."

"Mikhail," Father Samuka said. "Would you go into the chapel? The choir will start rehearsing soon. You might want to tell us how you like the music."

"But—"

"Now, *go*," he said in a good, firm tone.

Mikhail obeyed and scurried out of the room.

"You may not know, Miss Elena, but Mikhail loves music. He has sat through many concerts here and would like to learn to play the organ."

Elena smiled. "Good to know. So much has happened. I haven't had a chance to get to know my son."

"Yes, that is understandable. But now, will you please explain to the good brothers what has happened and why you need our protection."

Elena told them about everything. She held nothing back. The holy men looked at each other with raised eyebrows when she explained about the ghost but said nothing.

"Elena. You are now the owner of Dkany Castle. Yes, I have heard the rumors about some guests who come into the castle, but nothing as dastardly as heroin. That is bad, indeed." He rose from the seat, went over to the bookcase, picked out a book, and handed it to her. "This book? You may want to read. You understand it is not the church's position to recognize the occult. But I understand. I say no more than, I too, have seen it."

"You have?" Marina asked, mouth open. "You believe then?"

"Yes, I believe. However, if you say this, I deny. You understand?"

"Yes, we do," Elena said.

Father Samuka sat back at his desk. "Your good Alexander told me more. He asked something of me you may not know. He asked that I provide you knowledge of the silver cross. They think we may know more than what Gregory Balogh told you. So . . ."

"You do?" Elena asked.

"This is a long story—a long *history*." Father Samuka translated as Elena followed his Romanian laced with Ukrainian accent as best she could.

She followed him as he explained about the cross and the ruby, which Elena knew. He continued. "During the fifteenth century, monks from this monastery hid the cross from marauding Turks. The monks drew this map so the church could find it again after the wars ended. No such luck. An earthquake destroyed the part of the castle where the cross was reported hidden. The map, too, disappeared. At least that's what everyone thought. But, after a succession of communist and tyrannical governments finally fell in 1989, and the church gained independence and free movement, we were able to search for it again. Unfortunately, we couldn't find either the cross or the map."

"You weren't allowed to look for it before then?" Elena asked.

"We could. The government would have been all too happy for us to find the cross and then confiscate it. We were questioned. We never looked, so it was never taken."

"Oh," Elena said.

"Then, about a year ago, I read an old journal. I study historical documents, you see," Father Samuka explained. "I came across the letters concerning the whereabouts of the cross and the location of the map.

"I talked to some of the friars, who were here at the time, and we uncovered the map. It had been well hidden in the archive room, under floorboards. Somehow, Gregory Balogh got wind of it because he was on my doorstep, demanding to have the document. He said it was Dkany property, and he, as their executor, had a duty to return the cross to the family. I had no trust in this Balogh. The stories about his treachery to the townspeople made my blood boil. I believed if he got hold of that map, your family, Elena, would never see it or the cross."

"So, what did you do?" Elena was breathless, Marina on the edge of her seat.

"Well, naturally," he said, in good humor, with a wicked grin, "I forged another one."

Elena laughed so hard her insides hurt, and suddenly, she felt the need to run out of the room and into the token ladies room, where she threw up her breakfast. Oh crap, she thought. Why now, just when the good part of the story is coming up? Feeling a bit sheepish, she washed her face off and gargled with water, the only thing handy to take away the rancid taste. Then, she mustered up the dignity to go back into the room and hear the rest of the story.

"Are you all right?" Marina asked, frowning as she came back. The friars looked devastated with distress for her well-being. She shook off their concern and pleaded with Father Samuka to finish the story.

He looked apprehensive, as though concerned she couldn't handle the emotional stress of the story. Still, she smiled and asked him to continue.

"When Gregory Balogh came to get the map, there it was, written on ancient parchment in a concoction I believed to be similar to the ink used back then. I doubt he would have noticed the difference anyway. He took the false map and left. That's almost the end of the story."

"Almost?" Marina asked.

"All except for the real map. Brother Tibor, would you go over to the cabinet?"

Tibor took a key from around his neck and unlocked a metal cabinet door in the corner of the room. Inside, rolled up in a protective container, lay the ancient map drawn up by the fifteenth-century monks of Dkany.

"We've been waiting for a real Dkany to come along. Until then, we've kept it safe and secret. So, even we do not know what the document says."

Brother Tibor unrolled the parchment and spread it out on the table where Father Samuka got the first look. After a stunned silence,

Father Samuka said, "So, we've all been wrong." He laughed with a sound that seemed to go way down deep. A warm and pleasant sound. Elena laughed along with him.

They all stood around the desk as the friars cleared it off and lay the map flat.

The outside bell rang, and Brother Tibor ran to answer it. He came back, followed by Alex and Tony.

Alex's glance went around the room until it rested on Elena. His eyes didn't leave her.

"Alexander Brancusi and Anthony Donatelli," said Father Samuka. "This is Brother Tibor and Brother Benci, my assistants." They shook hands. "Brother Benci is in charge of the monastery archives. Would you care for a glass of wine, or shall we get down to business?"

"Please, we'd like to find out what you know," Alex said.

"We have some artifacts that might interest you. So, please come with me."

As he passed Elena, he pulled her to her feet and hugged her. "Oh, baby girl," he said, kissing her hair.

"Alex, I'm so glad you're here. I've missed you something awful."

"Me too. How are you feeling?"

"A lot of morning sickness at various times of the day. Other than that, just fine."

"Oh!" Alex said. "What's that?" He pointed to the map that lay on top of the desk.

Father Samuka explained, "That is a map of the location of the silver cross. Now we find it."

They walked to a bookcase, and Father Samuka pulled out a book. The entire case folded inward, similar to what had happened in the castle. Elena wondered whether the same architect had designed both the castle and the monastery. Next, they passed into a large archive room filled with crosses, pews, old robes, and first editions of bibles and other religious manuscripts. In the corner stood a statue of the Virgin Mary.

"Oh my, is this the original?"

"No, not the original. I would dislike destroying that."

"Destroy? Then this is where the cross is?"

"Yes, according to the map, this is where the cross lies."

"Clever. Very clever," Alex said.

"Is it not?" Father Samuka answered. "Now, Brother Tibor, would you hand me the chisel and hammer?"

The statute of the Virgin Mary replica stood twice the size of a person. Her arms stretched out as if calling to her people. They carefully dismantled her, leaving dust and debris and ceramic bits. Most of the inside was hollow, but Tibor hammered into the middle and hit something solid. By hand, the men dug in and pulled on something smooth and metal. They broke out the middle, and there stood the silver cross.

They stood in shock.

When they could breathe again, Alex whistled.

Father Samuka said, "Let's bring this into the office. Brother Tibor, put down a cloth over the table, if you please."

They carried the cross into the office and laid it over the cloth.

Parts of the cross still shone as sunlight came in through the window. Diamonds, emeralds, and sapphires were embedded in the silver. Only one indent for a missing stone remained. "That's where the ruby lay," Elena said. "My God, this is magnificent."

"It is priceless, and it is yours," Father Samuka said. "This belonged to your family. If it could be valued, I think it would be worth millions, although I doubt any organization could pay you that for such a relic."

"No," she said. "I don't think it does belong to us. Not really. This cross belongs to the church and should remain here, with the ruby replaced."

"That ruby was given to your family in the Fifteenth Century, Elena. It belongs to you."

"I insist you have it," Elena said. "It's only right. The cross doesn't look whole without it."

"That is very generous, indeed," Father Samuka said, intense pleasure crossing his face. "But what can we do in return?"

"I'm sure we'll think of something," she replied. The castle and her plans for a school came to mind. Maybe the monastery could build and provide for her school.

But that had better wait. Meanwhile, Elena needed to speak to Alex. The stress sent her stomach into more turmoil.

Oh no. She'd have to run to the bathroom again.

And now, everyone turned to her.

"Elena, what's wrong?" Tony asked. "You're turning green—or something. Flu going around?" His mouth turned up into a grin.

Alex raised an eyebrow but otherwise remained stoic.

"Ah, no. I think there is something more miraculous here, no?"

Elena made a beeline for the doorway.

"Father, please," Marina said gently. "Wait until Elena comes back."

Alex shook his head. "It seems everyone else knows anyway. I wanted to pass around cigars, but I guess you all beat me to it. Elena and I are going to have a baby. So, there you have it. I just found out today."

On that note, Elena ran for the bathroom.

"Oh, crap, Alex," Marina whispered when she came back into the room. "You look like you swallowed something rancid. She's going to have a baby, that's all. You know about that, don't you? You've done it before." She didn't say *you shit*—but he thought she'd like to.

"Marina, you don't understand." His grin turned downward. He had to keep up a positive appearance.

Elena walked back into the room, pale but smiling—until she looked at *him.* Then the smile turned downward into a frown. She'd caught his distress. He didn't want her to think that he didn't want the child. There were enough other things for them to worry about.

Alex caught her by her arm and led her out into the hall. "Are you sick?"

"Of course I am. And why the tight grip?"

"Oh." Alex let go. "Sorry. Something . . ."

For a moment, a chilled black silence surrounded them. Finally, Elena frowned and said, "You don't look pleased."

"Elena, I know we planned for this, but this is a bad, bad time."

"What? *Now* you tell me! My God, Alex. You don't want this child, do you?" She turned on her heels and headed for the chapel. "I need to be alone for a while. I need to think. I'm going up to the church. Don't follow me, okay?"

"Damn," Alex said.

"Maybe it's the hormones. It happens. Leave me alone before I get sick again."

Bitterness hit him like the persistent ghost of Elena's ex-husband. They hadn't taken precautions because they'd planned, hoped for a baby. He remembered what Magda used to say. *"Be careful what you wish for. You just might get it."*

He called out to her. "No, it's not okay. I want to talk this out. Why do you always walk out at crucial moments? Why do you always do this to me? You don't understand. Of course, I want—"

But Elena was already walking up the stairs toward the church. Then, she had turned a corner and was out of sight. So much for the positive appearance.

Boy, oh boy. A baby. Another case of the right event at the wrong time.

Chapter 38

Monastery

Elena walked up the stairs feeling Alex's eyes burning a hole in her back. She wasn't sure that he didn't want a child. In fact, she knew he did. But what had made him seem so adamant, so *scared?* It almost seemed he knew just being alive was a risk. How could she be in danger anymore? Gregory Balogh was dead, as was his gunmen. She thought for a moment maybe she should have stayed and listened.

Except for a choir of monks who chanted a Gregorian chant for evening vespers from the choir loft, quiet descended over the church. Glowing sunset flowed through the back of the stained-glass young Christ, where he continued to beckon, and this time aimed his grace on the end of a wooden pew. Elena sat far from where a solitary monk prayed.

She huddled into her leather jacket. Feeling sorry for herself and for her unborn child, she started to silently cry. It was such an internal, personal feeling of despair, she needed to savor it alone. If there had been any way she could have left the monastery and permanently disappeared into the shadows of the evening, she would have. Instead, she wondered how it would feel if she walked into that river and never came out. Why couldn't anything go right between her and Alex? Why did it always come to this?

The peacefulness of the environment, the chanting monks, sickness, and fatigue were enough to lull Elena into an uneasy, disturbing sleep.

Alex led priests in black robes and tall square hats with hoods down the aisle of the chapel. Elena stood in front of the cross wearing a white bridal gown, trimmed in lace, with pink and blue flowers. He approached her, and she thought he would take her hand and lead her to the altar, but he walked through her as though she didn't exist. Then, her white dress turned red, and she screamed. The men seemed not to hear her as Stefan approached, a gun in his hand. He aimed at Alex, and she cried out again. Alex paid no heed to her, and the gun blast cut through him, knocking him onto the altar and shattering a silver cross. A ruby shattered like glass. As she turned in horror, the specter of Stefan once more raised his gun and this time aimed directly into her womb.

Stefan? Why him? Elena awoke, her body shook with fear. She felt hot and feverish and something else—panic? The dream had been a premonition.

Oh God!

The singing had stopped. Elena sat alone in a nearly empty church. Her breathing became even more erratic as her anxieties increased.

The only other figure in the church was the lone monk covered with a black robe and hood. He'd moved closer than she'd remembered him from when she first came in.

Alex watched Elena walk up to the church. He was still reeling from the shock of the news she was pregnant, and Elena might have thoughts he didn't want it. He worried for their safety and for Mikhail's. He'd been scared about a lot of things, but never more than now. If anything should happen to her, he didn't think he'd survive. He didn't want to leave her alone, but with her being inside the church, he thought she'd be all right. He turned and walked back into the office.

Not a word was spoken. Alex sat in misery. He became increasingly worried as Elena's absence grew from minutes into a half-hour.

"So," Tony said, none too happy. "Elena is pregnant. That should be cause for a cigar and celebration, shouldn't it?"

Alex could have clunked Tony over the head. Instead, he was also growing worried. What the hell was she doing? Could she be throwing up her guts again?

"Marina, could you go check on Elena? Maybe she's back in the bathroom. I hope she's not sick."

A few minutes later, Marina returned. "She's not in there, Alex. Maybe she's still in the church speaking with one of the monks. You know her. She's always talking to somebody."

"It's dinnertime. The monks wouldn't be there right now," Father Samuka said.

"Maybe she got caught up in the service," Alex said. "I'll go up and look."

"Here, take this," Tony said, handing Alex his gun.

"A gun in our church?" Father Samuka frowned and shook his head. "I think not." He and Brother Tibor exchanged glances.

"I understand your position, father," Alex said, wondering what passed between these holy men. "But the bad guys aren't going to have those kinds of scruples if they should be able to infiltrate the monastery."

"Do you really think they know you're here?" Father Samuka asked.

"They might," replied Marina. "Mikhail was here when Brother Tibor picked us up. It wouldn't surprise me if one of his workmen saw us leave and told him."

"Oh no," Tony said.

"You think Stefan Baklanov has something to do with this?" the priest asked him.

"I'm convinced he's at the head of the organization," Tony replied. He'd been standing quietly at the table, looking at the map, fingering its authenticity and, frowning at all the comments made so far. "We got new information from Washington. He and Mikhail were out training in Afghanistan."

Father Samuka nodded his head. "Well, it's good that you got these young women out of there. Is that why you brought Mikhail with you? To keep him close?"

"Brancusi," Alex corrected. "Mikhail Brancusi."

"I told Elena not to tell him. I'm glad she didn't listen. It's better that he's here."

Tony went through his pockets and took out a photo that showed the priest the picture he'd taken of Mikhail and Stefan in military fatigues.

"Things are seldom what they seem," Father Samuka said. "The boy is a child. Stefan is his grandfather, for all intents and purposes. You need to take care of that young woman of yours, Alex. She's carrying a child who might be a threat to your enemies. She's in grave danger."

Alex went cold. "Could Stefan get into this monastery without your knowledge?"

"Easily," Brother Tibor said. "The gatekeeper is a relative of his. They're on intimate terms."

"Oh no." Alex had forgotten. Half the population was related to the other half.

"Alex," the old priest said. "Elena is the owner of the castle. So if she dies, the castle goes to you, no?"

The castle again. "We seem to keep coming back to the chain of inheritance, don't we?" Alex said.

"Yes. We do. At first, the Dkany family. With Freddy and Magda eliminated, and Elena's husband Jan—Mikhail's father—dead, if they killed Elena, there was no doubt Mikhail and Stefan would get ownership of the castle. It didn't work out that way. Do you not understand the danger all three of you are in? With your wife being with child, her child would inherit after Mikhail. If Elena dies before giving birth, Alex, you're the only other person that stands in the way."

"Except Mikhail, and he's one of them. So, the castle goes to them," Alex repeated.

"I've known Mikhail since he was a baby. I do not think the boy is a criminal."

"No, he's not. But he's under the influence of some evil men," Alex said, coming back to reality and getting out of the sofa. "They're assassinating their own people."

"Speaking of Mikhail," Tony said, "Where is he? I haven't seen him in a while."

"I'm going to find them and bring them back here," Alex said, leaving the room. He walked down the hall toward the stairs trying to picture his slender Elena, bulging with his baby, in about eight months. This would be the perfect time to tell her he loved her—really loved her—not for the sake of responsibility, but for love. The thought made him happier than he ever thought possible.

Elena prayed. She prayed for herself and her baby, for Alex, Marina, and Mikhail, keeping her family safe and together. They were the only family she had now. Nothing must disturb that.

She noticed the lone priest walking down the aisle toward her and felt strangely uneasy about his presence. She didn't like feeling that way. A priest should provide feelings of comfort and peace. Somehow this one didn't. Her stomach felt strange again, which wasn't the familiar morning or evening sickness type of nausea. This seemed to tug directly from her uterus. God, she hoped she wasn't miscarrying. Despite what the medical journals said, she'd read stories about how stress could bring about disastrous ends to pregnancies.

The priest who approached looked familiar, somehow. She'd seen him before and recently. Instinct forced her to move. She got up and walked across the church and through the pews into the next aisle. The priest followed. She turned and smiled at him, starting to speak when the man pulled something out of his robe. Then she remembered. He had the face of the priest in her dream. It was the face of . . .

"Stefan? Why are you dressed like a monk?" Stunned, Elena halted and faced her would-be adversary. Unlike Gregory, this man was anything but crazy. Eyes the size of slits and the color of cold, steel prison bars made him look like the devil incarnate—in the guise of a holy man. As she spoke, three other shadows appeared from behind the pillars, two man-size and the other boy-size.

"Mikhail? How did—?"

"Elena!" The boy almost shouted her name, half crying-half pleading while being hauled towards her by two heavy-handed thugs.

"Our gatekeeper found him playing outside in the garden," Stefan said. "After I told him to stay in the inn tonight. He did not listen." He pinched his lips together and place his fingertips over them. He sighed. "He *never* listens. He must take after his natural mother, I think?"

Mikhail whimpered like a boy who had lost his way, lost his family, and lost his trust in his world.

"Why did you make me go away?" Mikhail spoke softly, in almost a whisper. "I wanted to stay with you."

The two men shoved Mikhail up against Elena and held their guns on them. She thought they might be arranging a group execution. How could they, with a church full of monks? Then, she remembered something she heard Father Samuka mention after Vespers. They had a light supper in the main hall, clear across campus. Except for Father and the two brothers downstairs and Alex, Tony and Marina, nobody remained. They would be caught off guard.

No, but Alex and Tony are trained for such blitz attacks, so they'd know what to do.

She thought screaming might help, then decided Stefan and his henchmen would probably start shooting. She could try to talk—filibuster them until Alex or someone came looking for her.

Stefan spoke in a harsh Romanian dialect, his tone nothing like the soft, fatherly intonation. His two soldiers saluted him as a private might salute his superiors. Stefan nodded at them, and snapping his fingers, expecting to be obeyed, he pointed to the stairs.

Elena caught sight of something darting into one of the side pews before disappearing.

Tony was the first to hear movement in the hallway.

"What?" Father Samuka asked. "Alex and Elena, perhaps?"

"No," Tony said. "They sound like the squeak of army boots."

Father Samuka crossed himself. "Mother of God, protect us," he said. "Now, you come with me." He led them to the bookcase and pressed down on *The History of Wallachia*. The bookcase moved.

"You have the most unique bookcases in this town," Alex whispered as Samuka ushered him and Marina into a back room.

"We do indeed."

"The cross!" Marina started to run back.

Father Samuka pulled her back, and the door closed. "No. Is good. We use this as bait. Those men will want to come inside and look—maybe steal."

Tony showed the others how to breathe shallow—and quiet.

The door to the office burst open with some expletives in a Romanian dialect spewing from their mouths. "Where are they?"

Marina peeked from behind a volume of *Biblical Stories from the Old Testament*. She signaled *two* to Tony.

He mouthed, "Only two?"

Marina nodded and mouthed, "I hope so."

Tony crouched down with the others. "Does anyone know how to shoot a gun?" He almost breathed the words.

Marina whispered back, "Alex taught Elena and me to shoot."

Father Samuka pointed to a back denehole. The shaft led downward and opened up into an inner and larger room filled with church artifacts.

"Slightly updated since the ancient era, what?" The room was twice the size of the office.

"My God," Tony responded, staring around the room. Cobwebs filled the corners, and a heavy musky smell almost made breathing hard. He coughed, then sneezed. It was the contents that impressed him. Ancient artifacts, including altar crosses that appeared to date back for centuries, lined rows of shelves with volumes of old books of religious histories and services. One end contained a wall of cupboards secured with heavy padlocks.

"Surprised?" Father Samuka whispered. He smiled and nodded his head as though accepting an academy award for all the wonders displayed. "The friars hid many Romanian Jews and gypsies in here during the Nazi era. This hidden chamber contained the silver cross before the monks hid it inside The Virgin Mary for all those years. Too bad she's demolished. We could have used her again, someday. Now, follow me." He led them across the room to another cupboard. "You need weapons. We have them here." Father Samuka took the key from around his neck and opened yet another locked door. Weapons of all sizes and shapes filled the interior and lined the walls.

"Weapons? Here?"

"Come, pick something suitable. I do not know how many are out there, but we can take them."

"We can what?" Tony raised his eyebrows with surprise. Who were these men?

"We must hurry. They wait for our return but may soon search for us. Stefan knows about secret passages within the monastery, and he may have told his men."

"Where do these doors go?" Tony asked.

Father Samuka pointed. "The one over there goes into the hall. The one by the statue goes to the dining hall, and the far end door goes underground into the chapel. At the first sign of danger, the monks come running. These are trained soldiers, you see."

"Good. They won't be expecting an ambush from all sides. Marina," Tony said, as he handed her his gun, "are you sure you can shoot this thing?"

"Absolutely. I learned on one like it."

Tony took her hand. "You promise you won't shoot me instead of the bad guys?"

Marina smirked. "I wouldn't dream of it."

"Another weapon, I think," Father Samuka said. He picked one out for each of the brothers and one for himself.

"We have five against two—so far," Tony said. "I have a plan."

"You have a plan," Marina said. "A plan's good. What is it?"

"I'm going through the door to the front of the office. Maybe I can sneak up and surprise them. Father, I want you and the good brothers to come in through the hidden door on the other side. Marina, you stay here and aim your pistol through the books. Do not come into the room. Is that clear?"

"Pretty clear," she replied. She looked like she'd swallowed a sour grape.

"So, what's wrong?" Tony asked her. "You want to get shot up too?" He winked at her. "Just remember to shoot the bad guys."

"Well," she said, "I'm sure as heck not going to shoot *you.*"

"Good," he said. Then he acted. With a thumbs-up sign, he hurried out the door and cautiously sprung the opening. Looking out into the hall, he saw no one. *They're all in the office and will probably come out pretty quick. Now.*

Tony charged out the door.

Stefan's hitmen hovered over the cross. One of them held the map in his hands. They looked around as if following the map's directions. Tony came in alone, and they had a smirk and raised their guns. But the sneer froze when the wall on one side of the room slid out into thin air, and the bookcase behind them moved, giving the impression the place was moving. The gunmen screamed and shot wildly when three holy men dressed in black, wearing expressions like the devil, came straight out of a wall. They came apart when Marina walked through the other bookcase.

They didn't have to fire a shot. The gunmen gave up in fright before they realized they'd been had.

"Tough guys," Tony whispered, pointing his gun directly into one pair of angry eyes. "There's another one outside. I don't think he's going anyplace."

Father Samuka gave a reciprocal thumbs-up sign to Tony and delivered a broad grin. He disappeared back through the bookcase. Minutes later, he came back with an assortment of restraints that looked like they'd come out of a medieval torture chamber. Among the conglomeration were four pairs of shiny handcuffs.

"Holy sh— Um, sorry, Father," Tony said. "You get them the same place you got the guns?"

Father nodded, beaming. "For such occasions," he said. "Gentlemen and lady, a job well done."

"Is there anywhere we can lock these people up? I don't suppose you have a jail or anything?"

"As a matter of fact, we do."

Tony laughed. "Why should that be a surprise?"

Elena grabbed Mikhail and held on to him, instinctively pushing him behind her back, never taking her eyes off Stefan Baklanov. "You'd kill your own grandson?" she asked.

"Only if that grandson interfered with my business. Only if he decided he wanted to protect those who would be my enemies."

"Your accent—you don't have one anymore," Elena said, baffled by the change.

"I speak a dozen languages. I can have any accent I choose," Stefan replied. His humble demeanor changed along with his dialect. A gleam emerged from his eye, and his short, robust stature seemed to grow.

"So, who was working for whom?" Elena asked, intrigue masking fear. "Who was the boss of this group?"

"We like to think of it as a business corporation. I, Elena, am the head. The corporate CEO. Balogh worked for me. It was better for business when they were in the foreground. Unfortunately, his own sense of power and greed made him a total liability. This whole fiasco with you and Alex never should have happened. I am very sorry. You see, I do like you, Elena, and that man of yours, also. You should never have come over here nor found Mikhail.

"However, he did, and Mikhail became very fond of you. That was unfortunate for his position in my organization. I can't afford disloyalty from even our youngest member."

"Stefan, why don't you just give us Mikhail and let us go home. We don't want to interfere with your business. Besides, I'm pregnant. I don't think you want to kill a woman carrying a—"

"I'm afraid that doesn't even begin to influence me. I am sorry. If it didn't stop me from killing my own wife for interfering where she had no business, it certainly wouldn't stop me from dispatching you."

"Wait. You mean, you killed Jan's mother?"

The horror of this man just began to sink into Elena's mind.

"My organization set up the action which eliminated the competition that is all."

"Competition? Your wife was competition?"

"She was a threat to my empire. She, too, explored the castle and discovered that which she should not. And, so have you and, unfortunately, Mikhail. By now, my soldiers will be downstairs taking care of your friends. I will have the pleasure of seeing to the two of you personally."

"What about Jan? Did you have him killed too? Were you behind my husband's death?"

"Janek, my step-son, you understand, was a disgrace to the family. We do not tolerate homosexuality in the organization." Stefan shrugged off his statement. "Besides," he said, "Jan was not a warrior type. He was no use to us. Mikhail was never intended to be killed. He was to inherit the castle, become a warrior, sit on the executive board and take over someday. He is a smart boy." Stefan's eyes turned from a megalomaniac glow to dark slits in the space of a second. "However, he has no loyalty."

"He's nine years old," Elena said. "Besides, Stefan, the castle can't mean anything to you anymore. The earthquake destroyed half of it, and the governments know about your organization and where it is. You're finished here."

Stefan laughed. "Here, maybe, but not worldwide. We're all over the globe. There is something here that I want, and I believe you and your good priests have found it for me."

"The cross. But that can't be sold. It's priceless."

"No, it has a price. A very, very large price. There are always collectors. So, my dear young woman, I believe you and Mikhail, how shall I say, have had it?"

Mikhail huddled behind Elena, shaking uncontrollably. She'd die before she'd let anything happen to her son.

"Oh, kill me if you must, but please let Mikhail go. He's a Dkany boy. He can work at your Inn. I'm sure he didn't mean to be disloyal to you. He happened to be with me when we left."

"That means nothing to me," Stefan said.

"I won't let you do that to him," Elena said, forcing up a false sense of bravado. She wondered if she could run into this man and catch him off guard. Maybe Mikhail would help her. She made her decision and moved swiftly. She slammed into the old man with her total weight. Although unbalanced by the surprise assault, he managed to catch her by the wrist and fling her down to the concrete floor. Mikhail rallied to Elena's aid, but with the butt of the old man's gun, the boy was knocked out of the way. Stefan recovered the use of the weapon as Elena tried to rise.

"I wouldn't try it."

A familiar voice sounded from the pews, off to the side. Alex appeared, face terse, eyes deadly, holding a gun on Stefan. Just as gunfire echoed from the offices downstairs, Stefan screamed and shot Elena, while Alex fired a blast that not only cut him down but sent him flying. Stefan fell on his back, eyes wide open, staring up at the painting of The Arch Angel Michael throwing Lucifer out of heaven.

A Whirlwind gathered and grasped the dying Stefan, pulling him into the force. The earth opened, and the ghost of Janek Ivanov and the Arch Angel Michael hurled Stefan into the cataclysm below before the floor tile came back to normal, as though nothing had ever happened. Stefan's body lay on the ground.

Elena felt a burst of pain coming from her lower abdomen. Her dreams and terror for her baby now became ominously, too real. The last thing she saw was the horrified faces of Alex and Mikhail kneeling over her before everything went dark.

Chapter 39

Monastery Clinic

The monks rushed Elena to the monastery clinic, a facility used by the religious personnel and emergencies for local Dkany residents. It was not uncommon to see crying children emerge with arms in slings and legs in casts. The monastery was a Godsend to the community.

With a few gurneys, a wheelchair, and a nurse pushing a patient across the floor, the setting was elaborate as a hotel's lobby. Alex sat between Mikhail and Tony. Dr. James Swanson, M.D., from the United States, rushed down from nearby Cluj to confer with Marina.

Diagnosis: Gunshot wound to the abdomen. Although miraculously still alive, Elena lost a lot of blood and suffered from shock.

"What about her baby?" Alex asked, turning his back on the answer. He gazed through the waiting room window and over the mountains. So peaceful, he thought, in contrast to the turmoil in his soul. He wasn't sure he could stand to hear more bad news.

"The shot didn't go through her uterus. The baby's survived, so far." Dr. Swanson was abrupt but honest, a man of integrity and trust. There wouldn't be any false hopes given, as if any could be received. She'd been in bad shape when the make-shift stretcher had carried her from the chapel. "But, from loss of blood and shock, the baby may not make it. I'm sorry. We'll have to wait it out."

"Oh no," Alex whispered. "She wanted a little girl, so bad."

Marina took her brother's hand. "I'm sorry, Alex. For both of you."

He nodded slowly. "This was my fault. All my damned fault." Marina grabbed her brother and held him. "No, it's not, Alex. It's the fault of a very diabolical man."

"No. You don't understand. I think I gave the impression I didn't want the baby. I told her the timing was all wrong. I never should have said that." He shook his head. "I was so scared for her."

"And that's not the truth?" Tony asked.

"Yes, that's the truth. I was thinking about Stefan and the danger she was in. I didn't get a chance to explain. This wasn't about my lifestyle and certainly not the love I have for her. My freedom—that *freedom* has held me prisoner for years."

Dr. Swanson coughed. "Unfortunately, I have some other news." His following statement froze the smile off Alex's face.

"I'm not going to lie to you folks. She's lost a lot of blood. She's so weak."

"What's that supposed to mean?" Alex asked.

"It means, Alex, she may not live," the doctor said, compassion and sadness covering his face.

Fear and anger knotted up inside Alex. He wanted to hit the doctor, punch him between the eyes as though that spot held her prognosis.

Instead, he turned and hit his fist on the wall. He nursed his damaged hand, trying to drown out the real hurt with the physical pain. Then he noticed Father Samuka watching him. He nodded and shrugged.

"What can I do?" Alex asked.

"Pray," the doctor answered.

"I think that's something we all can do," Father Samuka said.

When the doctors finally allowed Alex to enter Elena's room, the lights were dimmed. Only the twinkling of the stars and streetlights lit the shadows of the mountains from the window. Rooms in the monastery clinic were different from some Romani hospitals. Spouses were encouraged to stay and provide comfort. Couches resided along the wall. The beds were big enough to allow the couples to be together if medical conditions permitted. Elena was hooked up to an IV, where blood was pumped into her veins. A once healthy complexion gave way to pallor of mixed white and gray. Her lively eyes barely opened upon his arrival. Robbed of her vitality, she had no strength, no life in her.

When he approached, Elena reached her hand out to him.

He sat on the bed by her side. "Hey," he whispered. "How are you feeling?" His hand caressed her forehead.

Elena managed a half-smile. "Like I've been run over by a truck."

Alex grinned, despite a tear escaping from his eye. "Good. You still have your sense of humor."

"If you can't laugh, what else is there?" she whispered back.

"I . . ."

"Shhh. Save your strength. You don't have to speak. You know the bullet missed our baby."

Elena smiled. "Yes, Marina told me."

"But I'd like to say something to you if you don't mind."

She was about to remove her hand, but he hung on. "I have a few things I need to tell you. And, as I have you as a captive audience . . ."

She laughed, then coughed and had a hard time catching her breath.

"Oh my God! I'm sorry," Alex said. "I didn't mean to—"

"I'll try to control myself," she replied.

"Good." He gave her as big a smile as he could. "The reason you were in the chapel at that time was my fault. I drove you away because—look, Elena, I was scared to death for you.

"I understood the danger, and you didn't. You left too quickly for me to explain. And, sometimes, I express myself poorly. But one thing is true. I love you." He made a motion with his hand. "I always have. I was a jerk ten years ago when I let you go, and I've suffered ever since. I've gotten so used to a lifestyle I hate, and I dumped it all on you. I need—I *want*—you in my life. I don't ever want to let you go again."

"Thank God. Oh, Alex." Her voice came as a whisper. "I love you, too. Please don't ever leave me." She sighed and turned her head. "I'm so tired," she said.

"You're my light, my soul," he said. He kissed her lightly on her forehead. Fear struck him as her breathing grew shallower.

"I'm so cold," she said. "Can't breathe."

Alex pulled the cord.

Marina hurried in. "What is it?"

"She can't breathe—"

"She's having a reaction."

Dr. Swanson hurried in. "Alex, out," he ordered.

"No, but—"

"Now!"

Alex waited along with Tony and Mikhail. Time went by and seemed like hours, but they'd only sat for a half-hour.

Marina came out and smiled at them. "It was just a mild reaction from the transfusion. It sometimes happens, even if the blood is compatible. She's resting comfortably. What did you say to her?"

Alex took Marina aside and told her.

"Good. Elena may just make it. You can spend the rest of your life making it up to her." Her tongue seemed planted firmly in her cheek. "And," she said, "vice-versa." She walked down the hall with Alex at her side. "Listen, I've never seen two people more at odds or more suited for each other. What's in the past, leave it there. Learn from it and move on."

Alex nodded and moved out of the way of two kids, one with a cast on his leg, the other a bandage over his eye, racing wheelchairs down the hall.

Marina told the boys to stop. They gave her a look but stopped.

"There, Alex. That's what life is really all about. Go back to Elena. Stay with her. I'll be here. Dr. Swanson will be here—hell, I want you *all* to be here when she wakes up."

With that, Marina walked back into the waiting room and sat next to Tony. He gave her his hand, and she held it.

Alex dozed with his head resting on Elena's bed. When he woke, he thought it must be morning, but it wasn't. He couldn't even be sure he was awake.

A man sat on the couch watching him. Tony? No. Not Tony. Then who? The doctor? No. Not him either. "Who are you? Why are you in Elena's room?" He reached for where his gun resided, but it wasn't there."

"No, Alexander. You won't need a gun. I'm not even real. You're asleep. I want to talk to you."

Recognition hit. The man on the couch—Janek Ivanov, Elena's ghost. He stared hard, expecting the specter to dissipate, but it remained.

"Why are you here? Why can't you leave Elena—us alone?" A horrifying thought occurred. "Are we still in danger?"

"No. No more danger, except that which comes from within."

Alex opened up his mouth to speak—to give this thing a piece of his mind—but his mouth snapped shut.

"No. I talk. You listen. We both love Elena. I loved her the way you love your sister. You love her the way a husband should love a wife. I do not think you know this yet, but you will. Elena has always loved you. She never loved another, only you. You must promise me you will love her, protect her and cherish her and Mikhail. Do you promise this?"

"Do you promise?" The ghost increased the intensity in his tone.

"My God," Alex whispered.

"Yes, the great God is here. He understands all. And now, I must go back to him. Magda and Freddy wait for me. She sends her love and asks you to protect Elena, Mikhail, and your new daughter. If you can do that, I will leave and will not return. You and Elena will not remember my presence here. You will forget."

"Janek—" Alex didn't know how to talk to a ghost, but he tried. "I'll never forget you. You made us aware of the dangers we faced. You saved our lives and brought down justice on Stefan. I'll always be grateful to you."

The man who sat on the couch no longer presented himself in solid form. He slowly turned into a vapor and gradually disappeared.

"God speed, Janek," Alex whispered.

Daughter. He'd said daughter. How could he know that? Alex did something he hadn't done in years. He cried until he gasped for air. Then, he curled up next to his wife and slept.

Alex woke up lying beside the love of his life. Her left arm was still hooked up to the IV, but the rest of her snuggled up against him. Her breathing was once again normal.

She woke and stretched. "Good morning," she said, looking around. "Are we in a hospital? Why am I hooked up to this thing? Why does my side hurt?" and "Was there a ghost in here?" Before Alex had a chance to answer, she said, "And why am I so hungry?"

After absorbing her new information, she asked, "Alex, why are you crying?"

Gently, he hugged her. "Because you're alive. You have no idea how much I love you."

Elena touched his cheek. "I'm glad. I love you too." She sat back and tilted her head. "I can see you're going to have to explain some stuff to me. I have no idea what happened. Just a chapel, a man with a gun, throwing myself over Mikhail, so he didn't get shot, my *getting* shot, and Lucifer and Janek Ivanov carrying the man down to hell."

"Yep," Alex said. "That about covers it."

Days became weeks before stretching into a month. The middle of August crept in, hot and humid with occasional hints of a fall that was yet to come.

Elena rested on the sofa in the cottage living room, wondering where everyone was and annoyed she wasn't allowed up except for emergencies. The doctors warned her if she didn't follow orders, she'd be confined to the bedroom—period, bedpan, and all. She was recovering, but not as fast as she'd like. She wanted to explore the town, the hills, take rides with Mikhail and Alex along the Dkany River. Her baby was okay—that's really all that mattered. *Resilient little critters when they are in the womb, aren't they?*

The plans excited her. She wished she could have seen the demolition of the ruins. The monastery picked up the expenses of the castle renovation. Magda's dream—and now Elena's—were in the hands of the Dkany Monastery. She could picture them teaching in Evanston during the winter months while living and working here during the summer. Mikhail would go to the International School in Evanston, a junior version of Briar Hill College.

But when would she be allowed out?

A rustle of activity came from the kitchen. Marina marched out with two coffee mugs in her hand. She put down the cups within reach and slumped onto the stuffed chair across from her. Her eyes shone in a way Elena hadn't seen from Marina in a long time. She didn't know why. Maybe Tony. He'd been paying a lot of attention to her. Whenever she was around, the man stared, bumped into things, smirked, mumbled, and brushed up against her whenever the opportunity arose. Marina grinned and looked demure. Love was definitely in the air.

Since Elena's release from the clinic, Alex hadn't left her side while she was in crisis or during her convalescence, but for the past few days, no Alex. Even Mikhail hadn't been around, and today, Tony hadn't made an appearance either. Another thing, her ring had disappeared. It was no longer around her finger. So, where was it, and where were they?

Father Samuka and the two brothers strolled in, the three wearing broad grins. Happy faces. Something definitely had happened to replace their generally stoic look with such pleasure. "Elena, we bring good news."

"Father," Elena said. "You look happy. Please sit down."

He pulled up a chair next to the sofa.

Marina gathered the kitchen chairs, and they all sat.

"We apologize for not being here during your convalescence.

But, we too, have been busy."

"Oh, that's—"

"We have been in Bucharest. You see, I took the cross to the head Patriarch of all Romania."

"You did?"

"I did, my dear Mrs. Brancusi. He had no words, *no words* for such a treasure. I tell him in return for the cross, you want only one thing. That is to make—no, convert—your castle into a school and to maintain its financial backing. You and Alexander will run the school, of course, and hire the professors. The details can be worked out by you and Alexander. He said that was not nearly enough gratitude for such a prize as the cross."

"But you had it all the time," Elena said.

"Yes, we did. However, it was not ours to give to the church, you see," Father Samuka replied. "With your gracious permission, we were able to give it back. You will be glad to know, the famous ruby arrived at our monastery this morning."

"The ruby is here?"

"That is not all. Our Father gave us the permission to let the cross sit on the altar at the monastery. It will be closely guarded, you understand. It will bring in more tourists to view the church and monastery. It is a priceless treasure, and I am so happy to have it where it belongs—has always belonged."

Elena bowed her head. "Yes, it's always belonged here. So, it's all working out the way I'd hoped—I'd *dreamed.* I'm so grateful to you, Father, and to your brothers."

Marina giggle. "Our partners in crime. God bless you. What's the old saying? 'Praise God and pass the ammunition?'"

Father Samuka laughed. "Yes, we too watch the old television movies. But I think it was a famous songwriter who said that?"

"Frank Loesser, I think," Marina replied. "But Elena, you don't look happy?"

Marina was right. Elena didn't feel much like keeping up appearances. She missed Alex and wondered what he and Mikhail had been up to.

The cottage door opened, and Alex strolled in, followed by Mikhail and Tony.

"Hey," he said to his sister. "Father—brothers. Glad to see you."

"Hey yourself," Marina replied. "Where've you been?" Tony grinned at her, and she stifled a laugh. But he didn't approach.

Mikhail skipped over to Father Samuka, who tousled the boy's hair. "Mikhail."

Alex, however, did. He shifted from side to side, looking nervous. *Uh oh, here it comes.* Elena looked down and smoothed out a blue satin robe Marina had brought to the clinic for her. She'd said it matched her eyes, and it did.

"How . . ." Alex started and paused. "How do you feel?" His tone was low, throaty, and infinitely sexy. Wow.

"Better than yesterday." She sized him up, curious as to what would come next. Tony carried a large box and handed it to him. He sat next to her and placed the box on her lap.

Elena raised an eyebrow.

"Remember the day after Magda's funeral?" he asked.

Elena replied, "How could I forget?" Not so long, but centuries ago.

"I handed you a box containing a costume and a photo album?"

She sighed. "Yes. Why bring that—"

"Wait," he said. "Open this."

Elena removed the top. Tissue paper crinkled. "What is it?"

He nudged her on with his eyes, first on her, then on the box, then back to her.

Under the tissue lay a white blouse with flowery sleeves and blue ribbons threaded into the elastic along the neck. Elena took in a breath of surprise. Her mouth just kind of came open, and for a minute, she couldn't shut it. Her eyes—she suddenly couldn't see anything through her tears. "Oh my."

"Here, look at the rest."

Alex started helping but got his hands twisted in the paper.

"Here, let me." Elena finally took a deep breath.

"Oh, the traditional Transylvanian wedding dress." The same, but not the same. This one was new and custom-made. The blouse was a white cotton skirt with a flower border, a matching apron, and black boots.

Alex nodded and took another smaller wrapped package from his pocket and handed it to her.

Elena looked at him, raised an eyebrow, and opened it. Her mouth opened as wide as the box when she saw a blood-red ruby cross on a silver chain, next to matching drop earrings. "Oh my God. This is from my ruby, isn't it?"

Father Samuka nodded. "We wanted you to have part of the stone to cherish. We have a jeweler who cut the stone down and placed it back into the cross. This is for you, my dear Elena."

"Oh, how exquisite. Thank you so much." Tears ran down her cheeks as she held up the stone. "This is too beautiful."

So intent on the cross, Elena hadn't notice Alex, who was now kneeling with something else in his hand. Elena put down the cross and stared at Alex. Alex wasn't a kneeler.

"Elena Dkany Brancusi," he said, his voice shaking. He handed her a smaller box.

"In front of our Mikhail, Marina, Tony, and our good priest and brothers—"

Pause.

He opened the box.

The missing ring.

"I want to officially ask you to marry me again. Renew our vows of eternal love, and for you to wear this ring until the day—no forever." Alex dropped his eyes. His expression eluded her. In a voice so soft she almost didn't hear him, he said, "I think I'll die if you say no, Elena. I love you—I've loved you since high school. I've never stopped loving you. Please, please marry me again. Stay with me—with us." He looked back at Mikhail. Mikhail beamed as though the joy bug bit him.

"Well," Elena said, regaining her composure, "since you put it that way. Yes!"

"You will?"

"I love you. I've always loved you, and I always will love you." She pulled him over to her and kissed him.

Alex shot up and looked around. "Damn. She said yes. The lady loves me. She wants to be my wife."

Mikhail shouted. "My Princess Elena is my mother!" He jumped up and down. "And now I have a mother, a father, and an aunt. Yippee!"

"And an uncle," Tony said. Everyone turned. "I asked Marina to marry me today, and she said yes."

The End

About Patricia A. Guthrie

"Every experience is potential fodder for a novel." Patricia A. Guthrie

Patricia A. Guthrie is the author of romantic suspense novels, mysteries, short stories, and non-fiction articles. Her published works include: *In the Arms of the Enemy*, *Waterlilies Over My Grave*, *Willed Accidents Happen, and Collection: Short Stories of Fantasy*, and are available at all major retailers and other online booksellers. She has short stories published on Amazon.com, Skyline Magazine, Affaire de Coeur, and non-fiction articles in the Collie Cassette and the online 'Nature Journal.'

An accomplished musician, Pat's sung in opera companies in Europe and the United States and been a church soloist and music teacher. An avid animal lover. she owns a horse (Dixie) and two black cats (Archie and Kitzy Kitty.) At one time, four collies owned Ms. Guthrie. They knew how to line up in a row and "sit-stay." (She has the photos to prove it.)

Pat's shown horses in Quarter Horse and local horse shows and collies in 'obedience' classes at dog shows. You'll find many of her experiences in her books.

You can find her works at all major retailers and online booksellers.

Patguth@aol.com
https://www.paguthrie.wordpress.com

Fresh Ink Group
Independent Multi-media Publisher
Fresh Ink Group / Push Pull Press / Voice of Indie

&

Hardcovers
Softcovers
All Ebook Platforms
Audiobooks
Worldwide Distribution

&

Indie Author Services
Book Development, Editing, Proofing
Graphic/Cover Design
Video/Trailer Production
Website Creation
Social Media Management
Writing Contests
Writers' Blogs
Podcasts

&

Authors
Editors
Artists
Experts
Professionals

&

FreshInkGroup.com
info@FreshInkGroup.com
Twitter: @FreshInkGroup
Facebook.com/FreshInkGroup
LinkedIn: Fresh Ink Group

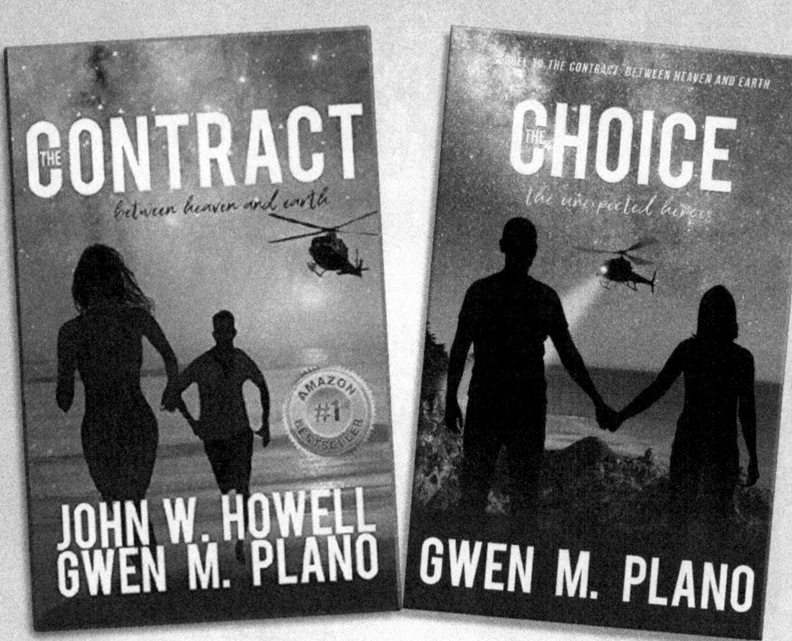

Paranormal,
Romantic,
Spiritual
Thriller
Trilogy!